SCAND
TRUTH

SCANDALOUS TRUTH

MONICA P. CARTER

URBAN CHRISTIAN

www.urbanchristianonline.net

Carter

Urban Books
1199 Straight Path
West Babylon, NY 11704

ISBN- 13: 978-1-60162-976-0
ISBN- 10: 1-60162-976-1

First Printing January 2009
Printed in the United States of America

10 9 8 7 6 5 4 3 2 1

*This is a work of fiction. Any references or similarities to actual events, real
people, living, or dead, or to real locales are intended to give the novel a
sense of reality. Any similarity in other names, characters, places, and inci-
dents is entirely coincidental.*

Distributed by Kensington Corp.
Submit Wholesale Orders to:
Kensington Publishing Corp.
C/O Penguin Group (USA) Inc.
Attention: Order Processing
405 Murray Hill Parkway
East Rutherford, NJ 07073-2316
Phone: 1-800-526-0275
Fax: 1-800-227-9604

14.95
10/8/09
NRN

6126623982   JG

Dedication

To Anubhav, who lets me fly and keeps me grounded

Acknowledgements

Another book. Another blessing. I would like to thank God, first, of course, for the ability, inspiration and guidance to create this story. Telling an engaging tale with a message is a profound joy.

I also would like to thank many people in my life, who continue to support my work and the dream I choose to walk in on a daily basis. My mother gave me my foundation and continues to shower me with the words to push me forward. My siblings and friends give me their love—and their honesty—so I stay on the right track. Readers give me warmth and continue to let me know my words create impact.

A special thank you to my publisher and my editor for working so hard to fulfill a vision of meaningful books that share universal themes, capture the imagination and make a difference.

And last, but certainly not least, thank you to my husband who walks with me each step of the way.

SCANDALOUS TRUTH

Chapter 1

Nikki Broussard nuzzled her young daughter's stomach and the child returned the favor, tickling her mother's midsection with slender fingers. Nikki swatted at the four-year-old and raced across the shiny, hardwood floor in the spacious living room, which was warmed by the glow of the late afternoon sunlight that washed through the wide front window. Psalm broke out into a peal of laughter as she chased her mother, who pretended to fall to the floor, just short of the decorative fireplace, and let the girl catch her. The two were tickling each other right there when William stepped into the living room, dropped his briefcase and stretched his arms wide, a smile showing off the dimple in his left cheek.

"Give me some love, y'all!" he said as mother and daughter peered up from their game.

Psalm scrambled to her father and he scooped her up, her ponytails and yellow ribbons swooshing from side to side. He kissed her and hoisted her to his right side, then pulled his wife close with his other arm. He gave Nikki a deep kiss, and a sexy groan escaped her upturned lips.

"I'm glad you're home," she said and let her tongue trail his lip.

"You and me both." He put Psalm down, then grabbed his wife's rear.

Nikki winked at him, the look in her eye hinting toward later, and sashayed to the kitchen. William followed, and Nikki knew his mind was already on the possibilities.

"I fixed spaghetti." Nikki lifted the top off the stainless steel pot.

"Smells good," William said, and took a bite from the spoon she held out to him. "Mmm, tastes good, too. I don't know how I got so lucky to be married to you."

Nikki was five-feet-three-inches tall, barely 112 pounds, with her natural hair in a fluffy, curly halo that flirted with her ears and slender neck. Her warm brown skin shone under the lights, radiant even without makeup. The toes on her bare feet were painted pink, while the nails on her hands were naked. She wore a fitted, sleeveless sky blue T-shirt over frayed jeans.

"I think I must have bumped my head or something," Nikki joked.

"Well, I believe it was God's blessing, all the way," William said. "The Word says a man who finds a wife finds a good thing. And I know my wife is good—through and through."

Nikki's skin grew warm as she let her husband's love radiate throughout her entire body, but she swallowed hard. A niggling thought challenged her husband's assertion that she was a good wife as visions of her past flashed in her mind's eye. She quickly pushed those thoughts away. She was saved now, and that's all that mattered.

"We're both blessed," she cooed to her husband.

"Well, feed your man, woman!" William bellowed with mock sternness.

"You are so silly." Nikki rolled her eyes and began spooning the food onto blue plastic plates. William wasn't done with her, though, as he bent and nuzzled her neck, letting his tongue trail lightly down her nape. Nikki giggled and twisted, ending up leaning into his chest.

"Psalm is in the next room," she whispered, "stop it."

William acted as if he couldn't hear, and Nikki's body awakened. The plate slid to the counter and William pushed her against the refrigerator, letting his hands roam under her shirt. "William, we really shouldn't . . ."

But her words died in her throat as he sucked them into his kiss. Nikki could feel her husband pressing into her through their clothes and her own body responded. She couldn't tell if the heat was from the stove or the Shreveport July, but she was on fire. William pulled at the strap on her tank, yanking it off her right shoulder.

"Mama, I want some juice."

Nikki heard the tiny voice from very far away. Her eyes flew open as reality assaulted her. She pushed William away and stepped around him, moving to the doorway, quickly jerking her strap back into place. She saw that Psalm was playing with dolls and trucks on the floor.

"Okay, baby, we're going to eat in just a little while," Nikki said. "Why don't you go wash your hands?"

William took this as his cue and went up the stairs to change out of his dark blue suit, squeezing Nikki's rear again as he went past.

The previous old one-bedroom apartment they had lived in down in New Orleans had been barely enough for one, let alone three people. The baby had often slept with them—except for when they felt like getting as naked and hot as the Louisiana night. Then they let her fall to sleep in their bed and later moved her to the rollaway in the living room. Psalm was an infant then. Now, four years later, in Shreveport, they were living in a four-bedroom house with more than 3,000 square feet. Nikki knew three of their old apartments could fit in it. Hurricane Katrina had wiped away so much of their lives, as it had thousands of others. They fled to the northern part of the state where William was from originally. It was only five hours from New Orleans, but felt like a different world in so many ways.

William's first computer business had been washed away with the rising waters of Hurricane Katrina, but they were now doing even better than before the natural disaster. He had started a new computer company, and had slowly built his clientele. Their income had taken a hit lately, though, as William was spending more time working on a political campaign for his pastor, and that meant less time finding clients. Nikki looked around the kitchen with its glass-top stove and double refrigerator and smiled. Yes, life was good.

That slightly unsettled feeling gnawed at the pit of her stomach, stealing her smile, and she tried, as she had over the years, to shrug it off. Her jaw tensed as she fought to bury the secrets that mocked her. There were things about her that would shake up her very existence if they were ever to come out. Panic bubbled in Nikki's throat as for a brief moment, she imagined her husband learning of the things she had done. But she closed her eyes and leaned against the refrigerator, willing her thoughts to settle. She knew there was a time when she wasn't living right, but she was trying desperately to live a better life now, and that just had to be good enough. Everyone has a past, she often reminded herself.

There was no way William could find out about her life before he entered the picture. Her secrets were safe. Yet, as she tried to assure herself of this fact, the knot in her stomach grew.

Nikki shoved away from the refrigerator and righted herself, letting out a tiny breath. A smile again creased her lips. Hers was the perfect life. Her husband adored her. He was her protector and her friend. That's why she had married him. She had known, even at 20, he would always be there for her. And she had worked hard to create the Nikki she knew he wanted. Now, seven years later, she had succeeded.

"Baby, I'm going to hop in the shower right quick," William called down the stairs.

"Okay," Nikki called back.

"Want to join me?" She could hear the hopefulness in his voice.

Nikki grinned. "I don't think so," she said. "And hurry up. We're hungry."

"Okay," William replied. "I just thought you wanted to have a taste of—"

"Will!" Nikki interrupted him. "Psalm is right here."

The start of the shower drowned out William's laugh and Nikki chuckled. Her husband could be so silly sometimes. They often bantered like this. They had been married seven years and there was no sign of an itch anywhere on the scene.

Nikki pulled out a carton of juice from the refrigerator for Psalm. She hummed as she thought back to how she and William had met. They became inseparable her sophomore year at a New Orleans private college, meeting at an off-campus fraternity party Nikki hadn't even wanted to attend, but had let her best friend, Danielle, drag her to one night.

Danielle had actually spotted William first. "You see that tall, goofy dude?" Danielle had pointed. "You see how he's dancing, like he has springs in his shoes? Looking like the Jolly Green Giant on crack? Why is he practically jumping up and down like that?" Danielle had whispered to Nikki behind her hand, laughing. "He keeps looking at me, but I keep ignoring him," Danielle said. "I know he'll be over here before the night is over, trying to get my number. Like I'd want to go out with some nerdy-looking goofball like him."

And he had come over. Only it was Nikki's number he was after.

"Hi, I'm William," he had said, extending his hand.

"I'm Nikki."

"I'm Danielle," Danielle asserted. "Did you come over here to buy us a drink or something? I saw you looking at me all night."

"Actually, I was looking at your friend, and no, I didn't come to buy you a drink," William said, then added, "though if your friend here wants one, I definitely will."

Nikki shook her head. "No, I'm cool. I don't need a drink." She surreptitiously pinched Danielle in the side. "And Danielle is just kidding."

She could tell Danielle wanted to protest, but she didn't. Danielle spotted one of her many boyfriends and disappeared into the crowd, and that conversation ended. Nikki turned back toward William, smiling up at him, still shocked that he had been checking her out. Guys never seemed to notice her if Danielle was around, and the attention caught her off guard.

"You don't seem like you're enjoying yourself very much," William surmised. "You want to go outside and sit in my car? We can talk for a while."

"What, so you can kidnap me?" Nikki gave him a side-long glance and a smile.

"Nah. I'm not going to kidnap you. But I am going to steal you away from here."

They ended up sitting in his car for the next two hours, talking and listening to old school music, while Danielle danced the night away. But Nikki hadn't minded. She and William seemed to click. William was the first man to make her feel safe and taken care of, and she had been drawn to him instantly. The fact that he had picked her—even with gorgeous Danielle standing there—made Nikki feel like maybe she could be beautiful too, that maybe she could be more than . . . well, just more. Even in that first meeting, she felt that way. He hadn't looked like much—he was tall and skinny, and told goofy jokes—but there was something about him that touched her.

Nikki shook her head at the memory, bringing herself back to the present as William came downstairs, the smell of soap enveloping him.

They sat down and bowed their heads in prayer before digging into their food. Husband and wife sat at the table, while Psalm sat on a Dora The Explorer blanket on the floor, just to the right of where the last of the July afternoon's sun bathed the floor. Sometimes they allowed Psalm to play on the floor while she ate—it seemed to make for a more peaceful dining experience. And today, Nikki needed peace. She wanted to discuss something with William.

"A magazine called today," she said carefully, watching her husband's reaction under lowered lashes.

"Oh yeah?"

"Yeah. They saw some of the photos I've taken and want me to interview for a photographer's position."

"You told them you weren't interested, right?" William glanced at her then took a gulp of tea.

"Well, I was thinking that maybe now would be a good time to go back to work," she said, looking down at the spaghetti strands she was twirling around her fork. "Psalm can get in the pre-kindergarten class and—"

"Nikki, haven't we talked about this? You're a stay-at-home mom."

"Yes, baby, I know, but—"

"So what's to discuss?"

Nikki's shoulders slumped in disappointment. She nodded and jammed a piece of bread into her mouth. "You're right." She drew a deep breath and tried to smile brightly. "I'm a happily married woman, able to stay home and take care of my husband and child. What else could I want?"

William leaned over and kissed her. "Exactly."

Chapter 2

Danielle stepped into her condo and icy air embraced her. She slammed the door against the heat of the oppressive summer evening. Tiny beads of perspiration dotted her nose on her otherwise perfectly made up face. She dropped the shopping bags to the floor, letting the box of sexy pumps in one spill open as her keys fell next to them. She kicked off her red Prada pumps, walked to the refrigerator, snatched a cola and took a swig.

Reaching for the cordless phone, she scrolled through her caller ID. Nope, Troy hadn't called. The message indicator was solid—no blinking light—but she pressed the talk button on the phone anyway, just to see if maybe . . . nope, he hadn't left a message. Danielle rummaged through her Fendi purse until she found her cell phone and looked at it again. Maybe it rang while she was shopping. But no, there was no missed call from Troy there either.

They'd had a fight the night before and he had slammed out of her condo as she flung razor sharp curses at his back. She spent all morning at work, trying to wait him out. She had been certain that he would call. But he hadn't. By afternoon, Danielle was alternating between seething and wondering. "He had better call me," she had railed to a coworker, but doubt gave her pause.

Not able to take it anymore, Danielle feigned a migraine and begged to be excused from work. She hopped into her car and zipped to her favorite in-town shopping spots. Buying beautiful, expensive things always made her feel better. She lunched at the Boardwalk, then cruised to Line Avenue to see what items the specialty boutiques offered. By the time she reached an upscale shopping center on Youree Drive, she had already spent more than she earned in a week. But she didn't care. She'd make Troy give her some money.

But now, that high was gone, and in its place was the blue Danielle had been wearing all day. She picked up the telephone and dialed her boyfriend's number, but quickly hung up. "I'm not calling him!" She hissed the words at the silent phone in her hand. "Danielle Esperanza doesn't chase men. Men chase me."

Male attention was nothing new for her. In fact, if Danielle went somewhere and didn't get hit on, then that would be news. "Every man wants me," she reminded herself. "And old silly Troy is no different. He just has a little attitude because I cussed him out last night."

Danielle dropped the cell phone onto the couch and flipped on the television. A reality show filled the screen, showing a woman with what looked like an artificially enhanced bust, whining to a man who then sloppily kissed her on the mouth. "What's so special about these people?" Danielle lamented. "How is it that they can get a show and I can't?"

She had tried to break into Hollywood, but couldn't seem to get a toehold. She even went to Los Angeles one summer, expecting to be immediately signed up to star in a show, but found no work at all, save for one solitary role as an extra. Now that Shreveport was becoming a budding destination for Hollywood producers, she was hopeful she could finally get going on her television or movie career.

Danielle felt that acting had to be her destiny. Why else would Shreveport have landed several high-profile Hollywood productions following Hurricane Katrina, as producers moved their projects from New Orleans? It seemed to Danielle that fate was bringing the opportunity for fame right to her doorstep. Shreveport had even developed a nickname as "Hollywood South." It was just a matter of time before some big-time producer spotted her walking through the mall or eating out somewhere.

"I know I could be a better star than these stupid people," Danielle muttered, flicking off the television. She wasn't in the mood to see someone else skyrocket to stardom while she wasted away as a nurse in a psychiatric clinic.

With the television off, her mind returned to Troy. She reached for her cell phone again.

"I know he's there, waiting for me to call him," she reasoned. "I'm going to call him, but I'm still going to make him beg me to take him back."

Chapter 3

William's rebuff silenced Nikki. *He works hard to provide us a good life so I can stay here and take care of Psalm*, Nikki chided herself. Many women would love to be in her position, she knew. "You're just being greedy," she muttered to herself.

"You say something, baby?" William asked.

"Oh. No," Nikki assured with a quick smile. "I was just agreeing with what you said earlier. We have a really good life." She craved a career, but she knew their plans couldn't be changed. They had agreed that Nikki would give up her work and raise their daughter—William had always wanted a home life like that.

"Daddy, I met a new friend at the park today." Psalm jumped into the conversation.

"Did you, now?" William glanced at Psalm with a wide smile.

"Yeah, we played on the swings," the four-year-old said, then scrambled up from her food and raced across the floor to William.

"Look at the polish Mommy put on my nails." Psalm showed off her pale pink manicure.

"Anything to keep from eating," Nikki said of her daughter's cunning escape from dinner.

William laughed. "Psalm, eat your salad," he said, which made his daughter wrinkle her nose.

The telephone rang and Nikki hopped up to answer it. "Hello?" She listened for a moment, licking butter from her fingers.

"Oh. Hi, Danielle," she said, holding up her index finger so William could see she wouldn't be long. "How are you?"

There was a pause, as Nikki listened, then she interrupted. "Hey, chick, I just sat down to dinner with Will and Psalm, so can I call you back in a minute?"

There was another pause, then Nikki held up her free hand, as if to stop the flow of words coming through the phone. "Okay, okay," Nikki said. "Let me call you back. Bye." She hung up.

Nikki returned to the table. "Danielle," she said by way of explanation, and William nodded.

"How is she doing?"

"Oh, fine, I'm sure," Nikki said and took a sip of tea. "She was trying to tell me about some man drama, but I told her I'd call her back."

"That Danielle always has a good story to tell," William grinned.

"Yeah," Nikki said. "One thing is for sure, it's never boring with her around. So, how was your day?"

William sighed and raised his eyebrows, letting out a long breath. "Baby, it was rough," he said. "The campaign is getting pretty heated and we had to fight off some crazy rumors."

William spent long days working on the mayoral campaign of Oliver Chance, a candidate he believed in fiercely, though the polls weren't too favorable to Chance at the moment. Chance was a pastor who had decided to run for office after becoming frustrated with the way many of his church members were too often treated by city government. This was his first political run and the incumbent, Lo Dark, had two terms behind him, money and a good support base.

William, who was a year older than Nikki, spent his first two years out of college building a computer services firm with a college buddy, but the company went under after a key investor pulled out following Hurricane Katrina. He now had another company and helped people with computer problems, though lately he was working less at his computer business and more at the campaign. Reverend Chance promised William a job in his administration if he should win. William liked the idea, because he wanted to hold public office himself one day.

Nikki had interned as a photographer for the local paper in Shreveport and had worked there briefly after fleeing New Orleans, but William did not want her working. He said she had her hands full taking care of their home, their daughter and finishing up her master's degree in art. Nikki knew he told her not to work out of concern so she wouldn't be unduly stressed, but she also knew this was a matter of pride for him. William felt more like a man when he could afford for his wife to stay home. Except now, bills were mounting and money was growing harder to come by.

Neither of their parents had wanted them to marry so young—her at 20, him at 21—after knowing each other for barely six weeks, but Nikki and William hadn't cared. Now, seven years and one child later, they had weathered a lot— struggling through college, building a business, seeing a business fail, having no money.

"Well, you know the Bible tells us that the enemy will

come at you from all sides when you are working for good," Nikki said. "And the pastor is running for office so he can make some real changes in this city. So I'm sure there are a lot of unhappy people out there."

"Yeah, it gets hard sometimes," William said.

"But I'm sure it will all work out. The Word tells us that no weapon formed against us shall prosper. And that's a promise. No weapon formed against us, you or Reverend Chance will prosper."

"I wish I could be as sure as you are," William sighed. "It's rough out there."

"Well, I'm certain you did an excellent job handling the situation." Nikki beamed at her husband.

"I tried." William rubbed his eyes. "Did I tell you Spencer Cason is working in the opposition's camp?"

Nikki's eyebrows shot up. "Spencer?"

"Yeah," William said. "It seems like I can't shake that dude. Every time I take one step, he takes two."

Spencer and William started off as friends their freshman year in college, but that soon changed as it became evident to William that Spencer seemed to covet everything William had.

"Are you serious?" Nikki regained her composure. She wrinkled her nose and tore apart a buttery piece of garlic bread. "I thought he had moved or something. Don't tell me he's still hanging around, chasing you."

"Well, I can't say for certain that he's still chasing me," William said, winking at Psalm, who picked at her salad with her hands.

"Well, didn't you start working on the Chance campaign first?" Nikki asked. "I bet you Spencer found out you were there and then went to work on the other side. What's that guy's problem? Seems like he would just get a life."

"My tummy hurts," Psalm said, pushing away her plate.

Nikki raised a brow. "Really, sweetie? Come, let Mommy make it feel better," she said, smiling knowingly at William. "Is it because you don't want to eat the rest of your salad?"

Nikki hoisted the child onto her lap and rubbed her stomach for a moment, but before Psalm could even get settled, she caught sight of her favorite DVD and bounced out of her mother's arms and raced to the TV stand. "Let's watch!"

Nikki smiled. She knew she had a good life. Why should she want anything more? William was right, she tried to assure herself. She didn't need a photography career.

But the longing remained.

Chapter 4

Danielle pressed the end button on her cell phone and slumped against the back of the black leather couch. Tears streaked down her cheeks and she bit down hard on her thumb to keep more from coming.

"I need to talk to Nikki!" she fumed. But she didn't call her friend back. When Nikki had asked if she was all right, Danielle had said yes, in a shaky voice. "I know she could tell something was wrong. But she was too wrapped up in her own stuff." Danielle forced herself not to feel let down by her friend's hurry to get off the phone. Nikki had been her first real female friend ever since their meeting freshman year. Theirs had not been an instant friendship, however.

Danielle, a year older than Nikki, had been forced to attend a mandatory tutorial session after she failed yet another English test. Nikki had been her tutor, though they were both freshmen.

"How are you going to tell me what to do when we're both starting out?" Danielle had groused, rolling her eyes.

Nikki shrugged. "Well, I've just always been really good

in English, and I scored really high on my college entrance exams in that subject. I needed a job and this was what was available. I don't know everything, but I'm here to help you as best I can."

"Well, why don't you just do my papers for me and we can let it go at that?" Danielle shot back.

"Because, that's dishonest," Nikki reasoned.

"So!" Danielle laughed. "Are you some goody-two-shoes or something?"

"No, I'm not a goody-two-shoes, but I know cheating on a paper is wrong and can get us both in a lot of trouble," Nikki had told her. "So, let's get to today's assignment. Let me see what you're working on in class. I know you can get this. I'm sure you're pretty smart."

Danielle had cut her eyes at Nikki before pulling out her notebook. "I don't want to do this mess. I'm wasting valuable time fooling around with this junk. I have a date tonight that I need to get ready for."

"Well, look, you have to master this first," Nikki insisted.

"Whatever. I have to do my hair, find something to wear, get my nails done—"

"It won't take you but a moment to get ready for your date," Nikki said and smiled. "You're beautiful."

Danielle's eyes narrowed. "What, are you trying to be funny? Are you trying to say something? I know you're jealous of me. Go on and say it."

"No, I'm just saying," Nikki said, taking in Danielle's long weave, carefully made up face and legs that seemed to go on forever, "it won't take you long to get dressed. You could probably go like that and the guy would still be blown away by you."

Danielle had stared at Nikki for a long moment, but realized Nikki was being sincere. Danielle's demeanor instantly changed, as she knew Nikki meant her no harm.

"So, you really think I look good? Do you like my hair? I bought these jeans last week."

Nikki had lavished attention on Danielle, and never seemed too busy for her—no matter what kind of crazy antics Danielle dreamed up. That's how the friendship started, but now that Nikki was married and had a child, Danielle sometimes had to share the attention.

"You'd think she would be tired of being with William after seven years, but no, she's still all up his behind," Danielle griped.

She picked up her house phone and speed-dialed Troy's number. Again, no answer. When the answering machine picked up, she spoke. "Hi, Troy, baby, it's me. Pick up."

Danielle waited for a moment, then hung up. Redialing, she paused for his outgoing message again and then said, "Hi, baby, I just wanted to talk. Give me a call."

She hung up again, waited a minute, and not able to restrain herself, dialed again. "Troy, I know your stupid behind is there! You'd better answer this phone or I will come over there and bust your head!"

When she called back a few seconds later, her voice full of syrup. "Troy, baby, I'm sorry. Please give me a call at your earliest convenience. I really want to talk to you. Love you."

Danielle slumped against the back of the couch, her chest heaving. "I have to talk to Nikki! And she's being so rude. She knows I'm having problems with Troy, but she's too busy with her own perfect life." Danielle uttered the words aloud as if speaking to someone. She dialed Nikki's number again, but it went to voicemail. Danielle hung up without leaving a message.

Thirty minutes later, her phone rang and she answered to Nikki's voice. "Hey, baby, what's going on? Sorry I couldn't talk earlier, but Psalm was talking and then Will started telling me about his day."

"Oh, I'm all right," Danielle said, still fuming on the inside.

"Are you sure? It almost sounded like something was wrong earlier. That's why I hurried up and called you back."

Didn't seem like you were in too big of a hurry to me. "No, it's fine. Sorry to disturb you," Danielle said, a bit coolly.

"Hey, look, if something is wrong, just spill it."

"I said I'm fine," Danielle snapped.

"Fine?" Danielle could hear the smile in Nikki's voice, but Danielle did not respond. Nikki prompted, "You know what 'fine' means." Still not getting a response, Nikki pressed. "Didn't you tell me yourself that you psychology types say someone who says they are fine really means they are fouled up, insecure, narcissistic and—"

"I said I'm fine!" Danielle snapped again.

"Okay, okay," Nikki backed off. "It was just a joke. Look, I'll be over there in a few minutes."

"You don't need to come over here," Danielle pouted.

"I said I'll be there in a few minutes," Nikki insisted. "Bye."

Nikki hung up. Danielle held the phone a moment. A tiny smile lifted the corners of her mouth. She knew her friend would come see about her.

Chapter 5

Nikki turned to William. "Look, I need to run by Danielle's for a sec. I think I hurt her feelings about something."

"You pay more attention to her than you do your own sister," William said.

"Well, she is my best friend—just like a sister," Nikki said. She had been surprised when the much prettier woman wanted to be friends way back during their freshman year of college. But Nikki quickly realized that as outwardly put together as she was, Danielle needed a friend. And living in a strange city, Nikki had need for one as well. She had moved to New Orleans from Houston not knowing much about the city, except this school offered her a scholarship and a chance to shoot pictures.

"I'm just saying. Every time that girl calls, you go running," William said. "She needs to realize you have a life and can't go traipsing all across town all hours of the night. You need to be at home with your family."

Nikki kissed William on the forehead. "I'll be right back."

"Okay, well, I'll make Psalm get her bath and go to

sleep." A mischievous sparkle lit William's eye. "So maybe when you get back, I'll have something waiting for you."

"Hmm," Nikki said, sidling up to her husband. "Will it be something . . . big?"

William smiled. "You just get ready. And don't do too much while you're out. You're going to need all your energy when you get back."

"Is that a promise?"

"You bet," he said, bending to kiss her. She slapped him on the rear and grabbed the keys to the Mazda Protégé they shared.

Fifteen minutes later, Nikki was letting herself into Danielle's spacious two-bedroom condo with the key Danielle had given her when she moved in two years ago. "Hey, Danny Boo, how are you?" Nikki employed the nickname she used when her friend was upset with her.

She found Danielle curled on the couch with the remote in her hand and a box of cookies on the floor. Danielle gave no indication that she heard her friend, so Nikki lifted the woman's legs from the sofa and sat down, placing Danielle's legs on her lap. "I'm sorry I couldn't talk to you earlier," she said.

"It's okay," Danielle pouted.

"You know if something is wrong with you, I want to know about it."

"I know you have your perfect little family, and can't be bothered with me and my little problems," Danielle sulked.

"It's not even like that, and you know it."

"Remember how we used to talk? We both said we'd never be one of those women who kicked their friends to the curb for a man," Danielle reminded Nikki.

"I didn't kick you to the curb."

"Right." Danielle's tone was dry.

"I didn't. I just had to pay attention to my husband for a

minute. He had a stressful day. I was going to call you back."

"You didn't know if I had an emergency or something," Danielle said. "I'm always there for you. I would never just kick you off the phone if I knew something was wrong."

"Come on, sis, I asked if you were okay," Nikki reminded her friend. "You said you were all right."

"Well, you could tell from my voice that I was lying."

Nikki sighed. "Look, Danielle, you can't be so sensitive. You know I love you like a sister. We've been tight for almost ten years. I would never push you aside."

"Humph."

"I wanted to share a word with you," Nikki said, pulling a devotional and tiny Bible from her purse.

Danielle held up her hand. "Girl, I am not in the mood."

"It'll make you feel better," Nikki coaxed.

"I know everything in that book." Danielle waved off the Bible. "I go to church just like you do—maybe not as often, but I do go sometimes. So I don't need you coming over here trying to preach to me."

"I'm not trying to preach to you," Nikki said. "I'm just trying to minister to you."

"Girl, please," Danielle snapped. "I was quoting the Bible before you were ever even saved. I certainly don't need you trying to tell me how to live. Remember, I know who you really are, so don't try to act like you're all holy in front of me."

Nikki looked down at her hands, then back up at her friend. "You didn't have to say that," Nikki said quietly. "Look, I know I'm not perfect. And I know you knew God way before I ever knew anything about the Bible."

"Yeah. So put your little devotional up," Danielle said, waving her hand in a dismissive fashion. "I don't need to get preached to by someone who has no room to tell me anything."

Nikki bit her lip. "I have no right to tell you how to live your life. I know that. I didn't grow up in a church. And I didn't have some of the experiences you had, always being around the Word."

"Exactly," Danielle interrupted. "My mama was always quoting some scripture whenever she wanted to get us to do something. Always dragging us to somebody's church service. I learned all that stuff while you were off being raised in your heathen family, so I don't need to hear it from you."

Nikki winced. "I wasn't raised in a *heathen* family. We just weren't very religious. But I can't change all that. All I can do is try and minister to you today. All I want to do is encourage you."

"Well, the only encouragement I need is for you to answer when I call you on the phone." Danielle's tone was sharp.

"Look, I will put the devotional up for now." Nikki shoved it back into her purse. "But I'm not going to let you talk to me like that. I came over here to help you. And I am here for you. Now will you let me be your friend—your sister—right now?"

Danielle didn't say anything, but Nikki could tell she was thawing. "Besides, I brought you something." She pulled a bag of Danielle's favorite candy, jellybeans, from her pocket. Nikki tickled her friend's foot. "Now, stop being a baby."

Her icy mood thawed and Danielle took the candy with a half smile. "Old meanie."

"Big baby."

Nikki twisted to get comfortable on the couch. "So. Tell me what happened."

Danielle dug her hand into the bag of candy and pulled out a palm full of jellybeans. She shoved them into her mouth, sniffling hard to keep from crying. "I think Troy is seeing that woman again," she said.

"Who?"

Danielle rolled her eyes. "The girl he was seeing when we started talking."

Nikki raised a brow. "Oh, yeah," she recalled. "Well, I told you to leave him alone, anyway. He's not any good for you. Besides, do you really want someone you picked up while he was putting gas in his girlfriend's car in the first place?"

"*Ex*-girlfriend," Danielle reminded her friend tartly.

Danielle had met Troy six months ago at the gas station as she sashayed across the parking lot when he called to her, complimenting her on how good her legs looked in her short red silk Gucci dress and Prada heels. Danielle had been instantly taken with him: his dark skin, tall, muscled frame and the shiny convertible he was driving. She later found out the convertible belonged to his girlfriend, but that didn't matter when he told Danielle he had ditched the other woman for her.

"Well, whatever," Nikki said. "Either way, he's a jerk."

"He's not!" Danielle smarted under the insult to her man.

"Well, if he isn't, then why are you over here crying, thinking he is fooling around?"

"Because . . ." Danielle said, then retorted. "Look, you wouldn't understand. It's been so long since you've been with anyone besides old William."

"Okay; so?"

"So, you don't know anything about anything."

"Well, I know enough to see when someone is getting played," Nikki said, waving off her friend's disparaging remark. "You're a beautiful girl. You're smart. Why do you keep dating these losers?"

"If you came over here to talk about me, you know where the door is," Danielle said. She had always known she was prettier than her friend, and that was part of why they were such good friends. Nikki never tried to compete with her, not like some of the other women Danielle knew.

Danielle was 5'11" with light, golden brown hair that hung past her shoulders and was carefully highlighted with honey blond, to perfectly complement her skin that was the color of milk-diluted coffee. She had put on more weight since college, but still had a good figure, with voluptuous breasts, a small waist and round rear.

"I'm just saying," Nikki said. "You deserve better."

"Don't worry about what I deserve," Danielle said.

Nikki could tell Danielle was slipping back into the mood she had been in when Nikki arrived, so she tried to change the subject. "Do you remember that time we almost got arrested when we went to the community college to visit that guy you were seeing? What was his name?"

"You're talking about Scooter?" Danielle smiled at the recollection.

Their freshman year, Danielle and Nikki sneaked into the dorm room of Danielle's newest beau and hung out late into the night. They bolted out the window when the resident assistant banged on the door, insisting he heard girls' voices. The security guard saw them crawl out the window and yelled at them, causing the girls to break into a run. They outran the rotund man who hobbled after them for maybe a few feet and stopped, out of breath, gasping at them to come back as he threatened them with a box of chicken and waffles in one hand and a flashlight at his waist.

"Yeah, that was some funny stuff." Danielle dissolved into giggles at the memory. "You remember that fat man's stomach looking like it was going to explode out of his shirt?" she guffawed. "Looking like a wave of wobbling Jell-O. I know he didn't think he was going to catch us."

"Yeah, girl, those were the days." Nikki laughed, glad her friend's mood had lifted.

"Back then, we wouldn't be sitting around crying over some stupid man," Danielle said, chewing on a mouthful of the sticky candy. "I had men for days. Everywhere I looked somebody was asking for my number."

"Yeah, you were it," Nikki said. "But you still are. Don't let this guy get you down. He's not worth your time."

"Yeah, you're right. He's not worth my time. He should be begging me to take him back."

Chapter 6

Nikki arrived back home to a darkened living room. She carefully placed her keys on the cherry wood table next to the door and tiptoed into Psalm's bedroom, where she found the child asleep in her canopied bed, her teddy bear in her arms. She leaned in and kissed Psalm's temple and stood over her, watching the child's chest move up and down as she slept. This child was Nikki's treasure.

She then walked to her own bedroom. Nikki burst out laughing when she saw her husband lying across the bed in red, silk boxers, giving her his best mock seductive look, with an exaggerated licking of his lips.

"What is this supposed to be?" Nikki asked, pointing.

William pretended to be offended. "I'm sexy, girl, I don't know what you're talking about." He threw an overstated kiss in her direction.

"You are sexy, baby," Nikki cooed stepping out of her dress, her zebra print bra and panties her only adornment.

She remembered how Danielle had thought William was goofy their first time meeting him, but Nikki had found his lankiness and boyish smile endearing. And he had filled out nicely as he got older, though he was still angular. He was long and lean, with butterscotch skin and teeth like those seen only in toothpaste commercials. He kept his hair shaved close and neat. William was the suit-wearing type. During his more casual moments, he wore khakis and loafers. He steered clear of throw-back jerseys and low-hanging jeans. He didn't have the animal magnetism or the jump-up-and-look-at-me handsomeness of some, but Nikki liked his clean-cut features. And she loved knowing she was secure.

William pulled her into his embrace, unhooking her bra at the same time. He kissed her mouth softly, then with more force. He leaned into her neck, breathing in the scent of her hair and skin, which still smelled faintly of peach blossomed shower gel. "You are so beautiful," he said.

William always made Nikki feel special. Most of the other guys she had met prior to him either were immediately drawn to her much prettier friend, or, if they liked Nikki, they didn't make her feel the way William had.

He explored her body as if for the first time, kissing her skin and letting his hands roam in all the places he knew she liked them to find. When she tried to reach for him to reciprocate, he gently pushed her back down. "Just relax," he said as she felt his breath on her neck.

They heard a muffled sound from Psalm's room and both instantly froze for a split second to listen for more. "She's still sleeping," Nikki whispered. Relieved they had not awakened their daughter, they continued the marital dance that never got old.

Afterward, they snuggled together, Nikki's head on her husband's chest. She lifted so she could look into his eyes. "I love you so much."

"I know what you love," he said and bit her ear.

She giggled. "Well, that too," she smiled, stroking him. "But seriously, I really do love you."

"I love you more." He let his fingers make lazy circles on her arm.

"I love you more than more," she said.

"I love you more than more than more." He kissed the top of her head. She giggled. But he had a strangely serious expression. "I'm for real. I thank God every day for you."

"Why are you so serious all of a sudden?" Nikki said. "Lighten up. I know you love me."

"No, baby, listen." William shifted so she could see him clearly. He cupped her chin in his hand. "I know you could have had anybody, somebody with more money, a nicer house, two cars. I really thought we would have been further along by now. I'm sorry for not being able to give you—"

Nikki put her finger to his mouth. "Shhh. Don't do that. We're in this together. I know you didn't plan on the computer business going bust, but it did. And it hasn't been easy, but we've made it. Baby, we made it when all those folks told us we wouldn't last seven months, let alone seven years."

"Do you regret getting married so young?" She heard the uncertainty in his voice.

"Not a single day," Nikki said, and a twinkle entered her eye. "Who else would I have this much fun with?" She shifted her position and pulled his face to hers, kissing his cheek. "Of course, I'll be glad when we get out of some of this debt."

William sighed. "Yeah, I know the feeling. But don't even worry about it. We're just doing what we need to for now, but our day is coming."

"I know, but sometimes I get scared," Nikki said. "This house—" she waved her hand in the air.

William put his finger to her lips. "Shhh," he said. "It's all right."

"I know," Nikki snuggled closer. "I know you've taken care of everything and always will."

"You got that right."

* * *

A piercing, pain-filled shriek jolted Nikki awake at four a.m. and she sprang from the bed, pulling on her husband's T-shirt in the same movement. She raced to Psalm's bedroom, with a groggy William at her heels, jerking on shorts.

"Baby, baby, Mommy's here," Nikki cuddled Psalm to her chest. The screaming got louder. "What's wrong?"

William flicked on the light. "Does something hurt?" he asked the wailing child.

Psalm's mouth was open wide and large tears flooded her cheeks.

"I thought it was a nightmare but these are real tears, and she's hot," Nikki said.

William got some children's medicine, but nothing seemed to work. No matter how much they held her, Psalm's wails continued.

"Baby, can you tell Mama what's wrong?" Nikki tried to sound calm, but panic made her voice crack.

Psalm seemed not to be able to get the words out, but she clutched at her stomach.

"Is it your tummy?" Nikki asked frantically, raising the child's shirt. She touched Psalm's abdomen, and the wails grew louder.

"Will, we've got to get her to the doctor," Nikki said, rocking her daughter in her arms.

William didn't answer, but disappeared into their bedroom. "Put your clothes on, we're taking her to the hospital," he said, emerging from the bedroom wearing jeans and sneakers.

"You think it's something bad?" Nikki asked, fear in her eyes. "I should have paid more attention to her earlier when she said her stomach was hurting. It's all my fault."

"Whatever it is, the doctors can fix it." William reached for Psalm. "I'll hold her while you get dressed."

"I don't want to leave her," Nikki shook her head. "Can you just pass me something?"

William grabbed underwear, jeans and one of her T-shirts. Nikki donned her clothing quickly, and they raced to the car, Nikki cradling the shrieking child to her chest.

Chapter 7

"Troy, I know you're in there!" Danielle hissed, her cheek pressed to the cool wooden door. She strained to hear movement, but could discern nothing. She knocked lightly, but insistently, on the door again, and then looked around. None of the neighbors came outside, thankfully.

"I saw your car in the parking lot!" Danielle said, this time a little louder, but trying not to raise her voice. "I know you're home."

Danielle had called Troy all day on his cell phone, but hadn't received an answer. Even when she called his job, she only received voicemail. She had tried to calm her mind while Nikki visited her earlier in the evening. Danielle had managed to put Troy out of her thoughts for a short while. She had even gone to bed shortly after Nikki left, but her mind raced with so many questions. Why was Troy ignoring her? Was he with that other woman? Who did he think he was that he could ignore her?

Finally, shortly after four a.m., Danielle could take it no longer. She climbed out of bed, quickly dressed and hopped into her gold Lexus coupe and sped to Troy's apartment to see if she could catch him and get to the bottom of this.

Boom! Boom! Boom!

Her balled fists pounded on the door, and this time when she spoke, her voice was no longer low. "Troy! I know—"

Before she could finish, the door jerked open and he stood before her, eyes red with sleep. "Girl, what's your crazy problem?"

"I know you have that woman in here." She shoved past him and flicked on the living room light. He held up his hands against the glare, cursing.

"You're out of your mind," he said. "Nobody is here, but your crazy self. Now stop trying to wake the whole neighborhood."

Danielle ignored him and stalked through the apartment, opening and slamming closet doors. She knelt and peered under the bed, where he returned, pulling the covers over his head.

"Well, why haven't you been answering or returning any of my calls?" she demanded, temporarily satisfied not to have found anyone, but still suspicious.

"Danielle, did it ever occur to you that something could be wrong, that I might be sick?" Troy asked in annoyance.

For the first time, she noticed the tissues on his nightstand and a half empty glass of orange juice.

"Oh, I'm sorry!" she said, her hand to her mouth. "Why didn't you tell me?"

"Because, I didn't feel like talking to anybody," he said through the covers.

"But, baby, I could have come over here to take care of you," Danielle cooed.

He grunted. "Right. You don't even like taking care of people at work, and that's your job."

"That's not true!"

"Okay, well, whatever," he said. "But look, I have a cold

or sinus infection or something. So can you let me get back to sleep? It's the middle of the night."

"Oh, well, I'll just stay here with you," Danielle said.

"Danielle, I'm sick," he said. "I wouldn't be any good company. And I don't want to get you sick." He let out a cough and she leaned away from him, grimacing.

"Yeah, you're right," she backed toward the door and rifled through her purse for antibacterial hand wash. "I'm sorry for waking you."

"Right."

Danielle fled from the apartment, slathering on antibacterial hand wash and never noticing the neighbor's door that stood slightly ajar.

Chapter 8

Nikki and William waited seemingly forever before the doctor emerged. "Is she all right?"

"She will be," said the kind-faced man. The lines around his eyes spoke of concern. His name tag identified him as Dr. Woods.

"Oh, thank you." Nikki visibly relaxed. "What made her cry like that? It seemed like she was in so much pain. I couldn't bear it."

"Well, she has what is called a choledochal cyst," Dr. Woods said. "It is a digestive condition."

"Is it serious? You said she will be okay, right?" Nikki's dark brown eyes searched the doctor's face. William put his arm around her.

"Yes, it is serious, and yes, there is a very good chance she will be okay," the doctor assured her. Dr. Woods included them both in his glance. "This is a situation brought on likely by an abnormality that's been there since birth."

"Since birth?" Nikki's voice cracked. "How can that be? You mean my baby has been sick and I didn't know?"

"Well, what usually happens is that by about the age

Psalm is now, bile begins to collect in the duct, forming a cyst, and this can cause a lot of other things," he said. "It can eventually cause abdominal pain and fever, though usually we don't see that in a patient this young."

"What can be done about it?" William jumped in. "It's curable, right?"

"There is a surgical procedure to remove the duct and use a piece of intestine to replace it," Dr. Woods said.

"My baby has to have surgery?" Nikki's voice quivered.

"Well, it doesn't have to be something that happens today, but the procedure can cure her condition. The sooner, the better, to prevent any further episodes like the one that brought her here tonight." His pager sounded. "Well, I've got to respond to this, but I'm available to you if you need to confer later. You are free to visit her room at any time."

As the doctor walked off, Nikki's breath caught in her throat. She let it out in a slow, ragged manner and turned, burying her face in her husband's shirt. "I can't believe I didn't know she was sick. I'm a terrible mother."

"Baby, you are the best mother in the world," William said. "The doctor said she will be fine. And she will be. We'll get her the care she needs and this will be behind us. God has revealed the condition so we have to trust Him for deliverance."

"What if the doctors can't do anything for her?" Nikki's eyes searched William's face for assurance.

"They will," William guaranteed.

"But what if they can't?"

"Things will be fine." William rubbed her shoulder. "You heard the doctor. We will pray for God's healing and that He directs the doctors to the best course of action. Now let's go see how our baby is doing."

"Okay." Nikki nodded. She squeezed William's hand, then walked with him to Psalm's room.

Nikki touched her child's arm while William prayed.

"Dear Heavenly Father, we ask that you show mercy to our daughter. We know you have the power of healing. Please deliver her from this terrible affliction. In the name of your loving son, Jesus. Amen."

"Amen." Nikki echoes the word, but nervousness crowded out confidence. As they stood next to Psalm's bed, watching her sleep peacefully, fear churned in Nikki's belly.

Chapter 9

Danielle dialed Nikki's number on the way to work the next morning, as was her habit. She didn't get an answer on Nikki's home phone, so dialed her friend's cell. Nikki answered on the second ring.

Danielle knew instantly something was wrong. "Are you okay?"

"It's Psalm," Nikki said. "We had to take her to the emergency room last night. We're still here."

Danielle gasped. "The emergency room? Is she all right?"

Danielle heard the breath catch in Nikki's throat. "I don't know," Nikki said. "The doctor said she has some birth defect and has to have surgery."

"Birth defect?" Danielle said. "She's four years old. How does she have a birth defect?"

"I don't know." Nikki's voice was small. "I'm just scared."

"Look, I'll be right there. What hospital?"

"No, don't come; we're about to take her home."

"Okay, I'll meet you at your house. I'll use my key."

* * *

About thirty minutes later, Danielle snatched the front
door open when she heard Nikki and William pull into the
driveway with Psalm. "Come on in and tell me what happened," she said as Nikki gently lifted Psalm from her
booster seat.

Danielle ushered her friend into the house, holding the
door as the smell of coffee and bacon greeted Nikki. Nikki
smiled and shifted Psalm in her arms. "Thanks," she said.
"You are so sweet. You didn't have to do this."

"Well, I know if you've been at the hospital all night,
you've not eaten," Danielle said, grabbing a cup of coffee
from the counter and handing it to William.

"Thanks," William said.

Nikki disappeared down the hall with the sleeping Psalm.

"You didn't have any syrup, so is jelly okay for your
bacon?" Danielle called to Nikki, knowing her best friend
always ate something sweet on her breakfast meat.

"I'm really not hungry," Nikki said, re-entering the kitchen.

"Baby, you need to eat," William coaxed softly.

Nikki nodded. "Yeah, jelly is okay." She sat down to the
food and they bowed in prayer.

"Dear Lord, thank you for this meal," William said, "and
thank you for even the blessing of this morning. Thank you
for giving us the knowledge of our daughter's condition and
we pray you guide us in the best course of action. Please
grant healing. Amen."

"So what is this about a birth defect?" Danielle asked,
her eyes moving from Nikki's grim face to William's.

"Well, the doctor said she has a condition that is the result of some birth defect she has had all this time." Nikki's
words came out softly and deliberately. "All this time, my
baby has been sick. I . . . I just don't understand."

"Well, I'm sure it's not as bad as the doctor said,"
Danielle assured.

"Well, birth defect sounds pretty serious to me," Nikki said.

"But that's all right," William reminded his wife. "God can do abundantly more than we can even think, much less ask Him to do. And that's in the Bible. So healing our baby is well within His capabilities, and I feel she will be delivered."

"I'm just going by what the doctor said," Nikki insisted. "I am so scared and—"

"Who are you going to believe?" William challenged. "The Lord or some human doctor?"

Nikki opened her mouth, then closed it.

Danielle nodded. "Yeah, listen to William. He's right. Remember when you came to my house last night trying to give me a word of encouragement to help me face my doubts? You wanted to tell me that God would see me through, right? Well, I'm trying to do the same thing here." Danielle raised a brow. "Surely you can take a few words of encouragement, can't you?"

Danielle saw the emotions play across her friend's face. She knew Nikki wanted to latch on to the words, but her doubts and concerns battled her faith. "Now tell me every single thing the doctor said," Danielle invited.

They told Danielle about the conversation with the doctor, and she nodded gravely.

When they finished telling her about that day's experience, Danielle shook her head and said, "I've never heard of this choledochal cyst, but maybe it's not as bad as you think it is."

"I'm going to look it up on the internet," Nikki said. "And we're going to get this taken care of as soon as we can."

"Can you call the insurance company today to get pre-certified?" William asked his wife. "That way, we can get the ball rolling and can go on and schedule the surgery, if we find it's necessary."

"You're not going to let her have surgery, are you?" Danielle asked.

"I'm sure it won't come to that," William said. "I'm praying she can be cured without that extreme measure."

"Well, the doctor said surgery is what would cure her," Nikki insisted.

"Well, still. . . ." Danielle wasn't convinced they should be so quick to consider surgery.

"Look, if surgery is the best thing, then that's what it'll be," Nikki said. "I can't let my baby get sick to where she is in as much pain as she was last night. It was horrible. She cried so much that her throat was sore and finally, all she could do was hiccup. I felt so bad. If I could have taken her pain as my own, I would have. I'll do whatever I have to for my child."

"Shouldn't you trust in God?" Danielle prodded. "Faith—"

"—without works is dead," Nikki interrupted flatly. "And I'm going to work on getting my child better, no matter what it takes."

Danielle shuddered.

Chapter 10

The insurance company's denial was immediate. The surgery wasn't covered. They said surgery wasn't the recommended treatment in patients Psalm's age, and that most people didn't experience ill effects from the condition until years later.

"Well, my baby was in terrible pain last night," Nikki said to the dry, bland voice on the phone.

"Well, ma'am, all I'm saying is this surgery is not considered the appropriate treatment, according to our experts," the insurance representative said.

"Well, ma'am," Nikki tried to speak calmly, "the doctor said—"

"Yes, I understand." The representative cut her off, speaking as if to a child. "Doctors sometimes over-treat. They often try to do the most drastic measure. Here, we want to be responsible."

"Responsible? What do you mean?" Nikki said before calming herself down. "Look, lady, I know you're just doing your job, but you've got to okay this surgery for my little girl."

"I'm sorry, ma'am."

"But I can't afford it without insurance!" Nikki said, clutching the receiver to her ear. Sweat beaded her nose. She could hear Psalm stirring in the other room. "Okay, look, I've got to go. Thank you for your non-help."

"You're most welcome."

Nikki stepped into Psalm's bedroom. The girl was just starting to awaken. "Good morning, precious," Nikki greeted with a wide smile. She didn't want Psalm to sense her anxiety. She leaned in and kissed the girl on the forehead. "Are you hungry? Do you want breakfast?"

"Yes, ma'am," Psalm said, stretching her tiny arms high over her head as she sat up in the bed.

Nikki's brows arched in surprise. She wasn't sure Psalm would be ready to eat, but the girl's assurance was a welcome response. Nikki reached down to help her daughter from the canopied bed, but Psalm sprang up and raced off from the room.

"Mommy, let's play hide and seek!"

Nikki followed the child in wonderment. It was as if Psalm had never been sick and had not spent hours at the hospital. Maybe her prayers were working, Nikki mused. She hadn't wanted to trust her daughter's care to a few random prayers, but maybe prayer was just the antidote. Relief coursed through her being as the anxiety of the past few hours began to dissipate.

Nikki's eyes fell on the children's Bible on the bookshelf. "Thank you, Lord." She breathed the words.

"Mommy!" Psalm's voice was insistent. "Come play with me!"

Nikki emerged from the bedroom. "Okay, okay," she said with a laugh. "Let's get you some food; then we'll play."

Nikki felt chagrin at her earlier dismay. "I'll never doubt you again, Lord."

Chapter 11

Danielle arrived at work an hour and a half late, but breezed in as if nothing was amiss. She gave her supervisor a quick explanation about a life-and-death emergency to stifle any complaints, then went about her duties.

Her mind went briefly to Nikki. It sure was a lot easier for Nikki to try to dish advice than it was for her to take it, Danielle mused. All Danielle had tried to do was give Nikki the same advice Nikki had wanted to give her. Danielle felt certain this medical issue wasn't that big of a deal. After all, how serious could it be if she had never even heard of the condition?

Danielle forgot about Psalm as she grabbed a stack of patient charts. She moved from patient to patient with little incident, until an altercation rattled her. Danielle escaped to her office for a few moments after a particularly harrowing confrontation with a patient. The man had tried to kill himself after losing his job and discovering his wife wanted a divorce. This was his third week of treatment. He shoved Danielle and she had almost gone crashing headfirst into the wall, but managed to regain her balance. She had to call in help to have him restrained. Now, back in her office to collect her thoughts, the restlessness she felt erupted.

"I can't wait to get out of this place," she fumed. "These people are working my nerves." Her phone rang the second she sat down. "Danielle Esperanza, may I help you?" she said in her professional voice.

"You know Troy was lying," said a female voice on the other end.

"Who is this?"

"You know who this is," the voice said. "I'm the woman you're so concerned about that you would leave your warm bed at four in the morning to come find."

"Look, I don't know who you think you are, calling my job—"

"Knock it off," the woman said. "I'm just calling to tell you, you can have Troy. I don't need some man who keeps trying to play me. I see you're into games. I'm not. My cousin just moved in next door to him and she told me about your visit last night. Troy and I spent the day together, in bed. I left to go home because that's the only way I could get some rest—he wore me out. He was probably exhausted when you showed up; he probably was asleep, I imagine.

"If I had known you were coming over, though, I would have stayed an extra fifteen minutes. I told Troy, if I ever caught him fooling around on me, that was it."

"Fooling around on you?" Danielle's blood pressure rose. "I'm the girlfriend. I don't know who you are. Probably some two-bit home wrecker."

"Well, name-calling isn't necessary," the woman said. "And for the record, the name is Chastity. Have a good day."

The phone went dead in Danielle's ear.

Chapter 12

Nikki telephoned the insurance company again, but still got nowhere. Another representative, this one a man with a thick accent, gave her the same news. Her child's surgery was not covered.

She plopped down on the couch, the silent phone in her lap. She knew she had to figure this thing out. Psalm seemed to be feeling all right, but Nikki wanted medical assurance. "Maybe I should go back to work, no matter what William says. At least then we'd have more money and good health insurance," she pondered out loud, but then stopped herself. "But no, that's not part of the plan. William wants me to be home."

Nikki recalled the feelings of loneliness she held as a child, especially when her mother remarried. The marriage had meant more material things for Nikki, but those things could never take away the feeling of losing her mother's attention. She even gained a sister, Carla, through the marriage because her stepfather brought with him a daughter, but even that didn't save her from the intense feelings of being by herself in the world.

Carla needed all the attention—first, because she was the baby, and then later, because she always seemed to get into trouble. Nikki's mother constantly rushed to Carla's aid, doing whatever it took to make her new daughter and new husband feel comfortable. Nikki remembered needing braces but her mother told her they didn't have the money. The next day, it seemed to Nikki's mind, Carla was wearing braces.

Nikki often stayed after school for activities, but Carla, who hated school, went straight home. If the after-school bus was late dropping Nikki off, it didn't matter. Her family would go out to dinner without her. On more than one occasion, she arrived to an empty house with only a dinner of peanut butter and crackers, while her family dined on pasta and steak in a popular restaurant.

She vowed she would never let her child know what it felt like not to have her mother's attention and concern. Nikki knew she had to find a way to get that surgery for Psalm.

Chapter 13

William tapped the keyboard for the final time and stood. "Okay, you're all set," he said and smiled at the blonde who looked relieved. "Your computer is good as new."

"Oh, thank you!" the woman said. She put her hand to her chest in an exaggerated expression of relief. "I was so afraid I had lost all my important documents. When the computer crashed I thought I would die."

They were at the woman's home office.

"Well, it was simple to fix," William said, taking the check the woman held out to him. He thanked her and left, his mind already on his work ahead.

The hospital visit had resulted in him missing his first computer appointment of the morning, so now he was headed to the campaign office, a tiny space on Jewella Avenue.

William dialed home. "Hey, baby. How is Psalm?" he asked when Nikki answered.

"She's fine. She's been playing for the last half hour. She hasn't eaten much, but she doesn't appear to be in any kind of pain."

"Oh, that's good to hear," William said. "How are you?"

"I'm mad!" The words were so loud, William pulled the phone from his ear for a moment.

"What happened?" he asked, putting the phone back in position to hear his wife.

"The insurance company," she said. "They are such jerks. The woman was talking to me like I'm stupid or something. Then I called back and talked to a man and he wasn't any help either. Bottom line is they aren't going to pay for this procedure."

"What did they say?"

"That it's not the recommended treatment."

"Did you tell them a doctor said this is what she needs?"

"Yeah," Nikki said. "You know all they care about is the money."

"Well, don't let them get you down, baby," he said. "Maybe she doesn't need the surgery after all. You just said she's been playing. Maybe God has already granted deliverance."

"She was playing all right early yesterday, too; but then we saw what happened," Nikki shot back.

"All I'm saying is maybe we're being hasty with this surgery idea," William said. "I've been praying. You've been praying. And really, what could one doctor know? God knows better and I believe He will heal Psalm; maybe He already has."

"William, I can't see her go through that again," Nikki's voice broke with emotion. "She was in so much pain. It hurt my heart. I hope she has already been healed, I really do, but I need to know for sure."

"Baby, it will be fine," William assured. "Just trust God."

"That's your answer to everything!" Nikki snapped. "Just trust God. Well, I think sometimes God wants us to act as well. It's not enough just to trust that miracles will rain down from the sky. We have to do our part."

"Fine," William said. "We'll write the insurance company a letter or something. We'll get them to change their minds. All of this will get taken care of. You'll see."

"Well, I just know my baby needs this surgery."

"Okay, baby, we'll talk about it later," William said. "I need to go, now. Love you."

"Love you, too."

William climbed from the car and saw a reporter walking toward him.

"Is it true that Reverend Chance has a gambling problem?" the reporter asked William, who laughed.

"Is that the best you guys can do over there?" William said, walking toward the office.

"You didn't answer the question," said Jimmy Vaughn, a short, balding reporter with ink-stained fingertips. He followed William into the tiny campaign office.

"No, he does not have a gambling problem."

Jimmy helped himself to coffee, pouring a cup. The reporter called or stopped by the office at least twice a week it seemed, with some query about the mayoral candidate. William did his best to deflate rumors and to deflect anything that didn't sound good. He believed in his candidate and wanted the city to see this was the right man for the job.

"Well, we have it from reliable sources that he has lost large sums at the boats," Jimmy said. "I'm doing some more digging, so this is your chance to get your side out."

"There is nothing to get out," William said. "Reverend Chance does not have a gambling problem."

"If you say so."

Jimmy shoved his notebook into the back of his pants, with the top sticking out. He took the last swig of his coffee, plunked the cup onto the counter, and left.

A moment later, Reverend Chance walked through the door, a cell phone to his ear and another one ringing in his pocket. He hung up that call, sent the incoming one to voicemail and gave a general greeting to everyone in the office. "Good morning, saints!"

A chorus of hellos greeted him in turn from those in the office: his daughter, Olivia, who was also his campaign manager; a new male volunteer who William had seen only once before; and William. Reverend Chance shook William's hand.

"How is it going, son?" Reverend Chance queried.

"Fine, Reverend," William replied. "And yourself?"

"Oh, I'm on the battlefield for the Lord," he said. "The devil will throw sticks, but the Lord keeps on breaking them."

Reverend Chance clapped and let out a booming laugh. William recalled the first time he saw the man. Chance had been the speaker at a student government function, challenging each of the students to work for right and to reach for greatness. He had been so powerful, so moving that William had been an admirer ever since.

"So, what's going on around here?" Reverend Chance asked. He was tall, well over six feet, nearly 300 pounds, with broad shoulders and wore neatly pressed suits that had to be tailored especially for his large frame.

"Well, the other side just released poll results showing we are behind by a significant margin." William hated to break the news.

"Well, we've fought uphill before," Reverend Chance said. "That just means we work that much harder to get our message out."

"We can order our own poll. I talked to the company yesterday. They are ready to go, if we want," William said.

"Yes, but we don't have the money for that," Reverend Chance said. "I think we'll wait another week or two and run the poll then."

"Well, we've got to know what the public is thinking," said Olivia, joining the conversation. She was stocky, with freshly permed hair and wore a dark blue suit.

"I know, dear, but we'll just trust the Lord for the next week or so and find out then," Reverend Chance said.

"We can't just leave this one to trusting the Lord," Olivia shot back.

Reverend Chance raised a brow and his tone grew stern. "We don't talk like that around here, Olivia."

She insisted. "Daddy, the general election is only a few months away. And, that's if we make it that far."

"I know. But I feel good about this."

William wasn't so sure. Lo Dark's signs easily outnumbered theirs and the media coverage seemed to favor the incumbent. There were a few other candidates running, but they didn't bear much mentioning, as they weren't doing much campaigning. William swallowed before breaking the latest news.

"Jimmy Vaughn from *The Times* just stopped by. I'm surprised you didn't see him leaving on your way in," William said. "They are trying to do a story about you and a gambling problem. I told them that was ridiculous, that you didn't have any such issues, but the guy seemed pretty intent on running something anyway."

"Okay, well, get them back on the phone."

"Do what?" William's eyes shot to Reverend Chance's face.

"Set a meeting, this afternoon if you can," Reverend Chance said.

"What do you mean, sir? We don't have to entertain foolishness."

"It's not foolishness."

William's eyebrows shot up. "Excuse me?"

"I don't mind talking about it," Reverend Chance said.

"I did waste a lot of money on the boats in my younger years, maybe ten years ago. But that's all behind me now. The Lord blessed me to overcome that."

Olivia let out a snort. "That's all we need; more bad stuff in the paper."

"Well, we can just come clean to the voters," Reverend Chance said. "Honesty—"

"Is overrated," Olivia said flatly. She put her hand on her father's arm. "Daddy, look. I understand that you want to be honest and tell folks about your past, but you and I both know you really don't want to go there."

Reverend Chance kissed Olivia's cheek. "You worry too much," he said.

"Well, somebody has to take control of things," she said.

Reverend Chance glanced around the campaign office, then back at his daughter. "I do have control." A slight edge crept into his tone.

"But, Daddy, you should just let me handle all of this," she said. "I know how to run your campaign. Don't mess it up."

"Olivia," Reverend Chance said, "This conversation is over. I have made my decision. I will go public and trust the voters to make the right choice."

William could tell Olivia wanted to protest, so he jumped in to steer the conversation away from a confrontation between father and daughter. "Maybe we should just wait and see." William glanced at Olivia, then he nodded at Reverend Chance. "Let's err on the side of caution and sit tight for a moment, maybe. And then if anything else comes up, maybe you go public then." He tried to broker a deal. William didn't want to see his candidate's numbers go even lower, and he knew a story about a free spending pastor would do just that. First his child, now his candidate. Could it get any worse?

"Just call them back, William," Reverend Chance said. "Tell them we have a statement."

Chapter 14

Nikki's Internet search yielded all manner of horror stories. Her first query produced a report that eased her mind, but subsequent searches gave her information about children and adults whose lives were forever compromised by their condition, of other disorders that resulted from the untreated condition, even cancer.

By the time William got home, she was near tears. "Psalm has got to have this surgery. Now," she insisted, before he even had a chance to take off his jacket.

"All right, baby," William said in a calm voice.

"Are you listening to me?" Nikki demanded.

"Yes, I am. I said 'all right.' " His voice remained calm.

"William, this is your child, your baby and you don't seem at all concerned for her well being," Nikki snapped.

"I thought you said she was up and playing earlier? That, to me, is a clear sign she is fine," William said.

"But what else did I say? I also said she was up and playing before all this happened, so we can't trust that to mean she is fine."

"Well, we can trust God to reveal to us she is fine, and maybe that's what He is trying to do," William said.

"Well, I think God wants us to do a bit more than sit around and wait on Him," Nikki said. "That's what you always do. You go and call on the name of God and then sit back and wait for Him to act."

"Well, I don't just 'sit back,' as you so note, but I do trust. And I trust Him to do amazing things for us. What is a little digestive condition? God can heal that instantly. Maybe He already has."

"But we don't know!" Nikki insisted. "I don't see why you can't get all this through your head. Our baby could be in that type of pain again, and I, for one, will not wait for that to happen."

"So you're saying you know better than God?"

"No, I'm not," Nikki said. "But what I am saying is that I want to do all I can. God wants us to act on our faith. I am acting. I'm trying to learn all I can about this condition, influence the insurance company as best I can, whatever is humanly possible. I'm not going to just sit on my hands."

"Nobody is sitting on their hands, Nikki," William said. "I just think we should wait and see."

Nikki threw her hands in the air. "I just don't understand you sometimes. I'd think you'd be at least a little concerned that your daughter could die."

William rubbed his eyes. "Die, Nikki?"

"Yes, die!" Nikki flung the words at him. "I sat right there on that computer and read some report about people dying from this thing."

"Well, you know the Internet has all sorts of crazy info on there," William said. "And yes, I'm just as concerned as you about Psalm, but I'm just trying to process all of this. That's all."

"Process?" Nikki said. "What's to process?"

"Nikki, it's been a very long day, can I just take my shoes off first?"

"Oh, *you've* had a long day?" Her chest was heaving. "What about me? I've been here, going back and forth with the insurance company all day—all day, Will—trying to save my child's life and to no avail. I've been researching this condition on the Internet and each story is more horrible than the one before."

"Okay, well, then get off the Internet," William said. "You know you can't believe everything you read on there."

"So, what, now you're saying I'm overreacting?"

William sighed. "Look, let's just chill for a few minutes and come back to discuss this."

"Oh, so you need a break from me, is that it?"

"No, baby; but nothing I say right now is going to work, and quite frankly, I'm tired," he said. "I just need a few minutes—just a few minutes—to breathe without being disturbed."

"So I'm a disturbance to you?"

William threw his hands in the air. "Impossible." He grabbed his keys. "Look, I'm going to hang out at Mac's house," he said. "I'll see you when you calm down."

"I know you are not just going to walk out while I'm talking to you!" Nikki said, her hand on her hip. "So you want to run to your brother's house to escape me, is that it?"

"Bye, baby."

William closed the door behind him and Nikki cursed. Every fiber in her being wanted to call William back and let fly every profanity she could summon. She speed-dialed Danielle instead.

"Hey, girl," she said when Danielle answered. "You won't believe what just happened."

"What?" Danielle said.

"Will can be so insensitive sometimes. He just came

home and I told him the insurance company won't pay for my baby's operation. And then I told him about all the horrible stuff I found out about this disease. All he could do was say he needed time to 'process.' What kind of mess is that? Then he walked out."

"Well, you know William always was a little slow," Danielle said. "He never does anything fast. He always has to think about things, or should I say, 'pray on it.'"

"Well, it's okay for him to think and pray, but I needed him to be as freaked out as me," Nikki said. "But he was just calm. Maybe he just doesn't care."

"You know that's not true," Danielle said.

"Sometimes, I just wonder why I married him," Nikki said.

"Well, I told you, you should have waited," Danielle said. She paused. "Hey, look, my other line is beeping, hold on for a sec."

A beat later, she returned. "This is old Troy on the other line, trying to apologize. I went off on him when some woman called my job about him earlier today. He knows he's in the doghouse. I'm going to make him beg, though. He can't just think he can treat me any kind of way and think that all will be well."

"So is he seeing the other girl?"

"I don't know," Danielle said. "He said she is stalking him and that's why she called me. She even made her cousin move next door to spy on him. He keeps saying he's not doing anything, so I guess he's not."

"Well, don't be dumb over a man," Nikki said. "You can let him go, you know."

"Oh, I know you're not giving me relationship advice, Miss I-can't-even-keep-my-man-at-home."

"It's not even like that, and you know it," Nikki said. "But hey, I'm going to let you get back to your man. Thanks for listening."

Nikki hung up. She let out a heavy breath, as she thought back over the argument with her husband. William seemed calm even at the idea that their daughter could have a serious condition. For him, prayer would take care of it. Nikki wanted that confidence; she wanted to give prayer a chance. She walked across the living room and grabbed a Bible from its spot next to a smiling photo of Psalm on a table. The Bible had lain there for weeks, untouched. She sat on the couch and flipped to Matthew. She read one passage and then another. Nikki closed the Bible and put her hand to her mouth, reflecting on what she had just read. She leaned her head back, staring into space. "Lord, you said, 'Ask and ye shall receive.' Well, I am asking you. Please deliver my child. That's what I need to receive. Deliverance for Psalm."

She swallowed hard. "I know you said if we just have faith the size of a mustard seed, we can move mountains. Well, I don't know how big a mustard seed is, but I'm having an issue of faith right now. Please heal my unbelief."

Maybe William was right. Maybe God had already delivered Psalm. Maybe that's why the child was playing so freely and showing no apparent effects of illness. Maybe the insurance had been denied because she didn't need the surgery. Nikki smiled a bit wryly. She knew she could be hasty to action at times, and a bit high-strung. Faith was still new for her.

Nikki had seen William's attachment to church and religion very early in their relationship and had worked to be a woman who had the same attachments. He was thrilled when she joined his church, the choir and even became an usher.

But sometimes that transformation showed a few cracks. Like now. Nikki went to church most Sundays and sometimes studied her Bible. She made sure to do what she thought to be right—she didn't cheat on her husband and she tried to treat people with kindness. But Nikki had a hard time trusting in what was outside of her control, and relying on prayer to heal her daughter just made her uncomfortable.

She had read about miracles in the Bible and had heard testimonies in church, but she couldn't cite any instance in her own life where she had let go and let God handle something dear to her. No matter what hard time she and William faced, she always tried to look for a practical solution, not a faith answer. She wasn't raised that way, and certainly life's hard knocks had taught her to be careful about trust.

Nikki fingered the outline of the frame around Psalm's photo and took a deep breath.

She would try this thing called faith.

Chapter 15

Danielle told Troy he could come over. She quickly showered and slithered into a new Victoria's Secret purple thong and bra set. She raced the vacuum across the floor and squirted Febreze in the air. Danielle sprayed Victoria's Secret perfume behind each ear, dabbed it between her breasts, and, for good measure, on her thighs. She popped an Altoid into her mouth. Old Luther Vandross ballads flirted with the air and a bottle of white wine chilled in the refrigerator.

Danielle always knew how to please a man. She had learned at an early age that she could get whatever she wanted if she acted nicely and looked pretty, both of which were art forms to her. Tonight, she would make Troy declare fidelity to her. After all, why would he want to be with anyone else when he had her?

Stepping into her Louis Vuitton red dress, Danielle had to twist a bit to zip it. "Hmm," she said, eyeing the faintest beginning of a love handle as she held her breath to let the zipper glide over it. "Oh, well, Troy won't care about that.

I'm still finer than whoever it is he was with before me. And I look good."

Knock! Knock! Knock!

Danielle quickly stepped into her pumps, took a last look into the mirror and walked toward the door. She waited for a second knock and fanned her face—there was no sense in looking as if she had been sitting around waiting for him.

She slowly opened the door and a smiling Troy pushed into her place. His skin was dark like midnight and the clearest she had ever seen on a man. His hair was cut close, with tiny waves making her want to stroke his head. His dark, strong, firm lips curved into that ever-present cocky smile that always gave her a slight rush. Danielle's eyes roamed over the rest of him. Troy was six-feet-four-inches tall, with rock hard arms that bulged out of his muscle shirt. A diamond studded Rolex twinkled on his wrist and a rough looking raised, black shoulder tattoo bespoke his earlier jailhouse years. She knew what was beneath the sharply starched expensive jeans. A shudder went up her spine as she anticipated his powerful body pressed against hers.

"What's up, girl?" he said, dropping a case of beer on the counter. "Get me one of them."

She rolled her eyes at his gruff manner, but grabbed a glass from the dishwasher. "Do you want something to eat?"

"Yeah, what you got?"

She hadn't really expected to fix anything, and indeed, didn't cook, but she smiled. "I could order a pizza."

"Okay, that's cool." He kicked off his luminescent white sneakers. "Make it a large, pepperoni."

"Pepperoni makes me sick."

"What are you telling me for?"

Forget about the stupid pizza, she told herself. "Oh, no reason. That's fine," she said, pouring beer in a glass. "I'll order it and then we can talk."

"I thought we already talked." Troy picked up her remote and flipped on her flat-screen television. Zooming through the channels, he stopped at a music video of scantily clad young women gyrating to heavy beats. "I thought I was coming over here for something other than some talking." He snatched Danielle onto his lap and jammed her hand to his groin. "That's what I thought I came over here for."

The touch excited her, but she knew she had business to take care of first. "Seems like you're feeling better," Danielle said, noticing the quick recovery. She passed him the beer. "Well, we still have a few things to iron out."

"Why don't you iron out that number to the pizza place and then come on back over here and sit on Big Daddy's lap?"

Troy shoved her off him. She shot him a dirty look when she stumbled to gain her balance. Danielle quickly found the number and placed the order. Then she sat on the couch next to him.

"So you ready to give me some?" He groped for the zipper on her dress.

She slapped his hand away and retorted, "Troy, you don't know if I'm going to sleep with you or not."

"Girl, stop playing!" He snatched her to him and kissed her hard. She sank into his bruising kiss, then twisted away.

"You're not just going to disrespect me and then think everything is all right," Danielle challenged, staring him straight in the eyes. She licked her bottom lip.

"You think you're calling the shots here or something?" Troy demanded, pinning her down and kissing her again. His hands roamed her skin. "Don't you know who is in charge here? Don't you know I always get what I want?" he said. When her breath began coming in ragged bursts, he snatched his hand away.

Danielle's eyes flew to his smirking face. She shoved him

off her and struggled to sit up. "And I get what I want. Now, we need to get a few things straight."

Troy instantly abandoned the harsh, demanding tone of a moment ago and charm oozed from his lips. "Come, on, baby, don't mess up the mood. We got plenty of time to talk about whatever you want."

"Troy, listen," she said as he began touching her again. "Troy, look, wait," she said, knowing her power of persuasion was in this moment. "What about that woman who called me? How did she get my number, and how did she know so much if you're not doing anything with her?"

"Baby, I told you, she's stalking me." His fingers again got busy on her skin.

Danielle wanted to melt under their touch, but she tried to clear her throat and regain the conversation. "Troy, listen. I'm tired of playing around. I'm twenty-eight, almost twenty-nine years old. I want a family—well, maybe a dog instead of kids—a house . . . all that stuff one day. But I can't have that with someone who is fooling around. So just tell me, are you seeing anybody else?"

"Baby, I'm into you right now." He kissed her neck.

"I mean, period, not just at this moment," she insisted, making one last effort to push forward her conversational agenda. She tried to shove his kiss away, but she didn't try too hard. "I'm not going out with anybody but you. And I need to know you're doing the same for me."

"Why are we even having this conversation?"

"Troy, I need someone who is going to be faithful to me," Danielle said. "I need someone who is going to do right. I need someone who will go to church with me."

"Church?" Troy said. "Is that what this is about? Half the time, you don't go to church yourself, and now you want to drag me up in there? C'mon, now. You know I don't get down like that."

"Well, I might not go to church every time the doors open—"

"Every time the doors open? You barely make it once a month."

"That's not true!" Danielle snapped, though she knew his words did have some truth to them. "Anyhow, this isn't about me. It's about you. I want a man who at least is making an attempt to live right."

"Well, when you start living right, then maybe I will," Troy said. "It just kills me that all the women I date want to start trying to change a man. And yet they aren't doing what they should do. How many times have you cussed me out? How many times have you done crazy stuff that I know is not in the Bible? So, why are you trying to hold me to a different standard?"

"I am not trying to hold you to a different standard!"

"Oh, really? Well, why is it that it's okay for you to lie— you lied to your boss earlier today, telling her you had a life and death emergency and had to be rushed to the hospital—but you get on me for lying? And why is it that it's okay for you to disrespect me, but you want to kick me to the curb for saying a few words to you? I'm just trying to see what makes you so special that you can live any way you want, but you want me to get a makeover."

"You are twisting everything all around," Danielle said. "I am saved, but maybe I'm not delivered from every single thing. I am human. If I make a few mistakes, so what? At least I believe in Jesus."

"Well, isn't being saved about a little bit more than that?"

"Well, that's the main thing," Danielle retorted. "I don't have to be a holy roller."

"Seems a bit hypocritical to me."

"Oh, well, you wouldn't understand," Danielle said. "Nonbelievers always want to hold believers up to an impossible standard. And it's not that simple. I don't have to be perfect. I just have to believe in Jesus and try to do all right."

"Well, how can you press me to do right when the best you can do is *try?*" Troy asked. "That's why I'm not down with all that stuff. I just live my life the way I want and that'll be all right."

"But, Troy, we can be really good together," Danielle pleaded. "You can join my church. We can get married. We can be happy."

"Baby, you knew what I was when you got with me," he snapped. "Now stop all this mess. I'm the same thing now as I was then."

"So what are you saying?"

"I'm saying that you are looking really good." He stood up and stepped out of his pants. He let the boxers slide to the floor and kicked them away. He disrobed, taking off everything else.

"Troy, so, is this just a little fling for you? Just a little piece?" she pressed. She gathered her composure and slid off the couch and stood, brushing her dress back down around her thighs. He reached for her and she jerked away, refusing to let him touch her. But he followed her and dragged her to the floor with him. "Troy, you can't do this."

He ignored her and tore off her dress. She gave a half-hearted resistance when her dress fell in a wrinkled heap on the floor, but didn't say anything when she, too, was naked as her body waited for him to finish what he started.

She mustered what little will she had left and repeated her question. "Am I just a piece to you?"

"Baby, baby," he said. "Look, don't get yourself all worked up. You got the music playing all nice, you're smelling good, looking good. Now, let's just enjoy the moment."

She waited for him to finish pleasing her, but he didn't. Instead, he peered into her face. "See, this is what I mean.

Don't your little Sunday School lessons teach you that having sex outside of marriage is wrong? I don't see you trying to stop doing that. So do you just pick and choose what rules you'll follow?"

"Shut up, Troy!" Danielle said, annoyance making her tone sharp. "I told you, it's complicated. You wouldn't understand. The Bible was written thousands of years ago. Not everything in it is to be taken literally."

Troy grinned. "See, that's why I like you. You always know what to say."

Troy kissed her again and a smile of satisfaction spread across Danielle's face. He was here with her now. Whoever he was with the other day didn't matter. She knew sharing her body was the key to affection. She had learned that skill long ago.

"Do you like that?" she asked, kissing his neck.

"Yeah, baby, you know how I like it."

"Are you going to get serious about me now?" she pressed.

"Yeah, baby."

Danielle grinned to herself. She pressed further. "So, do you love me?"

"Girl, come on!" he said roughly, leaning in to kiss her again.

She wrestled free. "Do you love me?"

"Yes, girl, now come on!"

I've still got it. Satisfied, she leaned into his kiss.

Chapter 16

William returned home two hours later, dropping the keys onto the table next to the door. "Mama sent you a plate," he said to his wife.

Nikki rolled her eyes. She knew his mother hadn't sent a thing for her. If anything, he had sneaked the plate out of the house. William's mother still blamed Nikki for snaring her son into marriage so young. His mother had wanted William to be free and independent of responsibilities and had even threatened to boycott the wedding. And if he insisted on marrying so young, she wanted her son to be with a girl who was raised in the church, not someone like Nikki.

"Thanks," she said. "I thought you were going over to Mac's?"

"I dropped by there for a minute but they were pretty busy. The kids were running around and Janice was fussing about something so I ducked out of there," William said. Nikki saw his eyes searching her face. "So, are you calm now?" he asked, kissing her cheek.

She wanted to pull away, but did not. "I was fine before," she said.

"Baby, you were wound pretty tight." He placed the plate on the counter in the kitchen.

"But Will, you can't just walk out on me because I'm upset or talking about something you don't want to talk about," she replied.

"I didn't leave you." William stepped out of his shoes in the living room. "I'll never leave you, but nothing was going to be accomplished by that conversation. You know I don't like confusion."

"So now I create confusion?" she asked, walking to the kitchen to peek under the aluminum foil on the plate he brought. It was loaded with greens, macaroni and ribs.

He walked up behind her and wrapped her in his arms. "Baby, let's not do this. You know I think the world of you. And I know you're stressed about everything that's going on."

"Well, why can't you talk to me about it then?"

"And say what? That I'm a lousy provider? That I can't take care of my family? That my child is ill and there is nothing I can do? That my wife is afraid and I can't comfort her?" He let go of the grip he had on her and stepped back.

"No," Nikki said. "But maybe we don't need all of *this*." Her hand flailed in the air, taking in the vaulted ceiling, the hardwood floors, and the expensive living room set. "Maybe we took on more than we could afford."

"But, baby, don't you see? I want to give you nice things," William said. "This and more!"

"Will, we're living in a four-bedroom house, three bathrooms, a pool." Nikki shook her head. "We were in a tiny one-bedroom apartment in New Orleans. And we were making do."

"Making do!" William shot back. "That's just it. I want to do more than just survive! I'm tired of struggling. And when we had the opportunity to move on up, we took it."

They had taken out an adjustable rate mortgage to move

into the house they could afford no other way. But now interest rates were rising and their monthly payment had already doubled.

"But why, Will?" This conversation wasn't new to them. "Why are we trying to keep up with the Joneses? Who are you trying to impress?"

"It's not about trying to impress," William said, "but it's a business decision. We have to look the part. I have to look successful, if I want to be successful."

"But, baby, you don't have to drive yourself into the ground," Nikki pleaded. "We are buried in debt here. We can't afford our life!"

"You just don't understand it," he told her. "God blessed us with this house. We had that hookup at the mortgage company. How else would you explain us getting approved for a house we certainly should not have been able to afford? That was a blessing."

"How can it be a blessing if it's stressing us out?"

"Don't talk like that," William said. "This financial strain is just a temporary inconvenience. You'll see. All this will change soon. Our business will really take off. Right now, we're just faking it 'til we make it."

"But, Will, we're only fooling ourselves. It's—"

"Look, what do you want from me?" William shot back. "I'm doing the best I can! I try to put a roof—a nice roof—over your head. I work extra hard so you can stay home with our daughter, so you can go to school. I am running myself ragged on this campaign so I can build important connections so we can meet the types of people we need. Everything I do is for this family. And you're telling me it's still not good enough."

Nikki turned to face him. She sighed. "Look, I'm sorry. I know this is tough on you too. I didn't mean to be so difficult." She touched his arm.

He sighed and smiled. "It'll be all right, baby. I promise."

She nodded. "I love you."

"I love you more."

Nikki's doubts remained. Love was great. But it wouldn't pay for her child's surgery.

Chapter 17

Pastor And Mayoral Candidate Has Devastating Gambling Habit.

The headline screamed from the top of the front page of the newspaper. Below it was a large, smiling photo of Reverend Chance.

William's throat constricted as he opened the newspaper bin to grab a copy. He stood right there and read the story. Passersby grabbed papers, too, and he could hear more than a few disparaging comments.

"I always knew that pastor was dirty."

"Aren't they all?"

"I know we are not going to elect a preaching crook."

The comments hurt. This story just seemed to fuel animosity toward a pastor these people knew absolutely nothing about, other than what they'd read.

"This is bad," William muttered under his breath. He had tried to talk the pastor out of speaking to the reporter, but Reverend Chance had insisted, saying he wanted to set the record straight.

The record is straight all right.

The story detailed Reverend Chance's gambling addiction ten years prior, with it culminating in the loss of his home and running up tens of thousands of dollars in debt. The pastor said he was free of the addiction now and hadn't set foot on a casino floor in years.

But all that seemed lost to William, who couldn't get that headline and large photo out of his mind. It seemed to be a sinking ship. But he knew he would stick with the pastor until the end.

William turned to get back into his car when he heard someone call his name. He looked up to see a beaming Spencer looking back at him. Spencer waved, and the light caught on his watch, making it sparkle. The watch had probably cost more than William's entire wardrobe.

"Great story in the paper this morning. I see you picked a real winner," Spencer called from his late model Mercedes. He let out a loud cackle and the window rolled back up.

William climbed back into his Protégé. He sat in silence behind the wheel, not turning the key in the ignition, not doing anything but listening to his thoughts. He had felt led to be a part of Reverend Chance's campaign, but how much longer could he remain? He was devoting more time to this campaign than he was to his computer business. And that meant he was generating even less income for his family than before.

"Lord, I believe you told me to help Reverend Chance on this mission, but I need some direction. Nikki is right. We have mounting debt. We're in a house we are having a hard time affording. Our daughter might have a medical condition that requires expensive treatment. I wonder if I should get off this campaign and get back to building my company on a full-time basis. But I know even as I entertain these doubts, sometimes you are working things we cannot see with the natural eye. So please help me to stay on course and keep going in the direction you have for me, even when I can't see the way."

William turned the key in the ignition and headed to the campaign office. He knew his wife sometimes thought he sat passively by and waited for God to manifest changes. But that's how William grew up. His mom taught him that faith was about trying to hear God's voice. And to do that often meant he had to wait.

William appreciated Nikki's declaration of love for God when they got married. He believed a couple should be spiritually on the same path, so her joining his church eased a lot of stress. Plus it took away one of his mother's arguments, because his mom constantly railed that William should not be with a woman who was not saved. So when Nikki got saved and baptized, that was a huge relief.

He knew his wife was a good, strong Christian woman. She had immersed herself in Bible studies and joined several ministries at church, including becoming an usher. She had dropped out of the choir and went to fewer Bible studies now, but she worked hard to do what she knew to be right. On this latest matter concerning Psalm, though, they disagreed. Nikki thought faith meant doing what she could first and letting God handle what she could not do. But William thought faith was about trusting God and waiting to see what happened.

William didn't want to think about that right now, though. He had more pressing and immediate concerns: Managing this campaign and earning money to support his family. He knew his pastor wanted to make some significant changes as mayor. Reverend Chance wanted to make real strides in meeting the needs of some of the most vulnerable people in the city. He felt he could do certain things as a church leader and pastor, but other changes had to come from making adjustments in how the city was being run.

William believed in the vision and wanted to help serve the needy. But he also wanted to serve the immediate needs of his family. He wanted to leave the campaign and focus on making serious money. It was the end of July, and for the fifth straight month, he knew revenue would be down from where it was a year ago. William had promised Nikki, even before the hurricane, that they would become multimillionaires, and they would live a life of luxury. But he didn't feel he was on that track right now, not with devoting so much time to the campaign.

"I'm having a hard time making a distinction between your voice and my own desires right now, God." Stopping at a traffic light, William dialed Reverend Chance's cell number.

The candidate picked up on the first ring. Without even saying hello, Reverend Chance inquired, "Where have you been?"

"What do you mean?"

"I've been trying to call you all morning. The phone immediately went to voicemail each time," the candidate said, sounding a bit irritated.

"I'm sorry, Reverend Chance," William said. "My phone didn't ring, or at least, I didn't hear it."

"Well, whatever the case, we are having an emergency meeting," he said. "We're going to have it at Two Sisters Kitchen, away from the office."

"Two Sisters? That'll be just as bad as going to the office," William said. "Everybody will be there. You won't be able to get anything done for all the folks coming up to speak."

"Well, I still need to be out in the public eye as much as I can. So meet us there in a few minutes. We've got to strategize. This story is being blown way out of proportion and presented in such a bad way."

William wanted to say, "I told you so," but instead, he simply replied, "Yes, sir."

Chapter 18

Nikki furiously typed away on her homework assignment for her class, knowing she was behind because of everything going on in her life lately. The report had been due yesterday, but the professor had extended the deadline to this evening. It was a paper dissecting the artistic style of painter Clementine Hunter. She was enrolled in a graduate program and the summer semester was wrapping up at the end of next month, August. After that, she had one more semester before she would receive her Masters degree.

"Maaaamaaaa!" she heard the wail coming from the bedroom and sprang to her feet, knocking over the chair. Psalm was stretched out, reaching for her mother with one hand, her other hand planted gingerly on her abdomen.

"Oh, baby!" Nikki gathered Psalm into her arms, and the child's cries grew louder. Nikki didn't know if she should let the girl lie still so as not to make her stomach hurt even more, or if she should run from the house with her now, in search of a ride to the hospital. She let Psalm lie still.

The cries grew more intense and Nikki quickly pulled on sneakers. She grabbed her purse and gently picked up

Psalm, trying to comfort the child, but knowing she had to get her to medical care. She walked quickly to her neighbor's house.

Nikki banged on the front door until the neighbor opened it. "Mrs. Carrie, can you please give me a ride to the hospital? My baby—"

"Oh, I don't know," Mrs. Carrie said, slowly shaking her head. "I'm in the middle of—"

"Please, Mrs. Carrie!" Nikki begged. The woman looked as if she might say yes, but she retreated inside her air-conditioned living room.

"It's so dangerous out there these days," Mrs. Carrie said, closing the door except for a crack. "I watch the news. So many shootings and muggings and murders. I don't go out much these days. I'm sorry. I want to help you, but I just can't."

"Come on, Mrs. Carrie, please!" But Nikki knew the plea was to no avail. Mrs. Carrie's car barely moved all week, save for a trip to the grocery store or church.

Nikki banged on the door of the house next to Mrs. Carrie's. No one answered. She looked around frantically, cradling her crying child. "Please, somebody!" She tried to hold back the tears from her own eyes.

"Are you okay?" Nikki looked up, grateful for the acknowledgement. It was the man who lived on the other side of her. He was sticking his head out of the door.

"Please, can you give me a ride to the hospital?" she asked. "My baby is sick."

"Oh, sure," he said. "Let me get my shoes."

He disappeared into the house. Nikki raced to his car as quickly as she could, taking care not to jostle Psalm any more than necessary. Psalm's wails tore at Nikki's heart.

A moment later, her neighbor reappeared, quickly snatched the passenger side door open, and helped Nikki and Psalm into the car. He raced around the front of the car and hopped in, threw the car into reverse and skidded down the drive-way. They sped to the hospital, neither saying anything, as Nikki held her daughter to her chest, praying for relief as Psalm's tears soaked her skin.

Nikki frantically dialed William's cell phone, but it went straight to voicemail. She tried calling him at the campaign office, but got no answer.

"You trying to reach someone?" her neighbor asked.

"Yeah, my husband," Nikki said. "But he's not picking up."

When the car pulled up at the hospital, she forgot about the calls, intent on getting treatment for the wailing Psalm. She climbed out of the vehicle and walked quickly through the doors of the hospital. "Please, can you help my baby?" she begged the woman who sat at the emergency room reg-istration desk.

"What is wrong, ma'am?" the clerk asked in a flat tone.

"Her stomach hurts," Nikki informed her.

"You brought her to the emergency room for a stomach ache?" The clerk's voice betrayed a touch of annoyance. "The emergency room is for emergencies, ma'am. You uninsured people can't continue to use the emergency room as a sub-stitute for a regular doctor's visit."

"Ma'am, I have insurance!" Nikki snapped. "That's not the point. My daughter is in severe pain because of a seri-ous health condition. Just admit her, please!"

The woman rolled her eyes, but began typing on her computer. "Name?"

Nikki quickly rattled off all the relevant information, in-cluding noting that her daughter was at this same hospital two days ago for this same condition.

Once Psalm had been admitted, Nikki tried to reach William. Again, the phone went straight to voicemail. She left a frantic message, then called the campaign headquarters and left a message there, too. Nikki swallowed hard to calm her nervous stomach.

"Ma'am, you can't use a cell phone in here," a passing nurse said, peering into the open doorway of the room in which Psalm and Nikki sat sequestered since another nurse left after taking Psalm's temperature.

"Oh, sorry," Nikki apologized, but quickly dialed again when the nurse disappeared down the hall. This time, she punched in Danielle's work number.

"I'm sorry; she's on the floor right now. May I take a message?" the attendant asked.

"Tell her it's an emergency."

"I'm sorry, ma'am," the attendant said, "I don't think—"

"Just page her!" Nikki was insistent.

"Oh, all right." The attendant's voice was full of attitude.

A moment later, Danielle was on the phone. "What's wrong?"

"I'm at the hospital with Psalm," she said, her voice cracking.

"She got sick again?"

"Worse this time." A flow of tears started to flow down Nikki's cheeks. "I'm so scared."

"I'll be right there."

Twenty minutes later, Danielle arrived at the hospital, walking quickly into the waiting area. She immediately hugged Nikki. "Have you talked to the doctors?"

"One just came out and said Psalm was stable," Nikki informed her. "They let me go back with her for the initial consultation. Then they moved her and told me to come back out here and wait."

Danielle turned to Nikki's neighbor, who was standing close to Nikki. "Who is this?"

"Oh, this is Julius," Nikki said, sitting down on a plastic

chair. "You know, the guy who lives a couple of doors down from me. He brought me here."

Danielle looked him up and down, then spoke in crisp tones. "Okay, well, Julius, thanks for helping her out. That was really generous of you. You can go now. I'll take her home."

Julius looked from Danielle to Nikki. Nikki was sitting on the edge of a chair, her head in her hands. "Nikki, do you want me to hang around?"

"I said I've got it from here," Danielle said. "I'm her best friend in the world."

"I wasn't talking to you," Julius said. He turned back to Nikki. "Nikki, do you . . . ?" His voice trailed off into the question.

"Oh, whatever she says is fine," Nikki mumbled, distracted.

Danielle smirked at Julius, who glowered at her and left.

Danielle sat down next to Nikki. "It's going to be okay," she said.

Nikki shook her head. "Danielle, she's got to have that surgery. She can't keep having these episodes. She was in so much pain."

"I know it can't be easy seeing her like this," Danielle said. She didn't have any children and had no desire to have any, though she was generally fond of her goddaughter.

"I don't know what I'm going to do. We can't afford this surgery."

"How much is it?"

"More than we have." Nikki sighed. "It's really just a few thousand dollars, so as far as surgeries go, it's not that expensive. But for us, that may as well be a few million dollars. We don't have any money."

"I don't know why you don't just get a job," Danielle said. "Forget what that broke behind William says. Tell him when he can start taking care of his family like a real man, come see you then."

Nikki squirmed. "It's not that easy," she said. "William has really strong views. He was raised by a mom who worked herself nearly to death because his dad wasn't around. He sees it as his role as a man to take care of his family."

"Yeah, well, in case you haven't noticed, he's not doing much of that," Danielle said. "I mean, if he was, you'd be driving a Mercedes, not hitching rides to the hospital. You'd be able to afford to get your hair done every week. You'd—"

Nikki held up her hand. "Look, forget all that. I just need to figure out a way to get my child proper medical care."

"Well, what about faith? Don't you believe God will heal?"

Nikki chose her words carefully. "Yes, I believe God has tremendous power. I do. But I don't believe I'm supposed to idly sit by and watch my child suffer."

"So, what are you saying?"

"What I am saying is I need to find a way for my child to get the care she needs. Period."

Danielle studied her best friend and then lowered her voice. "Well, you know, I could talk to Troy."

"What do you mean?" Nikki asked.

"I mean, he has a couple of hookups. He might be able to get you a hookup at the hospital."

"How so?"

"Well, he might be able to get somebody to help you with your payment," Danielle said.

Nikki's eyes widened. She didn't know all the details, but she knew if it had anything to do with Troy, it couldn't be good. She had heard about Troy's "hookups" before. They all seemed to involve some kind of shady dealing.

"What would Troy do, exactly?" she asked, suspicion in her tone.

Danielle waved off the question. "I don't ask all those questions. Haven't you ever heard, sometimes, you shouldn't look a gift horse in the mouth? Just take the gift and keep on moving."

"Well, I just want to know exactly what Troy will do," Nikki said. "I know he can get involved in some crazy things, and I'm not trying to get caught up."

"Look, do you want this surgery for your child or not?" Danielle snapped.

"I do, but—"

"But nothing!" Danielle said. "All I have to do is say the word, and Troy will get it taken care of."

"But how? That's all I'm asking," Nikki insisted. "I just want to know what he will do."

"What does it matter?" Danielle said. "All you need to know is Troy can give you a way to pay for this surgery."

Nikki shook her head. "I don't want to do anything illegal," she said. "I don't want to. That's not me."

"Well, you weren't saying that a few years ago," Danielle said sharply.

Nikki quickly looked around and moved closer. "I never did anything like this! It's wrong."

"Wrong is relative," Danielle said. "What's wrong is letting that precious baby suffer like that when you could do something about it. You just said that yourself. You're not above doing something crazy to get what you want."

Nikki shook her head again. "That's not me; not anymore."

"Tell that to somebody who doesn't know you."

"Danielle!"

"Well, you can put on this innocent act with everybody else, but I know you," Danielle said.

"I'm not acting!" Nikki said, then lowered her voice to a whisper. "And stop talking like that."

Nikki's chest heaved in quick bursts as her mind took her back all those years ago, to her freshman year of college. She was new in New Orleans, broke and on the verge of having to quit school because her scholarship covered only half her tuition and her part-time tutoring job didn't pay nearly enough. She found a way to get the money. But she didn't want to think about the lengths she had gone to back then to get it.

She shook the thoughts from her mind and looked Danielle in the eye. "Well, I don't want to do anything dishonest. Besides, Will would never go for that."

Danielle shrugged. "William doesn't have to know."

"I don't want to start lying to my husband."

Danielle gave her a disdainful look, and said, "Fine time to start thinking about that."

"Well . . ." Nikki's voice trailed off.

Danielle raised a brow. "Besides, is it really a lie if you just don't tell him the truth?"

"Yes, it is," Nikki said flatly. "This is a crazy idea, Danielle. I want to save my child; you know I do. But I have a feeling that whatever scheme Troy cooks up will have something illegal or bad attached to it. "

"Look, I'm just trying to help you. I'm not the one with the broke husband and sick kid."

Nikki touched her friend's arm. "Look, thanks. I really appreciate you for trying to help. I do. But I think there are some lines we can't cross. I'm really surprised you'd make this suggestion. Is this what being with Troy has brought you to? You really need to get rid of him because you are going down a dangerous path."

"Don't start judging me, Nikki." Danielle's voice shot up and heads all over the waiting room whipped around to see what was going on. She lowered her voice. "Troy is fine and I don't need you to start telling me who I should be dating.

He gives me nice things and would even be willing to help you out, I'm sure. Don't act so ungrateful. It's really not very becoming."

"This is all so stressful," Nikki said, twisting a strand of her curly hair. She had been absent from Bible Study lately, but she knew what Danielle was suggesting couldn't be cool. "I don't want to break the law. The Bible—"

"Look, I already told you, I don't need you lecturing me on the Bible," Danielle warned. "I know the Bible inside and out and you can't take it literally. You just use the parts that make sense and go on. You don't see anybody running around here chopping off hands because somebody stole something, or stoning somebody because somebody had a little bit of sex, now do you?"

"No, but—"

"Okay, so be quiet," Danielle said. "I was quoting scripture before you knew what the Bible was, so I know what I'm talking about. Now, back to the matter at hand. You know William's mom is broke. His brother has too many mouths to feed and can't spare a dime. Your folks have their heads so far up your stepsister's rear end that they wouldn't be able to afford to give you any money . . . and I just don't have it. So this is probably your best option. Troy can hook you up with a way to pay for this surgery."

Nikki opened her mouth to offer a retort, but the doctor stepped into the waiting area. She instantly forgot her argument with Danielle and sprang to her feet, hugging her arms around her body. Danielle stood at her side.

"What is it, doctor?" Nervousness made Nikki's voice come out in a whisper.

"Well, we'll want to keep her for a few hours for observation, but she is all right for the time being," he said. "Her condition is taking a very irregular course in that it seems to be quite aggressive. I've never seen such a case in one so young."

"What does all this mean?" Danielle barged into the conversation.

The doctor hesitated, but Nikki nodded. "She's family."

"Well, she needs to have the surgery pretty soon, if at all possible," he explained.

"And if she doesn't?" Danielle asked.

Nikki searched the doctor's face as she waited for his answer.

"Well, if she doesn't, she could see quite a few of these attacks," he said. "It's taking a toll on her tiny body."

"Oh, my baby!" Nikki wailed and Danielle squeezed her friend's hand.

Nikki knew she had to find an answer. She looked at Danielle.

Chapter 19

William's cheeks hurt from smiling so hard, as he had to do once they entered the restaurant. He knew all eyes were on the Chance party and they all had to look as if it was just any other day. Everyone was watching to see how they were handling that day's front page story. Reverend Chance looked unaffected, but William could tell Olivia was upset at the bad coverage her father was receiving.

William's eyes narrowed when he spotted Spencer seated at a corner table with Jimmy Vaughn, a folded copy of the day's newspaper among a stack of papers between them. *I bet you that's where the story came from*, William thought.

"William, this is what we'll do," Reverend Chance said. "Let's immediately go on the offensive. I need you to schedule as much press as you can—radio, TV, print—and I will just hammer my message. We won't address this story. We will just talk about our own message. We will talk about what we will do to change this city, what we will do to help every citizen."

"So you want a media blitz, starting now?"

"Yes, as soon as possible," Reverend Chance said. "And don't miss an outlet. Get the black newspaper. Get the paper that ran that story. Get everybody. Try to even catch up to the political bloggers. Let's hammer our message home."

"Daddy, don't you think we need to have other people out there instead of you?" Olivia asked. "That way, you won't be caught in the awkward position of being asked a bad or embarrassing question. If we are out there speaking for you, we can push forward your message, but not expose you to tacky reporting."

"No, I think I should be the one out there," Reverend Chance said, and Olivia rolled her eyes. "Olivia, I know you disagree, but this is the right course of action."

"No, it's not!" Olivia retorted. "You keep making these wrong moves. You came clean about that gambling story, which got us into this mess to begin with. And now you want to expose yourself even more by being directly interviewed. Just listen to me. I can run this campaign and I can get you elected. But you can't keep going against every piece of advice I give you. You've got to let me do my job. You wanted me to manage the campaign. Well, let me manage it."

"Olivia, I appreciate your management; I do," Reverend Chance said, "but ultimately, the decisions are mine. And this is a decision I've made and it's final. I will be the one going on the interviews."

Olivia pursed her lips but said nothing more.

"So what do we need to do to make these interviews happen?" Reverend Chance asked the table at large.

"William, I need you to get back to the office and prepare mock questions from every possible angle," Olivia said, casting a glance at her father. "Since our candidate is going to do these interviews, we'll need to do some quick run-throughs so he can be prepared and have the right answers."

"It'll take a while to get ready for that," William said. "His schedule is pretty booked for today and I have to make appearances as well."

"This has got to be priority," Olivia stressed. "Clear the schedule for the next couple of hours and let's get this done. I want to control this message, and to do that, my dad needs to be prepared as he goes on this insane mission. I need you to pull this together now. Immediately."

William raised his hand. "But—"

"It can't wait," Olivia snapped. "We've got to hop on this now. We want to have the best impact we can, so we've got to move now. So let's clear his schedule and get him prepared for these interviews he is so intent on having. We can't let him go out without having gone through a series of questions, so we can properly structure his responses."

Reverend Chance grimaced but nodded. "She's right," he sighed. "Okay, well, clear my appointments and let's make this happen. I can't believe we're having to scramble over something that happened ten years ago."

"Yeah, the media can be pretty rough." William felt for his pastor. "I'm glad I've lived a pretty straight life. Some people would call it boring, but at least I know there won't be any skeletons falling out of the closet, helped by nosy reporters."

"Yeah, keep your closet clean, William," Reverend Chance said. "Don't do anything you wouldn't want to see on the front page of the newspaper."

Chapter 20

Nikki ripped open the envelope. The words on the page were exactly what she had expected, but had hoped against. Their mortgage was two months late and a third month would mean serious trouble. They had been in this position once before and had to save the house from going into foreclosure.

"What are we going to do?" she wondered out loud. Their financial burdens seemed to be growing rather than shrinking. When they were in New Orleans, they weren't being faced with losing their residence. That apartment had been tiny, but at least it hadn't stressed them.

Their mortgage money had been spent on getting the Protégé fixed last month. It seemed that there was always something going wrong. Nikki looked around the large living room. The house was way more space than the three of them needed. But it was in a good neighborhood and beautiful. They had both fallen in love with it the instant they saw it. She and William had been surprised to find they could afford it. Of course, "afford it" was subjective. They had been able to get in, thanks to a zealous loan officer who provided them some creative financing—a no-money down loan. They had been able to get into the house, but Nikki was afraid they wouldn't be able to stay in it. This letter from the bank pretty much told her that.

The weight of a sick child and a pending foreclosure pressed into her, giving her a headache. Nikki rubbed her temples with her fingers. *I just don't know how we're going to handle all this.*

Nikki put the mail to the side and went upstairs to get on the computer and work on her class assignment. The hospital had sent Psalm home with her, and now, the child was sleeping soundly in her bedroom.

Nikki was finishing her paper when William walked into the house just after 9 p.m. and dropped the keys on the table next to the door. She heard him enter the house, but made no move to greet him. He climbed the stairs and walked into the office.

"Hey, baby," he said, sighing and then stooping to kiss Nikki, who continued to work on the computer. She jerked away from him.

"Hey, what was that for?" he asked.

She continued typing. "I hope you had a good day."

"It was brutal," he said, rubbing his neck. "We had—"

"I don't care, Will!" she said, turning away from the computer for the first time. "Your child was laid up in the hospital half the day, and could I get into contact with you? No."

William's face registered alarm. "What happened? Did she have another episode?"

"Yes, she did," Nikki said. "But where were you? Nowhere to be found. I called your cell phone all day. Left messages there. And I left a message at the office as well."

William slapped his forehead. "Dag, Olivia gave me a note saying you had called," he shoved his hand into his pocket and pulled out the crumpled pink square, "but in the rush with everything going on, I forgot to call you back. I meant to."

"So, why didn't you have your cell phone on?" Nikki demanded.

"It was on."

"I called, Will, and it went straight to voicemail."

"I think something's wrong with it."

"Whatever!" she said as she got up and stalked out of the room. "I can't believe you made me go through this by myself."

"Baby, I'm sorry." William followed her into their bedroom. "I didn't realize you were trying to reach me. My phone—"

"I don't want to hear it!" she snapped, plopping down on the bed. "Apparently whatever you had going on was way more important than your child."

William crossed the room in two long strides and sat next to her on the bed. "Baby, I'm really sorry I wasn't available to you. And I'll stop by the cell phone place tomorrow to get them to look at it and fix it." He paused for a moment. "Now, tell me what happened. How is Psalm?"

He rubbed the small of her back and this time, she didn't pull away. Instead, she sucked in and slowly let out a ragged breath, then told him about Psalm's rush to the emergency room.

After discussing the day's events—both her time at the hospital and William's campaign work—they decided to take a shower and go to bed.

As Nikki stood in the shower while her husband washed her back with a soapy sponge, Nikki's mind wandered. The shower felt good, but her enjoyment was muted by pressing concerns. She knew there had to be a way to deal with these bills and this medical issue.

"Will, I really think I should go back to work," Nikki

said. "Psalm will be turning five soon and going to kinder-garten."

"Nikki, let's not talk about that right now," William said, turning her so the spray from the shower washed the soap off her back.

She wanted to say more, but held her words. The day had been stressful for both of them. Maybe now wasn't the time to have this talk.

"I'm tired," she said, twisting her body so the water ran over her head, but not her face. "I'll be glad to get to bed."

"Yeah, me too," William said. They switched positions and Nikki lathered up his sponge and began soaping him.

They finished the shower and quietly dressed for bed. William pulled on shorts and Nikki donned a T-shirt. They knelt together on the floor next to the bed, praying in silence.

Nikki's prayer was pretty brief, but she remained on her knees and waited quietly for William to finish his. Her prayers felt more like robo-calls to God these days, as she ran through the template she uttered every night, thanking God for life and asking a generic blessing for her family. As she knelt next to her husband, her mind was on the stress of bills and her child's illness. She knew it was up to her to solve her own problems. She couldn't depend on William or a God she could not see. She felt guilty at the thoughts, but she could not change them. She didn't want to change them.

From childhood, Nikki had tried to rely on others, but they had always let her down. Her father. Her mother. Friends. No, she couldn't trust anyone. She had learned that a long time ago.

When they rose from their knees, she asked William, "Do you want me to fix you something to eat? Are you hungry?"

"Nah, I'm just going straight to bed."

"Mommy!" They both jerked into action at the sound of Psalm's voice. They raced to her bedroom.

"Yes, baby?" Nikki said, standing next to the bed. William stood in the doorway.

"I want to sleep in your bed," Psalm said.

Nikki scooped her into her arms. "Oh, sure, sweetie," she agreed. "Come on."

They returned to the bedroom and all three climbed into bed. "Good night, Psalm," William said, kissing his daughter. Then he leaned over and kissed Nikki. "Good night, baby."

"'Night," Nikki said.

She snuggled next to Psalm. "Good night, little girl," she said, and nuzzled Psalm's neck.

"Good night, Mommy," Psalm replied before closing her eyes.

Before long, Nikki heard the soft breathing of her daughter and the heavier breathing of her husband, but sleep, for her, would not come. William was on one side, and Psalm was on the other. Listening for the slightest sound of discomfort from her child at her side, Nikki tried prayer. *God, you know I've really tried to be a good wife, a good mother. Please show me the way to fix this.*

Psalm's breath was soft against Nikki's cheek. Tears welled in her eyes. She wanted to trust. *Please heal my baby.*

Nikki raced across the living room to grab the phone, hoping its ringing had not awakened Psalm from her afternoon nap. "Hello?"

"Hey, Sister Broussard."

"Hey, Sister James," Nikki said. "How are you doing today?"

"Baby, I'm fine," the head of the usher department said.

"I was wondering if you could run over here and take a few pictures for me? I'm trying to get some things ready for a presentation."

"William has the car," she said. "So I don't have a ride."

"Oh, that's all right. I'll send my son to pick you up. I really need to get these done today."

Nikki glanced at her notebook which was turned to her class assignment, then at Psalm, who was sleeping on the sofa. "Sure. I'll be happy to come."

"Good," Sister James said. "I knew you'd agree, so I already sent him to get you. He's on his way, so he should be driving up shortly. You're such a sweet thing. Thank you, baby."

Nikki hung up the phone and sighed. She went into the kitchen to turn off the oven, and put back into the refrigerator the chicken she had been ready to bake for dinner. She raced to change from the t-shirt she had been wearing into a sundress, not wanting to keep Sister James's son waiting. Only a few minutes later, she heard the crunch of tires in the circular driveway out front. Nikki gently shook Psalm. "Come on, baby, we have to go somewhere."

A groggy Psalm protested with a groan. "It's okay, baby," Nikki purred. "Somebody from church needs some help. So we have to go. Come on."

She hoisted the child into her arms and grabbed her keys. Her homework for class would have to wait. The doorbell rang and Nikki smiled as she answered. "Hi, David. So nice to see you."

Chapter 21

William sat across the table from Reverend Chance and Olivia. "I thought we were going to be on the front page in this paper?" Olivia's question was more like a demand. Her fingernail stabbed at the paper as she pointed.

"Well, we gave the interview," William said. "We can't make them place a story in a certain section."

"You should have done something, William," Olivia insisted. "They ran that horrible story on the front page. They should have run this one there, too. It was positive. It hyped our message. It should not have been buried inside."

"Well, at least we got in the paper," Reverend Chance said. "I think you did a good job, William, making that happen."

He smiled at William, but Olivia wasn't having it. "Look, we have to be aggressive. It's not good enough for us to be buried inside. The next time I say I want a story in the paper, I mean on the front page. We are not second-class citizens. This is unacceptable."

She shoved her chair back from the table and stomped over to the coffee pot. Reverend Chance's eyes followed his daughter. "She's just looking out for me," he told William. "She really wants me to win. So don't let her hurt your feelings. She doesn't mean any harm."

William waved off the words from Olivia. "Oh, that's all right, Pastor," he said. "I know Olivia is just a very driven, hard working woman. She's strong."

"Yes," Pastor Chance agreed. "She is."

William's cell phone rang. He picked up. "Hello?" He paused to listen. "Oh . . . um, sure," William said. He hung up and turned to the pastor. "That was a client. She is having a problem with her computer. I told her I'd go and check it out. I'll be back as soon as I can, okay?"

"Sure, go take care of your business," Reverend Chance said.

Olivia butted into the conversation. "William, try not to be gone long. Next to my father, you're one of the most important people to this campaign. You've been out in the public eye almost as much as he has. I have a few projects I need you to tackle today."

"Okay, Olivia," William said, standing. "I'll be back as soon as I get this thing taken care of."

"I really appreciate the sacrifices you are making, William," Reverend Chance said. "When I'm in office, I'm going to remember your faithfulness."

"Thanks, Pastor. I'll see you in a bit."

Chapter 22

Nikki wrapped up the photo shoot for Sister James.

"I'm going to send these pictures to that mission magazine," Sister James said. "I always see those other churches' pictures in there, so I decided to get our church in there, too."

"Oh, that will be a really good thing," Nikki said. "Give our church some exposure."

"Indeed!" Sister James said. "All those big-city churches can't be the only ones showing off." She glanced at Nikki. "I've been missing you at usher meeting lately. And I didn't see you at church Sunday."

Nikki blushed. "Oh, I—"

Sister James pulled out a catalog. "These are the new usher uniforms we'll be getting." She pointed to a blue and white ensemble that looked pretty similar to the ones the ushers already wore.

"Oh . . . these are nice," Nikki said, while thinking to herself that she could not afford to buy another usher's uniform. Especially since she hadn't been participating much lately anyway.

"Yes, they are," Sister James said. "They'll get here just in time for the Usher Appreciation Day. I'm going to tell everybody about them in our next meeting. I hope you'll be able to make it to that one."

"Oh, um, yeah," Nikki said quickly. She knew she had to do better.

"Good," Sister James said. "I'm going to have all the information ready. Everybody can place their orders then."

"Well, isn't that kind of soon?" Nikki asked. "I mean, some people may have to wait for payday. Or they may not have the money at all."

"That's nonsense!" Sister James waved off that idea. "We should want to look our best for the Lord."

"Right," Nikki said. "I'm not saying that. I'm just saying it might not be that easy for some people."

"Easy?" Sister James laughed. "Serving the Lord isn't about easy, child! We should be grateful to be able to make the sacrifice. And if someone does not have the money for the new uniform, then sacrifice is what they should do. They can give up a dinner out one night to pay for these beautiful uniforms."

It's a bit more expensive than a pizza, Nikki thought. "Well, I'm just saying that maybe we should take into account people's finances and give them a bit more time to place their order than at that meeting."

"Humph!" Sister James huffed. "I say if they can't afford to buy a simple little uniform, then maybe the usher board isn't right for them. I can't stand a lazy Christian! Somebody who isn't willing to make a tiny sacrifice for our Lord when He gave His whole life for us!"

Nikki knew there was no dissuading the woman.

"Too bad all our members can't be as sweet and giving as you," Sister James said, lightly tapping Nikki on the cheek. "You always do what I ask. You might not come to all the usher meetings, but I know I can always call on you to help me when I need it."

Just as she had dropped whatever she was doing today to respond to Sister James's call, Nikki had done the same thing many times over the past four years, offering to baby-sit for single mothers, visiting the elderly, and serving food to the homeless at Thanksgiving.

"You are such a delight," Sister James said.

Nikki managed a smile. "Thank you, Sister James."

"And you are doing a beautiful thing, staying home to raise that precious child," the woman complimented. "So many of these young mothers stick their babies in daycare the first chance they get." Sister James glanced at Psalm, sat at the table, quietly drawing on a sheet of construction paper.

"Thank you," Nikki said, growing increasingly uncomfortable with the conversation. She didn't want to be a stay-at-home mom, but knew she could not voice that. "As a matter of fact, I need to get her on back to the house. She's not been feeling well lately."

"Nothing serious, I hope?" Sister James inquired.

Nikki started to downplay her daughter's condition, then decided to come clean. "Well, to be truthful with you, Sister James, I don't know how serious it is. We just found out she has a medical condition that may require surgery."

"Surgery! My word!" Sister James's hand flew to her chest. "Well, I will certainly lift her up in prayer. Our Lord is still in the healing business. He healed a woman with an issue of blood when doctors gave her no hope. He healed Hezekiah and extended his days. He will heal your child. You just keep the faith."

"Sometimes it's hard, Sister James," Nikki admitted.

"Hard? There is nothing too hard for God, child!"

"No, what I mean is—"

"Shhh," Sister James said. "Don't speak doubt. You just

go forward and trust the Lord to bring healing to that girl. Now go on home. Get in the Word."

Nikki wanted to say something more. She wished she could talk to someone about her doubts and her fears, but who would listen? Those around her seemed to be so much further along in their spiritual lives than she. "Come on, Psalm, let's go home," she said, and the child climbed off the chair.

They said goodbye to Sister James and called for David, who was somewhere out back. They climbed into his car for the second time that day. Psalm began whimpering on the way back home. Nikki turned around to touch the child in the backseat. "Oh, baby, it's all right," she said.

"My tummy hurts," Psalm whined.

"She had too many cookies at my mom's house, huh?" David asked with a smile.

"No, actually, she's been sick the past couple of days," Nikki said, rubbing the child's leg.

"Oh, I'm sorry to hear that. Did you put in a prayer request at church?"

"No. I just—"

"Oh, you should put in a request," David said. "Let the prayer team offer your family up."

"Yeah, I should," Nikki said weakly. "I just hadn't gotten around to it."

"Oh, that's a shame. That's the first thing I do if ever I need something. The Lord can't bless us if we don't ask."

"Well, I've been praying on my own," Nikki said.

"It's not the same," David chided. "You need prayer warriors working on your behalf."

"Yeah, you're right." Nikki didn't want to argue.

"Moommmyy!" Psalm's wail pierced the air.

"Oh, that child is in some serious pain," David said, and clucked his tongue. "It's a shame you have been holding off on getting your blessing, Sister Broussard. You should get the prayer warriors praying for you soon. Stop standing in the way of your child's blessing."

By the time they returned home, Psalm had calmed down. She ran to play on her Dora the Explorer blanket. Nikki closed herself in the bathroom and sat on the edge of the double vanity. She buried her head in her hands. She broke down in tears and no words could get around the lump in her throat. The fear for her child's life knotted her stomach and the heartbreak she felt at seeing Psalm suffer made her raise her fist toward the ceiling. "God, please!" She managed to get the words out.

"Mommy, are you okay?" A concerned Psalm knocked on the bathroom door.

Nikki quickly wiped away her tears. She mustered false cheer and called back. "I'm great, sweetie! Go back and play. Mommy's in the bathroom. I'll be out shortly."

"Okay, Mommy," Psalm called. "I love you!"

Nikki's heart melted. "I love you, too, baby."

She could hear the child scurry away. Nikki could not imagine letting her daughter go through another painful episode. Psalm didn't deserve this pain. Nikki opened the door and walked to the nightstand next to her bed. She picked up the phone and dialed Danielle's number. She knew what she had to do. She had put it off long enough.

Chapter 23

Danielle let her hand trail lightly across Troy's naked stomach as he lay on his back next to her, the sweat still warm on his skin. "So, baby, do you think you can get a hookup at the hospital for Nikki?"

"What do you mean?"

"I don't know," Danielle said. "Do whatever you do. Nikki needs some help paying for a surgery and she doesn't have any money."

"What? Don't tell me Miss Goody Two Shoes wants a hookup."

"Well, she's not as innocent as she pretends." Danielle toyed with the idea of laying her best friend's laundry out before Troy, but refrained. "Yeah, she's in kind of a bad way. Her baby is sick and she needs some money kind of fast. And you know I've got to help my girl out."

"I don't know if I want to give her anything," Troy said. "She don't like me too much."

"If you do this for me, this could really help things along," Danielle said suggestively. Troy had been on his best behavior as he tried to smooth things over with her.

Troy thought about this for a moment and then nodded. "Okay," he said. "But she needs to keep this under wraps."

"Oh, she won't say anything," Danielle assured and leaned in to kiss him. "But look, let me get out of here so I can scoot on to work," she added and climbed out of the bed.

She hopped into the shower then slathered on thick, peach scented lotion as she got dressed for work. She rolled her eyes as she looked at the clock. Yep, she would be late, again. "I have got to get married so I can quit this dumb job," she groaned inwardly as she heard Troy rustling about the next room.

"I'm headed out now!" Troy called to her.

"Okay, bye, baby!"

She heard the door slam, and then the condo was again silent. Danielle admired herself in her full-length mirror, pushing out her breasts and nodding at her flat stomach— well, it wasn't as flat as it was a few years ago, but it wasn't bad. She saw the beginnings of a pooch. *At least I don't look like some of those big, fat nasty women who act like they've never heard of a gym.* The only workouts she had gotten lately, though, were always on her back. Her firm cheerleader's body was morphing into a soft roundness that was still decent, but could easily get out of hand. But she shrugged the thoughts off; after all, she had always been beautiful. That was how she made her way in the world.

She worked hard to look good—she got her hair done every week, and nails too. Spa treatments kept her looking refreshed and expensive, designer clothes showed off her body. A woman's power is in her looks, she had always believed.

Danielle knew many women shunned such a statement and looked upon her with disdain for taking it to heart. "Those are just the ugly trolls," she mumbled to herself. Danielle knew definitively where her power was. She recalled the first time she realized her looks could get her what she wanted. She had been five years old. She and her sister had been playing in the mirror while waiting for ice cream. Her sister wore a pink dress with the most beautiful lacy rose-colored ribbon Danielle had ever seen. Danielle's dress was the same design, but yellow, with a matching ribbon. She thought her sister's pink ribbon was prettier and tried to snatch it from her hair. When her sister protested, Danielle shoved her to the floor, causing the girl to bump her head. Their mother had spanked her and fussed, telling Danielle to go outside. The heartbreaker was when their mother said Danielle could not have any ice cream because she was on punishment for being mean. Danielle flounced out to the porch, angry and pouting. Her uncle smiled at her. "What's the matter?"

"Mama says I can't have any ice cream," she said, looking at him with sad eyes.

He smiled and hoisted her onto his lap. "Well, a pretty girl like you can't ever be found crying," he said, situating her narrow behind over his lap. "Let me hold you just like this for a little while and I'll take you to get some ice cream. You're so pretty I'd do anything for you."

And he had.

Danielle shook her head to clear the memory. *Yes, looking good will get you anything you want.* And now, finally, she had snagged someone who would give her what she wanted: a big house, a Range Rover, and enough money to quit that Godforsaken job. Troy was fine and had a good job in sales. That little cheating episode—or whatever it was—was behind them. He knew he had a good thing. He wouldn't dare be so ungrateful as to cast her aside. "As soon as I get back from my honeymoon, I'll be telling that hospital where they can get off," she mumbled.

Danielle hated nursing, and had only entered the field to be closer to doctors, thinking she would be able to snap one up in pretty short order. Nobody told her, though, when she signed up for nursing school, that most of the doctors were already married. That plan hadn't worked.

She ran through a series of men and wasn't sure how she ended up still single. *Nikki goes out to one party not even caring about finding a man and ends up with a guy who immediately marries her. I go out every week and can't meet anyone to take me down the aisle. But that's all about to change now.* The relationship with Troy was coming along nicely—that minor cheating episode aside.

Danielle had barely made it through nursing school, and would have flunked out if she hadn't zeroed in on her advisor's admiration of pretty things—or at least, pretty young women. Through a series of carefully placed coy comments and "accidentally" brushing against him, she had managed to get him thinking about her. She flattered the balding and overweight man with attention, and blew his mind with short skirts that showed off her lack of undergarments. Before long, she had convinced him to steal tests for her so she would have the answers and even to change her grades. In exchange, he got to taste her young body.

"You know, I think I'm starting to feel really bad about all this," Danielle had said to the advisor, her eyes lighting on the smiling photo of the professor with his wife and two children. She touched his wedding band, which was nearly hidden in the fleshy folds of his hand.

"Oh, you're just a sweet girl, you shouldn't feel bad," he had said, zipping his gray pants after a lunchtime quickie in his cluttered office.

"I'd really hate for your precious wife to be so hurt by all this." Danielle straightened her clothes and fluffed her hair.

His eyes shot to her face. "What are you talking about?"

"I'm just trying to look out for your family," she said sweetly, trailing her hand over his chest. The white shirt was transparent with big, sweaty spots. "Your dear, loving wife really has a right to know what's going on. Maybe I should tell her."

He grabbed Danielle by the arm. "You'll do no such thing!" His breath was hot on her face.

"What *you* will do, is get your fat hands off me," Danielle said. Her voice was low, but deadly. "Because, you see, I am the one with the power in this situation. You owe me."

"Owe you? Owe you?" he sputtered, letting go of her arm. "I am the reason you even passed nursing school. If it had not been for me, you would have flunked out two semesters ago."

"Precisely," she said, stepping to the door with her purse in hand. "Which is exactly what I will tell the dean of the department if you don't find me a job."

His face slacked and looked deflated as he slumped back onto the desk they'd just used as a makeshift bed. Moisture beaded his pasty white forehead and he let out a defeated sigh. "Okay, okay. Let me, uh, make a few calls. I'll have you a job by week's end."

She blew him a kiss. "Thanks, baby."

And now, her affections would land her Troy. Already, he was doing her bidding by getting this surgery taken care of for Nikki. It would be only a matter of time before she got him down the aisle, Danielle mused.

Chapter 24

The next few days had seemed to crawl by for Nikki. She had just wanted the surgery to be done already. For once though, she had been glad William was so busy with the campaign and the computer business that he barely had time for anything else. Even the other day, when Nikki had told him she had found the money for the surgery, he had only half listened.

"Really? That's good, baby," he had said, kissing her absent-mindedly as he pored over poll results. "I knew you'd make the insurance company see things our way."

She had not corrected his assumption. Even when they had driven to church Sunday, William's mind had seemed to be elsewhere. They had ridden in relative silence.

But today was Monday, Psalm's surgery day. Troy had told her to speak to a certain person at registration, and that's what Nikki did when they arrived ten minutes early.

"May I speak with Denise, please?" she asked now as the woman at the counter prepared to pass her a clipboard. A woman quickly hurried over to where Nikki stood. Nikki checked the woman's nametag to confirm her identity. Yes, this was Denise.

"Oh, I'll take care of her paperwork," Denise said to her co-worker, who shrugged, dropped the empty clipboard on the counter, and walked away.

"Suit yourself."

"Baby, can you go get me some water?" Nikki looked for an excuse to get rid of William.

"Sure," he said. "I need to make a call right quick, anyway. I'm going to step outside, make the call, then I'll get you a water. Okay?"

"Sounds good," Nikki said hurriedly.

William disappeared.

The woman pulled out paperwork that was already filled out. "All you have to do is sign here," she pointed to a line.

Nikki held her breath as she scribbled a name on the line. Troy had told her what name to use. He had told her that this was the person who was going to take care of the bill for her. Nikki let out her breath when the woman took the paperwork and nodded. "Okay," she said. "You're all set."

Nikki glanced around to make sure William was still nowhere around when she saw Spencer's wife coming her way. Nikki had forgotten the woman worked there. Nikki quickly lowered her head. Denise handed Spencer's wife Nikki's paperwork.

Spencer's wife never flinched. Nikki and the woman had met a long time ago, shortly after Nikki and her family relocated here from New Orleans. The woman hadn't taken too kindly to Nikki then, and Nikki wasn't interested in developing a relationship with anyone connected to Spencer. Now, Nikki let out a shaky breath to steady herself. *Maybe she doesn't recognize me.* Nikki knew that was close. While she didn't know all the details of Troy's hookup, Nikki knew enough to be afraid of being found out—especially by Spencer's wife.

William returned from his errand and extended a bottle of water to Nikki. "Here you go, baby," he said.

Nikki shook her head and held up her hand, forgetting she had requested the beverage.

William frowned. "I thought you wanted some water?"

Nikki, remembering she had sent him for it, apologized. "Oh, yeah," she said. "I'm sorry. I'm just so nervous about the surgery."

William put his arm around her. "It'll be fine. You see, God blessed us to get the surgery. He would do no less than bless the hands of the doctors."

Nikki nodded. William didn't know about her part in making the surgery happen, and that made her wince inside.

William's mother was standing next to a window when they entered the waiting area. "Hey, Ma," William said and leaned in and hugged her. "Thanks for coming."

Nikki smiled at the woman and gave her a stiff hug. They waited the entire morning to hear word. Nikki paced the waiting room and William stood stoically near the door.

"Stop all that pacing," William's mom chided Nikki.

"Mama, leave her alone, please." William defended his wife before Nikki could respond. His mother folded her arms across her chest but said nothing more.

As Nikki strode from one end of the room to the other, she tried to comfort herself by reciting scriptures, but kept getting the words mixed up as she fished in her memory for specific references. She could not concentrate. Each time someone entered the waiting room, her eyes flew to the doorway. But none of those who arrived came with news of Psalm.

Sister James and two other ushers stopped in and prayed

with them. Reverend Chance dropped by briefly and gave a few words of encouragement before heading to a campaign event.

William strode to his wife. He put his arm around her and they embraced without words. Stepping back, William smiled. "It'll be all right."

Nikki tried to smile back.

"Mr. and Mrs. Broussard?"

They whipped around to see the doctor standing before them.

"Yes?" they said in unison.

"Your daughter came through surgery beautifully."

Nikki slumped into William with relief. She hadn't realized how tense she had been, but hearing that Psalm was doing all right made her burst into emotion.

"Oh, thank you, doctor!" Nikki exclaimed.

"Thank you, Jesus!" Sister James shouted and William's mother and the ushers called out praises of their own.

"So she'll be all right? Can we see her now?" William asked.

"Yes, and yes," Dr. Woods said with a broad grin. "She is a tough little girl."

The next few weeks passed quickly. Things returned to normal for Nikki's family as Psalm recovered from her surgery and seemed to suffer no ill effects. Nikki wanted to take a late summer vacation to relax, but William shot down the idea. He couldn't afford the time away, and gas prices were too high to be touring the country, he told her. When Danielle asked Nikki if she wanted to ride over to Dallas with her for a shopping trip, Nikki said yes, knowing William would never even miss her.

They piled into Danielle's Lexus and made the three-hour westward drive. They went to Northpark Center in the central part of the city, then Danielle insisted on heading up to Plano to check out a new shopping center. Nikki tried to decline when Danielle offered to buy a pair of pink sandals for Psalm, but Danielle ignored her, buying the girl shoes that were more expensive than anything else Psalm owned. She also knew Psalm would outgrow them before the seasons changed, but Danielle didn't care. Danielle was shopping, and doing it with her best friend, so she was in a generous mood.

When they returned home late that night, William was still gone. Nikki sighed. She had known William was too busy to miss her, but it would have been nice if he had.

August was zipping by with William working still longer hours than Nikki would have liked, but she knew he was giving the Chance campaign his all. Especially now that it seemed the pastor was taking a beating in the polls. Just the other day, a newspaper story had come out broadcasting all of Lo Dark's so-called accomplishments, though Nikki knew Dark hadn't done much—certainly not for folks who were not his political friends. He had browbeaten the city council into approving a plan for a new entertainment complex with a convention center, movie theater and shopping center that was now coming to fruition. But even that project hadn't been all that great as it had been delayed more than six years because of various problems with the site. But the entertainment complex had now become a reality and it seemed no one cared its arrival meant an increase in taxes to pay for it. That the mayor had given the go-ahead for the construction of a parking lot at a soccer field in the rich part of town without the council's consent, seemed not to have raised any eyebrows either, even though that meant less money for a city-funded feeding program for needy, elderly residents.

Reverend Chance had a small piece of the story as he touted his plans for a project that would give more contracting opportunities for businesses owned by women and minorities. He also supported a project to direct more faith-based funding to social programs, but his opponent received twice as much ink—as if Dark needed any more free publicity.

Reverend Chance kept a positive attitude, pointing to the fact that he was included in the story at all as a good thing. The other challengers weren't even mentioned. Reverend Chance may have been optimistic, but Nikki could tell William was worried. She tried to encourage him, but she was lonely and missed her husband.

She telephoned Danielle a couple of times to get together, but Danielle always seemed busy. Danielle made time, however, to stop by Nikki's one afternoon with a bit of news.

"I'm getting married," Danielle grinned and flashed a nice-sized princess cut diamond in a platinum setting.

"To whom?" Surprise was etched on Nikki's face. Her eyes moved from the ring to her friend's visage.

"What do you mean? Troy, of course!" Danielle said with irritation, snatching back her hand.

"You can't be serious!" Nikki said, staring at her friend in disbelief.

"Yes, I am. Now, don't go and rain on my parade."

"Girl, you need to think about that," Nikki insisted, shaking her head. "Just a few weeks ago, you were convinced he was cheating on you."

"Well, we've gotten past all that," Danielle said, moving around her friend to the hall mirror where she fluffed her hair over her shoulders and then admired her ring. "Just be happy for me. He's a good man. And he's changed. He loves me. And I love him. He appreciates me and all I've done for him. And he is going to join church."

Nikki doubted the miraculous change Danielle described, but she knew this was not the time to be skeptical. She swallowed her words and pasted on a smile. "Well . . . congrats!"

Chapter 25

MAYORAL CANDIDATE CHANCE FOUND DEAD IN RED RIVER. The headline ripped through William's consciousness like a bullet. His eyes widened as he snatched the paper out of the bin, hungrily devouring each word. The story wasn't very long, but it was the lead piece on the front page. It didn't say much, just that Reverend Chance had been found floating in the river near the casinos.

"Oh, my God," William said. His head hurt as he took in the story. He drove to the office as if in a trance. If he ran a red light, he didn't remember. If he rolled through a stop sign, it didn't register.

He stepped into the somber office just after 7:30 in the morning and was greeted by a red-eyed Olivia.

"What happened?" he asked.

She hunched her shoulders. "I don't know. All I know is what I read in the paper. Someone from the police department stopped by my house last night, but they didn't have many details. I wanted to go to the scene but I had to be with my mother. It was really late when they discovered him. I guess that's why there isn't much in the paper."

William gave her an awkward hug. "I'm so sorry."

"William, my dad is dead." She said the words as if she couldn't believe them.

The door flew open and a gaggle of reporters stormed into the office. The bright light of a camera momentarily blinded William, who threw up a hand to block the glare.

"So, was the reverend losing all his campaign funds at the casinos? Is that why he committed suicide?" a reporter asked.

"You guys, get out of here!" Olivia demanded.

"Was your father afraid of losing the election or was he afraid of facing the public with the truth about his gambling habit? Is that why he jumped?" Jimmy Vaughn demanded, standing in front of Olivia. A TV reporter thrust a microphone into her face.

William stepped in front of Olivia and spoke. "Reverend Chance did not commit suicide. We are investigating all of this. Of course, we are quite distressed at the news we've just found out. You'll have to excuse us as we absorb this very sad and shocking turn of events. That's all we have to say."

"So, are you denying the reverend killed himself over gambling debts?" a reporter insisted. "I thought the reverend said he hadn't set foot in a casino in years. Can you explain why his body was found near them?"

"No comment," William said sternly. "We will have a statement later. Until then, good day."

He pushed them toward the door. When they were safely on the other side of it, he turned to face Olivia.

The sadness in his eyes mirrored her own. "I can't believe he's dead."

William didn't have time to stop and grieve, as he immediately began to look for answers to the questions. How did

Reverend Chance end up face down in the muddy river—outside the casinos he said he hadn't visited in years?

The idea of suicide just didn't sit well with William, but the stories flew around like confetti on a gusty day. It just didn't seem that the man he had worked so closely with these past few months could have done this. What if there was more to this story? What if Lo Dark's people had something to do with it?

"Surely, you don't think Spencer, I mean, Mr. Dark, would do such a thing?" Nikki asked after listening to William speculate. "That is so unreal."

"I don't know what to think," William said. "But I'll figure it out. Something just doesn't sit right about this whole thing. And I wouldn't be surprised if the other side is behind it."

William demanded an investigation, but the police department said they had no resources to devote to something that was so obviously a suicide.

"Those guys are on Lo Dark's payroll, so of course they would say that," William fumed. The police chief liked the mayor because the mayor made sure the department got all the money the chief wanted. "Of course the chief wouldn't care about what happened to the mayor's challenger."

William was surprised when Thurston Hicks, pastor of the city's largest black church, approached Olivia about having the funeral at his big church. "Why does he want to have the funeral at his church?" William asked when Olivia told him about the conversation.

"He says my dad had a lot of supporters and my dad's own church would be too small," Olivia said.

"So. Your dad's church is fine. He's just thinking about the publicity. He probably wants to step into your father's shoes or something. Maybe he wants to run for mayor himself."

Olivia didn't say anything for a moment, then she spoke. "I don't know. Maybe he is right. Maybe we do need a bigger place."

William knew Olivia was taking most of the responsibility for arranging her father's funeral. Her mother had taken to her bed after hearing the news and Olivia's brother, who had been deployed to Iraq, hadn't come home yet, though he was due any day. William knew Olivia was strong—at 29, she had already buried a husband—but he couldn't imagine being in her position now.

"Well, I'm here if you need me," William said, giving her a one-armed hug.

Olivia leaned her head on his shoulder and smiled. "Thanks."

"You know you don't have to move the funeral to that other church if you don't want to. Your dad's church will be good enough."

"What if Pastor Hicks is right though?"

"Well, if there are that many people, then they can stand."

In the end, Olivia's mother settled it when she finally pulled herself from the bed and said the funeral would be at the church her husband had built.

William wondered what lay ahead.

Chapter 26

Nikki typed the last word of her graduate school assignment and logged off the computer. She was glad she had only one more semester after this long summer term. Nikki walked down the stairs to her husband, who was reclining on the couch, a sleeping Psalm on his chest. It was just after midnight.

"You didn't have to wait up on me," she said, gently picking up the girl. "It's coming down to the wire. I don't want anything standing between me and graduation."

William stood and stretched. "You know I don't like going to bed without you."

"Well, I'm sorry I had to finish my assignment."

"It's cool. I didn't mind. I'm so tired, I could have fallen asleep right there on the couch."

"You know, I was thinking that maybe after graduation, I should go back to work full time," Nikki said casually.

"We've already discussed this," William said. "It's my job to take care of my family. Besides, Psalm needs you."

"Psalm will always have my attention," Nikki said. "But

we got another notice about the house the other day. And we both know how tight our money has been."

"Baby, how many times do we have to talk about this?"

"What good is a degree if I'm not going to use it?" Nikki prodded.

"You'll use it plenty," William said. "There will be plenty of volunteer committees to sit on. Think about the intellectual conversations you can have. And when is the quest of knowledge simply for the sake of it a bad thing?"

"I want to do more than just show off my degree in a conversation," Nikki said. "And what about my photojournalism degree? It's a shame not to use it."

"Don't you take pictures sometimes?"

"Will, you know what I mean," she said. Nikki went to the kitchen and put the last of the food in the refrigerator. In her mind, she saw her mother rushing to do her stepfather's every bidding, constantly telling Nikki that a wife's place was to obey her husband and keep the peace. Nikki, in all her teenage glory, had sworn she would never be like that. She would be fierce and independent, and if her husband didn't like what she did, well, he could just get lost. She'd never be more concerned about her husband's bidding than about her own happiness. But now, she swallowed her desires, pulled out the broom and swept the already clean floor, then wiped down the counter. William walked to the refrigerator and grabbed a soda.

"So are we going straight to the funeral tomorrow or do you have to go by the office first after we drop off Psalm at your mother's?"

"I thought I'd get there a little early, but no, I don't have to stop by the office," William said, opening his soda and taking a swig. "I still can't believe Reverend Chance is dead."

"I know. It all seems so unreal," Nikki said, pulling out the ironing board they kept in the hall closet. "I spoke to him just last week when I dropped you off at the office. He was so upbeat, so positive."

"Yeah," William said. He stayed his wife's hand with his own. "Don't worry about ironing. I'll get that done in the morning."

"Are you sure? We might be pressed for time."

"It's all right. I know how you hate ironing anyway."

Nikki smiled. That had been the longstanding arrangement since early on. William did the laundry. He insisted, after his new white T-shirts disintegrated in his hands following Nikki's first load of laundry as a new wife. He had to tell her that too much bleach wasn't a good thing. And she didn't like ironing, so he usually ended up doing that chore as well, though she did more of that now that he worked so many hours.

"Okay, thanks," she said. "I guess we can go to bed."

He smiled. "Just what I was thinking."

Good thing we got here when we did, Nikki thought as she looked to the end of the crowded pew to see a couple trying to enter. She scooted over to make room, squeezing closer to William. Not an empty seat could be found. Nikki didn't know a lot of the faces, but recognized two city councilmen, several pastors, president of the NAACP, and a senator. Her eyes widened when she spotted Spencer Cason. She quickly looked away.

Her husband saw her tense and followed her gaze. "I can't believe he showed up at the funeral!" William hissed under the funeral music. "I should go kick him out."

"Baby, just ignore him," Nikki whispered back. "He's just paying his respects."

"He and his boss are the reason Reverend Chance is dead," William said. "I guarantee they had something to do with what happened."

Nikki nodded and didn't say another word as the funeral

began. There were people even in the fellowship hall, watching via closed circuit television.

Reverend Chance's wife cried throughout the service and Olivia kept her head down. A young man in military dress—whom Nikki discovered was Reverend Chance's son—kept clearing his throat and breathing deeply.

Nikki put her arm around her husband's waist as they waited to file out of the church. William reached down and squeezed her hand.

"Let me speak to Mrs. Chance once more and make sure Olivia is okay," William said once outside.

"Do you want me to go with you?"

"No, it's crowded. Here are the keys." He handed them to her. "I'll be right back."

As she turned to head to the car, she bumped into a young woman carrying a sleeping boy who looked about three or four years old. "Oh, I'm so sorry!" Nikki apologized, her hand instinctively flying out to steady the woman.

The woman smiled. "It's okay. It's so crowded, you're bound to bump into someone."

"Yes, it's very crowded," Nikki said. "Are you a family member of the Chances?"

The woman shook her head. "Oh, no. I just met him one time. Years ago, when I was pregnant with him," she gestured with her head toward the sleeping boy in her arms, "Reverend Chance helped me out when I had nowhere to turn. He gave me a place to stay and helped me find a job. I just wanted to come to his funeral. It's the least I could do."

"Wow," Nikki said. "He touched a lot of lives."

"Yeah, he really did," the woman said. "But you'd never know it because he didn't brag about what he did. It makes me so mad when I read the newspaper and they are talking about all the stuff Dark did for all those rich people and never say anything about what Reverend Chance did. All they talk about is that gambling he did all those years ago."

Nikki could see the woman was riled. "Hey, I'm sorry for getting you so upset." She extended her hand. "I'm Nikki."

"Oh, I'm so rude," the woman said, adjusting the boy in her arms. "I'm Keedra. I would shake your hand but, well . . ."

Nikki smiled. "I understand. I have a little one myself, so I know what it's like to have your hands full. Fortunately, my mother-in-law agreed to keep her so we wouldn't have to bring her to this."

"You're married?"

"Yes," Nikki said. "My husband works—worked—for Reverend Chance."

"Oh, it must be nice . . . being married, I mean."

"It is," Nikki said. "I feel really fortunate. We got married pretty young, but we've stuck it out. We're pretty solid."

"I don't have anybody here," Keedra said. "I just graduated from college and had to stay in town because I can't afford to move. My family members all live in Texas. And my son's dad is nowhere around."

Nikki felt a tug inside. She could not imagine what it would be like to be alone with a baby. On impulse, she pulled out a strip of paper and wrote down her number and handed it to Keedra. "Hey, give me a call sometime. Maybe we can do something. Maybe take our kids on a play date, even."

Keedra's face lit up. "Are you serious? Oh, that would be awesome," she said. "Here, write my number down, too."

She rattled it off and Nikki programmed it into her phone. It would be nice to have another friend. Maybe Danielle would want to hang out with Keedra, too.

Chapter 27

The day following Reverend Chance's funeral, William immediately got back to pressing the police for an investigation into the candidate's death. William couldn't get anything accomplished that way, so he went to the newspaper; maybe he could force the police to investigate the matter if he went public with their reticence. He asked to see Jimmy Vaughn and was stunned to see Vaughn usher Spencer out of his office.

Spencer shot William a smirk as he left. William's eyes narrowed.

"William, it's good to see you in these parts," Jimmy said, patting him on the back. "What brings you here?"

"I want to talk about Reverend Chance's death."

The meeting with Jimmy netted nothing that William could see. Jimmy said if William brought him proof, any information, he would have something to go on.

"I thought your job was to get the proof? Don't they call you an investigative reporter?" William asked.

Jimmy laughed but simply repeated what he had just said.

William left the office, dejected, not knowing what else to do. How could he prove his boss was murdered and had not killed himself? Reverend Chance would have never taken so drastic an action. William knew the pastor did not believe in taking a life, whether it was his own or another's. William drove aimlessly to the headquarters, and was startled to see a bunch of empty boxes waiting for him. "What is this?"

"We're getting ready to pack up the office. With no candidate, there is no campaign," Olivia said. Her brother nodded.

"Yeah," William said slowly, taking in the scene. "I suppose you're right. I guess it just hasn't sunk in that not only is Reverend Chance gone, but so is all his hard work."

"Yeah," said Oliver Jr. "It's a shame. My dad would have been so good for this city."

"I can't believe that Lo Dark is going to get re-elected," William said.

"That really makes me angry," Olivia added. "I know my dad didn't kill himself. And I bet those people in the other campaign had something to do with it. They are the only ones who would have benefited from seeing my dad dead. My dad was going to beat them, and they knew it."

"Whoa, sis," Oliver Jr. said. "Those are serious allegations. We can't go around spewing stuff like that."

Olivia pounced on her brother. "Don't tell me what I can say, and what I can't! You've not been the one here busting your tail day in and day out! I was the one who created that campaign. I was the one who came up with a strategy, and who worked as hard as I could to get Daddy elected. I've earned the right to say whatever I want."

"Okay, okay." Oliver Jr. held up his hands. "Just calm down. And stop acting up in front of company."

"William isn't company," Olivia said. "We've all become like family here. But you wouldn't know that."

"Look, don't blame me for not being here," Oliver Jr. snapped. "I had a job to do."

"Well, if you had been here, you could have done something!" Olivia's voice rose. "You could have stopped all this. And Daddy would still be alive!"

William cleared his throat. "Hey, guys, I hate to butt in, but maybe we should all leave and come back later. There is no need to start packing so soon. Emotions are running high. Maybe we'll come back tomorrow or the next day and pack all these things and shut down the headquarters."

Olivia sighed. "You know, he's right. I'm going to see Mama."

William walked out with Oliver Jr. and Olivia. William got back into the Protégé and pulled onto the street, but he wasn't sure where he was going.

What do you do when your boss has been murdered and your life's mission has suddenly evaporated into thin air?

The next day's newspaper reported that with Dark's main opponent now out of the race, Dark would likely be re-elected with ease for his third term. William slammed the paper down on the couch and Nikki looked up.

"What's wrong?" she asked.

"The man isn't even cold yet and they've already moved on to talking about Dark's third term," William said. "Don't they have any decency?"

"Well, Dark only gets a third term if he doesn't have a serious challenger, right?"

"Yeah, but in case you missed it, his serious challenger just died."

Nikki joined her husband on the couch. "What if you run?"

"What?"

"You heard me."

"Nikki, are you crazy? I can't run."

"Why not, baby?" She put her hand on her husband's. "Hasn't that always been your ultimate goal anyway? You were working on this campaign because you believed in the candidate, but also to get experience. How many times have you said you wanted to run for office?"

"Yeah, but—"

"There is no *but*," Nikki said. "This is the perfect opportunity. You know the work Reverend Chance started. Why don't you finish it for him?"

William's eyes were wide. He blinked and rubbed his forehead. "Are you serious?"

"I've never been more serious," Nikki said. "You would be the perfect candidate."

"Well, baby, I'm too young—"

She cut him off. "Age ain't nothin' but a number."

"And we don't have any money."

"That's never stopped us before. You'll get out there and work dog hard to raise funds like you were doing before, only they'll be for your own campaign." Nikki nodded in assurance.

"But we don't have enough clout yet, baby, to run for office. This is Shreveport. I know things are changing, but it's still about power and who you know—and who knows you. Nobody knows me," William reasoned. He knew he was fishing for excuses. "According to my plan, this run would be at least another four or five years off. After the computer company was a bit more stable and I had worked in Reverend Chance's administration and we had more money."

"Well, life rarely goes according to plan," Nikki said. "Baby, this is what you've wanted for years."

"We might not have time to qualify."

"You and I both know qualifying is another few weeks off. It's the end of August right now. Qualifying isn't until, what, early to middle of September? As long as you get your paperwork in by the qualifying deadline, your name will be on that ballot for the November election." Nikki shot down each excuse.

"I'd have to make it past the October primary election first," William said.

"Oh, you would make it." Nikki shrugged off the resistance. "Those other people running aren't serious contenders. The media doesn't even report on them all that much. Your focus would be the general election."

William didn't say anything for a moment. Nikki knew she had to speak his language. "Maybe this is where you have to step out on faith," she said. "Maybe this is an opportunity God is presenting. He wants you to continue the work the pastor started. You can do this."

William slowly shook his head. "I appreciate the support, baby, but I don't think we're ready. We can't win an election like this."

"Are you saying there is something too hard for God?"

A tiny voice mocked her: *Didn't you think healing your child was too hard for God, so you took matters into your own hands? Who are you to talk about faith?*

Nikki blocked from her mind that hookup and how she had paid for Psalm's surgery. That was different, she reasoned. "We must have faith."

"Yes, I know but . . ." William's words trailed in the air.

"This is your chance, honey," she said. "Step out on faith."

The next day, William arrived at the office before the others to begin packing. He knew this would be hard on Reverend Chance's family, so he wanted to get much of it out of the way before they came. He was on the second box when Olivia and Oliver Jr. entered the office.

"Can we talk to you for a minute, William?" Olivia asked.

William smiled. "Sure. What's up?"

Olivia looked to her brother, who cleared his throat. "We got a call from Reverend Hicks last night."

"Okay."

"He wants to place another candidate on the ticket," Oliver Jr. said. "He said we've got to have someone to seriously challenge Dark and he is willing to help find the money."

"Okay. . . ." William said slowly, not sure where this was going.

"We think it should be you," Oliver Jr. announced, looking at his sister.

"Me?" William's brows shot up.

"We think you should run," Olivia blurted. "You've had almost as much face time as my dad since you were his spokesman. And you know all of the issues inside and out. Reverend Hicks is right. We can't let all of our work be in vain. Daddy wouldn't want that. The other candidates in the field are just jokes; nobody can even take them seriously. You would be the only serious competition to the incumbent. You're the only one."

William grimaced. He just did not know. "Well, I'd have to get through the primary and then get to the general," he said. "That's two elections."

"Oh, the primary won't be a big deal at all," Olivia said. "Those few challengers are nobodies. And whatever votes they would get would be so split among the lot. You'll get through the primary. And I'm sure you'll win the general. I'll see to it."

William's mind flashed back to last night's conversation with Nikki. Could he really do this? He shook his head. *No, I can't run. I wouldn't know what to do. I don't have the experience or the money*, he told himself.

"What do you say?" Oliver Jr. said. "My family has discussed it and we're in full support of you."

William continued shaking his head. "I don't know what to say. I'm honored that you would think of me, but really, I think you have the wrong guy."

"Come on, William," Olivia said, touching his arm. "You have to do it. You're our best chance. If not, Reverend Hicks will throw his money and support behind someone else. And don't you want to see my dad's work continue? There is no guarantee another candidate would feel about the community the way my dad did. And besides, we've got to have a viable candidate; someone to beat Dark."

"I'm not viable," William insisted. "I'm too young. I don't have any money. My company is floundering along at best. I just—"

"William, we need you." Olivia looked into his eyes.

He saw the pleading in her eyes and looked away. "I really don't think so."

William stepped away from the siblings and stared out of a window, watching cars pass by on the street. His thoughts were a jumble. What should he do? Could he run this race? Could he win it?

The room was starting to close in around William. Half-filled boxes dotted desks, Olivia and Oliver debated in a corner; a clock ticked loudly near his ear.

"I'll be back later," William said abruptly, and grabbed his keys. He hopped into the car and found himself parked in his mother's driveway twenty minutes later. He knocked on the front door and heard her call from inside.

"Come on in, it's open!"

He pulled the screen door and stepped inside, immediately hit by the pungent smell of onions and greens cooking on the stove.

"Hi, Ma," he said, bending to kiss her on the cheek as she chopped peppers.

"Boy, can't you see how hot it is in here? Get away from me, trying to kiss me," she said. "This stove is burning up and you're here all crowding me."

William stepped back. He opened the refrigerator, hunting for some iced tea.

"Hurry up and close that door," Mable Broussard said. "Don't be letting all of my cool air out. You don't pay bills around here. Electricity ain't free."

"Yes, Ma," he said, wondering why he had come.

Mable Broussard had raised her sons hard. Life hadn't been easy for the single mother. She felt proud of herself for raising them to adulthood—a good tongue-lashing or whipping helped keep them in line. Neither son had ever been arrested, she was quick to tell anyone who listened; and one had even gone to college. She didn't like that William ran off and got himself married to a fast tail girl who surely must be the reason he was still broke. At least Mac had gone to barber school and made a nice living cutting hair. And at least Mac had married a church girl, not some heathen he had to convert.

"So what's on your mind?" she asked her younger son, casting a sidelong glance at William.

"What makes you think something is on my mind?"

" 'Cause I'm your mama and I know when something is bothering one of my children," she said. "What's that girl gone and done now?"

"Nikki? You know Nikki doesn't ever do anything bad. We're cool."

"Uh-huh," she pursed her lips. "Is she still lazing around the house? I don't see why she can't seem to get a job. I had two children to raise, and I worked. Sure didn't sit around the house all day, sucking up all the air and not doing nothing."

"Ma, Nikki does plenty; you know that," he said. "She's in school and she is raising our daughter."

"Well, I just don't think it's right that you have to go out and work 'til midnight, breaking your back while she sits at home all day," Mable went on.

"Look, Ma, I didn't come over here to talk about my wife," William said. "She's doing a wonderful job at being my wife and raising our daughter. And she's almost finished with grad school. She's going to graduate with a near perfect grade point average."

"Humph," Mable said and dropped the bell peppers into hot grease. She added tomatoes and sausage. "Well, I never had no man sitting around taking care of me. I worked, and I worked hard. Ain't never heard nobody tell of me being lazy."

"Anyway, Ma, we're just trying to figure out the next step as far as the campaign is concerned," he told her.

"What campaign? Your candidate is dead," William's mother said with a wave of her hand.

"I know that, Ma. Some people think maybe I should run."

"You?" She cocked her head to the side. "What people?"

"The Chance family, for one. Reverend Hicks, for another," he said, shrugging.

"Reverend Hicks? The one with that big ol' church they show on TV? Really? Well, that's all right," she said with approval. "You'd be a better candidate than any of them other folks."

"I don't know," he said slowly.

"The Lord works in mysterious ways," his mother said. "This could be your blessing in disguise."

"Yeah, maybe. It's a big step, though, running for mayor. I just don't know that I have what it takes," William voiced his doubts.

"Well, you won't know 'less you try," she said.

"That's what Nikki says," he said.

"What? She think you should run?" Mable Broussard's

tone changed. She didn't like knowing she was agreeing with something her daughter-in-law had suggested.

"Yes, she was the first one to encourage me to do it," he said. "Yesterday."

"Uhn. I should have known she was the one pushing you to this. Should have known it was her idea. I think it's crazy. You're too young and you ain't even got money for some stupid campaign."

"But, Ma, you just said—"

"What I said is it's stupid. You can't win nobody's election. Stop letting that girl put that foolishness in your head."

William took a deep breath as he weighed his options. He didn't know whether to follow his wife's advice—or his mother's.

Chapter 28

Danielle sat on the couch in the Broussards' living room, playing Patty Cake with Psalm while Nikki took cornbread out of the oven. When Nikki returned to the living room, Danielle looked up.

"So, I found a couple of cute designs for the bridesmaids' dresses," she said. "Pass me that magazine under my purse. I want to show them to you. And I found one for you as the matron of honor."

Nikki bit her lip to keep from saying anything. She wasn't thrilled about her best friend's wedding but didn't want to spoil Danielle's excitement. Danielle had dropped in after work so she could show Nikki the wedding party dresses and talk about the upcoming nuptials. Nikki passed the magazine to Danielle, who instructed Psalm to go and play on the other side of the room. Danielle flipped through the magazine, removing a sticky note from the page she had marked.

"See? What do you think of these?" she shoved the book at Nikki. The floor length dresses were a beautiful mauve with spaghetti straps.

"Most folks try to make their bridesmaids wear ugly dresses," Nikki joked.

"Oh, see I'm not even concerned about them outshining me," Danielle said. "Their dresses are going to look good, but my dress is going to look even better. I'm going to look better than any of them. All eyes will be on me."

"Yes, that's true. All eyes will be on you," Nikki said dryly. "It'll be your day."

"I can tell you're still not all that happy for me," Danielle said. "And I just don't understand. I was happy for you when you got married."

Nikki swallowed, not sure what to say. She conjured up the best smile she could muster. "If you're happy, I'm happy."

"I am," Danielle said. "And besides, at least I won't be fornicating anymore. Shouldn't that make you happy? You know how you used to always fuss at me about that."

"Well, I don't think—"

"Anyway, forget all that," Danielle said and leaned over to hug her friend. "I'm putting a lot of energy into getting ready for this wedding. I really want this day to be special. And you're my girl. I need you in my corner."

"I'll always be in your corner, Danny Boo."

"You know you're my only true friend."

"You have plenty of friends," Nikki said. "What about the bridesmaids?"

"Those trolls?" Danielle said. "I'm letting Cecelia be in it because I was in her lame wedding. You know she's always been jealous of me, ever since college. And the other two are Troy's sisters."

"What about your sister?"

"What about her?"

"Well, don't you think it's about time you made up with her and the rest of your family?" Nikki could see her friend's jaw tense. "I mean, ever since I've known you, you have been at odds with your family. Whatever happened, it was so long ago. Let it go, Danielle. Your family loves you. Lots of people do."

"Girl, stop talking all crazy," Danielle said dismissively. "I don't need them. As long as I have Troy and as long as I have my best friend, I'm cool. You're the only two people who appreciate me. Everyone else is either jealous or just hateful."

"That's not the right attitude," Nikki said. "God didn't make us to be all by ourselves. You should forgive your family—for whatever they did."

"Girl, don't start preaching to me. I'm really not in the mood." Danielle rolled her eyes.

"Well, I'm just saying God doesn't like that you're like this," Nikki said.

"Please don't lecture me about God," Danielle stressed. "I know you're a holy roller now, but give me a break. I know who you were before your little spiritual makeover."

"Look, I did do some crazy things back in the day, but that doesn't mean—"

"What it means is that I don't want to hear about God from somebody who has sinned as much as you have!" Danielle snapped.

Nikki bit her lip and swallowed hard. *She's right. Who am I to tell her what God wants? I am just fooling myself.*

"When you can live without sinning, then you come talk to me," Danielle said. "Until then, shut up."

"Well, I just hope you forgive your family," Nikki said. "That's all I'm saying."

"I don't want to talk about all those haters. So many people are just jealous of me. It's ridiculous. I can't help it if I'm beautiful and smart and have money."

"Danielle." Nikki sighed. She hated it when Danielle talked like this. Even after all this time, sometimes Nikki felt as if she did not understand her friend. "I don't know why you always say things like that. Nobody is jealous of you or hates you. Plenty of people adore you."

"See, you're just so sweet," Danielle said with a smile. Her earlier derision of her friend was gone. It was as if the exchange had never happened. "You think the best of everybody. That's why I love you. But see, I know people better than you do. And I know I have to keep my guard up. Besides, I don't need a lot of friends. That's why I have you."

Just then, they heard a light knock on the door. Danielle looked up. "You're expecting company?"

Nikki scrambled to her feet. "Oh, yeah. I have a friend who said she'd stop by."

"A friend?" Danielle cut her eyes toward the door, but Nikki was already scrambling across the room.

She opened the door to Keedra. "Hi, girl!" Nikki said, and embraced the woman.

Keedra stepped into the living room, holding her son's hand. "Hi, thanks for inviting me over."

"No problem," Nikki said. "I was so glad you called to say hi. We have plenty of space, so it's always nice to have a friend over. Dinner will be ready in just a sec."

Danielle looked the woman up and down. "I see you made it to K-Mart's end-of-season sale," Danielle said to Keedra sardonically.

"Huh?" Keedra frowned. "What do you mean?"

"She doesn't mean anything," Nikki said quickly. She shot Danielle a sharp look.

Danielle wanted to retort, but didn't.

Nikki smiled at Keedra. "Keedra, this is my best friend, Danielle. Danielle, this is my friend, Keedra, and her little boy, Josiah."

Keedra extended her hand. Danielle pretended not to see and turned back to flipping pages in her magazine.

Keedra hesitated, then said, "Nice to meet you."

"Yeah. You too." Danielle didn't bother to look up.

Nikki jumped into the conversation. "Would you like something to drink, Keedra?"

"Sure. What do you have?"

"Sweet tea."

"Oh, that's great. It's so hard to find good sweet tea! And this is the South. I just don't understand."

Nikki laughed. "I know what you mean. It surprises me that more places don't have sweet tea around here. Going out to eat is tough. Nobody seems to serve it. That's probably why I stock up on it at home! I love Red Diamond tea. I buy it by the jug!"

"Oh, you have Red Diamond? I love that stuff, girl!" Keedra grinned.

Keedra glanced at Danielle, trying to invite her into the conversation. "So, do you like sweet tea, too, Danielle?"

Danielle pretended she hadn't heard the question. She continued flipping through her magazine.

"Danielle, Keedra was asking you a question," Nikki prodded as she stepped into the kitchen.

Danielle glanced up, an innocent expression on her face. "Oh, I'm sorry. What was that?"

"Oh, I was just asking if you like sweet tea, too," Keedra repeated. "I love me some good sweet tea."

"Oh, no, I don't drink sweet tea," Danielle breezed. "It has too much sugar. I try to watch what I put into my mouth." She looked Keedra up and down. "But I can see not all of us do."

"She's just joking," Nikki said quickly, returning to the living room with a plastic jug of tea in one hand and a glass in the other. "Danielle drinks sweet tea." Nikki poured Keedra's tea into a glass and handed it to her.

Danielle frowned. "You didn't ask me if I wanted something."

Nikki laughed. "Girl, you're not company. This is like your second home. You can get your own."

Danielle rolled her eyes, but stood. Then she sashayed to the kitchen and grabbed a cup then retrieved the jug of tea from Nikki and poured some for herself. She turned back to Keedra. "Yeah, she's right. This is like my second home. I even have my own special cup, see." She held out the white, plastic cup she had gotten from one of the city's many Mardi Gras parades. "Nobody drinks out of this but me. Neat, huh?"

"Yeah, that's nice." Keedra smiled.

Nikki quickly fixed plates of cornbread and jambalaya and they all sat at the dining room table and ate, Danielle next to Nikki. Keedra sat across the table. The children fussed about sitting at the table, so Nikki let them sit on a blanket on the floor near the adults.

"Did you see the new photography at that black bookstore on Linwood?" Keedra asked.

They had discovered during their first phone conversation that they shared a love of photography. Keedra was a recent graduate with a photography degree and worked for a local newspaper.

Nikki's eyes lit up. "Girl, I did! I went by there the other day when I stopped by the campaign office. It's amazing. The lighting. The colors."

"I know," Keedra said. "If I had half that talent! Did you see the expressions on those faces? The photos made me want to cry, I could just feel what those people were going through."

"Me too," Nikki said. "Especially the one of the mother holding the baby sitting on the front row at the funeral."

Danielle listened to the conversation as she quietly drank her tea, then stood, brushing nonexistent wrinkles from her chocolate skirt. "Well, I'm going to head on out. Seems that you two friends have lots to talk about without poor little old me hanging around spoiling the party."

Nikki looked up, startled. "You haven't even had dessert. I made your favorite, bananas Foster."

"I'm not hungry," Danielle said, gathering her keys. "On second thought, just stick me some in a bowl and I'll be going. Seems like three's a crowd."

Chapter 29

William stopped by the deputy coroner's house the next evening. Francesca Garcia was one of the sharpest people he knew, someone he had known since childhood. She had been one of his brother, Mac's, classmates, and now, at 32, she could have a shot at the coroner's post if she wanted to run—making her the youngest person to ever hold that position in the parish.

"Hey, come on in." She smiled when she opened the door for William.

He stepped into the spacious living room of her two-story, antebellum home. "Good to see you again," he said. "Things have been so hectic, what with the funeral and all, that I've not had a chance to get back with you. What can you tell me about Reverend Chance's death?"

Dr. Garcia sighed. "Well, you know I really can't say anything."

"Come on Fran. You've got to give me something to work with. I just can't wrap my head around the idea of suicide."

Dr. Garcia thought for a long moment, as if trying to decide if she should say anything. At last, she spoke. "Well, all

I'll say is this: There are some people in the city who have been pressuring our office—my boss—to declare it a suicide so there won't be an investigation."

"So, you're saying it wasn't a suicide?"

"All I'm saying is there are people with a vested interest in it being ruled as such," she said. "They don't want this thing dragged out any more than it has to be."

"So, what does your work show?"

"William, my name can't be attached to this." Her tone was serious.

He nodded eagerly. "Okay, it won't. Just tell me what I need to know."

"There was no water in his lungs."

William stared at her, his eyes narrowed. "So that means—"

"He was dead before he hit the water."

The revelation struck William hard. He had known in his gut that his boss hadn't killed himself, but having it con-firmed sent shock waves through his being. That meant only one thing: Someone had indeed murdered Reverend Chance.

But who? William told Nikki about his conversation with Dr. Garcia that night as they lay in bed.

"Murder? Are you serious?" Nikki was shocked.

"Yes, baby," he said. "Somebody killed Reverend Chance."

Nikki let out a slow, low breath. "That's some serious stuff. Who could it be?"

"I don't know," he admitted. "But I have my suspicions."

Nikki shook her head. "Surely you don't think Spencer, or the Lo Dark campaign would stoop so low? I mean, that's crazy, right?"

"I don't know," William spoke slowly. "I really don't know."

Silence enveloped them for a moment, each processing the information.

William mused. "You know, there always were those rumors that Dark has mob connections."

"Yeah, but those are just rumors. I mean, this is Shreveport, not some big, overpopulated city." Nikki twisted to look at him in the glow from the moon that sliced through the curtains. "Do you think that whoever killed Reverend Chance would come after you if you ran? Will, I'm getting freaked out by all this."

William didn't say anything for the longest moment. She jabbed him. "You sleep?" she finally asked.

"No," came the answer. "I'm just thinking."

"Okay, tell me."

"You know what this means?"

She slowly nodded. "Yeah. You've got to find answers, one way or the other. And if the current police chief and administration are the ones blocking you, then you've got to get in there and become the administration yourself. You've got to run."

William met with the Chances and Reverend Hicks, telling them of his tentative decision to run. Maybe if he won the election, at least then he could open an investigation into Reverend Chance's death. He still wasn't hundred percent certain he wanted to do this, but he knew he couldn't let someone get away with murder. Maybe his wife was right, maybe this was God pushing him to follow his political dream. *Well, Lord, I sure wish you would have given me a nudge into my political career, not a shove like this*, he mused.

Reverend Hicks seemed pleased William would run and told him he would see to it that William's family moved into a larger home immediately and got another car.

"Why?" William asked.

Reverend Hicks looked at Olivia, who shrugged. "Well, you know politics is very much about appearances," he said. "And we really must make sure your image is appropriate."

"My image is fine," William said, feeling his face growing hot. He worked hard to put his best foot forward. He was living in a house that was already more than he could afford. He couldn't take on any more expense. And he didn't want handouts.

"Well, your house is all right," Reverend Hicks said. "It's decent, but it's not truly a 'wow' factor. For that, you need to change zip codes. And that little car you drive?"

Olivia jumped in. "What he means is that we need to give your image some punch. You need to look like you have already arrived, like you've made it."

"Yes, not like you're hanging on by a thread," Reverend Hicks insisted. "It just isn't right. You've got to look self-sufficient and your car—"

"I *am* self-sufficient," William said stiffly. "I take care of my family. I don't need some handout."

"William," Olivia said, touching his hand. "Reverend Hicks didn't mean any harm. We all want what's best for the campaign. And he's right. You can't be a mayoral candidate driving around in some budget college-student looking car."

"Besides, I understand you are in a bit of a financial bind," Reverend Hicks said. "I believe your home is on the verge of foreclosure, is that correct?"

William's eyebrows shot up in surprise edged with embarrassment. How did Reverend Hicks know about that? "Oh, uh, we—"

"Never mind all that," Reverend Hicks interrupted. "My point here is that it seems this new residence will be right on time for you. We can arrange a quick sale of your house so you don't have that foreclosure on your record. I know someone who can help with that. And we can get you moved."

William's jaw was tight. All the feelings of inadequacy came flooding back. Nikki deserved to live better than having to struggle to keep a roof over her head or to share a breakdown-prone car with him. And his child deserved access to the best. "I'm not taking somebody's handouts."

"Don't look at it as such," Reverend Hicks said. "It's not a handout. Just think of it as something to tide you over until better things come along. And you're a bright young man; better things will come along soon for you."

"Well, what about campaign finance rules or something?" William said. "I can't—"

"Well, you're not a candidate yet," Reverend Hicks said. "You're just a young man trying to provide for his family. And I'm a pastor interested in helping young families. Olivia and I have it all arranged."

William glanced sharply at Olivia, who smiled, but said nothing. Reverend Hicks continued. "The house belongs to a friend who is out of the country and needs a house sitter. And I have a friend who owns a car dealership who is just waiting for the word. He owes me a favor. Olivia has seen to it that you have a new bank account."

"Well, let me think about it," William said finally.

William mulled the idea over for another few days. He and Nikki spoke about the upcoming election in hushed tones after Psalm went to bed at night. This would mean so many changes for them.

The first few days of September seemed to speed by as the qualifying deadline drew near. And now, time had run out. William had to make his decision public. Today was the last day to qualify for the upcoming elections. If he went through with signing up, there would be no turning back.

"You sure this is okay, Nikki?" William peered into her face. "If you don't want me to run, I won't. I know it's asking a lot."

Nikki's temples began to pound, but she smiled. "It's okay."

William smiled back, glad to have her support. He grabbed the car keys from the table. "Well, I'm going to sign up to run for mayor."

The story came out in the paper the next day, broadcasting a new challenger for Dark. The frenzy was immediate. "Who is this young kid?" Someone from Lo Dark's camp was quoted as saying in the story.

William read the story through three times before putting the paper down. It didn't bother him that they had questions about him. They'll know who William Broussard is before long, he mused, the excitement of his decision finally taking hold. He had always thought he would be older by the time he ran for office, but he was finally wrapping his head around the idea that he could become the city's youngest mayor. He had worked all his life for this—he didn't even have a single speeding ticket. "Keep your nose clean," his old political science professor had told all the students. And William had taken that to heart. He didn't want to be compromised like so many candidates; by some skeleton clanking out of the closet.

Even before he officially declared his candidacy, so many things had happened at lightning speed. The family's move had been a hurried one, as they tried to get everything settled before his announcement. In a matter of days, they were living in a four-bedroom house in one of the city's mixed race, nicer neighborhoods—though, purposefully not the wealthiest—and driving a shiny Yukon. He had decided to keep driving the Protégé, though, and leave the Yukon for Nikki. His new home was in the wealthiest part of town, but not the wealthiest neighborhood. Reverend Hicks said this would give him the credibility with the Whites but not alienate him from the Blacks.

The house was a shade smaller than their other one, but

it was a lot nicer, with its landscaped lawn and newer construction. Just last week, they had celebrated Psalm's fifth birthday with a party under the gazebo on the back lawn. Mac and his family had attended, as had William's mother, with the woman inspecting the house and giving a nod of approval, as she thought her son had finally begun making some real money. William basked under her smile. He had seen Nikki trying to put on a smile as well, though he knew without being told that she was disappointed when her mother called the morning of the party to say she and her husband would not be able to make the drive up from Houston, because Carla had some type of emergency.

The house would be great for entertaining, William knew, as he envisioned the many political meetings and social engagements they would have. As for the vehicle, it wasn't new, but it looked good. He had insisted on keeping the Protégé, though. It was the first big purchase he and Nikki had made together and it meant a lot to them.

He would hire a couple of people to help him run his computer business. That way, his business could grow while he focused on the campaign. Now that he didn't have the pressure of the monstrous mortgage, William could have a little breathing room. He would use the money he had been directing to the mortgage to now pay a couple of part-time employees.

I told Nikki we would be all right. We've suddenly moved on up like the Jeffersons, William mused, humming a few bars from the old television show.

"Who is William Broussard, indeed?" he chuckled at the question the newspaper had posed. "Just wait till they find out."

His eye caught sight of something else on the page. He squinted and peered closer. *Photo by Nikki Broussard. What is this?* He frowned as he read the story that accompanied the photo, about a big-rig that crashed into an SUV, sending a woman and child to the hospital and killing the driver of the rig.

"Nikki didn't even say anything about this," William muttered, jabbing his finger at the photo. "But I know she's not trying to start working again. We've already settled that."

Before he could call Nikki, his cell phone rang. William did not recognize the number but answered anyway. "Hello?"

"So, are you ready to get your rear end kicked?"

The voice was unmistakable. It was Spencer.

"How'd you get this number?" William demanded.

"You must have forgotten. You're a political candidate now. I can get any information on you I want."

"Well, there is really nothing to get on me, so I'm not concerned. And to answer your question, the only kicking that'll be going on is the thrashing you'll get on Election Day." William hung up. Excitement coursed through him, but so did trepidation.

"What have I gotten myself into?"

Chapter 30

The doorbell rang and Nikki quickly put down the apple pie she had just removed from the oven, its scent of cinnamon and spices wafting throughout the house. She dusted a bit of flour from her chin with the back of her hand, and wiped her palms on a dish towel as she crossed the expanse that was the living room of her new home. The move from the old house had been quick, as Olivia and Reverend Hicks insisted on removing all vestiges of a struggling middle class family from William. Now, they lived in an expensive Southeast Shreveport home.

"Who is it?" Nikki called.

"Trudy McWilliams."

Trudy McWilliams? "Who?"

"It's Trudy, dear," the voice called. "Please open the door so I do not have to continue standing out here."

Who is Trudy? Nikki wondered. She opened the door and her eyes widened. Oh. *Trudy.* Trudy McWilliams was among the city's black social elite and often appeared in the newspaper. She stepped into the living room, unbidden, her expensive perfume softly tickling Nikki's nose, as her pearl earrings and upswept hair drew attention to a long, elegant neck. Trudy's posture was perfect and her dress impeccable, as she checked out the newly decorated house Nikki and William had moved into only days before. Trudy's eyes trailed over the furnishings.

"Not a bad start," she said, a slight frown creasing her brow. "Before long though, we will need to replace that couch with this season's version."

"Pardon?"

Trudy turned. "Olivia asked me to stop by your home to help refine your tastes and to groom you, as you'll now be traveling in some very prestigious circles," Trudy said, again looking around. "I see we're going to have our work cut out for us."

"Oh . . . I. . . ." Nikki said, flustered. "We just moved in. We're still working, though I thought the decorating project was coming along nicely."

William had told Nikki that Reverend Hicks had a friend who needed a sitter for this Victorian-style house with its pitched roofs and high ceilings. Some of the furnishings belonged to the owners, but Nikki had redecorated the living room. She had brought in a contemporary vanilla leather love seat and couch set, and had placed an Oriental rug in front of the couch, flanking it on both sides with lamps. She created an intimate setting in the large space.

"Well, I'm sure you did your best," Trudy said. She held out her gloved hand. "My throat is parched, dear."

Nikki snapped into action, her mind whirling. Olivia sent Trudy? But why? *I have taste and I know how to act in public. I don't need some high-class tutor*, she thought to herself. Nikki immediately moved to the kitchen. She turned to face the woman again, though. "Oh, forgive my manners," she said. "Please, have a seat. Would you like sweet tea?"

Trudy's brows shot up ever so slightly. "Sweet tea? Do you have any hot tea? Any golden needle perhaps?"

"Oh, I can make it hot," Nikki said, smiling. "That's not a problem. What's golden needle?"

"It's a black tea."

"Oh, yeah, I have black tea right here," Nikki said, pulling the bags out of the cabinet.

Trudy looked aghast. "No, darling; surely you're not referring to those supermarket tea bags? The tea I'm interested in costs at least $80 an ounce, not ninety-nine cents for a whole box."

Nikki gulped. "Oh . . . I . . ." she looked at the tea box in her hand, embarrassed. "I'm sorry. I don't have anything like that."

Trudy sighed and fanned her face. "Oh my," she said. "We must get started quickly on your refinement. I'll pass on the tea. Do you have any scones and a bit of marmalade or spread?"

Nikki squirmed. "I don't. But I do have apple pie I just made."

Trudy pursed her lips but nodded. "Very well. I'll take a bit of the pie."

Trudy insisted Nikki have a spa date with her the following afternoon. Nikki didn't want to go, but she knew William wouldn't like it if she alienated these new people who were prying into her life, so she arranged for Keedra to baby-sit Psalm after school.

"I can't do anything to jeopardize my husband's new career," Nikki reminded herself. It didn't matter if she preferred an afternoon at home so she could work on her thesis for her final degree requirements. Nor did it matter if she wanted to spend time helping Psalm with her kindergarten assignment, now that the girl was in school. Nikki needed to get out there and start mixing and mingling with Trudy and her friends.

As she stood on the steps of the spa the next day, Nikki had to admit that some of the high life wasn't so bad. This was her first-ever spa visit. She strode into the foyer and was immediately met by a smiling attendant.

"Good afternoon," the lady said, gesturing for Nikki to follow her. She seemed to know who Nikki was, even without an introduction. "Mrs. Broussard, please come this way."

The woman led Nikki into a back room with reclining seats. "Please wait right here. Make yourself comfortable."

Nikki received a little jolt at the personal attention, and sneaked a peek around. The green and white colors seemed to spell serenity and the plush furnishings bespoke the luxury of the moment. "Has Mrs. McWilliams arrived?"

"She telephoned just before your arrival to say she is running a tad late, but she will be here shortly."

Nikki sighed with relief, glad it was McWilliams who was late. The attendant left Nikki and her stomach immediately rumbled loudly. She tried to suck her midsection in to squelch the sound, thankful she was alone.

She sat in the soft chair to wait for Trudy, but her stomach squealed again. Nikki rummaged around in her purse for gum, candy, anything. Her eyes fell on a bowl of cucumber slices and a basin of water with lemons. "Oh, they have refreshments," she said and walked over to the bowl. "People with money are so weird. Who wants to just eat a bowl of cucumbers? And where are the napkins and forks?" The hunger pangs reminded her that she didn't care about napkins right now.

Nikki didn't want anyone to see her dig into the bowl with her fingers so she quickly glanced around to make sure no one was coming, and then fished a few cucumber slices out of the bowl. She said a hasty grace and stuck them in her mouth. The cool crispness felt good on her tongue.

She stood over the bowl, eating a few more. She was chewing a slice when the attendant and Trudy stepped into the room. "Good afternoon, Nikki," Trudy said, eyeing the bowl of cucumbers.

"Hi," Nikki said, swallowing the last bit and moving away from the bowl.

"When are you going to do something about that nappy head?" Trudy whispered when the attendant showed them to their changing area.

Another attendant placed cucumber slices on the eyes of a woman reclining in a robe on a plush seat. Nikki gulped in embarrassment. *So that's what those cucumber pieces were for,* she realized.

"Did you hear what I said?" Trudy repeated.

"Huh?" Nikki drew her attention back to Trudy.

"Your hair. When are you going to do something about that nappy head of yours?"

"What do you mean?" Nikki touched her natural hair, which was pulled back into a puffy ponytail.

Trudy rolled her eyes. "Surely, you can't expect to walk around looking like a pickaninny."

"Pickaninny?" Nikki was offended.

Trudy waved off the protest. "Spare me the righteous indignation," she said. "I know you think you're being vogue by going 'natural' but the nappy hair has got to go. You're going to have to get a perm in that head of yours. Surely you don't want to be photographed looking like some little refugee child?"

Nikki's back stiffened. "I don't believe I look like anyone's *refugee,*" she told the older black woman stiffly. Her mother hadn't liked when Nikki began wearing her hair natural five years before, and even Danielle had disliked the look. But Nikki had insisted on the natural look. At the time, she had done it because she detested spending all day in a beauty shop and it was a bit of a financial decision as she couldn't afford to have regular beauty appointments after she got married. Besides, Nikki thought she was cute with natural hair. She cut her eyes at Trudy.

"Well, be that as it may," Trudy said, "we must do something about that head. I can understand your affinity for Mother Africa or whatever, but you've got to look at the big picture. What you look like is quite important to this campaign. And do you want to help your husband or hinder him?"

"I want to help him, of course."

"Then you'll need to get rid of that hair," Trudy said. "This campaign is not about what you want. It's about what will get your husband elected. And if that means sacrificing a bit of yourself, then you'll need to do that."

Nikki looked down at her hands. Sacrificing for her husband was nothing new. She nodded. This was yet another piece of herself she had to give up.

Nikki picked up Psalm from Keedra's later that evening and took her to the campaign office. She let the child play in a corner, while Nikki designed posters, flyers and yard signs on the computer. Olivia would take them to be printed the next day.

The office was abuzz with activity. Some of Oliver Chance's volunteers had stayed on and the small office had an air of purpose.

"We may be small and few in number, but we are going to do this!" William said, rallying his troops.

"Yeah!" a volunteer yelled. Another clapped.

Nikki looked up from her work and smiled. Reverend Hicks had promised to help raise funds and to send his church members to vote for William, but Nikki knew pulling off this campaign in so short a time frame would still be difficult. William's days were even longer than when he worked on Reverend Chance's campaign. And now, Nikki found herself at the campaign office often.

The volunteers started leaving one by one around 10 p.m., until only Nikki, William and Olivia remained. Olivia and William were hunched over a table, scouring a city map and planning strategy.

Nikki rose from her seat to take a stretch. Psalm was playing with a doll, but Nikki could tell the child was sleepy. She stretched and walked to William. "Baby, it's getting late." Nikki rubbed his back.

William looked up. "Huh?"

Nikki smiled. William could be so one-track. "The time. It's after eleven," she said. "Psalm is getting antsy. She has school tomorrow."

"Baby, we just have a few more things to discuss," William said, looking at Olivia, who held no expression.

"I know, sweetie, but you'll stay out here all night if I let you," Nikki said. "Everybody else is gone. I know we have a lot of work to do on this campaign, but we also have a life."

"Baby, this campaign is my life right now," William said.

"William, we really have a lot of work to do," Olivia said quietly.

"William, it's almost midnight," Nikki said. "I'm tired. Psalm is tired."

"Oh, well, you don't have to stay. That's one of the good things about having two cars now. Why don't you go on home? I'll finish this up with Olivia and be right there."

"I was thinking we could *all* go home," Nikki insisted.

Olivia stood and smoothed her charcoal skirt over her round hips. "Well, maybe your wife is right. Maybe we are putting too much time into this campaign. All the volunteers have left. We can pick up tomorrow. I guess just because we got a late start and have to play catch up is no reason for us to work so hard, huh?"

William held up his hand. "Wait, Olivia, don't go," he said. He turned to his wife. "Baby, Olivia is right. We are in a race against time."

Nikki's shoulders slumped. "Okay, baby," she said. "Fine. But I'll wait around with you. We'll stay for a while longer."

Chapter 31

Danielle sat in a tub filled with jasmine-scented bubbles, with lavender candles lining the edge. She leaned her head on the pillow and breathed deeply. "You've got to stay calm," she told herself as she felt the warm water swirl around her body.

It seemed that her supervising nurse was out to get her. Just today, the woman had tried to test Danielle's knowledge by asking her random questions about medications and their dosages.

"Like she's trying to give me a pop quiz or something. But she's not going to get me. She thinks she's slick, trying to make me look dumb. But I'm smarter than all of them." Danielle spoke the words aloud.

The pop quiz had been interrupted by Peggy, the downstairs receptionist, who paged Danielle over the loudspeaker. "Danielle Esperanza, you have a visitor in the first floor lobby."

Danielle flashed a quick smile at her supervising nurse. "Well, I have to go downstairs." She turned to leave. "And for the record, I do know how to do my job."

Danielle grabbed her stack of papers and found the elevator. When she stepped off, she was surprised to find Troy waiting at the front desk.

"Hey, baby," he said, kissing her cheek. "Brought you something."

Their relationship seemed to be going smoothly. Troy still hadn't made good on his promise to go to church with her, but no more strange women were calling her number.

Troy held out a white bag from her favorite deli. She took it and looked inside, smiling when she saw a Philly cheese steak sandwich, fries and cookies. "Thanks, baby." She gave him a quick peck on the lips.

"Anything for my soon-to-be wife," Troy grinned. He stayed for a moment longer, and they chatted. "Hey, I've got to get back to work."

"Okay, well, I'll see you when I get off, baby," Danielle purred. She tiptoed and kissed him on the lips. A few heads turned, and a nurse standing nearby frowned. Danielle didn't care if any of those people saw her kissing her man. *They're just jealous*, she thought with a touch of defiance.

"Bye, baby," Troy had waved as he walked toward the exit.

He had been doing lots of nice things lately, but Danielle couldn't get the notion out of her mind that something wasn't right. She felt he was cheating on her. She vowed that if she caught him, it would be over.

The memory of that afternoon produced mixed emotions as Danielle now sat in the tub. She tried to use the breathing exercises a counselor had once taught her. She knew she would break out in hives if she continued to let the stress control her. The feelings began to rise in her chest, crushing her breathing, causing her breath to come out in sharp, jagged thrusts as the room started to spin. *One* . . . *two*. . . . Pant, pant. *Three* . . . *Four*. . . . Pant, pant. . . . *Five* . . . *I can't breathe!*

She flailed about and splashed out of the tub, dripping water all over the carpet. She fanned her hands in front of her face, but the breathing kept coming in sharp, shallow bursts. Danielle grabbed on to the edge of the counter with soapy hands, trying to steady herself. It took a few seconds, but the room slowly stopped spinning. Her breathing began to slow down and she realized she was cold as the water dried on her body.

She grabbed for the phone on the counter and pressed speed dial. "Hello?" A strange voice answered. She looked down at the phone to make sure she had dialed the right number, knowing she had.

"Uh. May I speak to Nikki?"

"Oh, is this Danielle?"

A chill shot through her. "Yes," she said coolly. "Who is this?" Why was somebody else answering Nikki's cell phone?

"Oh, this is Keedra," the chipper voice said. "I met you a while ago."

"Why do you have Nikki's phone?" Danielle demanded.

"Oh, she's just down the hall," Keedra said. "She's putting Psalm to bed. She asked me to answer the phone for her. Do you need me to give her a message?"

Danielle's tone was icy. "No." She hung up with narrowed eyes.

Chapter 32

Broussard Being Investigated For Identity Theft and Fraud.

William did a double-take at the morning's headline and sucked in his breath. He almost laughed at the absurdity, but anger coursed through his being. How could these guys print these lies?

He read the story through. It claimed he was being investigated for using a stolen credit card to pay for some medical procedure. He slammed his hand down on the desk when he saw they had brought his wife into it, implicating her as well.

"What is this craziness?" William wondered aloud. "It's bad enough for them to attack me, but they can't do this to my wife."

He dialed his attorney and had a terse conversation. Then he called Olivia.

"I am pulling up outside. I'll be inside in a sec," Olivia told him and hung up.

William reached to dial Nikki's number, but the office phone rang. He snatched it up. "Broussard headquarters."

"Is this William Broussard? This is Channel Seven News," the person on the other end said. "We'd like to get your comments about the theft allegations."

"I have no comment." William slammed down the phone.

The phone rang again, but he ignored it as Olivia stepped into the office.

"William, I saw the paper," Olivia's face was grim. "What is going on?"

"I wish I knew," William said. "It's some kind of witch hunt."

"Well, we need to pull together our team and get on this immediately," Olivia said in crisp tones. She placed her purse on her desk and picked up her phone. "I'm calling Winston now."

Winston was William's spokesman. Winston, an old college friend, owned a public relations agency and had signed on to help the campaign.

"Okay, good," William said. "I've already called the attorney, who should be here shortly."

"I'll schedule a press conference for mid-morning, after we've had our strategy session," Olivia said.

William smiled gratefully. "Thanks, Olivia. I don't know what I would do without your help."

She didn't say anything. William walked to the back room and punched in Nikki's cell phone number. He waited for her to pick up. He knew she was just returning from dropping Psalm off at school. "Baby, did you see that craziness in the paper?"

"No, what?" she said.

"It's a bunch of lies. You'll have to find a copy and read it. I can't even tell it to you, it's so ridiculous. Some mess about us using some stolen credit cards to pay for a surgery."

"Did you say stolen credit card?"

"Yeah, that's what I'm saying. Stupid stuff. I'm ticked off.

But I'm going to sue them for this. It's just not right. I don't know how that rag continues to survive, publishing this garbage. I'm sorry you had to be dragged into this. I'll straighten it out."

"Wow, that sounds serious," Nikki said and William could hear the worry in her voice.

"Hey, baby, don't worry about it. I'll get it taken care of. They said in the last line that they tried to reach me but calls were not returned by press time. I had one missed call from the newspaper yesterday. I didn't get a chance to call back but they should have tried a little harder to reach me. They know where I work and where I live."

"William, everybody is here. The meeting is about to start," Olivia called sharply.

"Be right there!" William replied. He lowered his voice. "Look, baby, I have to go. We're about to have a press conference and squash this. Then I'm going to light into that newspaper with a lawsuit for libel. Don't forget to read the story when you can."

"I will."

He hated to hear Nikki sound so forlorn. "It'll be okay, baby," William said once more. "I love you."

William hung up the phone and walked into the main area of the headquarters. Tension was thick. They all sat around a table in the center of the room.

"So, is there any truth to any of this?" Winston asked.

William looked at him as if the man had lost his mind. "Of course not!"

Winston held up a hand. "Hey, man, I meant no disrespect. I'm just trying to see how much of this is true so we know how to respond. I'm not accusing you at all."

"Yeah, William," Olivia said. "I know the news media can be vicious, but usually they don't just flat-out make up stuff."

"Well, that's exactly what happened!" William snapped. "I can't believe you guys think I did any of this."

Olivia touched his arm. "No, we don't think *you* did this. Is it possible your wife—?"

William cut her off before she could finish her sentence. "Olivia, I'm going to interrupt you so you don't say something really stupid right now. There is no way my wife had anything to do with this. And anyone who says otherwise will have to answer to me."

Olivia held up a hand. "Sorry. I wasn't trying to insult your wife."

The attorney scribbled notes on a legal pad. "Well, you just give me the word and I'll have a lawsuit drawn up before you can even finish your sentence."

"Thanks," William said. "I definitely am going to sue. But for now, we need to figure out the media approach."

They began strategizing, but ultimately settled on issuing only a prepared statement. Winston advised against a press conference, but William insisted. Like Reverend Chance before him, he felt compelled to speak on his own behalf.

The press conference was a brief affair. Reporters flung questions at William, but he refused to answer or acknowledge. Instead, he simply read from the statement he, Winston and the attorney had prepared.

After answering the basic questions, William quickly pivoted around and left the room following the reading, even as reporters hurled more questions. Winston held up his hands and told the reporters that would be all for the day.

But while William could push off the members of the press, he had no such luck with Reverend Hicks, whose eyes were red with fury at the story. "Look, I'm suspicious of that White newspaper just like you are, but I've been around a long time, and I've never known them to completely make up a story."

"Well, I'm telling you, that's what they did," William said, resenting the fact that he had to defend his wife to this man. But Hicks had pulled many strings to get him to this point.

"Well, is there any portion of truth at all to this?" the preacher asked, staring at William.

William refused to be intimidated, and stared right back. "I told you before. No."

"You need to watch your tone, now, young man," Hicks glanced around the campaign office, but nobody made eye contact.

William sucked in his breath and let it out slowly, trying to calm himself. He knew he couldn't offend the man who questioned him. "Sorry, sir." William cleared his throat. "I will get to the bottom of the story. Believe me, somebody will pay for this."

Chapter 33

Nikki raced to the computer and typed in the address for the newspaper's website. The top story was the one she feared. She got knots in her stomach as she read the report, proclaiming she and her husband used a stolen credit card to bilk a local hospital out of thousands. She sat down hard in the chair and dropped her head in her hands.

She knew Troy's hookup was probably not the best thing to do, but at the time, she had convinced herself it was all right. After all, her child had been in such a serious condition.

Now, two months later, Nikki knew the day she had been dreading had finally arrived. "And you call yourself a Christian," Nikki chided herself. "Danielle is right. Who are you fooling? You just can't get it right. You knew what you were doing was wrong. You can't walk in the Word. At every turn, you make the wrong choices. Why do you even try? Just give up. Go on back to your old ways. Stop pretending."

Nikki's insides quivered as she realized the magnitude of what she had done. She wanted to call on God's name, but shame held her silent. How could she pray now when she had done something so bad? This wasn't a tiny thing. This was against both God's law and man's.

She cried bitter tears until her throat hurt. Finally, with no more tears left, she wiped her face. Nikki knew she needed to talk to someone. And there was only one person who would understand. She washed her face, grabbed her keys and drove to Danielle's job.

"I'm here to see Danielle Esperanza, please," Nikki told the woman at the front desk.

"I'm sorry, she's on the floor right now." The woman's tone was pleasant.

"Okay," Nikki said, trying to keep the panic out of her voice. "I have an emergency. Can you just get a message to her?"

The woman nodded. Nikki quickly scribbled a note and handed it to the woman, who disappeared into an elevator. Within minutes, Danielle was standing before her.

"What's wrong?"

"Have you seen today's paper?" Nikki whispered, glancing around.

"Girl, you know I don't read the newspaper."

"Well, you should start," Nikki said and pulled out a crumpled copy of the story she had printed from the website. Danielle read it and her eyes widened.

"You've got to be kidding me!"

"No," Nikki said. "What am I going to do?"

"What about me?" Danielle said. "I could get in trouble, too, if my name comes out."

Nikki soothed her friend's concern. "Your name wouldn't come up. You know I wouldn't bring you into this. But I'm scared. What do I tell Will?"

"Well, just tell him you don't know what these people are talking about," Danielle said. "Who is he going to believe? His wife or some stupid reporter?"

"Well, I can't keep lying to him," Nikki said. "I feel horrible as it is now for lying to him to begin with."

"Well, it's a bit late in the day for that," Danielle said. "You did what you had to do. Your child is all better, isn't she?"

"Well, yeah, but—"

"So," Danielle said. "If he gets mad at you for protecting your child, then forget him."

"Well, it's not that simple."

"Yes, it is," Danielle said. "Listen to me. You are a great mother. You did what you had to for your child. If he can't understand that, then obviously he doesn't care about you or Psalm."

"Well, I didn't exactly tell him the truth," Nikki reminded her friend.

"So?" Danielle said. "Big whoop-ity-do. If you had told him, you knew he would have been acting all goody-good and would have tried to keep you from doing it. He would have beaten you over the head with God and whatnot. And really, this had nothing to do with God. This was about you and your baby."

"Well, let's say even if I can get him to forgive me, what about the story? It could ruin his career."

"Look, you can't spend your life worrying about other people all the time," Danielle said. "William will be all right. Do you know how they found out anyway?"

"No," Nikki said, then she snapped her finger. "You know what? I remember seeing Spencer Cason's wife at the hospital when I registered for Psalm's surgery. You know she works there."

"That old, bad-built hussy? You think she snitched on you?"

"Well, her husband is working for the opposition."

"So, what, you want to go get in her face?" Danielle said,

pushing up her sleeves. "We can do that. It's been a minute since I've fought a girl, but we can get down, you know."

Nikki rolled her eyes and let out a short laugh. "Girl, you are so ghetto. We are not getting ready to go fight some woman. That's the last thing we need to do."

"Okay," Danielle said. "But I'm just saying. We can handle this."

Nikki shook her head. Worry laced her voice and lined her face. "I don't know what I'm going to do. I have really messed up this time."

Danielle squeezed her shoulder. "It'll be okay."

"How do you know?" Nikki asked.

"Just deny your involvement. They probably can't prove anything."

"And what about Will?"

"What about him?" Danielle asked. "You saved his child's life."

"But will he see it that way? Will he forgive me?"

Nikki paced the large dining room with its hardwood floor, her socks muffling any sound. She had put Psalm to bed early and prepared William's favorite meal. Her stomach was in knots as she practiced what she would say, and how. She sat on the couch and read over and over that day's devotional, about God granting strength against adversity. She felt it must have been written for her. She felt she needed to muster strength from somewhere.

She jumped when the key jiggled in the door at a quarter to nine. William entered, and immediately let out a sigh.

Nikki scrambled up from the couch and quickly walked to him, reaching for his jacket, but he pulled her close. "Hey, baby," he said. "How was your day?"

"All right." Her voice came out in a squeak. She cleared her throat. "How was yours?"

"That doggone story consumed my day," he said, walking to the stove where he saw macaroni and cheese, chicken fried steak and cabbage. "This looks good."

"I thought you'd want some of your favorites after such a long day." Nikki tried to make her voice sound light and casual.

"Well, I don't even know if I can eat after dealing with that mess all day," William said, pulling off his tie and letting it fall to a chair. "It just burns me up that I had to lose a whole day of campaigning to deal with this. I don't have a lot of time to let the voters get to know me and now, not only do I have to play catch-up, but I've got to do damage control."

Nikki scooped the steaming food onto a plate and poured him a glass of tea and placed the plate at his spot on the table.

He raised an eyebrow. "You're not eating?"

"Oh . . . I . . . uh," she stumbled. There was no way she could eat anything; her stomach felt like somebody was tap dancing in it. "I already ate."

"Oh," he said. "I guess it is kind of late."

He briefly bent his head in prayer, then scooped up a forkful of macaroni. "Baby, this is so good. Just what I needed after a stressful day. I hope you didn't catch too much flack from all those lies today. Has anybody called you?"

She picked at the polish on her fingernails. "No. Well, the neighbor from across the way acted like she didn't hear me when I spoke to her when I was outside checking the mail. I could tell something was up."

William put down his fork and gestured for her to come close. When she did, he put his arm around her. "I'm so sorry you have to deal with all this," he said. "I guess it's the first bit of dirty politics we're facing."

"Yeah, I guess so," Nikki said, feeling guilty.

"Well, don't you worry," William said, taking a bite of cabbage. "This thing is going to blow over in no time."

Nikki took a deep breath. It felt like a grapefruit was lodged in her throat. She wished they were talking about something benign, like the good report Psalm had just received from her kindergarten teacher today. "Um, baby? There is something I think you should know."

William looked up from his food. "Sure, what's wrong? You're not looking too good."

She cleared her throat and tried to swallow, but it felt like cotton was sticking to her tongue. "You remember when I told you I found the money for Psalm's surgery?"

"Yeah, you said the insurance company finally agreed to pay."

"Well, that's not really what I said."

"You sure?" he took a swig from his glass. "That's what I thought."

"I know that's probably what you thought," she took a deep breath. "And I probably didn't correct that assumption. What really happened is that I, uh . . ."

Her voice trailed off and the words wouldn't come out. William's eyebrows drew together in concern. "What's wrong, baby? Just spit it out. You can tell me anything."

She clenched her teeth and sucked in another breath. Then she blurted: "The story is true."

"What are you talking about?"

"The story. In the paper. About the, um, credit card, um, fraud."

William laughed. "Girl, you had me going for a minute. Stop joking."

She planted her hand on his shoulder. The smile evaporated from his face when he saw how serious she was. He sprang from the chair. "Nikki. You're not serious!"

"Baby, I didn't know what else to do."

William put his hand to his head and rubbed his eyes. "How, Nikki? And why?"

"Danielle's boyfriend said he could get me a hookup and help pay for the surgery."

"Danielle's boyfriend? You mean that little low-life thug you said she is dating?" William was incredulous. "The one you said is always into some scheme?"

"Well, I didn't know exactly what he was doing, but—"

"You didn't know?" He yelled the words.

"All he told me was to sign the paperwork and somebody would take care of it," Nikki said.

"Sign the paperwork? The story said there was forgery involved. You signed someone else's name?"

"Yeah, but—"

"And you're telling me you didn't know what was going on?"

"Well, I mean, I suspected, but I, well, he never just came out and told me what—"

"Nikki, I can't believe you're telling me this now!"

"But, baby, I didn't think—"

"Of course you didn't think!" William flung the words at her. "Nobody in their right mind would come up with some craziness like that! You let this man go and get you caught up in one of his stolen credit card schemes. What person in their right mind uses stolen credit cards?"

"But Psalm had to have the surgery," Nikki pleaded. "I was just trying—"

"I keep telling you, I will take care of this family!" William said. "We would have figured something out. Did you think I'd let my child die? Did you think I'd let my wife go and get herself—get us—into some stupid trouble? Nikki, I wish you'd listen to me sometimes!"

"Look, you're not my boss!" Nikki said. "You can't keep me under your thumb and tell me what to do all the time."

"Obviously, somebody needs to!"

"Will, I did what I thought was best."

He glared at her. "Is that why you lied to me?"

She cast her eyes down. When she looked up, he was putting on his jacket.

"Will, I'm sorry. I didn't mean to lie to you."

"Oh, yeah, I saw your picture from the accident in the paper the other day," he spat. "I guess that's another thing you kept from me. What else have you lied to me about?"

"No, baby, it's not like that," she said, following him to the door. "I was caught in traffic when the accident happened, and since I had my camera, I just took a few shots. I didn't mean to—"

"Forget it, Nikki. I've got to get out of here. I don't want to say another thing to you right now, or it might be something we'll both regret. I can't believe you lied to me."

Nikki sat down hard in the overstuffed lazy chair after William stormed out. *I didn't have a choice. I had to take care of my child*, she reasoned. But uneasiness bubbled in her stomach.

She knew she had acted hastily because she hadn't trusted God to clear the way for the insurance company to approve her request or for God to provide another answer. The way had seemed so dark, and her child's needs had seemed so pressing that she had convinced herself that this "hookup" was the best way.

Nikki bit her lip and she sucked in a deep breath through her nose to keep from crying. As she sat there in the silence of night, she remembered one of the first conversations she and William had. It had been on their first date. Following a movie, they decided to go to one of the city parks since they couldn't have members of the opposite sex in their dorm rooms at night. It was late, after midnight, but she hadn't minded.

As they sat on the swing, sipping Icees and enjoying the breeze, he told her about his childhood, growing up with a mother trying her best to take care of his brother and him. His father had shown up infrequently, and had made numerous promises to get his brother and him for various holidays, events and occasions. He always got William's hopes up. William finally realized the promises always fell flat, as their father made excuse after excuse for not making good on his word.

Watching his mother struggle to take care of her family had produced in William a strong desire to take care of his own family — if ever he had one. His father's lies had made him especially averse to being lied to—about anything.

Now, not only had his wife broken that all-important rule, she might very well have cost him his career. And perhaps their chance for a better future.

Her husband had walked out the door. Would he come back?

Chapter 34

William drove around, angry thoughts swirling in his mind. He didn't know where to go. He didn't want to go to his mother's and knew his brother's family was likely getting ready for bed, and with four small children, they had no room to spare anyway. His good friend Winston would welcome him, but after spending so much time working with Winston on controlling the spin on this story, he knew the man likely needed some time away.

"I don't know what she was thinking!" William jabbed at the horn to urge the car ahead of him to get going after the light turned green. He drove aimlessly, too angry to return home. "I don't know why she does stuff like this. If she'd just listened to me in the first place."

He seemed almost startled when he shut off the engine and stepped out of the car at the campaign office. There was a cot in a back room. Maybe he would crash there for the night. He let himself in, but stopped short as he realized the light was on.

"Hello?" he called, immediately on guard.

"Oh, hi," Olivia said, looking up from a thick stack of papers.

"What are you doing here?" he asked, smiling and letting his muscles relax again.

"I could ask you the same thing," she said, wryly. "Looks like you're not too happy of a camper right now. What's got you in a funk?"

Olivia could always pick up on his moods. "Oh, it's nothing," he said, shrugging off his jacket.

Olivia strode to the coffee pot and poured a cup, which she extended to him. "Want some coffee? It's fresh. I just made it when I got here. I figured I'd get a few hours of work done, since most of the day was lost to that silly story."

At the mention of the story, William's countenance clouded.

"Hey, don't look at me like that," Olivia said, cutting her eyes at William.

He took a sip from the coffee. "I'm sorry," he said, sitting down heavily in a chair. "I just found out the story has merit."

"What do you mean?"

He quickly told Olivia the highlights of the conversation with his wife. Olivia's eyes widened. "Wow," she said. "What was she thinking?"

"That's just it. She wasn't." William slammed his fist down. "I can't believe she would do something that didn't make any sense at all."

Olivia spoke carefully. "Well, I'm sure she had her reasons."

"Yeah, I guess."

"Well, it's not something I would have done," Olivia said, pulling up a chair next to William. "But then, I guess she and I are different that way."

Olivia rubbed William's shoulder. "I sure wouldn't do that to my husband."

Chapter 35

Nikki stood next to the burgundy curtains in the living room, staring out the window into the darkness. Each approaching car made her hopeful, but none slowed. Where was William?

He had never stayed away longer than a couple of hours, and now five hours had passed and it was after two in the morning. She tried his cell again, but it went directly to voicemail. She sighed and walked back across the living room, hugging her arms around herself. "He might really be gone this time."

She tried to ignore the fear in her gut. She shoved a movie into the DVD player to distract herself, but she couldn't pay attention to it. "Did I hear a car in the driveway?" She sprang from the couch and rushed to the window, but sagged in disappointment as she realized it was not William.

Nikki finally fell asleep as the sun started to peek through the curtains. When a playing Psalm awakened her hours later, she realized it was after nine a.m. "Oh, baby, Mama's sorry. I've made you miss school today," she said, rousing from the couch. She stretched, trying to get rid of the ache in her neck for having slept in an awkward position. "Let me fix you something to eat."

William hadn't come home all night. The realization made her lightheaded. Her mind raced as she quickly scrambled some eggs and made toast. He had never stayed out all night before, no matter how angry he had become. *Oh man, this is serious*, she worried. *He really has gone. He has left me.*

After Nikki cleaned the kitchen and settled Psalm in front of the computer on a learning game, she decided to see what was up with her husband. She tried him again on his cell. He answered on the first ring.

"Hi," she said.

There was a pause.

"Hey, baby. It's me," she said, in case he hadn't heard her the first time.

"Nikki, I'm in a meeting. I need to talk with you later."

"Oh. Okay."

The phone went dead in her hand.

Nikki's mouth drew into a tense line as she dialed Trudy's number. She didn't want to call the woman, but knew Trudy could be the only person to tell her how she should proceed. Nikki was almost certain the socialite would know how to do damage control so Nikki didn't ruin William's image. Nikki thought that if she could fix this situation, perhaps William's anger would dissipate. Nikki waited for someone to answer Trudy's phone.

"McWilliams residence."

"Trudy, please?"

"May I tell her who is calling?"

"Nikki."

Nikki could hear the phone being placed on a hard surface. A moment later, whoever had answered the phone returned and spoke again. "I'm sorry. Mrs. McWilliams is unavailable."

"Can you tell her it's an emergency?" Nikki's tone was desperate.

"She will not be able to speak with you, ma'am."

"I have to talk with her," Nikki insisted. "Please tell her I'll only take a moment."

The person placed the phone down again. A moment later, Trudy was on the line. "Oh, Trudy, I need your help!"

"I'm sorry," Trudy said. "I won't be able to help you anymore."

"What do you mean?"

"Surely you do not think I can associate with someone who so obviously flouts the law," Trudy said. "I realized you were among the middle class, but I didn't realize the criminal element was so entrenched in your character. I cannot be associated with credit card thieves."

"But, Trudy, you don't understand!" Nikki pleaded.

"I'm sorry, but I must be going now," Trudy said in a matter-of-fact tone. "Please do not call my home again."

The line went dead in Nikki's hand. She stared at it, dumbfounded. It took her a moment to collect her thoughts, but when she did, she knew she had to reach her husband.

"Come on, Psalm, let's make ourselves pretty," Nikki said with forced brightness. She dressed Psalm in a pink dress and ribbons. She herself donned a navy pantsuit and quickly washed her hair to make the natural curls more pronounced. She smoothed on lipstick and gave herself one more look in the mirror. *I'm no Danielle, but I look okay.*

"Come on, Psalm, let's go see Daddy!"

"Yea!"

She stepped outside. Nikki quickly buckled Psalm in and stopped by a nearby deli and bakery.

Thirty minutes later, she waltzed into the campaign headquarters. Nobody noticed her quiet entrance. She quickly spotted William, bent over a table with Olivia, studying what looked to be a map of the city.

"Hi, honey!" She smiled brightly at a startled William, who quickly regained his composure.

"Hello," he said to her and opened his arms wide for Psalm. "Hey, little girl!"

Psalm hopped into his arms. Nikki offered a sandwich to Olivia. "I just thought I'd bring everyone lunch."

Olivia glanced at William and took the sandwich. "Thanks, Nikki," she said. "I'll leave you two alone."

Olivia went to speak to a volunteer.

Nikki turned to William. "You didn't come home last night."

"I know."

"I was worried." Nikki could read nothing into William's tone or expression.

"No need to be."

She touched his arm. "Will, I'm sorry about . . ." her voice trailed off as Winston approached.

"Hey, boss, we've really got to get moving," he said. "Hi, Nikki." He turned back to William. "You have to be at the TV station in thirty minutes."

William held up a hand. "Okay, give me a second."

"Sure thing."

Winston left and William turned back to Nikki. "Baby, look, now isn't a good time," he said. He saw her expression of worry. "Look, we'll work it out. I was really ticked off last night. You know I can't stand lies. And for you to do something like what you did, well, I just didn't understand it."

Nikki opened her mouth to say something, but he stayed her with a light touch on her arm. "But look, I'm a bit cooler now. We'll talk about it when I get home. I know it's a lot I don't get, but Olivia helped me understand it a bit more from a woman's perspective."

"Olivia?"

"Yeah, we both stayed here last night."

Chapter 36

"Danielle, your latest report was sloppy," her supervising nurse, Jody Smart, said in the afternoon staff meeting.

Danielle looked around, wondering why the supervisor insisted on embarrassing her in front of her co-workers. "My work is always impeccable," she countered.

"Well, you transposed numbers and some of the dosages were off—I trust the patients received the proper amounts," Jody said. "And you left off a patient's last name."

"I did no such thing," Danielle snapped, looking around at her peers. *I do better work than all these stupid people*, she thought.

"Danielle, it's right here." Jody held up the paperwork and tapped her finger against it.

"Well, then, somebody must have changed it," Danielle snapped.

Jody rolled her eyes. "I'm noting this in your file. Meeting adjourned."

Danielle waited until the other nurses had dispersed, then approached Jody. "Are you sure about that report?" she asked, this time with sugar dripping from her tongue. "I try so hard to do a good job and I can't imagine I'd be so careless."

"Well, like I said, it's right here," Jody said, flipping through the patient records.

Danielle touched the woman's upper arm. "You're right. I am so glad you caught that. You're such a lifesaver. I don't know what I'd do without you. You're such a good supervisor."

Nurse Smart smiled and her voice softened. "Well, you just have to be more careful, Danielle. I'm sorry for pointing out your mistake in front of the group, but that's what these meetings are for."

Danielle put on a cheery smile. "It's all right. You were doing your job. I'll make sure I pay closer attention next time."

Danielle gathered her notebook and pen and walked out of the room. She paused just outside the door. "You look really pretty today. Wearing your hair down like that really becomes you."

Chapter 37

Nikki went back home after the brief conversation with William. The phone was ringing when she stepped across the threshold into the house. She dropped her keys and rushed to pick up. "Hello?"

"Hey, Nikki, this is Keedra."

"Oh, hi, girl," Nikki said. "How are you?"

"I'm fine. I was calling to see how you were doing, though."

"I'm hanging in there," Nikki said, sinking onto the couch. She snapped her fingers to get the attention of Psalm, who had opened the bottom of the entertainment center to look for her favorite DVD. "Go change your shirt. You have mustard on it."

Psalm looked up from her search. "But, Mommy—"

"Psalm, I don't want to have to tell you again," Nikki threatened, the stress of the day making her temples throb.

Psalm scrambled from the floor and disappeared.

"Sorry about that," Nikki said, returning to her phone conversation. She held the phone away from her mouth and yelled: "And don't make a mess in that room! Don't put your clothes all over the floor!" She put the phone back to her mouth. "Sorry," she apologized again.

"It's okay," Keedra said. "I didn't get a chance to call you after I saw all that weird stuff in the newspaper. I meant to, but I had some assignments that kept me busy."

"It's all right," Nikki sighed. "And unfortunately, the weird stuff is true."

"Really?" Nikki could hear the shock in her new friend's voice.

"Yeah," Nikki said. "I was pretty desperate a while back to get some money for a medical procedure for Psalm. And I used a stolen card to pay for it."

"Well, I'm really sorry to hear all that," Keedra said. "We all make mistakes. I know you were just trying to protect your baby."

The compassion she heard in her friend's voice drew a lump to Nikki's throat. She hadn't expected Keedra to understand. After all, Nikki was beating herself up so much, she expected everyone else to do the same.

"It just got really out of hand," she said. "I knew better. But I just let my emotions get in the way of my common sense."

"Well, you and William must have been backed into a corner," Keedra said.

"Actually, William didn't know about the card until I told him last night. After the story."

"What?" Keedra was confused; Nikki could tell.

She quickly filled Keedra in on the details, including the part about William storming out of the house.

"Well, it probably wasn't the best thing for you to do, but like I said, we all make mistakes," Keedra repeated. "You just ask for forgiveness and pray God helps you grow so you are stronger next time."

"Well, I haven't felt too close to God lately," Nikki confessed. "I mean, I've done some really bad things and I can't see how He can keep forgiving me. Besides, I feel like such a fake sometimes."

"We all do," Keedra assured her. "But we just keep trying."

"Easy for you to say, you probably haven't done anything really bad," Nikki said.

"We've all done our dirt," Keedra said. "But enough about all that. You will be fine. And I know William will calm down and get over being mad at you."

"What if he doesn't?"

"I've seen the way that man looks at you. He couldn't stay angry with you."

"I hope you're right."

Chapter 38

Danielle had a lot on her mind as she left work. She wanted to just take some time and sort through her thoughts. "Maybe I should go out to eat, have a nice bottle of wine and unwind," she mumbled as she crossed the street to her car. She didn't like eating out alone, though, and never had to do it. She could always call any number of men to take her out, and of course, there was always Troy. But she didn't feel like being bothered with him right now.

She picked up the cell phone and dialed.

"Hello?"

"Hey, Nikki, it's me," Danielle said. "Come meet me out. Let's get something to eat."

"Hey, let me call you right back, okay?"

"Call me right back?"

"Yeah, I'm on the phone with Keedra."

There she is, talking to that Keedra again, Danielle groused silently. "Well . . . okay," Danielle said, her voice catching in her throat. "I just really needed to talk to you. I had a terrible day. I just found out my mom died."

"Your mom? Oh, Danielle, I'm so sorry! Hold on."

A moment later, Nikki was back. "Okay, I'll be right there. Tell me where to meet you."

Chapter 39

"Hey, have you noticed anything weird?" William asked, walking to Olivia's desk, a frown on his face.

"Weird like what?" Olivia asked, quickly putting away the lipstick she had just reapplied.

"Well, it just seems like I can never find any of my signs in any yards," he said.

"You know, you're right," Olivia said. "I had a few people call to say the signs we placed in their yards were gone. And Winston mentioned he passed a couple of places where we had signs, but they are no longer there."

"You mean to tell me somebody is stealing our signs?"

"That's what it looks like. That, and I think we have another issue as well."

"Which is?"

"Some people who were supporting us are now backing out," she informed William. "This credit card situation really hurts. We're losing support right and left."

"So, why wasn't I informed about this thing with the stolen signs?"

"Well, we just knew you had a lot on your mind—"

"Olivia, when things happen, I need to know," William interrupted, slapping his palm on the table. A few heads turned. His voice lowered. "I don't need people keeping things from me."

"Hey, I'm sorry," Olivia said. "Look. It was an honest mistake. I know you're stressed about your home situation, but that doesn't mean you can take it out on us here."

"I'm not taking anything out on you," William snapped.

"Look, I'm your manager." She touched his hand. "That means I manage. And that's what I was doing."

They stared each other down for a moment, then William breathed deeply. "You're right. I am wound tight. Thanks for looking out for me. You're a good woman."

Olivia rubbed William's back. "It's okay. I'll take care of everything."

Chapter 40

Nikki drove to the restaurant Danielle had suggested, hopped out of the Yukon, grabbed Psalm from the back and raced inside. She spotted Danielle immediately, and rushed right over to the table. Nikki hugged her friend and then sat down.

"Hey, Dee Dee," Psalm said and hugged Danielle.

"Hey, Psalm," Danielle said, leaning in for a quick hug. She then picked up her wine glass and took a sip.

"I can't get over what you told me," Nikki said. "What happened?"

Danielle put down her wine and hunched her shoulders, looking sad. "I don't really know," she said in a tear-filled voice. "You know they don't talk to me. I just found out by chance. I tried to call them today when I was at work, to, you know, just reach out. And my sister answered the phone and told me in a cold voice that nobody wanted to see me and why did I keep calling. Then she told me Mama died."

Nikki gasped and put her hand to her chest. Danielle rarely spoke of her family and had actually forbidden the topic. Nikki didn't know much about the Esperanzas, except Danielle didn't talk to them much because of some kind of dispute. Nikki knew the estrangement must hurt Danielle. And now this.

"I don't know what to say," Nikki said softly.

Danielle's hand shook as she took another sip of her wine. "I feel so bad," she said. "I know we didn't have the perfect relationship, but I had hoped one day we would be able to get back to being a family."

Nikki moved from her side of the table to where her friend sat and put her arm around her. "It'll be okay. I'll help you through this."

"I can't believe my mom is gone."

"I know, sweetie," Nikki said. "When is the funeral? I'll go with you."

"Oh, they've buried her already. The funeral was yesterday."

They talked quietly throughout the meal, and when the check came, Nikki insisted on paying. She knew her bank account was rather anemic, but wanted to lend whatever support she could.

"Do you want us to stay with you tonight?" she asked, walking out of the restaurant, holding Danielle's hand. Psalm walked a bit ahead. "Psalm, baby, slow down."

"No," Danielle said. Her voice was heavy and tired. "It's all right. I think I just want to spend some time alone."

"You sure? It's really okay. I don't mind coming over."

"No," Danielle said, unlocking her door. "I'm just going to take a bath and go to bed. But thanks for tearing yourself away from your conversation with Keedra to baby-sit poor lil' ol' me."

Nikki frowned. "Stop it," she said. "Of course I was coming to spend time with you. I'm here for you, no matter what."

Danielle stared at her for a long moment. "No matter what?"

"No matter what." Nikki said emphatically.

"Thanks," Danielle said with a watery smile.

"You're welcome," Nikki said and hugged Danielle. "Now, get some rest. And if you need anything, please call me."

Nikki kissed her on the cheek. Psalm gave Danielle another hug and they separated. As Nikki drove back home, her heart hurt for her friend.

"She's trying to be strong, but I know she's got to be in so much pain," Nikki mumbled.

"What did you say, Mommy?" Psalm asked.

"Oh, nothing," Nikki said. "I was just saying how sad I feel for Danielle. Her mommy just passed away."

"I'd be sad if you went away," Psalm said in a serious tone and Nikki caught her daughter's eye in the rearview mirror.

"It's okay, sweetie," Nikki reassured the child. "Mommy's never going to leave you."

Even though Danielle never spoke of her family, Nikki knew the broken relationship caused her pain. Nikki had never pried, knowing that Danielle didn't want to discuss the details. And that, to Nikki, meant it hurt too much.

And to lose your mother and not even be able to go to the funeral? It was just beyond Nikki. She punched the numbers to her own mother's phone.

"Hey, Ma," she said when Nancy answered.

"Hey, what's going on? You know I never hear from you anymore."

Nikki rolled her eyes. "I was just thinking about you and wanted to say 'hi.'"

"Oh, well, that's nice," her mother said. "I'm trying to set the table to have it ready when Steve gets home from his golf game. I need to get his bath ready so he can get cleaned up before we eat. He likes to change the moment he gets home. I'm going to have to talk to you a bit later, okay, dear?"

Nikki sighed. "Okay, Ma. You take care of yourself. And tell him I said, 'hello.' "

"All right, sweetie," her mother said. "You be good. I'll give you a call another time."

Nikki pressed the END button on the phone. Even after all this time, her mother's sole purpose was taking care of her husband and making sure his every whim was fulfilled. "He's not going to leave you!" Nikki wanted to scream at her mother. "You don't have to kill yourself trying to be the perfect wife."

Steve had been a good provider and a welcome addition to their world after Nikki's father walked out. But it was hard to compete with him for her mother's attention. And any attention her mother may have lavished on her was taken up by Nikki's stepsister, Carla.

But she's still my mother. And I'd feel so horrible if I lost her, Nikki knew. Her mind went back to her friend who had just lost her own mother. "Danielle and her mom may not have gotten along these past few years, but that doesn't mean they didn't love each other," Nikki mumbled. "I've got to be a better friend to Danielle. She's been through so much."

Chapter 41

Nikki returned to an empty house. She had half-hoped William would be there. Would he spend another night away? Was he really gone? She had tried not to think too much about the tension between them and had allowed the visit with Danielle to distract her. But now, as she drove up to the darkened house, the knot in her stomach returned.

She and Psalm walked inside and the space felt so cold. The rooms seemed twice as large as they actually were and her steps across the hardwood floor seemed to echo. She looked at her daughter to see if the child noticed anything different, but Psalm raced into the house, bouncy as usual. For the child, her father's absence felt like any other late night on the campaign trail. For Nikki, it felt like the beginning of the end of so much. She ran her hand over her head, sighing heavily.

When she finally heard the crackle of tires on the driveway outside, her heart leaped. Nikki scurried to the window and peeked out. It was the Protégé. She quickly walked to the bathroom and splashed water on her face. She swished mouthwash and rubbed floral scented lotion on her arms and hands.

She stepped out of the bathroom just as William walked down the hall.

"Hi," she said, tentatively.

He responded. "Hello."

He proceeded to their bedroom. She followed. "Can I get you a glass of water or anything?" she asked, helping him off with his coat.

"No, I'm cool," he said.

"Daddy!" Psalm raced into the room and hugged William about the knees.

He picked her up. "Hey, little girl!"

"I'm not a little girl. I'm a big girl," Psalm retorted.

William laughed. "Well, you're right. You are a big girl." He held her over his head. "And now you're bigger than me. You're big and tall."

"Yea!"

Nikki smiled at the attention William gave their daughter, but she wondered if she would ever again evoke such light-hearted affection from him herself.

When William placed Psalm down, the child tugged at his hand. "Let's play horsy. I want to ride your back."

"No, Psalm, let Daddy get undressed and rest a bit," Nikki said, gently easing Psalm away.

"We'll play later," William said and winked at the girl.

"Yeah, it's time for you to go to bed, anyway," Nikki told Psalm. "You missed school today because I overslept. But that won't happen tomorrow. Go get your gown."

Psalm left the room and Nikki closed the bedroom door. She and William stood in silence.

"Baby, I'm really sorry about everything that happened," Nikki said.

"Okay." William's tone was flat. He stepped into the walk-in closet and disrobed.

Nikki followed him. "I feel horrible," she said.

"You should."

His unforgiving tone stopped her. She opened her mouth, then closed it.

William walked past her. "Excuse me," he said.

She stepped to the side.

"I need to take a shower," he said, walking naked across the bedroom into their private bathroom.

"You want me to join?" He always liked when they showered together.

"No."

Chapter 42

Danielle scribbled on paperwork as she sat at her desk following a confrontation with a patient. The man had shoved her and she had to call in help to restrain him. These crazy patients are getting on my last nerve, she fumed. She signed the last piece of paperwork documenting the incident. "We should lock all of them up in a room and throw away the key. That fool scratched me."

"Are you all right?"

Danielle looked up to see Raymond, a fellow nurse with whom she shared this office, stick his head into the room. She quickly erased the anger from her face and pasted on a bright smile.

"Yeah, I'm okay," she said. "Come on in."

Raymond entered. "That last patient was pretty rough with you."

"Yeah. But I know he's in so much pain, so I don't take it personally. I care about my patients so much, so it just hurts to see them go through all these things," Danielle said, putting her hand to her chest.

"Well, you can't get emotionally involved," Raymond said.

She looked up at him with wide eyes and smiled sadly. "I know, but it's so hard for me. I just care so much."

Raymond nodded. "I know you do."

"And now, with Smart on my tail—"

"Yeah, she did kind of put you out there in the staff meeting."

"I've just been working so hard lately," Danielle said. "I've been under so much stress. My best friend's little girl is dying, and I've been trying to be strong for them. I've been trying to reach out to my own family lately, but they won't speak to me because of some things they did a long time ago. And I've been really stretched thin to take care of so many patients."

"Wow, that's a lot on your plate," Raymond said.

She hunched her shoulders and started working on another report. "I know, but everyone has their own issues, so I just try to do the best I can and not complain. I just wish I could help my friend get through this tough time with her child or help my family heal from the past. It's just so hard. And when I get to work, I know I take on too much sometimes. It's so hard to ask for help, you know. I don't want to be a burden."

He walked around the desk and put a hand on her shoulder. "Maybe I can help you out," he said. "I can look over your reports in the evenings before I leave."

Danielle shook her head. "No, I couldn't ask you to do that."

Raymond insisted. "It's okay. I know you're strong and independent, but it's okay to have help. So let me help you."

Danielle gave him a tiny smile. "Well, since you put it that way."

Chapter 43

When Nikki rolled over the next morning, she awoke to find William already gone, and the spot where he had lain was cold. She didn't like this distance between them, but at least he had stayed home last night. The night had been full of tension, with few words exchanged. If she asked him a direct question, he gave a one-word answer, but it was clear to her he did not want to engage.

Nikki felt bereft at the knowledge William had purposefully left early to avoid talking with her this morning. She stopped short of getting dressed and knelt at the edge of the bed instead. It had been quite a long time since she had spent any time in morning prayer.

She had felt ashamed at her actions and unsure of whether God would hear her. But this morning, her burden was too heavy to carry alone. She opened her mouth to pray, but shut it against the words. God didn't want to hear from her. Not now. Nikki knelt there for a moment longer then quickly rose. She raced through her morning routine, then got Psalm up, gave the child breakfast and drove her to school.

When Nikki returned home, she tried to work on her thesis, but the phone rang.

"Hello?"

"Nikki Broussard, please," the voice on the other end said.

"Who is calling?"

"This is *The Times*, calling about—"

"I have no comment."

Nikki hung up. The phone rang again, ten minutes later. She checked the caller ID this time, but received no clue as to the identity of the caller, as it read UNKNOWN CALLER.

"Hello?"

"Is this Nikki Broussard?"

"Who is this?" Nikki demanded.

"I am calling to get a comment about a recent story about stolen credit cards. I have a few questions," the caller explained.

"I have nothing to say about that," Nikki said.

"But, we just want to give you an opportunity to share your side of the story," the caller insisted.

"I'm not interested."

Nikki slammed down the phone. She finally took all the phones off the hook after a fifth call from a reporter, asking for her comment on the credit card fraud story.

I never meant for any of this to happen, she thought.

Nikki gave up on working on her graduate school project for the time being, and instead, went to clean Psalm's bedroom. She was in the midst of dusting when she heard the doorbell ring. She quickly put the dust cloth aside and walked to the door. "Who is it?"

"This is Amy Collins, with Channel Seven," the person replied.

Nikki leaned against the door. "Look, will you people please leave me alone! I have no comment."

"Ma'am, we'd love to get a few quick comments from

you, just so you can clear your name." The person's voice was insistent. "Just open the door. We can talk."

"No, just go away!"

"Well, at least take my card," the woman said.

Nikki sighed. Maybe they would leave her alone if she just grabbed the card. She opened the door and the bright light of a television camera blinded her. She blinked and held up her hands to block the light, stumbling to close the door with her body. But Amy Collins stuck her foot in the doorway and blurted out questions.

"Were you part of a vicious credit card theft ring? How many identities did you steal?" Amy rammed the microphone in Nikki's face.

"No, I wasn't a part of any ring!" Nikki spat the words out. "You people leave me alone! You make me sick!"

She succeeded in ducking back inside the house and slamming the door. She leaned heavily against the wall, her breath coming in sharp thrusts. Her heart was beating furiously. She wiped her sweaty palms on her shirt.

Nikki hid out in the house for the rest of the day until it was time to pick up Psalm from school. The day did not get any better. As she walked to the entryway of the school, she noticed adults staring at her.

"You'd better hold on to your purse," a tall, thin woman warned her friend in a loud whisper. "That's the woman who steals people's credit cards."

"Look at her, with her lying, thieving self!" said another woman, this one dressed in a smock over ill-fitting sweat pants. "I can't believe she would show her face around here."

Nikki tried to ignore the pointed looks, and pretended not to hear the whispers. She found Psalm and loaded the girl into the vehicle as quickly as she could.

"Mommy, what's an ID thief?" Psalm asked from the backseat.

"ID thief?" Nikki asked?

"Yeah, Morgan told the other kids not to play with me because my mom is an ID thief. What's that?"

Nikki almost drove the vehicle into the other lane, but steadied herself. She tried to regain her composure as she realized her daughter was talking about her legal woes. "Do you mean identity thief?"

"Yeah, something like that," Psalm said. "It sounds bad. I told them my mommy didn't do anything bad, but they didn't believe me. They all laughed at me."

Nikki ached for her child. She tried to smile. "Don't you worry about it," she said. "Your classmates will forget about this in no time. The next time someone tries to make fun of you, you just tell them they don't know what they are talking about. It'll be okay."

Psalm seemed mollified at the response. She grinned. "See, I knew my mommy was no ID thief."

Nikki drove the rest of the way home in silence. She felt horrible at putting her daughter through this. How much worse would it all get?

She had just finished fixing dinner when William walked in, dropping his keys on the table next to the door. "Daddy!" Psalm raced to her father, who picked her up.

Nikki carefully walked to him, too. She moved to share a kiss with him as was their custom, but he ignored her.

"So, tell Daddy about your day," he leaned to put Psalm to the floor.

"The kids in my class were making fun of me," Psalm said, her lower lip trembling.

"Really? Why?" William knelt in front of her. "What happened?"

"They kept telling me my mommy was an ID—I mean, identity—thief," she said.

William glanced up quickly at Nikki, who looked away guiltily. He looked back at Psalm and gave her a hug. "Well, you just tell those kids to leave you alone. Tell them your mommy is a good mommy and makes better cookies than their mommies."

Nikki felt a small sense of relief that he took up for her, but she knew that was really for Psalm's benefit.

"I learned a new thing on the computer," Psalm announced.

"Oh, really?" William said, removing his tie. "Well, you'll have to show Daddy sometime."

Finally, Nikki tried a greeting: "Hi, baby."

"Hello."

"How was your day?"

"Fine."

"William, I—"

"Nikki, I don't feel like talking about all that right now."

"But, sweetheart—"

"Psalm, let's get on the computer. Show Daddy what you learned today."

Nikki watched as her husband scurried away with their child.

Later that night, they each retreated to a corner of the bed, Nikki on one side, William on the other. The silence covered them, but she knew he wasn't asleep.

"Baby, I wish you'd talk to me." Nikki's tone was plaintive.

Silence.

"Will, I'm really sorry."

Silence.

"If you'd just let me explain," she said, reaching to touch his shoulder. He shifted away. Nikki rolled closer to her husband and put her arm around him.

He climbed out of the bed. "I'll sleep on the couch."

Chapter 44

For the third day in a row, Nikki and William were the top news of the day. The television news had a shot of a wild-eyed Nikki shouting "You make me sick!" at a reporter, while the newspaper quoted the district attorney as saying he was preparing to file charges against the couple for a host of wrongs—including identity theft and credit card fraud. One news report even speculated that William had killed Reverend Chance in order to take the man's spot as a candidate.

William cursed as he read the story. Already, three of his volunteers had quit and Reverend Hicks had been hinting that he wanted William to withdraw from the race, with the primary election bearing down on them in mere weeks.

"I saw the news and read the paper," Olivia said sympathetically. "It's really bad. How are you holding up?"

"Not well," William said. "I'm so angry that I've got to spend time dealing with this instead of doing what I need to do. And now, I have serious problems. We could go to jail."

"You don't really think you'll have to serve time, do you?" Olivia asked. "I mean, you didn't do anything."

"But my wife did."

"Well, but you and she are separate individuals. I'm sure if you struck a deal with the DA—"

"I can't turn on my wife like that."

"Of course not," Olivia said quickly. "But I'm sure your wife wouldn't want to see you go down for something she did. I'm sure she'll make it right and tell the DA it was all her."

"I don't know, "he said, changing the subject. "I don't really want to talk about my wife, though. How are the polls?"

"Not good." Olivia sat down next to William, and leaned in close.

Chapter 45

Raymond placed a report on Danielle's desk. "Hey, I'm about to head out for the day, but I thought I'd help you with your last report first. Here it is."

Danielle smiled into his eyes. "You are so sweet. She picked up the document and flipped through it. When she saw a couple of changes to it and some additions, Danielle added, "You really didn't have to do that."

"It's no problem," Raymond said. "I know you're under a lot of stress. I just wanted to help you out. How is your friend's child doing?"

Danielle's eyes immediately filled with tears. "Things aren't going too well." She put her hand to her chest.

Raymond stepped around the desk and put an arm around her shoulders. "Hey, hey," he said gently. "I didn't mean to make you cry."

She waved her hand and sniffled. "It's okay. I just get so emotional when I think about all that little girl is going through. Doctors don't know how long she has to live."

Raymond's eyes widened with concern. "Wow. I didn't

know it was like that. Is she in a hospital? Maybe we can send her something."

Danielle spoke quickly. "No, no. But that's a nice thought. Her parents are kind of private. They wouldn't want all the attention."

"Well, if you need anything," Raymond said, stepping away. "Anything at all. You just let me know. And I'll be there."

Danielle dried her eyes. "You're so sweet to me. I couldn't ask for a better office mate." She kissed him on the cheek and pulled back slowly, letting her perfume tease his nose. "Thank you."

Raymond seemed to blush under her gratitude, and Danielle stifled a grin. Pretty soon, she would have him doing more of her work, she knew.

Chapter 46

"Psalm, stop running in the house!" Nikki snapped at the girl and Psalm instantly started wailing. Nikki shook her head and pushed away from the computer. "Baby, I'm sorry," she said, holding the child close. "Mommy didn't mean to yell."

Psalm's tears were gone in an instant and Nikki sighed as the girl's attention was diverted to the markers and crayons and poster board Nikki handed her. She knew stress was causing her to take her frustrations out on Psalm. William wasn't speaking to her. His campaign was in jeopardy and so was the life they had built.

The newspaper proclaimed the district attorney was hot on her trail and each time she heard a noise outside, she was afraid it was police coming to get her. The tension made her nerves brittle. She dodged phone calls unless they were from friends.

Nikki punched in Keedra's phone number. When the woman answered, Nikki voiced her question. "Can you look after Psalm for a couple of hours? I just need some time to think and—"

"Sure," Keedra said, even before Nikki finished the question. An hour later, Psalm was gone, and Nikki had the house to herself. She was sitting on the couch when she heard a knock at the door. She sat perfectly still, hoping whoever was there would go away. The knock sounded again, insistent and menacing.

"Who is it?" Nikki asked with trepidation.

"Police."

Her eyes widened in fear and a lump formed in her throat. She stood riveted to the spot. "One moment," she said weakly, willing herself to move. She opened the door and tried to smile, but failed. "May I help you?"

"Nikki Broussard?"

"Yes."

"We have a warrant for your arrest."

Chapter 47

Moments later, after reapplying her lipstick, Danielle sashayed out of her office, her report in hand. Raymond had done a really good job. She was so glad she had found somebody to do her crummy work for her. *I don't have time to waste on these stupid patient files*, she thought with a smile.

"Hi," she said, stepping into Nurse Smart's office. "I just wanted to give my last report before leaving."

Nurse Smart smiled and took it. She glanced at it and nodded. "Your work has really improved lately," she complimented. "This is excellent."

"Yes, I really took to heart what you said," Danielle said. "You're so brilliant and I'm just thankful you pulled me aside to help me."

Nurse Smart beamed. "You're most welcome."

"Well, I guess I should be going," Danielle said. She turned, then paused. "I bet you get a lot of compliments on your eyes. They are absolutely beautiful."

Nurse Smart blinked in surprise and sat up a bit straighter in her chair. "Oh. Well, not really," she said and let out a small giggle. "I've always thought my eyes were my best feature."

Danielle seemed to have a sudden thought. She dropped her purse on Nurse Smart's desk and rummaged through it, pulling out a makeup case. She quickly walked around the desk and closed the gap between them. "They are beautiful," she said. "You really should play up your mouth, too. You have great lips."

She held up a lipstick. "You mind?"

Nurse Smart shook her head, startled, then puckered her lips.

Danielle smoothed the lipstick on slowly, taking her time. She could feel Nurse Smart's breath on her hand. The other woman was quiet, and Danielle held back a smile as she could feel the woman's breathing quicken. Danielle touched the woman's hair and then pulled out a mirror. "See, look at yourself!"

Nurse Smart did a double take. "Oh, thank you!" she said. "I can't believe that's me staring back in this mirror."

Danielle grinned. "See, you are a knockout, and didn't even know it." She put her makeup case back into her purse. "You've got to loosen up. You're always so uptight. But you're beautiful. Well, thanks again for looking at my work with such a favorable eye."

"Oh, anything you need, you let me know," Nurse Smart said, her voice a bit husky. She cleared her throat.

"I'm really trying to get a good review so I can get that raise," Danielle said.

"Oh, don't you worry about that," Nurse Smart said. "You'll get a good review."

"You think so?" Danielle said, letting a tiny line cross her forehead. "I've been so worried. What, with that bad report I received the other day and all."

"Oh, don't be concerned about that," Nurse Smart said, waving. "I'll go back into my records and correct that. We'll just say I had time to, uh, review the situation. And I see your work is exemplary." She held up the latest report. "You have nothing to worry about."

"Oh, thank you!" Danielle said and hugged the other woman. Then she stepped back. "Oh, I'm so sorry. I hope you don't mind. I just got so excited."

"It's okay," Nurse Smart gushed. "I didn't mind. I'm glad to see you so happy."

"Okay, well, I guess I should be going now," Danielle said, gathering her purse.

"Danielle, wait up," Nurse Smart said, springing from her chair. She cleared her throat again. "Do you . . . would you like to have dinner tonight?"

Danielle quickly sidestepped the question, with a smile. "Tonight, I can't, but I'd love to get together sometime. Well, I've got to run. See you tomorrow!"

Danielle quickly walked out of Nurse Smart's office, with a self-satisfied grin. *Yep, I am going to get my raise*, she thought. But her visage quickly darkened as her mind went back to the half dozen phone calls she had made to Troy all day. She hadn't been able to catch him at all.

She hopped into her gold Lexus and sped to Troy's apartment, bouncing off the curb in her haste to turn into his complex. "See, I knew he was there!" she yelled the words to the emptiness of her vehicle. His Navigator was parked in its usual spot. She jumped out of her car and rushed to the stairs, then paused. She decided she was going to see what he was up to first.

Instead of climbing the stairs and knocking on the door, Danielle slipped around to the back. She climbed over prickly hedges, trying to balance on one foot. She gathered her skirt around her thighs and twisted until she was next to the wall, then tiptoed around the building until she got to just beneath Troy's second floor apartment.

She stepped onto the patio of the bottom apartment, looking for a foothold to hoist herself up.

Rrrrring! Rrrring! She quickly looked down at her cell phone. She didn't recognize the number, but picked up anyway. This had better be Troy's sorry behind, she groused. "Hello?"

"You have a collect call from . . ."

"Collect call?" Danielle hung up. A moment later, the phone rang again. She thought to ignore it, but answered. "Who is this?" she said in a hushed tone.

The recording started again, announcing she had a collect call. " . . . call from Nikki. Will you accept?"

"Yes, I'll accept," Danielle said, curiosity in her tone.

A moment later, Nikki's voice came over the line. "Danielle, I hate to bug you but I am in jail."

"In jail?" Danielle's pitch rose and she tried to lower her voice as she stood on the patio of someone's apartment. "What are you doing in jail?"

"They arrested me behind that credit card mess," Nikki informed her.

"You didn't say anything about me, did you?" Danielle's voice was laced with worry.

"No, no," Nikki said quickly.

"Oh, okay, cool," Danielle said, now more relaxed.

"But I need you to bail me out," Nikki said.

Danielle heard movement from above. Troy was on his deck. She quickly stepped back, inching as close to the wall as she could. She could hear him talking; it sounded like he was on his cell phone.

"Nikki, I'm going to have to call you back," Danielle whispered.

"You can't call me," Nikki said, but Danielle had already hung up.

Chapter 48

Nikki didn't know what to do. She was fresh out of options. Danielle had hung up and William wasn't answering his cell. What if they had taken him in, too? Nikki would never forgive herself if William went to jail over this. Fear gripped her gut as she faced a night behind bars. And what about her child? Who would care for Psalm? She couldn't call Keedra because she was out of her allowed phone calls.

Nikki was ushered back to her cell, where she sat on a cracker-thin mattress, staring at gray walls. All around her, she heard conversation, some raised, some muffled. No one seemed to pay attention to her, and she had no cell mate at the moment. Her palms became sweaty as a thought hit her: What if she had to stay here overnight? They had processed her as if she would be there for a while—they had taken her fingerprints and mug shot and even confiscated her clothing and personal items.

She didn't have an attorney or anyone else to call for that matter. She thought to pray but shook her head at the idea. *God doesn't want to hear from me*, she thought.

Nikki was alone.

Chapter 49

Danielle crouched in the shadow right beneath Troy's apartment, straining to hear his conversation. After a moment, he went back inside. She waited for a beat to be sure he wasn't coming back out.

She took her shoes off and stuck them into her purse, which she looped over her shoulder, then carefully stepped onto the thick, wooden rail, balancing on one foot as she hooked her other foot in a rung. She managed to shimmy up the splintered column. Then her foot slipped and she flailed her arms wildly, knocking over a plant that clattered to the ground. As she fell, she stuck her hands out to brace herself. The fall didn't hurt, since it was only a couple or so feet, but a splinter got lodged into her thumb. She squeezed it out, sucking the spot where it had broken her skin, before climbing more carefully again.

This time, she managed to flip her leg over the bar and get a good grip and pull herself up the column. Her skirt hitched about her thighs and her bare feet anchored her.

At last, she stood on Troy's deck. She paused to catch her breath, and wiped sweat off her forehead. *I'm going to* make him pay for my clothes. They are ruined, she lamented, taking in the sweat stains and torn hemline. She tried the glass doors. They were unlocked, as she knew they would be. Troy never locked those doors.

She quietly slid them open and stepped into the cool kitchen. The place was silent and dark. She paused. She could hear a sound, but couldn't make it out. She inched closer to it, holding her breath.

Oh, it was the shower. She breathed, relieved she hadn't walked in him doing anything that would upset her. She saw no telltale signs of another woman being there. Maybe he wasn't cheating. But he still needed to answer the phone when she called.

An idea occurred to her. If Troy hadn't been cheating, then she needed to get out of there—like now. She didn't want Troy to think she was crazy. She backed into the living room and heard the shower stop. She froze. A whisper of, "Oh, shoot!" escaped her lips. What should she do? Where could she hide?

Danielle knew if she ran, she could hop out the doors and disappear. But as she debated the unpleasant thought of shimmying back down that splintery wood, she heard muffled voices coming from the direction of the shower. Her eyes narrowed. She inched closer to the bathroom door and pushed it open.

Water cascaded off Troy's long, lean, naked body as his arms enclosed an equally naked woman, pinning her against the shower's wall as he pressed his body to hers.

Danielle stared at the two, unable to move.

Chapter 50

William's attorney called to let him know a warrant had been issued for his arrest.

"What do we do?" William inquired.

"Well, it's going to be a lot of drama either way," Jonathan said on the other end of the phone. "Media folks are going to be hot on your trail. I'm working to handle things from the legal end, but there is no way around this warrant. I've tried, but there are some folks who have a vested interest in seeing you go down. And this is too good for them to pass up."

"Yeah, I know, the mayor is doing all he can to influence this process," William said.

"Yeah, he has been pressuring the DA," Jonathan said, "and unfortunately, the evidence is pretty incriminating. They have the hospital's video showing you standing there at the counter and in another frame, it shows your wife signing the paperwork."

William recalled the day at the hospital as they registered Psalm for the surgery. He now understood why Nikki had sent him on an errand to get some water. "Yeah, I'm sure it looks bad," he said. "Well, let's get this over with. I'll surrender. So the sooner I get in, the sooner I can get out."

"Okay," Jonathan said.

They talked a bit more and then Olivia drove William to the parish jail, where he met Jonathan to surrender. He bonded out shortly thereafter.

Cameras flashed as he walked out of the parish lock-up next to his attorney, but he stared straight ahead, as if they were not there. He climbed into Olivia's waiting pearl-toned Cadillac.

"Are you okay?" she asked.

He only glanced at her. She started the ignition. "Sorry."

As they pulled off, William leaned his head back onto the headrest. "I'm going to have to drop out of the race."

Olivia didn't say anything for a moment. "I wish there was some way to salvage this."

"Me too," he said. "But let's face it. It was a long shot from the beginning, and now, with this bad press and all these things, I can't win."

Olivia turned to look at him as they stopped at a light. "William, if anyone can pull this off, it's you."

He smiled at her. She was so loyal and sweet. "I appreciate you, but it's hopeless."

"Well, let's not give up just yet. Don't pull out," she continued, "I get so mad though, when I think of all the hard work we've put into this. First, someone robs my daddy of his life and of his campaign, and now it's happening all over again. I don't know Nikki all that well, but I really wonder if she realizes just how much she has hurt you—hurt any of your chances of ever winning a race. She seems rather shortsighted."

"She . . . ." William's voice trailed off as he didn't know what to say. He wanted to defend his wife, but anger wouldn't let him. They had spent so many years having each other's back, rooting for each other, pushing each other, and just when he had the prize within reach, she had snatched it away.

Maybe she wasn't the wife he had always thought her to be.

Chapter 51

"What is this?" Danielle screamed as her momentary paralysis vanished. She charged toward the couple in the shower. Troy scrambled to right himself. The woman looked startled and confused.

Danielle stopped short of hitting them, instead, she looked for something to throw. She knocked the woman's bracelets off the counter and kicked one of the woman's heels across the room. "Troy, who is this?" Danielle demanded, grabbing the other shoe.

Troy held up his arms to shield himself from Danielle's assault as she wielded the woman's footwear. She came down with it, slapping his water-soaked skin, hard.

"Girl, you better watch it, with your crazy self!" Troy said and snatched the shoe from her.

"See, I knew you were cheating!" Danielle yelled, punching at him. Troy knocked her against the wall, and stepped out of the bathroom, water dripping on the oversized plush blue rug.

The woman hastily wrapped a robe around herself, her

eyes moving from Danielle to Troy. "Troy, I thought you said your girlfriend was out of town."

"She is," he snapped. "Let me handle this."

"Your girlfriend? How about your fiancée, you jerk? And I'm right here," Danielle shot back, jamming her finger in his chest.

He grabbed her hand. "You touch me again, and I will break that finger."

"Troy, I told you if you mess over me, I will kill you!" Danielle screamed, her wild eyes flashing. "I'll cut you up in little pieces and scatter you from here to Mexico. I'll burn you up and dump you where nobody can find your sorry behind. I'll—"

"Shut up!" Troy said, "You don't even know what you're talking about."

"You've got too much drama," the other woman said, stomping out of the bathroom. "I'm going to get my stuff and be gone."

"Yeah, you do that!" Danielle flung the words at her. She turned back to Troy, fire flashing from her coffee-colored eyes. "How could you do this to me? Don't you know how many men want to be with me? How many men wish they could be with me? How dare you cheat on me! On *me*!"

" 'Cause you're crazy!" he said. "What sane person breaks into some dude's place?"

"That's 'cause I thought you were up to no good!"

"Okay, so now you know."

"Well, you're going to have to beg me to marry your sorry tail!" she said, staring him down. "I'm through with you."

"That's the best thing you've said all day." Troy jerked on his boxers and walked into the living room, Danielle at his heels. The other woman marched back through the living room, dressed in jeans and a tank. "I'll call you," Troy said.

"Don't bother," she shot back and rolled her eyes, then slammed the door behind her.

"Troy, how can you disrespect me like this?" Danielle demanded.

"You know what, you need to get up out of my spot." He turned his back to her and dug into the refrigerator.

"Okay, okay, I'm going!" Danielle said, nodding hard. "I don't need your sorry behind. You need me. And you'd better watch your back."

Danielle stomped out of the apartment and slammed the door, breathing hard. The nerve of Troy, to treat her like that. He should have been grateful she would even go out with him, as far as she was concerned. *To think I was going to marry him*, she fumed. She stopped halfway down the stairs and turned, walking back up to his door. She pulled out a red lipstick and scrawled onto the wall next to his door. *Ladies: beware. Tiny man behind these doors. Don't waste your time, unless you like them small.*

She underlined the word "small" and then stomped back to her car. She eyed the Navigator. She dialed information and found the number she wanted. She quickly hung up and dialed the number the information service had just given her.

She glanced back up at Troy's window. "Hi, I need to have a vehicle towed."

Chapter 52

Olivia offered to order William something to eat, but he declined. He thanked her for the ride back to the campaign office, then climbed into the Protégé. He would just go home. He was drained. The day's embarrassment weighed on his shoulders. He had never even so much as had a speeding ticket, and now he was on his way to being a felon. How could Nikki have done this? William had never been angry with her this long, and even now, being mad at his wife was hard. So many emotions coursed through him. This was the woman he had pledged to spend the rest of his life with. This was the woman who gave him a baby.

But this was also the woman who had lied to him. When he thought of the lie, his temperature rose. He tried to put the last few days out of his mind.

William turned on his cell phone. When he checked his voicemail, all he heard was a recording, something about a collect call.

He pulled into the driveway beside the SUV. As he climbed out of the Protégé, he realized he still wasn't ready to forgive Nikki. He stepped into the living room. It was quiet. Nothing was cooking on the stove. Neither his wife nor daughter greeted him.

He looked around; something wasn't right. Her keys were there. So was her purse. The hairs on the back of his neck stood and his scalp tingled as a thought suddenly hit him. Had they arrested his wife, too?

His heart beating fast, he snatched his wallet out and flipped through the business cards, searching for his attorney's number. What did he do with that card? He threw his wallet down on the table and his eyes hungrily roamed the room, looking for the phone book. He found it and flipped through until he found the number.

He quickly dialed. When Jonathan answered, William was brief: "I need you to see if they arrested Nikki," he said. "Find my wife."

Chapter 53

"That jerk has made a fool of me for the last time," Danielle fumed as she sat in traffic on her way back to her own place. The last guy she dated had tried the same thing. Come to think of it, she had been cheated on by everybody she'd ever been with. That sudden realization hit her.

When she was little, maybe seven, Danielle knew she was her uncle's favorite. He would always tell her she was pretty and let her sit on his lap. He'd hug her tight and even gave her grown-up kisses, but only if she would be good and not tell anybody.

It was their secret.

The kisses made her feel gross, but he was her favorite uncle and she didn't want to say anything about them. And he seemed to always be buying her nice things. But then one day she heard him telling her twin, Gabrielle, just how pretty Gabrielle was. Danielle emerged from the next room. "You think I'm prettier, though, right?"

Her uncle had laughed. "You're both very pretty little girls. And very special. You're both my favorite."

"But you can't have two favorites," Danielle had pouted.

"I can when they are as pretty as you two."

"But I'm prettier, right?" Danielle pressed.

Her uncle looked from one to the other. "Well, I can't really say," he said. "But I think your sister here is prettier today."

Gabrielle had stuck her tongue out at Danielle in victory and scrunched her nose. Even with all the uncomfortable things he did to Danielle, that wasn't enough to make him choose her. But it wasn't just her uncle. Everyone in her life chose someone else over her. And she wasn't going to keep letting that happen.

This latest betrayal had her mind racing. She wanted to lash out in so many ways, but she tried to calm herself. You can't get yourself worked up, she reminded herself. She needed to talk to her best friend. Nikki would know just what to say. She pressed the key Nikki's cell number was stored under. But when the call connected, it went straight to voicemail. Danielle's eyes widened and she slapped her palm to her forehead. "Nikki! I forgot. She's in jail! She wanted me to bail her out," Danielle remembered.

In Danielle's one-track pursuit of Troy, she had forgotten her friend's desperate call. "Well, I'm sure she won't be mad. It's not like she was going anywhere. I'll just go get her now."

Chapter 54

William saw Nikki emerge from the lockup, tired and worn. He knew she had spent stressful hours in the uncomfortable cell, waiting, hoping someone would come for her. Her skin looked sweaty and grimy and she wiped her hands on her pants, trying without success to get rid of whatever was on her palms. He could see her swallowing back tears, demanding they not come.

He saw her brows shoot up in surprise as she discovered William and his attorney waiting for her. She hadn't known who had bailed her out.

A pang shot through him as he realized she hadn't expected him to come for her. How had they gotten to this point?

William extended his hand to her when she walked into the open area. He put his arm around her. "You okay?"

"I am now," she said in a voice barely above a whisper.

They bade goodbye to Jonathan and they walked to the Protégé.

Seeing Nikki brought forward so many feelings. He had been terrified at the thought of her in jail, alone, not knowing what to do. But it was her own fault, he thought. But that was quickly replaced by another thought: *She's still my wife, though, and I can't see her hurting.*

He could tell Nikki wanted to talk, to say something, but she was holding back. He was glad she didn't press for conversation because he didn't know how he felt. He had come for her, but he didn't know what that meant.

"Where is Psalm?" he asked when they got into the car.

"At Keedra's."

"Where is that?" William asked.

Nikki rattled off the address

Nikki reached to touch his hand, but William moved it away. Nikki let her hand fall back into her lap and they rode the rest of the way in silence.

Chapter 55

Danielle arrived at Nikki's house shortly after the family got home.

"Hey," she said, pushing past Nikki into the house.

"Hi," Nikki said, cutting her eyes in her husband's direction. "We just got home. I need to talk to Will for a bit."

But William didn't have the same thoughts. "I'm getting ready to get back to the headquarters," he said, grabbing a soda out of the refrigerator. He kissed Psalm.

"But baby, we just got home," Nikki said, startled. They had so much to discuss.

"Well, in case you haven't noticed, I've got to do damage control because of my wife's foolish actions," he said. "So, if you don't mind, I'll be leaving to do that."

"But, I thought—"

"Check you later, Danielle," William said, cutting Nikki off. "I'm out."

He slammed the door. Nikki stood stunned. "Danielle, I don't know what I'm going to do," she said, sinking into a chair and placing her head in her hands.

"Yeah, well, it'll blow over," Danielle said. "Back to the matter at hand. By the time I got to the jail, you were gone. You could have told me so I didn't waste a trip looking for you."

"Well, I didn't realize you were coming," Nikki said, walking to the kitchen. "After it took you so long and all. And I was just glad to be free. I forgot to call you."

"I bet you called that Keedra, didn't you?"

"Well, yes, as a matter of fact I did."

Danielle pursed her lips but said no more. Nikki saw her friend's pout but didn't care. She didn't feel like dealing with Danielle's tantrum tonight. The woman had left her stranded.

Nikki would never have done the same thing to Danielle. *She is so selfish*, Nikki thought. Moments later, Nikki chided herself: *I'm the one who caused this mess. It's not her fault I got myself arrested. At least she did come to get me. I'm such a terrible friend.*

"Hey, I'm sorry," Nikki said. "Thanks for having my back."

"No problem," Danielle said. "That's what best friends are for."

An hour later, Danielle left. Nikki flipped through the channels and stopped when she came to an image of her husband walking swiftly from the parish lock-up, a grim expression on his face. The screen then switched to a shot of Lo Dark in some cheesy photo-op, holding a baby.

The announcer's voice came over: "The city's mayoral campaign is shaping up to be about corruption and promise. The little known Broussard has been wrapped up in a most bizarre case of identity theft—and possibly the murder of another candidate—while the incumbent Dark spends his time serving his constituents."

Then came Dark's smiling visage, looking directly at the

camera. "I'd certainly prefer not to have to spend so much time campaigning. I'd rather handle the business of the city. I'm sure the voters are smart enough to realize I am the better choice; the one who has been working on their behalf. But even so, I realize I must be out there hitting the streets, educating anyone who may be tempted to vote otherwise. Though, who would vote for one wrapped up in such legal issues, I do not know."

The reporter switched to a voter, chattering away. It was a woman, in her mid-30s, with a big, floppy hat on her head. "Oh, no, I sure wouldn't vote for that Broussard. He's been mixed up in some bad things. We definitely don't want our city to go back to those days of corruption and scandal. No sirree!"

Nikki flipped to another channel. She was sick of the coverage and drama. These people didn't even know the whole story, yet they speculated and were sullying her husband's name. "It's my fault he's in this bind," she reminded herself. William's popularity was down to single digits. The newspapers, TV and radio stations, and especially Internet bloggers, were having a field day. He seemed to be the punch line of every joke. He was the poster child for Shreveport corruption.

The next channel was playing a Lo Dark commercial, asking voters, in an ominous voice, if they wanted to continue to move forward for progress with the current mayor or go backward with a candidate who stood for the "old Shreveport" and corruption.

"But he's the king of the corrupt!" Nikki fumed, switching off the television. Unsubstantiated reports insinuated that William had a hand in Chance's death—that he had possibly murdered the man to take his spot on the campaign trail. The story had unnamed sources speculating that William would stop at nothing to get what he wanted; whether that was to steal a credit card or kill a competitor.

Nikki knew she had to do something. She felt it was her fault that everyone was looking at her husband as a lying, thieving murderer. "I've got to find out who killed Oliver Chance."

But where should she begin?

Chapter 56

Winston walked into the campaign headquarters, carrying a stack of William's yard signs.

"What's this?" William asked.

"I found a whole pile of these at an old building across town," he said, dropping the signs to the floor with a loud thud.

"Are you serious?" Olivia asked, stepping closer. She picked up a sign. "These cost good money."

"Yeah, I was networking with some contacts and someone told me I should go look," Winston said. "And get this, the property is owned by Lo Dark's brother-in-law."

"I knew he was behind all this!" William said, snapping his fingers. "He's behind this whole thing. The murder. The stolen signs. The bad press."

"But he's not behind the credit card scam, and right now, that's our biggest worry," Olivia reminded him. "For that, we have only to look to your dear wife."

William stopped short. He wanted to look elsewhere as the cause of his woes, but he knew his biggest headache originated with his wife. William turned to his computer and began typing. He had several speeches coming up and he was working on the outlines himself, now that so many of his staffers had quit.

He didn't have the luxury of allowing someone else to write his speeches for him. He couldn't ask Olivia to do it. She was already doing so much. And Winston had his hands full with keeping the press at bay, and trying—in vain, it seemed—to get a positive story out about William.

Olivia was right. He had only to look as far as his wife to find the source of his problems.

Chapter 57

Danielle had expected to hear from Troy, but he didn't call. I know he misses me, she thought as she paced the floor in her condo. He'll come begging, and when he does, I will squash him like an ant.

Danielle thought back to her childhood. Her biological father had traded her and the rest of her family in for another one, and they'd had little to no contact with him after he left. It was her stepfather who raised her, the only man she knew as a father, really, and he hadn't been much better. She remembered all the nights he would return home smelling like sickeningly sweet perfume. At first, her mother would say something and the couple would argue furiously, with doors slamming and lots of yelling, but as the years wore on, her mother said less and less.

One night, the day before Thanksgiving, Danielle's stepfather returned home from work with a jaunty step and a whistle. Thirteen-year-old Danielle, at first, was happy to see him in such a good mood because that meant tension would not rule the house that night. But her joy soured when she saw him emerge from his bedroom a half hour later, freshly showered and shaved.

"Daddy, where are you going? It's the night before Thanksgiving," Danielle had asked.

"Look, don't you get in grown folks' business," he had shot back, grabbing his hat and keys.

Tears welled in her eyes. "Daddy, it's Thanksgiving. It's the time for families," Danielle said, grabbing his arm. He shook her off and walked toward the door.

Tears streaming down her cheeks, Danielle whirled to her mother. "How can you just stand there? How can you let him leave us like that?"

Danielle's mother's hands never stopped moving up and down in the basin of dressing she was mixing. "Danielle, there are just some things a woman has to put up with in this life."

"What do you mean, 'Put up with?' You know he's going to see somebody else! How can you stand there and let him do this to us? How?"

Danielle's mother looked up, and with an expression Danielle remembered clear to this day, said, "Sometimes you can do all you know how to do, and a man will still leave. But if you just be patient, he'll come back."

"I hate you! I hate you! I can't believe you're letting him do this to us! I'll never be like you!" Danielle flung the words at her mother and stomped to her bedroom, fell on her bed and wept into her pillow.

She shook her head as if to clear it of that bad memory. "Yeah, Troy will be back."

Chapter 58

Nikki kissed a sleeping Psalm lightly on her forehead and got up from the edge of the child's bed. With one last glance, she closed the girl's bedroom door, except for a crack and walked quietly up the hall to the kitchen. She sighed, and ran some warm dishwater. She washed the few dinner dishes and put up the leftovers, save for William's plate, which she covered and put in the microwave. William had missed dinner again, as was his usual custom now. She missed her husband.

When William entered the house at a quarter to ten—without a greeting—she silently walked to the microwave and heated his plate. She set it on the table.

"Thanks," William said, and dipped his fork into the spicy dirty rice.

"You're welcome." She poured him a glass of tea.

William ate in silence. The oven-barbecued chicken was so tender it fell from the bone. Nikki sat across from him, sipping water.

"Baby," she began, "how is the investigation into Reverend Chance's death coming?"

"It's not."

"What do you mean?"

"Just that, Nikki," he said. "Nothing's being done."

"But I thought that's one of the reasons you wanted to get elected."

"Well, I'm not elected yet, now am I?" he glared at her. "And, thanks to you, I might never be."

She bit her lip to keep from saying anything. She had thought his anger would have dissipated, but it was still there, even after two weeks. She knew her marriage was falling apart.

Nikki had never been one of those little girls who dreamed of getting married. She grew up watching her mother cater to her stepfather, and to young Nikki, it seemed a ridiculous act. She couldn't understand why her mother closed herself off from her own dreams and desires to take care of her husband.

Yet, Nikki knew she was doing the same thing. For one, she was harboring this secret, this past that would tear apart the life she had so carefully built. And even now, she wanted to get out there and pursue her photography dream, but she knew her husband wouldn't like it. She wanted to say something about the investigation, to press, but she bit back her words, knowing he would disapprove.

Instead, she busied herself with taking care of her home and tiptoeing around her husband.

She had become her mother.

Nikki sat down at their home computer and began typing. She was no computer expert, but after years of watching her husband repair and network computers, she had picked up a few things. Within a few minutes, she was hooked into the system at William's office. She shook her head, wondering how it was that he did not have a firewall.

She hoped she could find some clue to Oliver Chance's

last days. She scrolled through the system, looking for an electronic calendar. She paged through file after file. Her eyes widened.

She had to break into William's office.

The next day, Nikki donned an olive green pants suit with a crisp white blouse, and low-heeled pumps. When she dropped Psalm off at school, she drove to the district attorney's office and parked. Nervous and uncertain of her next move, she walked up to the door, taking a deep, calming breath. She summoned all the confidence she could and told the receptionist she was there to see an assistant district attorney.

The receptionist, calm and professional, asked a few questions. "What is it concerning?"

Nikki wanted to turn, to rush back out the doors, but she spoke in a level voice. "I have some information concerning a pending legal action."

"Are you a witness to a crime?"

"Sort of," Nikki said. She took a deep breath. "I'm the defendant."

The woman's expression never changed. "Do you have legal counsel?"

"No. But that's not necessary," she said. "I am here on my own behalf."

"Okay, ma'am, well, have a seat, and I'll have someone come speak with you."

"Thank you."

Nikki sat down on a brown leather chair. A few boring landscape paintings decorated the walls and worn home and garden magazines dotted the coffee table. She flipped through one of the magazines blindly.

"Mrs. Broussard?" she looked up when the receptionist called her name. "Luke Marks will see you now."

Nikki stood and smoothed down the front of her jacket.

This was it. She flashed a tiny, tight smile at the receptionist and followed the woman down the hall. The woman
stepped aside and held out a hand. "This is Mr. Marks's office."

"Thank you," Nikki told the woman.

"Mrs. Broussard," the man said, standing. He was about
five feet eleven inches, with sandy hair and a pronounced
tan. Biscuit brown is what came to mind. She could tell he
spent a lot of time outdoors. "How can I help you?"

"I want to get my husband out of trouble."

His right eyebrow shot up quizzically. "Get your husband
out of trouble?"

"Yes, I did a very bad thing and he got arrested," she said.

"Well, why don't you sit down and tell me exactly what
happened?"

She took the seat across from him as he leaned back in
his chair, staring intently into her face as she took a deep
breath. She told her story. Her husband had nothing to do
with the whole setup.

"I'll face whatever punishment, but please drop the
charges against my husband," she said.

"Well, we'll need your sworn statement, but we make no
promises," Luke Marks said. Nikki knew lots of people
came across his path proclaiming their innocence, but few
confessed all their misdeeds and yielded themselves to the
mercy of the court. "We may be able to work out a deal, if
you can tell us who supplied you with the card information
in the first place."

Nikki's eyes widened. She wasn't prepared to incrimi-
nate her best friend. She looked at her hands in her lap and
then back up. "I can't do that."

"Can't?" Luke echoed. "Do you realize you are facing
some serious charges?"

"I know," she said, "but I can't drag anybody else into
this. Anyone who helped me did it out of kindness."

"Kindness?" Luke said. "We're talking about felonies, Mrs. Broussard."

She said nothing. He pressed. "Look, if you can help us out with some names, I can help make these charges against you and your husband disappear."

Tears welled in Nikki's eyes, but she breathed in and pushed them away. "I can't do it," she said. "All I'm here to do is to clear my husband because he had nothing to do with this. As for me, I'll take whatever punishment. But I can't speak against anyone else."

Luke sighed. "Okay, Mrs. Broussard," he said, standing. "Have it your way. But I must tell you, you're making a mistake."

Chapter 59

Nikki waited until William settled in for the night before slapping herself on the forehead. "Oh, I almost forgot," she said. "I have to run an errand."

"At this hour?" William questioned. "It's eleven o'clock at night."

"I know," she said. "But it won't take that long."

"Okay, well, I'm going to bed," he said and walked to the bedroom.

For once, Nikki was glad of the tension, for it meant not much conversation. She quickly pulled on her sneakers. She cast a quick, furtive glance down the hall and took her husband's keys. She backed out of the driveway and sped toward the campaign office. She knew no one would be there at this hour.

Heart pounding and palms sweating, Nikki quickly sifted through the keys on William's chain until she found the ones to the building. She jammed the key into the lock and let herself in. She flicked on a light and looked around.

She didn't know exactly what she was looking for, but knew she had to get a good, uninterrupted search of the office. She knew most of Reverend Chance's items were long gone, but hunted anyway.

She rifled through drawers, turned on computers, even looked under desks. There had to be a clue! She felt certain the charges would be dropped against her husband, now that she had taken all the blame. Now, if she could solve the murder on top of that, surely she and William could get back on track.

She saw an overstuffed box in a corner. She picked up something from the top and realized it was a pile of Reverend Chance's things. Nikki carefully went through the items. Her hand paused over a thick, black book. It was his planner! She started to flip through it. No, searching through it now would take too long. She would just take it with her. She slipped it into her purse. She carefully placed all the items back in the box and stood up.

"What are you doing?"

Nikki jumped at the words, and whirled around. Her eyes widened, and she froze.

Chapter 60

Danielle lounged in bed, sipping a glass of wine, flipping though channels under the soft light of candles. She had earlier been listening to mellow music, but turned from it to see what was on television. She stopped her channel surfing to watch an entertainment show, catching up on the celebrity gossip. She had to know these details, because one day she would be one of those celebrities. She would be traveling in those circles.

She had let the drama with Troy and the shenanigans at work sidetrack her, and she hadn't thought much about her movie star aspirations lately. But watching that entertainment show reminded Danielle of her dreams of fame.

The stars on all those shows seemed so hollow; none of them could measure up to her, as far as Danielle was concerned. She felt confident that if she could just have a few minutes with a director or producer, she would be on her way. That was all the more important now that she had dumped Troy. Landing a gig in a movie or on a show would be the only thing to rescue her from her life now.

She was daydreaming about walking the red carpet when

she heard a knock at her door. She wondered who it was as she sat motionless for a moment. She wasn't expecting any company, so whoever it was could just go on back home.

Knock, knock, knock.

She got a chill. She quickly got up, swiping her hand over her hair. She ran to the bathroom and sprayed a bit of body spray over her midsection and thighs, then pulled her dress back down.

She walked to the door. She opened it. And smiled.

Troy snatched her to him and kissed her hard on the mouth.

"I knew you'd be back."

Chapter 61

"What are you doing in here?" Olivia demanded.

"I—I was just looking for something," Nikki stammered weakly.

"Does William know you're here?" Olivia asked, looking around suspiciously.

"Well—"

"I thought so." Olivia's eyes narrowed. "You know, you've caused William enough trouble, don't you think? And now, what are you, adding breaking and entering to your little criminal resume?"

"I didn't do anything!" Nikki said. "I just wanted to come down here and look for something."

"Something like what?"

"Clues to your father's murder!"

Olivia stopped cold. "What do you know about my father's murder?"

"Nothing," Nikki said, "but I'm trying to help."

"You leave my daddy's name out your mouth!" Olivia spat the words. "I'm calling William."

"No! Wait!" Nikki rushed to the woman and grabbed her hand.

"Are you attacking me?" Olivia's eyes were large and wide.

Nikki dropped her hands. "I'm sorry. But please, can we just talk?"

Olivia was not in the mood to entertain Nikki's request. She punched the memorized digits to the Broussards' home phone. After a moment, she spoke. "William, I just walked into a break-in at the office." She paused. "No, no. I'm fine . . . No, it's not like that . . . But you have to see this . . . Yes, I think you should come down."

Nikki wanted to hop into her car and rush back home, but she stayed rooted to the spot. She slumped down on a chair and waited. A hostile Olivia stood with her arms crossed over her chest, silently glowering at Nikki.

Fifteen minutes later, Nikki heard a car door slam. And the door to the office tore open. "What's going on?" William demanded.

Olivia pointed. "I stopped by here to get some notes I forgot earlier and I found her rifling through our things."

"Nikki, what are you doing here? I thought you said you had an errand?" William demanded. Before Nikki could speak, he held up his hand. "No, let me guess. Another one of your lies, right?"

The words cut Nikki deeply, but she struggled not to show the hurt. She spoke clearly. "No, William. I didn't lie. I told you I had an errand. If you'll recall, you showed no interest in my whereabouts and told me you were going to bed. So I didn't think you'd care."

"You didn't think I'd care to know you were coming down to break into my office?"

"I didn't break in!" Nikki's voice rose. She struggled to remain calm. "All I was trying to do is find a clue to the murder."

"What, you're Sherlock Holmes now? I had to get my child out of bed for this? I had to rouse her from her sleep, pack her into a cold vehicle and drive across town, and for what? This is so unreal. I don't even know you anymore."

"William, yes, you do know me," Nikki cried. "I'm your wife. I'm the woman you swore you'd love, but you've been treating me like I'm not even there. I thought if I could help you figure out who killed—"

"I don't want to hear this!" William said in disgust.

He shook his head and stared pointedly at his wife. "I think you should leave now."

Chapter 62

William moved out the next morning. He packed a duffel bag of clothes.

"Where will you go?" Nikki asked, wanting to beg him to stay. But she held her tongue.

"I don't know," he said. "I'll crash somewhere. Maybe at the office."

"But, Will, please let's not do this," she finally uttered what was in her heart. "You can't leave."

"I can, and I am," he said, zipping the bag.

"But, Will, everything I've ever done, it's been for you," she said. "I gave up my dreams for you. My world revolved around you."

"Well, then you should be relieved to have some free time on your hands," he said, picking up the bag.

He slung it over his shoulder and hoisted a box under the crook of his arm. Nikki felt her heart pound hard in her chest. She wanted to fling herself at his feet and beg. She wanted to hold on to his leg and make him stay. She wanted to stretch out across the doorway and block his exit.

But she did none of these things.

Instead, she sat on the edge of the bed and said nothing as her husband walked out of her life.

Nikki could not believe her husband had left her. She had refused to let tears flow last night. And now, this Saturday morning, as she scrambled eggs for her child, none fell from her eyes.

She served Psalm breakfast and then sat at the kitchen table with a calculator. Her heart hurt terribly at the thought of losing her husband, but she knew she still had to be practical. What would she do about money? How would she support herself and her child? The thoughts swirled around her mind.

She wrote down expenses, and then the thought came to her. The newspaper. That's it. She snapped her fingers. She would apply for a job as a photographer.

The photo editor had told her several times that he'd love to have her on staff. When Nikki shot that photo of that accident right around the time William signed up to run for office, the editor had been impressed with her work. She had been on the interstate when she saw the accident. Instinctively, she had grabbed her camera. She recalled now that William had been angry after seeing that photo in the paper. He hadn't let her explain that she had taken the photo on a whim, not as a deliberate act of defiance. But maybe that photo, and all her previous work, would be enough to land her a job. Nikki's hand shook as she dialed the number to the paper. She doubted if the photo editor would be in on a Saturday, but called anyway, as she knew newspaper folks often had erratic schedules.

"Joe Smiles, please," she said when someone answered.

"This is Joe."

"Hi, Joe," Nikki said. "It's Nikki Broussard."

"Hi, Nikki," he said. "How are you?"

"I'm doing great. I was actually calling to see about getting some work, maybe if you had some freelance assignments. Or even a full-time position."

She heard Joe sigh. "Well, Nikki, we have a slight problem with that right now," he said. "I'd love to hire you—full-time, even—but unfortunately, this latest business with the credit cards is posing a real problem. I don't know that I can bring you on, on even a freelance basis, with that thing hanging out there."

Nikki closed her eyes a moment and let out a deep breath. "Joe, it was a crazy situation," she said. "I'm really sorry that all happened."

"Yeah, Nikki, I couldn't believe it when I heard it," Joe said. "We were all shocked. We've enjoyed working with you in the past. You were a great intern and you've done some good freelance work for us."

"Thanks, Joe," Nikki said, "but I really need a job."

"Nikki, I just don't know—"

"Joe, my child was sick and I couldn't think straight," she rushed to explain. "I made a terrible call. I was desperate."

Joe's voice lowered. "You know I understand. If it was my kid, I might have done the same thing. Hope I never have to find out. But right now, I can't do anything for you."

"Thanks, Joe," Nikki said sadly. "Have a good day."

The phone slipped from her fingers and the tears finally came.

Chapter 63

Bₗₐcₖ Male Found Burned In Car

Nikki wouldn't have paid any attention to the headline, but the smiling face of Troy caught her attention. Why was Troy's picture under this headline? *Don't tell me he's gone and killed somebody. I told Danielle he was bad news.*

But as she read, her breath caught in her throat. Troy wasn't the assailant. He was the victim. Troy was dead! She snatched up her cell phone and pressed Danielle's number.

When her friend answered, Nikki's words came out in a rush. "Danny Boo, are you okay? I just read the terrible news in the paper. Why didn't you tell me? I'm so sorry!"

"It's okay," Danielle said in a toneless voice.

"I've been so wrapped up in my own problems, I didn't even realize anything was wrong. When did he go missing? What happened?"

"I said, 'It's okay,'" Danielle said. "Look, I really don't want to talk about this."

"I know you're in shock. I'll be right over."

Before Danielle could say anything, Nikki hung up. She snatched up her keys, grabbed Psalm and raced to the SUV.

Nikki had no time to think about her own life that was falling apart. Her best friend needed her.

Nikki arrived at Danielle's condo and let herself in. Danielle was polishing her toenails.

"Danielle, I am so sorry for your loss," Nikki said, hugging her friend.

"I told you, it's all right," Danielle said.

"The story didn't say a lot," Nikki said. "What happened?"

Danielle shrugged. "I really don't know. Just whatever they said in the paper. He was shot in the head at close range."

Nikki gasped. "Poor Troy."

"Yeah."

"What are they doing about funeral arrangements? Have you spoken with his family?" Nikki asked.

"Well, I went by his mama's house only to find two other women over there, both claiming to be his grieving girlfriend," Danielle said. "So I left."

Danielle's hands fluttered lightly in the air, their movements seeming to belie the seriousness of the moment. Nikki looked around her friend's place. The walls were covered with photos of Nikki and Danielle at various functions over the years. But not one photo was of Danielle's family. Nikki's heart ached for her friend who was so enclosed in a lonely world estranged from her own family, especially now as she struggled with the loss of her fiancé. I've got to work harder to be there for her. I'm all she has, Nikki told herself.

Nikki grimaced at Danielle's news. "That's pretty bad," she said, casting about for some words of comfort. "I'm sure that was just a misunderstanding. You were his fiancée."

Danielle fastened the top back onto the red polish. "Well, it's a shame, what happened to him. I guess he must have been dealing with the wrong type of people. It's really a shame."

*   *   *

Nikki drove back home, thinking about her next move. In a matter of two months, she had gone from a happily married woman with a man who adored her, to someone who could very well be headed for divorce. "Oh, and don't forget, you're on your way to being an unemployed felon," she said to herself, recalling her legal woes.

Depression crouched on her shoulders, and she gripped the steering wheel tighter. And now, her ace in the hole—the job at the newspaper—had fallen through. She knew she had brought this on herself.

"I didn't trust God," she muttered to herself, finally admitting for the first time the full magnitude of what she had done. It was her own impatience and haste to do something—anything to find an answer for Psalm's condition. She hadn't truly prayed over her situation. "I talked about faith, but when it mattered, I didn't have it. And now, look what happened."

"I have made a mess of my life."

The realization hit her hard.

Nikki roused Psalm from bed. "Come on, let's get ready for church," Nikki prodded.

"I'm sleepy," Psalm protested.

"Girl, if you don't get yourself up," Nikki warned, "talking about you're sleepy. Come on."

Psalm made unhappy noises, but slowly climbed out of the covers. Nikki quickly fixed breakfast and did the girl's hair into a ponytail at the top of her head and let her wear the rest of her hair down in the back, a decision that made Psalm forget her earlier protests.

"Where is Daddy?" Psalm asked as they walked out the door. "Is he going to church with us?"

Psalm still did not understand that her father had moved out. Nikki hadn't tried to explain too much. She had just said William was working a lot and would be at the office. But Psalm was used to the family attending church together.

"Well, your daddy is still working," Nikki clutched about for an explanation.

"Will we see him at church?"

Nikki didn't know, but tried to distract the child. "Maybe so," she said. "Do you want to have pizza for dinner after church?"

"Oh, can we really?" Psalm's eyes lit up at the thought.

"Sure," Nikki said.

When they arrived at church, service was already under way. Nikki dropped Psalm off at the children's church service. Sister James caught up with her as she got ready to enter the sanctuary.

"I didn't see your name on the list of those who have purchased their new usher uniforms," she said.

"Oh . . . I . . ." Nikki had forgotten about the order. With so much going on lately, usher uniforms were not very high on her list of priorities.

"I tried to call you twice last week," Sister James said. "I guess your voicemail must have been messing up, because I didn't get a call back."

Nikki had avoided contact with most people lately. "Yeah, I know, I'm sorry I didn't get a chance to call you back," she said.

"Well, I guess I should just be happy you're at church today," Sister James said pointedly. "I wasn't sure if you were coming, seeing as how it's so late."

"Oh, I . . . uh . . . yeah," Nikki stammered.

"Well, don't just stand out here," Sister James said. "You're an usher; you know better. Get on in and find a seat."

The usher on the inside of the door slowly pushed it open. Nikki was about to step inside when Sister James grabbed her arm. "And don't you worry about all these things they put in the newspaper. You just keep God's Word in your heart and He will see you through."

Nikki smiled gratefully. She quickly stepped into the sanctuary and allowed the praise and worship to envelop her being. She remained standing and swayed to the music, clapping and singing along with the choir and others in the congregation.

The burden of a crumbling marriage, impending legal woes, and the stress of being an out-of-work single mother almost made her sit down, but she refused to give in to the temptation. Instead, she sang with more gusto than ever, as if willing away her troubles.

The new pastor preached about prayer and its healing power. As Nikki sat and listened, she felt encouraged. Her sadness seemed to lift a little. But as she drove home following service, a dark cloud again settled over her spirit. Doubt battled the confidence she wanted to feel. Doubt told her maybe it was too late for prayer to work for her.

Maybe she had gone too far. Maybe God would no longer hear her cries.

Chapter 64

The late afternoon sun peeked through the blinds, casting a glare on William's computer screen at the campaign headquarters. He had just returned from a full day of debates and had given two speeches on opposite ends of town.

"Winston, didn't I tell you to make sure I got to speak last at that debate?" William snapped.

Heads jerked up as everyone looked at William. He never exploded like this.

"I'm sorry, boss," Winston said. "Remember, they flipped a coin. There wasn't anything I could do about that. I told you ahead of time that I wasn't able to arrange the order."

"I don't care about that, you should have been able to do something!" William said. "I swear, do I have to do everything around here?"

Olivia put her hand on William's arm. "Hey, what's gotten into you?"

"I'm just tired of all this!" William said. "And why is this big glare on my computer screen!"

Someone quickly closed the blinds.

"William, you've got to calm down," Olivia said soothingly. "I know you're just upset about your lousy home situation. But that's no reason to take it out on the staff. Winston does really good work for you. And the debate went beautifully."

"I need some air." William stood abruptly. He strode across the room and flung open the door, slamming it behind him. He found himself staring at the potholed parking lot, his mind a blur of emotion.

September was drawing to a close and the primary election was coming up in a few short weeks. But that wasn't the big one. William knew it would be a much harder fight to win the big general election in November when it was just Dark and him. Even as William tried to focus on the upcoming elections, it was his wife at the top of his mind. He had skipped church yesterday because he didn't want to bump into her there. He knew that wasn't the best approach, but he couldn't risk running into her because he knew if he saw her, he may give in and come back home. And right now, he just didn't know if he could go back home.

She had lied to him repeatedly, it seemed. When had she become so deceitful? When had she started going around behind his back? It was a good thing he did have this campaign to keep him occupied.

William knew he could not take his pain and frustration out on his staff. He walked back into the building and took a deep breath. "Hey, I'm sorry for blowing up earlier," he said to Winston, who gave him a thumbs-up sign and went back to work.

To Olivia, he confided, "I guess I'm just in a bad mood. I don't understand what's going on with me and my wife; we've never been like this before. I'm angry with her, yet I love her. I keep wanting to reach for the phone to call her, but then I think maybe it's all a waste of time."

Olivia chose her words carefully. "Well, you're a good

man," she said. "And maybe all of this happened for a reason. Maybe she's not the type of woman you need to have on your arm when you get elected mayor."

William paused for a moment. "You think I'll get elected?"

Olivia smiled into his eyes. "Yes, I do. You'd be the perfect mayor."

Chapter 65

Nikki didn't want to make the phone call, but necessity compelled her. *I've got to know who leaked that stuff about the credit card. I can't believe he would do this to me . . .*

It had been so long since she had talked to him . . . years, in fact. She wanted to never speak or see him again. He represented her past. And she wanted nothing to do with it. But now she had no choice.

Her fingers hesitated over the buttons on the phone, but she pressed them down firmly.

A receptionist or someone picked up the telephone.

Nikki exhaled, then said: "Spencer Cason, please."

Nikki plunked her purse down on the floor and the thud reminded her of the book inside. She pulled Reverend Chance's calendar out and set it on the table. It would have to wait. First, she had to get Psalm settled with lunch.

She fixed a grilled cheese sandwich and cut it into quarters, slicing off the edges. She put orange pieces on the side and poured milk. "Psalm, come eat, baby. I fixed your favorite—grilled cheese!"

"Grilled cheese! Yea!" Psalm raced into the kitchen.

Nikki smiled quizzically. "Didn't you forget to do something?"

"Oh," Psalm said and rushed down the hall. A moment later, she returned, with water dripping down her elbows. Nikki smiled and handed the child a paper towel, along with her food.

"And what else did you forget?"

Psalm immediately clasp her hands together and said her grace.

"Very good," Nikki said when the child was finished. "Now, eat all your food. Be a big girl for Mommy."

Nikki settled on the other end of the table, slowly flipping through the planner. Reverend Chance sure couldn't write, she noted with a wry smile. His handwriting was atrocious. She struggled to read the appointment entries. He seemed to have been meeting lots of community groups, of course, and seemed to still manage to do a fair amount of marital counseling and general ministry. And on top of all that, he had been running for mayor.

Something fell to the floor and she picked it up. She flipped it over and frowned. It was Danielle's business card. Why did Reverend Chance have Danielle's business card?

She continued to flip through the planner and stopped short. "Dinner with Danielle Esp."

Nikki re-read the entry, trying to see if had made a mistake. Danielle Esp? Was that short for Esperanza? She slowly fingered the entry and again looked at the business card. How did Reverend Chance know Danielle? Danielle never said anything about meeting him. She picked up the phone to call her best friend, but put it down.

She'd visit her instead.

Chapter 66

"**I** didn't know you were friends with Reverend Chance," Nikki said casually, when she stopped by Danielle's condo the next day. It was Danielle's third day of being off work for bereavement.

Danielle lay on the couch, her hand in a box of chocolate-covered peanuts. "Reverend Chance?"

"Yeah, I got a copy of his appointments the other day and one entry had your name on it." Nikki watched her friend.

"Oh. Yeah," Danielle said. "I met with him a couple of times. So?"

"Nothing. I just never knew."

"Do I have to check in with you at every turn?"

"Hey, why are you getting all smart with me?" Nikki said. "I was just asking a harmless question."

Danielle rolled her eyes and popped another nut into her mouth. She shifted on the couch, and then stretched for the remote, but could not reach it.

"Pass me that remote," she said, and Nikki did.

"So, what were you meeting with Reverend Chance about?"

"Nothing! Why are you all in my business?"

"Look, I'm sorry. It's no big deal. I was just curious is all."

"Well, if you must know," Danielle said with a shrug. "I was just going to him for some counseling. I was depressed a while back and needed to talk. I was missing my family and having some issues at work. He was giving me advice."

"Why didn't you come to me?"

"Because you were too wrapped up in your perfect little life," Danielle said, her tone hardening on those words. "I met him, actually, at the grocery store a while ago and he invited me to his church. I never went there, but when I got depressed, I called him for counseling."

Nikki hadn't realized her friend was having so many emotional issues. "So are you better?"

"Well, let's see. My fiancé just got killed. And then I found out he's been cheating with a bunch of other women. I don't know. What do you think?"

"Oh, that was a stupid question, I'm sorry."

"It's all right," Danielle said. "Seriously, I am better. Reverend Chance helped me through a lot. It's a shame what happened to him, though."

Nikki nodded. "Yeah, it is," she said, but still felt Danielle knew more than she was telling.

Chapter 67

"You know, you're welcome to sleep in the guest room at my house," Olivia said, as she gathered her purse to leave the office for the evening.

"No," William said, "I'll be fine here."

Olivia shook her head. "I really hate for you to have to sleep on that cot. As hard as you work all day, it's a shame you have to be so uncomfortable at night. I really hate your wife is putting you through this. It's a shame you have to sleep here, not even on a real bed."

"Well, I don't have much of a choice right now," William said. "I don't want to barge into my brother's place and my mother would raise too much of an *I told you so* fuss if I crashed at her place."

"Well, just know that you always have a bed at my place," Olivia said.

"Thanks."

"Well, have a good night," she said. "I'll see you in the morning."

* * *

It had been more than a week since William left home. He had called twice to talk with Psalm and stopped by her school once, but he had not spoken with his wife.

And now, after another night away from home—and sleeping on that uncomfortable cot—William was getting updates about his wife from the newspaper, of all things. He finished reading the news story, and then read the title of the article again.

CHARGES DROPPED AGAINST MAYORAL CANDIDATE FOLLOWING WIFE'S CONFESSION.

He wondered if he should call to thank Nikki for talking with the district attorney's office. But he did not. William was still angry with her for what happened before, but he felt tenderness at her gesture. *I should have known she'd try to fix this herself, even at personal risk.* He picked up the phone and dialed his attorney. "Did you see the story in today's paper?"

"Yes. Congratulations!" his attorney said.

"Yeah, thanks," William replied, "but what I'm calling about is this: I don't want my wife to have a hard time. See what you can find out at the DA's office about this case."

Olivia materialized at his desk as he hung up. "Hey, great news on the charges being dropped!"

William's voice held no jubilation and his eyes no light. "Yeah, that's great."

"Hey; why the sour mood?"

"Well, I'm just worried about Nikki."

Olivia's frown was instantaneous, but just as quickly, she smoothed her brow. "Well, she did bring it on herself."

William opened his mouth to protest, but closed it. Maybe he wasn't the one to try to fight his wife's battles anymore.

Maybe this separation was for the best.

Chapter 68

Nikki looked around cautiously and slipped into the booth at the back of the restaurant, a baseball cap pulled down low on her head. Large sunglasses covered half her face.

"I didn't expect to hear from you," Spencer said coolly.

"Yeah, well, I didn't expect to have to call you." She had scheduled this meeting with Spencer at this out-of-the-way restaurant after calling him the other day. The waitress approached but Nikki waved her off.

"Hey, hold up," Spencer said to Nikki, then to the waitress, said "She'll have a sweet tea with two lemons."

Nikki's brow raised but she said nothing. Spencer smirked. "That is still how you like it, right?"

Nikki ignored him, but nodded to the waitress, who scurried off.

"So, to what do I owe the pleasure?" Spencer smiled. "I guess you've realized you made the wrong choice, huh?"

He was still so smug.

"Whatever, Spence. This has nothing to do with my husband. This is about you."

"Well, seems that your husband has been in a lot of hot

water lately." Spencer leaned in. "Makes one wonder just what is going on with him. See, if you had stayed with me, you wouldn't be getting dragged through the mud like this."

"Well, if I had stayed with you, there is a lot I wouldn't be doing right now," Nikki snapped. "Namely, living. I'd probably be dead."

Spencer grimaced. "Now, Nikki. Don't be so harsh. We were young and dumb. That was a lifetime ago. A past that's tucked away."

"Yes, which is why I thought you'd be the last person to double-cross me."

"What are you talking about?" Spencer frowned. "How could I have possibly double-crossed you? Remember, you've not even spoken to me in years."

"So, you're going to try to sit here and tell me you didn't rat me out to the newspaper about that credit card bit?"

Spencer's eyebrows drew together. "Is that what this is about?" He lowered his voice. "Don't you think I would think twice about doing something that dumb? No, I had nothing to do with that. Besides, I had no idea you were involved in that thing until it hit the news. How could I have known that?"

Nikki studied him for a beat. Spencer had done a lot of lying to her and had taken her through a lot, but she knew he was telling the truth. "So, your wife didn't tell you she saw me at the hospital back in the summer?"

"My wife? No."

Nikki abruptly stood. "Well, thanks for answering my questions. I've got to run."

"You're not going to stay for lunch?"

"No, I'm picky about who I keep company with."

Chapter 69

Danielle chose not to attend Troy's funeral that weekend, but Nikki still knew her friend's mind would be on the service. She dropped Psalm off at Keedra's and took a bag of groceries to Danielle's.

"I thought I'd fix us something to eat and we could hang out and watch movies or something," Nikki said.

"I'm not really in the mood."

"Well, that's okay," Nikki said. "I know you're probably preoccupied. You can go lie down if you want and I'll just be in the kitchen. I just wanted to be with you today. Because . . . well, just because of everything."

Danielle peeked into the bag. "Did you bring any ice cream?"

"No, you want ice cream?"

"Yeah, I'd love pralines and cream," Danielle said, taking a bite of a slice of pizza she pulled from a plate in the refrigerator.

"Okay. Well, I'll just run back to the store."

Danielle smiled. "Thanks. Get some potato chips too."

Nikki had thought the food she brought would be enough,

but she didn't want to upset Danielle anymore than she already was. So she grabbed her keys and left to get ice cream and potato chips for her friend. Her mind raced as she drove to the grocery store. So much was going on that it was hard to keep it all straight. She was really worried about Danielle, especially because her friend didn't talk much about what was truly bothering her. Losing Troy had to have been a tough blow.

That thought reminded Nikki about losing her own man—maybe not to death, but it hurt just as much. And that thought prompted another one: If Spencer wasn't behind the leak to the press about the credit card scam, then who was?

Nikki fixed a lunch of smothered chicken, mashed potatoes and corn on the cob. She also prepared bananas Foster, one of Danielle's favorite desserts. As she washed the dishes following their meal, Nikki could see her friend's mood seemed to have lifted.

"So, how is work going?" Nikki struck up conversation.

"Girl, don't even ask," Danielle replied. "I have this lesbian nurse hot on my tail, and I'm trying to keep her at bay."

"Is she harassing you? Why don't you report her?"

"No, it's nothing like that," Danielle said. "She's not harassing me. She just keeps dropping hints that she wants to go out."

"What, are you giving off gay signals now?" Nikki laughed.

Danielle grinned. "Maybe. I'll do whatever I have to, to get what I want. And if that means skinning and grinning in some lonely woman's face, then I will."

"Danielle, you've got to stop playing with people's emotions."

"Well, you just have to know what people want. Then you tell them what they want to hear. If I happen to make a comment here and there about how pretty she is and she gets confused and thinks I like her, is that really my fault?"

"Well, just be careful. I'm just glad we're friends because I know you could be one dangerous sista," Nikki said.

"You got that right."

Chapter 70

Danielle lay on the couch, staring at the ceiling while Nikki vacuumed. It was such a shame about Troy. Danielle shook her head. She recalled his visit following that blowup at his place. He had barged into her condo, and after they satisfied their lust, he told her he knew she was the one who had his car towed. He had gone outside ready to drive to work the next morning, only to find an empty parking space. He had cursed at first, sure thugs had stolen his SUV. But a few phone calls to some questionable associates had revealed the car wasn't stolen, but was at a scrap metal lot. He paid big bucks to recover it.

"I don't know what you're talking about," Danielle had feigned innocence.

"Right," he said, "and I'm Santa Claus."

"I'm serious," she had insisted, but he shook his head.

"You are one slick woman," he said, running his hand along her thigh, "but I'll let that slide, 'cause you know how to hook a brother up."

She licked her lips and the conversation was forgotten.

And now he was dead, shot to death and burned. Somebody must have been pretty upset with him about something.

Poor Troy.

Chapter 71

The October primary election was just as Olivia and Nikki had predicted. William collected enough votes to keep him in the race for the big election in November. He didn't even take time to celebrate, because that smaller election felt just like a dress rehearsal—he hoped the general election would produce the win he wanted. Now the contest was between Lo Dark and him.

He had to commend Olivia. In just a short time, she had helped raise his visibility and had given him the edge among the mostly unknown lot running against Dark. Reverend Hick's church had turned out in huge support, as had the members of several other congregations. Now the campaigning kicked into a higher gear as William closed in on Election Day.

Winston kept William busy with back-to-back appointments. William thought if he had to eat one more rubbery piece of chicken and dry potatoes at some civic club luncheon, he would assault the next person who came bearing the offending meal.

But this was all part of the process. And now that the

charges had been dropped and he was the lone challenger to Dark, he was working furiously to get people to forget about their earlier suspicions. Now, as he sat at his desk and read over polling data, he shifted in his chair and rubbed his neck. Pain radiated up and down the right side, into his shoulder. He couldn't even turn to his right, without feeling as if something were pressing into him. He sighed, and stretched.

Olivia looked up from her work. "You okay?"

"Yeah," he said. "My neck is just tight after sleeping on that cot again."

William had been tempted to return home at the prospect of spending yet another night on the narrow cot in the corner of his office. But he pushed the thought from his mind.

"It's no wonder," Olivia said. "You've been sleeping on this ridiculous cot for what, two weeks now? You're coming to my house, and I'm not going to take no for an answer."

He held up his hand and shook his head. "No, it's okay. I'm fine sleeping out here."

"No, you're not. Now, when I leave tonight, you're coming with me."

Chapter 72

Nikki was in no hurry to return to the home that seemed so quiet without her husband, but she knew it was time. She gathered the movies and her purse.

"So, are you sure you're going to be all right?" she asked Danielle.

"Oh, I'm super," Danielle said.

Nikki hesitated, but knew she had to ask. "Danny, would you mind if I ask you a question?"

Danielle peered at her. "Sure. What?"

"I spoke with Spencer the other day."

"You talked to Spencer?" Danielle sat up on the couch. "For what?"

"I asked him if he spilled it about the credit card. He said he didn't."

"Well, what did you expect him to say?" Danielle snapped.

Nikki shook her head. "I don't know," she said. "But I think he's telling the truth. Which brings me to my question. Are you sure nobody else knew about what we were doing?"

"What, do you think I had something to do with the leak?" Danielle looked hurt.

"No, no," Nikki quickly backtracked. "I mean—"

Danielle let out a disgusted grunt and lay back down. "I can't believe you're questioning me like this," she said. "There is no way I would have done that to you. I didn't go and blab to the newspaper. Besides, why would I do that? I'd get in trouble too."

"I'm really sorry," Nikki said. "I was out of line to even question you like that."

"Yeah, you were," Danielle said. "After all this time, you're acting like you don't trust me."

What Danielle had done all those years ago to make Nikki doubt her trustworthiness was in the past, Nikki reminded herself. "Forget I said anything." She leaned down to hug her friend. Nikki turned to leave, then stopped. "You know, I've been wondering something."

"Yeah, what?"

"Is anything that Reverend Chance told you back then helping you cope now, with this new tragedy in your life and all? Is that why you're so relatively calm?"

"Reverend Chance?"

"Yeah, you know, from your counseling sessions."

"Oh. Yeah. He gave me a lot of really good information. I'm so glad we bumped into each other that day at the mall."

"At the . . ." but Nikki bit off her words. Instead, she hugged her friend. "If you need anything, just call me."

Driving home, Nikki's eyes narrowed. She had suspected Danielle was lying about her acquaintance with Reverend Chance, but now she knew for certain because Danielle must have forgotten she had told Nikki she met the pastor at the grocery store. The second time, she said it was the mall.

And what about the credit card leak? Surely Danielle wouldn't go to the newspaper about that behind Nikki's back. But Nikki had to admit, Danielle had betrayed her before. Nikki tried to push from her mind how she felt when she found out Danielle had slept with Nikki's boyfriend while Nikki was home on semester break visiting her family. They had been young and immature then. They had been through a lot and Nikki had forgiven Danielle.

But nagging doubts remained. Her best friend was lying about something. But what was it? And why was she lying?

Chapter 73

William pulled up to the house. He was surprised at the twinge of disappointment he felt at seeing Nikki wasn't home. He let himself in and walked to the bedroom. The house was neat. The cream-colored bedspread covered the bed, with pillows crowning the top. He pulled open a drawer and grabbed more clothes.

He shoved the clothes into his bag and zipped it. He slung it over his shoulder and turned to walk to the door when he almost bumped into his wife.

"Oh. Hi," she said. "I saw the car outside and was wondering what was up."

"Yeah," he said, shrugging the bag on his shoulder. "I needed some more clothes."

The hopeful smile Nikki had disappeared at his words as she spotted the bag on his shoulder. "Oh. You were just getting some more of your things?"

"Yeah," he said, clearing his throat at the awkward moment. "I needed some more underwear and shirts."

"So where are you staying?"

William's eyes shifted just over her head then back to her. He cleared his throat. "Oh, you know, here and there."

"You're not still sleeping at the headquarters, are you?" Nikki frowned. "That won't do your back any good."

"I'm fine." He didn't want to discuss where he was sleeping.

"Well, if you're not there, I know you must be at your mama's house." Nikki tried not to roll her eyes. "I'm sure that's all she needs. She's probably badmouthing me every day, telling you to run to get your divorce."

William let the conversation die, and silence hung between them. Looking at her standing there, looking as pretty as the day they met, he wanted to take her in his arms.

But he didn't.

They stood for a moment, both wanting to say so many words, but neither knowing exactly what to say.

"Well, don't let me hold you up," Nikki said. He knew she thought she was sounding cheery, but the sound was shrill. "I know you were on your way out when I walked in."

"Oh. Yeah," William said. "Well, I'll see you around."

Chapter 74

Nikki sat down hard on the bed in the room William had just so casually left. How could he look her in the face and act as if she were a stranger? She had tried to be nonchalant with William, though her heart felt as if it would split with every syllable he uttered as he said, "Well, I'll see you around."

Like I'm a freaking dog he saw on the street, she thought despondently.

She reached for the cell phone. The distance was too much to take. Nikki couldn't stand being separated. She would just apologize again, even beg at his feet, if necessary. She just wanted her husband back. Nikki felt as if she could not live without him.

"Hello?" William's quick hello startled her.

"Hi," she said.

"Yes?"

"I . . . was. . . ." She cast about for the words. How could she let him know that she would simply die if he didn't come back to her? Didn't he already know she couldn't survive that?

"Spit it out, if you have something to say," William said.

"Will . . ."

"Look, Nikki, I'm on the phone with Olivia. What do you want?"

"Oh. Well, I'll let you get back to your call."

"Thanks. Bye."

Nikki felt her mouth go dry and a lump lodge in her throat. She could feel the distance between them growing. Would William ever love her again?

Chapter 75

Danielle stepped into her office and found a bouquet of flowers on her desk. *I know this woman didn't send me flowers!* she thought. She quickly snatched the card out and read it. "Thinking of you, Raymond."

"Hi, do you like the flowers?" Raymond said, stepping around the desk.

"Oh, they're beautiful," Danielle said, a careful mix of appreciation and grief crossing her face. "It's so hard to believe Troy is gone."

"I was quite disturbed to hear of your bereavement," Raymond said. "You've been through so much. Your best friend's little girl's death, so much at work, your family, now this."

"Yes," Danielle said, lowering her head. "It's been very rough for me."

"Well, I don't mean to intrude, but do you have someone helping you through this?"

Danielle shook her head. "No . . . not really," she shook her head sadly. "My best friend is pretty shaken up from losing her little girl, and my family . . . well, like I said, they don't speak to me. I've been home alone, crying."

She shuddered, and tried to smile. "But I'm not going to let anything get me down. I'm just going to try to get back to work and do the best job I can."

"Oh, don't worry about your case load," Raymond said. "I've handled some things on your desk. And Nurse Smart said she would divvy up your active files until you are back on track. She's been really accommodating to you lately. It's like night and day."

"Yes, she's been kind," Danielle said softly. Then she made an exaggerated effort to smile. "Well, I'll go and reclaim my work. I don't want to be an unfair burden on anyone."

"Oh, it's no problem at all!" Raymond said. "I'll help you in any way I can."

She patted his arm. "Thank you, Raymond. If you can, get my reports to me at least an hour before shift change, so I can go over them and at least be aware of what's in them." She flashed a quick smile. "You're so sweet."

Chapter 76

MAYORAL CANDIDATE DIVORCING WIFE FOR MANAGER.

The headline slapped Nikki. What was this? She snatched up the paper, her eyes hungrily consuming the words next to a smiling photo of William. "Beleaguered Mayoral Candidate William Broussard has dumped his wife, an admitted identity thief, and has lately been seen sporting around town with his campaign manager, the Ivy League educated daughter of the late Reverend Chance."

"Ma'am, are you going to pay for that?" the agitated clerk asked, pointedly eyeing the newspaper in Nikki's clenched fist.

"Oh . . . yeah," Nikki said, struggling to regain her composure. She added the newspaper to her tiny stack of groceries, hurriedly paid and fled the store. Back in the SUV, she jammed the key in the ignition, then opened the newspaper again.

"This can't be true," she mumbled, the words on the page blurred. She sniffled back the tears, though, again refusing to let them fall. During this latest ordeal, she had refused to break down or even to let a tear escape her eyes.

But this time, it was hard.

I'm going to get to the bottom of this! She gunned the engine and tore off for the campaign office.

Nikki hopped out of the vehicle and strode quickly to the door. She paused for a moment to regain her composure, then stepped into the building. The air outside had a light touch of coolness, but the air conditioner whirred as if the calendar said July and not October.

Winston flew by her. "Hi, Nikki, excuse me," he said, stepping around her. "I'm on my way to meet our candidate at a briefing."

"William isn't here?"

"No," Olivia said, stepping next to Nikki. She waved Winston off. "William is a very busy man. Especially now that his wife has almost single-handedly destroyed his career. But we are working to repair the damage."

Nikki recoiled as if slapped. "Excuse me?"

"You heard what I said," Olivia said coolly. "You have wrecked William's life. I don't know why it took him so long to finally realize you're just some backwoods, low-class girl. Certainly not the caliber of person he needs on his arm as the future mayor."

Nikki regained her voice. "William's and my relationship is of no concern to you."

"See, that's where you are wrong," Olivia said, quickly glancing around and then lowering her voice. "Your relationship with William is every bit my concern. William is a good man. A good, strong man. And he is going places. I have sat around and watched him follow behind you. But I knew if I just played it cool long enough, you would do something to mess it up. And then he'd see clearly that I am the better woman. I have education. I have status. I have money."

Nikki swallowed. She knew from speaking with William

that Olivia was Ivy League educated and had spent some time working in the former president's administration before moving back home following her husband's death.

Nikki felt she was just a country girl who got a scholarship to go to college. She'd never even been to Washington, much less worked for a president. Nikki's insecurity made her shift from one foot to the other.

Olivia's pumps probably cost more than Nikki's entire outfit, Nikki knew. Olivia was in her late 20s or early 30s, Nikki wasn't sure, and had a solid build. The woman wasn't small by any means, and in fact, the jacket on her navy suit was just long enough to hide heavy thighs. She wore diamonds in her ears, heavy makeup and big hair. The combination commanded attention.

Nikki touched her own natural hair, with its curls that grazed her neck. Maybe she should have taken Trudy McWilliams's advice and straightened her hair. She looked down at her own jeans and T-shirt. Her face was devoid of makeup, and her slender frame had never held an extra ounce of fat. Nikki knew some men liked women with "meat on their bones," and she would never be that woman.

"Well, you just stay out of our business," Nikki finally managed to say. "I'll take this up with my husband."

Olivia smirked. "Yes, I'll be sure to tell William you stopped by. Do you have a newspaper, by chance? I was wondering if there was anything interesting in there today."

Chapter 77

Reverend Hicks pulled William aside as the media event wrapped up. "You've still got a decent shot at winning this mayor's office," the older man said. "That's as long as you don't get into anymore trouble."

"Yes, Reverend, I know," William said. "I'm doing my best to just focus on my campaign and not worry too much about the negativity out there."

"Well, all that negativity was created by your own poor decisions," Reverend Hicks chided. "Yours and your wife's. You two need to get it together. Don't let all the work I've done for you be in vain."

"Thank you, Reverend," William said, assuming Hicks was fishing for appreciation.

"You can thank me by winning," Reverend Hicks said. "Just keep doing your speeches and meeting with as many folks as you can. And stay out of trouble."

"I will, sir," William said, looking for a way to exit. He hoped Winston would arrive soon. Just as William's eyes scanned the room, he saw Winston enter. William smiled at Reverend Hicks.

"Sir, Winston is here to take me to my next engagement," William said. "It's been a pleasure talking with you."

Reverend Hicks spotted Winston. "Okay," he said to William. "I'll see you later."

William quickly walked toward Winston. "Let's go!" he hissed, and Winston followed William out of the building. William climbed into the car with Winston. He rubbed his eyes. "Man, so many people have pinned their hopes on me, but I just wonder if I'm making any difference."

"Sure, you are," Winston said. "I got numbers this afternoon. Your points are up, now that you've gotten rid of the PR problem Nikki was causing."

"Well, I didn't *get rid* of anything," William said. "Did you find out how that story got in the newspaper to begin with?"

"No, I didn't, but it's a good thing," Winston said. "It at least distances you from the issue of the identity theft. You know I like Nikki. She fed me plenty of times when we were in school. But right now, she's a liability."

"Man, don't talk about my wife like that!"

Winston raised an eyebrow. "Well, according to the paper, she won't be your wife for long."

William shook his head, recalling the latest story. "I will fire whoever told that to the press. I can't believe that stuff ran. There is nothing going on between Olivia and me. And I certainly don't need Nikki to see that story. We already have enough problems."

Chapter 78

Nikki's eyes fell on a copy of the newspaper with the offending story in it. Her face threatened to crumble as her eyes again took in the story that announced the demise of her marriage, but Nikki managed to keep her composure. She turned on her heel and quickly walked back to her vehicle. Her breath came in short bursts as she struggled to control her emotions. Hurt, anger and fear churned in her heart. This was something she had never expected from William.

But then reason prevailed. *Olivia is lying. My husband would not do this to me,* Nikki told herself. She backed out of the parking lot, then hit on the brakes. She would find out what was going on.

Things had never been like this between them before, but she wasn't sure how to fix any of it. It seemed that one bad thing led to another.

Nikki would wait in the parking lot until William arrived. She was glad Danielle had offered to pick up Psalm from after-school care when she got off work. It was a surprising move from Danielle, who rarely baby sat Psalm, but Nikki knew the woman's motivation: Danielle felt threatened by Keedra and had insisted on picking up the girl today, as if to stake her claim.

The offer gave Nikki the freedom to force a confrontation with William. She would ask him about Olivia and that news story as soon as she saw him this evening. He would tell her the news story was wrong and Olivia was a liar. Then they would go home and work out their problems.

Nikki pulled into a corner parking space and waited for William to return. Nervousness filled her stomach.

Chapter 79

Danielle sat at the back of the cold room, silently observing as Nurse Smart led a group session for patients. The air conditioner clanked loudly and Nurse Smart had to raise her voice as she moderated this special session. This was really one of Danielle's responsibilities, but Nurse Smart had insisted Danielle take it easy.

You don't have to tell me twice. Danielle leaned against the wall, crossing her arms over her chest. Even in her scrubs, she knew she looked good.

A patient glanced around the room and his eyes rested on her for a split second. *I know he wants me,* Danielle mused. She casually averted her glance, though not before she smoothed her hair with one hand.

I don't know what it is. All my life everybody has tried to get with me, she thought. It all started with her uncle, who let her bounce on his lap and later, played grownup games with her. And then growing up and even in college, so many guys had hit on her. She shrugged when she thought of all the girls who had gotten mad at her when their boyfriends came sniffing around. It wasn't her fault she was so beautiful. Besides, something must not have been right on the home front to begin with if their men came to her, is how she saw it. It wasn't her fault, she had always told herself.

The most imperceptible twinge niggled at her conscience as she recalled the summer between freshman and sophomore year of college when she slept with Nikki's boyfriend—this was way before William—one weekend when Nikki went home to visit her family.

She still wasn't sure how the two had ended up in his bed. And really, it wasn't her fault he wanted her, she thought. Just like it wasn't her fault Nurse Smart wanted her and kept dropping all those hints. Even Raymond was smothering her with attention. Then there were the patients. They wanted her too, Danielle was certain.

Everybody craved her. Everybody it seemed, except for Troy.

It's so sad, what happened to him, she thought, absentmindedly twisting a strand of her hair.

Chapter 80

Nighttime was falling when Winston pulled into the parking lot of the headquarters and William stepped out of his car. He already looked like a polished politician, in his charcoal gray suit and freshly shaved head. He had a sophisticated air about him, as if he had been wearing suits all his life. The sight of him jarred Nikki, and she longed for what they once shared. She longed, even, for that goofy William whose skinny arms seemed to extend forever and his elbows seemed to get all over the place. She'd take anything. Before she could move, though, Olivia deftly emerged from the office, her purse in hand.

"Why don't we knock off early?" Olivia said. "Come on, gentlemen, let's go grab something to eat. I know you're exhausted."

Nikki fumbled with the latch on the door and jerked. Her eyes flew to the lock and she realized it must have automatically clicked when she first got in. She pressed the lever and sprang from her vehicle, then quickly crossed the parking lot to her husband. "William, we've got to talk."

"William, I must update you on a critical situation," Olivia said, moving a step closer to William—too close, Nikki thought—and taking on an imperious tone.

"William, I need to talk to you. Now." Nikki's tone was urgent.

William looked from one to the other. Winston cleared his throat. "I'm not much feeling like going out to eat, Olivia. I'm going home. I'm going to work on some things on my laptop."

He quickly climbed into his car and sped off.

"Let me just get inside and put these things down," William said, picking up his brief case. He moved stiffly, and Nikki could tell he didn't want to be there, to have this conversation.

Desperation gave her energy and boldness. She grabbed his arm: "William, it'll only take a moment."

She felt him hesitate, but he twisted away from her and continued into the building. Olivia tried to elbow her way into the door first, but Nikki slipped past and raced to William's desk.

"What's up with that story in the newspaper?" Nikki demanded.

"Can we discuss this later?" William asked, looking around the room. It was empty, save for the three of them and an obviously eavesdropping volunteer in a corner. Nikki knew William hated discussing his private life in public, but what choice did she have?

"No," Nikki said. "What's up with you and Olivia?"

William frowned and looked disgusted. "Nothing is up with me and Olivia," he hissed. "I know you didn't believe that crap you read in the paper."

Uncertainty crossed Nikki's face and she relaxed as she realized her fears were misplaced. Of course those reports were false. William loves me. She breathed the words to herself.

Olivia touched William's arm, letting her long nails drag

down his arm a bit too long, and Nikki's heart sank. "Okay, well, I'm leaving," Olivia said, cutting her eyes at Nikki. "I'll see you at home. Should I hold dinner?"

Hold dinner? Nikki's eyes flew to William's face and he tried to shake his head, but she didn't wait around to listen. So it was true. And he was living with Olivia? Nikki raced from the room, this time, letting tears run down her cheeks. Olivia's voice from their last encounter seemed to mock her as it owned the space in Nikki's consciousness. "*I'm the better woman. I'm the better woman. I'm the. . . .*" Nikki tried to shake the other woman's words from her mind.

She saw the Protégé parked at the edge of the lot and instinctively, she fled toward it. She wanted to touch nothing that had anything to do with that campaign, and that included the Yukon she had been driving. She found her key and unlocked the door. Nikki hopped inside and backed onto the street, the tires squealing. She could not believe the rumor was true.

She couldn't believe William was sleeping with Olivia.

Chapter 81

William slammed his hand down on his desk and cursed. "Why'd you do that?"

Olivia looked at him with big, innocent eyes. "What are you talking about?"

"Why'd you go and say that?"

"I only asked a question," Olivia said. "I was trying to be nice. I just needed to know if you wanted me to save you something to eat."

"Olivia . . ." he stopped. "Forget it."

"What's wrong, William?" Olivia pressed. "All I've tried to do is to be helpful to you. And now you're biting my head off. Might I remind you, all this is your wife's fault. If she hadn't—"

"Hey, don't worry about my wife," William spoke, and his tone was sharper than he intended. He sighed. "Look, I'm sorry. I know you were just being nice. I'm just stressed. And I can't believe that story showed up in the paper. Like I need more problems between me and my wife."

"Well, surely you don't think she believed that story, do you?"

William looked at her sharply.

"Well, I just know that if I were married, I'd trust my man," Olivia said. "And I would know the type of man he was. I certainly wouldn't believe some newspaper over his word. But I guess maybe your wife doesn't know you at all."

"My wife knows me fine," William said, but he was beginning to wonder.

Olivia sidled up to William and rubbed his forearm. "I hate to see you like this," she said. "Come on, let's go home. I'll fix you something good to eat and rub your shoulders."

Chapter 82

Nikki went straight to Danielle's house, thoughts tripping over each other as they chased around her head. All this time, she had thought her marriage was strong, better than everyone else's. But now she could see she had been wrong.

Forget William! She railed silently.

She climbed out of the Protégé and banged on Danielle's door. Danielle opened the door and Psalm raced out. "Hi, Mama!"

Nikki struggled to put on a bright smile. "Hi, precious. Did you have fun with Auntie Dee Dee?"

"I did," Psalm said. "We watched TV and she let me put on makeup."

"That's nice, dear." Nikki patted the girl's head.

"What's wrong with you?" Danielle asked, taking a quick glance at Nikki before going back to working her hips and legs with Billy Blanks and Tae Bo on the TV screen.

"I'll tell you later," Nikki said. "Thanks for keeping her for me. I'll just grab her and get out of your hair."

"Hey, you look upset," Danielle said. She did a lunge

and kick combination. Her voice came out in short bursts. "Just . . . wait . . . 'til . . . I . . . . finish . . . . this."

Nikki plopped down on the couch, grateful to have a listening ear—even if she had to wait.

Ten minutes later, Danielle flopped down next to her, wiping sweat from her forehead. "Psalm, go pass me my water from the refrigerator."

Taking a swig from the bottle Psalm had brought, Danielle turned to Nikki. "Now, what's wrong with you?"

Psalm raced off to the bathroom to continue playing in makeup. Nikki rattled off the news about William and Olivia, careful to speak in low tones so Psalm would not hear.

Danielle's mouth fell open. "With Olivia?"

"Yeah."

"I should have known she had a hand in this," Danielle said with a faraway look in her eyes.

"You know Olivia?"

"Oh, no," Danielle said quickly, refocused on her friend. "I was just speaking . . . in general. You know how women are. Always out to get your man."

"Yeah," Nikki sighed. "I can't believe William would allow himself to be drawn in though."

"Boring old William? That's unbelievable. I thought he was one of the good guys."

"Yeah, me too."

"Well, look, you don't need him anyway. You don't even have to go back to that funky house he put you up in. Why don't you and Psalm crash here?"

"Really?"

"Yeah, I know you don't want to have to go back to that house and look at all those memories. Besides, you don't need anything from William Broussard."

Nikki's smile was watery. "Oh, thanks, Danny!" she said, "You're right, I don't want to go back to that house."

"Then, it's settled," Danielle said. "You know where

everything is. You and Psalm can get the guest bedroom. You can just go get your stuff tomorrow. It'll be fun, just like a big slumber party."

Nikki nodded. At least she still had her best friend. And to think, she had doubted Danielle a few days ago. Nikki felt ashamed.

Chapter 83

William went into Olivia's spare bedroom that had become his resting place for the moment. He shut the door and leaned back on the bed, his legs extended over the edge. How had his life gotten so complicated? Here he was estranged from his wife and in a campaign he felt he would lose.

His mind turned over all of the developments of the past few weeks and his head hurt. He now had more access to money than ever before, a nice home and people were beginning to know who he was. People like Reverend Hicks were showing up in his life, offering him the means to attain things he would not be able to have on his own.

But was all this worth it? Was it worth his marriage? He had a house he was not even living in. He had a wife he couldn't communicate with anymore and a campaign he was not sure how he wound up in to begin with.

William's eyes roamed the room, landing on a Bible in a bookcase. He sat up and reached for it, pulling it onto his lap as he perched on the bed, his back against the headboard.

He had to admit, his prayer life had suffered quite a bit lately. He couldn't even remember the last time he had studied the Bible—not since Reverend Chance died, it seemed. William opened it now and his eyes fell on James 5:13: "Is any among you afflicted? Let him pray."

He sure did feel afflicted. At every turn, William had trouble. Maybe he should take some time to pray over his situation. But what should he even pray for? William sighed and closed his eyes. "Lord, I just need help."

He paused. His mind went back to the dreams he and Nikki had spent hours weaving. They would chase their political dream. He would run for a small office at first in city government, gain favor, do a good job, then move on to bigger and better—a statewide office, on the way to a national post.

Nikki would be home with their children and she'd sometimes travel with him during school breaks. He would give her a big house, vacations in The Hamptons . . . the works.

But why was it that they were at odds?

He stood up, and after a moment of silence, announced to the empty room: "I'm going to get this thing straight with my wife."

Chapter 84

Danielle went to her bedroom and quietly shut the door. She looked around, taking in the walls, floor and ceiling. This was supposed to be her sanctuary, but she couldn't be too careful.

She picked up the cordless phone from the night stand and examined it, then carefully placed it back on its base. All her life, she had known she had to watch her back. And with what happened between Troy and her, she had been feeling lately like she had to be on her guard even more.

She couldn't let anything slip past her. She heard a sound and stood perfectly still. Not hearing anything for a moment, she eased next to her door and stood next to it, listening. She thought she heard Nikki whispering in the other room, but couldn't be sure. "Did I just hear my name?" she wondered out loud.

Danielle inched even closer to the door and slowly eased it open. Silence. *I know they're talking about me. I know they're watching me. But they're not going to get me*, she vowed.

She closed the door and locked it, then wedged a chair under the knob.

She stretched out on top of the covers, fully dressed, and fell asleep with the light in her face.

Chapter 85

William sat in his favorite chair in the living room at the house he had briefly shared with his wife, waiting on Nikki to return. It was late. He glanced at his watch. He had been sitting there for two hours.

He knew she had to come home soon. She would not want to keep Psalm out too late. When she arrived, he knew they would be able to talk through this thing and put it behind them.

He sprang up when he heard tires crunching on rocks outside. He looked out of the window and his heart sank as he realized it was just somebody turning around in the driveway.

William sat back down. His mind turned to the years he had spent with his wife. They had been through so many hard times, but they had never quit. And he almost had quit on them this time. But he was ready to set this right. The discord between them had gone on too long, and it was time he put an end to it.

"Where is Nikki?," he wondered as the minutes ticked by.

He pulled out his cell phone and dialed. A sleepy Nikki answered. "Hey, it's me," he said, surprise in his voice. "You asleep?"

"Yes, I am. And why are you calling me?"

"Why am I calling you?"

"You heard me."

William frowned. He wasn't used to this tone from Nikki. She usually catered to him, and now she was being rather short. "I'm at the house, waiting on you."

"Well, wait all you want," she retorted. "I'm not going back there."

"You're not coming back?" William asked in surprise.

"Did I stutter?"

"Baby, we need to talk. We've got to settle this thing between us."

"Seems like you already settled it when you got in Olivia's bed."

"Baby, it's not even like that. I—"

"Save it, Will."

The phone went dead in his hand.

William sat in the easy chair, stunned. She couldn't really believe that. But he knew infidelity was the one thing Nikki would never tolerate. He could still hear the anger in her voice when she told him about the time Danielle had slept with her boyfriend. But Nikki said she forgave her friend, though she dumped the boyfriend.

She knew him better than that, William reasoned. Surely Nikki knew he wouldn't do that.

She's just mad right now. I'll talk some sense into her in the morning.

He had to.

Chapter 86

Nikki put the cell phone back on the chair next to the bed, sleep now gone. She slowly eased out of the bed, trying not to awaken her daughter. She tiptoed to the door and squeezed out of it. William's call had jarred her.

Why was he calling now? She had pleaded with him for weeks to try to talk this thing through, but he wouldn't have it. "Oh, but now he wants to talk to me after he's been sleeping with old what's-her-name. I don't think so," she hissed as defiance blazed in her heart.

Nikki knew she had to get her thoughts together. She pulled open a kitchen drawer, searching for a pen and paper. She grabbed a blue pen and found a small spiral notebook. She flipped through it, searching for a clean page.

Danielle sure has some ugly handwriting. Good thing she types most of her stuff, Nikki mused with a half smile. Her best friend was beautiful but this writing was not. It reminded Nikki of someone else's but she couldn't place it. She frowned as her eyes slid over words on one of the lined sheets. "Chance funeral. 11 a.m. Olivia has details."

Why did she write down info about Reverend Chance's funeral? Nikki wanted to know.

"What are you doing in my drawer?"

Danielle's voice startled Nikki and she jumped. She laughed, a bit nervously. "Girl, I didn't know you were right there."

Danielle walked to the counter. "I see," she said, taking in the notepad and pen. "What are you looking for?"

"Oh, I just needed something to write with," Nikki said, holding up the pen and paper, grinning sheepishly. "William woke me up, so I decided to come in here and just try to jot down some things floating around in my head."

Danielle eyed Nikki for a long moment, then nodded. "Oh. Okay."

The next morning, Danielle did a final inspection of her room before grabbing her purse and keys to head to work. She did a mental check of her duffel bag, making sure she had a good change of clothes. She always kept the bag in her car in case she wanted to ditch her work scrubs in favor of something sexy after she left work.

"I fixed you some pancakes and eggs," Nikki said, stepping into Danielle's bedroom. "Do you want orange juice or milk?"

"Oh, don't worry about me, I don't need anything," Danielle said. "I'm already late."

"When has that ever stopped you?" Nikki laughed.

"Well, I've been late a lot these few months so I need to try to do better," Danielle said. "My boss has been really cool lately, but still, you know there is a limit."

"You mean the boss you've been flirting with for the raise?"

"I already got the raise," Danielle said, "and I can't help it if people think I'm desirable."

Nikki cast her eyes skyward. "Okay. Well, I'm going to fix Psalm something to eat then."

When Nikki stepped out of the room, Danielle's eyes returned to her own reflection in the mirror. "I know she's spying on me," Danielle told the image staring back at her. "I saw her going through my drawer last night. But they're not going to get me."

Chapter 87

Nikki's cell phone rang and she saw the call was from her husband. She sent it to voicemail. She was not going to talk to him. Instead, she finished washing the breakfast dishes. The phone rang again ten minutes later.

She pressed the button and again, the call went to voicemail.

The phone immediately rang again. Nikki sighed in annoyance. She knew William would keep calling until she talked to him. She grabbed the phone. "Hello?"

"Hey, it's me," William said.

"I know who this is."

"So are you going to talk to me now?"

"For what?" she said, sticking her hand into the warm soapy water to pull out the stopper and let the sink drain.

"So we can reconcile," William said, as if the answer should have been obvious.

"Oh, now you want to reconcile?" Nikki needled. "So, you're tired of Olivia's bed already?"

"I told you, nothing is going on between us."

"So why are you staying at her house?"

"Because I needed a place to crash."

"What, you didn't have a home? You didn't have a wife? William, I don't want to hear this mess. Leave me alone. Goodbye."

Again, she hung up on him.

"Why is she being so difficult?" William fumed in frustration, letting the phone clatter onto the desk.

"William, we've got to get a move on. You have to give a speech in forty minutes," Winston said. "Let's get out of here."

"You didn't come home last night," Olivia accused, walking to his desk. She had been on the phone when he arrived at the office 30 minutes ago.

"I was at home. My home," William said coolly.

Olivia's eyebrows shot up and a vein pounded in her forehead. "You went back home?"

William looked at her sharply. "Yes, is that a problem?"

"Oh. Oh, no," she said, but he could tell she was agitated. "I just didn't know. You didn't tell me."

"Olivia, you're not my keeper," William chided. She was starting to get on his nerves.

"I'm not trying to be," Olivia shot back. "I'm just trying to be a friend."

"Well, just chill. I have a lot going on, as you well know."

"So, are you moving back into your house then?"

William opened his mouth, then shut it. He had no idea. If his wife wasn't there, what was the point?

"I need a job," Nikki said flatly. She stood in Joe Smiles's office; on the wall in front of her was a line of dramatic photos, even the accident photo she had taken more than a month ago. "Joe, you've got to hire me."

Joe chewed his bottom lip and slowly shook his head, his ruddy cheeks flushed. "Nikki, I've told you before, I would if I could," he said. "But I can't. The newspaper is really concerned about liability."

"But the charges have been dropped against my husband and those against me have been downgraded to misdemeanors; and I'm paying restitution." She paused, frustration creeping into her voice. "Well, I would be paying restitution if I had a job."

Joe continued to shake his head. "I wish there was something I could do. I really do."

Nikki stood in front of him, despair written across her face. She leaned over his desk. "Joe, come on," she pleaded. "We go way back. How many times have I freelanced something for you? How many times have I gotten you out of binds with a photo here or a photo there? You know my work."

"Nikki, it's not about your work," Joe said in a regretful tone. "You are one of the most talented photographers I've seen in my whole career. That's not the issue. The issue is that legal thing. If it was up to me, I'd hire you in a sec. But it's not up to me."

"Joe, isn't there something you can do?" Nikki searched his face. "I have a daughter to support. She needs things—food, clothes. I really need this job, Joe."

But Joe shook his head. "I'm sorry, Nikki. I can't help you."

Disappointed, Nikki walked with leaden steps out of Joe's office, climbed into her vehicle, and let her head fall to the steering wheel. What would she do? She had to get a job. She had to be able to provide for her child.

Bitterness crowded into her consciousness as she thought back just a few short months. She had been docile and sitting by while her husband practically forbade her to get a job, even declining a photography position at a magazine. And now here she was, almost begging to work and couldn't get anywhere.

I don't know what made me trust my whole future to a man, she thought in anger. I'll never do that again. I don't care how in love I feel. I'll always be able to take care of myself.

Thank God. At least I have Danielle.

Chapter 88

Danielle wrapped up her last session and ushered two patients back to their rooms. As she turned to leave them, Nurse Smart materialized at her side. "Hi," Danielle said, surprise registering on her face.

"I've been trying to catch up with you all week," Nurse Smart said, with a bright smile. "If you're not doing anything after work, maybe we can grab dinner somewhere."

Danielle searched her mind for an excuse, but knew she had run out a long time ago. She nodded and patted the woman's arm. "That sounds great. Where do you want to go?"

Danielle sat across the table from Nurse Smart, nodding as the woman chatted in animated fashion about her last relationship. The woman's voice seemed to drone on, and every now and then, Danielle would mutter encouragingly as she let her eyes roam around the room. It never failed, no matter where she was, people would be watching her. *Look at them, checking me out. They don't think I notice, but I do*, she observed, lightly touching her hair and straightening up in her chair.

Moments later, they had their plates. Nurse Smart dominated the conversation, but Danielle did not mind. She didn't have much to say. All she wanted was to get through the meal and return home so she could take a long, hot shower and relax. She was constantly on edge these days and knew she needed to find a way to calm down.

When they parted after dinner, Nurse Smart smiled. "It was really nice spending time with you," she said. "Maybe we can get together again soon."

"Sure," Danielle said and quickly ducked into her Lexus. She waved at Nurse Smart and drove off.

Nikki sat in the middle of the floor at Danielle's, a plastic cup of sweet tea at her side and the newspaper classifieds spread in front of her. Ink stained the tips of her fingers as she scoured the ads, searching for jobs. She picked up the telephone, eyeing the number of a listed vacancy.

"Do you still have the opening for the receptionist?"

"No, I'm sorry, we just hired someone."

Shoot! "Okay. Thank you."

She scratched that off the list and called the next. "Is the position for a cashier still open?"

"No, we're not hiring at the moment."

"But the ad in the newspaper—"

"Ma'am, we're not hiring."

Nikki sighed as she pressed the END button on the phone. She had tried getting a photographer's job at the newspaper, had even called the small weekly newspaper to see if they were hiring, but both turned her down. *I don't know how to do anything*, she thought sadly. *Who wants to hire some housewife whose only skills are changing diapers and fixing dinner?*

Despondent, broke and near tears, she sighed. She refused to let the tears fall, though. That, she would not do. "I will beat this thing."

She looked at Psalm, who was sucking a grape Popsicle. "Don't get that on Auntie Dee Dee's carpet," she told the child.

"I want to see my daddy," Psalm said.

Nikki stifled a sigh. Of course the child missed William. Nikki touched Psalm's arm. "Okay. We'll call him in a minute, all right?"

"No, I want to call him now," Psalm insisted.

"Psalm, Mommy's busy right now," Nikki said. "I'm trying to make some phone calls."

"I want to call my daddy!" Psalm stomped.

"Psalm, stop that whining," Nikki said. "We will call your daddy in a moment. For now, finish up your Popsicle and then go on back over there and finish coloring. And please, be quiet. I'm trying to make some important phone calls so I can get a job and get us a new place to live," Nikki said, wiping a purple droplet from her daughter's chin.

Psalm poked her lip out but did as she was told.

Nikki turned her attention back to the classifieds. She picked up the phone but it rang before she could dial out. "Hello?"

"Hello? I'm looking for . . . is this the Danielle Esperanza residence?" the male voice asked with hesitation.

"Oh, yeah," Nikki said. "Yes, this is the right number. I'm just a houseguest. I'm her best friend."

The voice on the other end instantly warmed. "Oh. Nikki," concern dripped from his voice.

"Do I know you?" Nikki asked, intrigued that he knew her name.

"No, you probably don't," he said. "I'm sorry. I'm being rude. I'm Raymond. I work with Danielle."

"Oh, well, nice to meet you," Nikki said. It felt good to

know her best friend had apparently spoken so well of her, if the warmth in the man's voice was any indication. "Hey, I know this is a really bad time for you, but I just want to let you know I'm so sorry to hear about the passing of your daughter," Raymond said.

Nikki almost dropped the phone. "The passing of my daughter?"

"Yes, Danielle told me she died a few weeks ago, from a birth defect, I believe? I know it's been hard on you. Danielle has taken it hard too. We've all been pitching in at work to help her out. Between your child's loss and the murder of her fiancé, she's been through so much."

Raymond's words clanged around Nikki's head. She managed to mutter a few words to Raymond and tell him that she would let Danielle know he called.

What was going on? Why did Danielle lie about Psalm? A chill ran through Nikki.

Chapter 89

William high-fived Winston and a volunteer rushed to hug him. Olivia eased next to him and planted a kiss on his right cheek. "Congratulations," she said softly.

"Thanks," he said and turned to face the room. "This is the break we needed," he told his staff, with a Tiger Woods fist-pump in the air. "This is excellent news. Thanks to each and every one of you for your hard work and for sticking by me with so much going on."

The most recent poll results were the first significant pieces of good news for the campaign. His numbers had shot up, he was getting good name recognition and positive identification.

The election was only days away. As chatter erupted around him, William eased down into his seat, and reached for the phone. He had to share his good news with his wife.

"What are you doing?" Olivia asked, staying his hand. "You've just gotten the best news of the season and you're just sitting there? Come on, let's get out of here and go celebrate!"

He put the phone back down.

* * *

Danielle stepped into her condo. "Hey, girl," she greeted Nikki, dropping her keys to the counter.

Nikki slowly stood from where she sat on the floor, pushing aside newspapers. Danielle cast a sidelong glance. "You all right?"

"Danielle, we need to talk." Nikki's tone was grim.

"Okay, what?"

"I've seen some really weird things going on lately, and I need to know what's up."

Danielle grabbed a diet soda from the refrigerator, then turned to face Nikki. "Well, stop acting so secretive. What are you talking about?"

"Someone named Raymond called here for you."

"Oh, Raymond," Danielle said, smiling. "He's so cute. He works with me. I'd maybe even be into him, but he is just too nice. What did he want?"

"Well, he asked me how I was doing."

"So?"

"Wanted to express his condolences for the death of my daughter."

Danielle stood perfectly still for a beat. "What was he talking about?"

"That's what I want to know. Why would he think my child died?"

Danielle shrugged and turned up her soda, taking a long, slow swig. "He must have gotten you mixed up with somebody else."

"No, he seemed pretty certain he meant me," Nikki said, closing the gap between them. "And then I know you were lying about meeting Reverend Chance."

Danielle's eyes flashed and she slammed the soda down on the counter, spilling a drop. "What are you accusing me of? You trying to call me a liar?"

"Danny, I don't know what's going on." Nikki reached to

touch her friend's arm. "I'm just trying to figure it out. Is there something here you're not telling me?"

Danielle jerked away. "I can't believe this! I've opened my home to you and you come in here snooping around and accusing me of being a liar! I don't have to take this."

"I feel like there is so much going on, so many questions," Nikki said. "You seem so . . . different. You're lying. You're being evasive."

"Don't try to flip this around on me! I'm not the one who is tripping," Danielle said. "That's you! All I've tried to do is be your friend."

Nikki held up a hand. "You know what? We're both getting out of control. Let's just take a step back and calm down."

"No, you calm down!" Danielle said, stalking to her bedroom. "I'm going to bed. I don't need this stress."

She slammed the door so hard the pictures on the wall shook.

Chapter 90

Danielle stood in the shower for a long time, letting the hot water wash away the argument with Nikki. "See, I knew something was up," Danielle nodded. "She's spying on me, they all are. But I'm going to beat them." She turned off the water and grabbed her towel to dry off.

She stepped from the shower and bent to look under the sink. Not finding what she was looking for, she opened the cabinet and searched. "Where is my padlock?"

She still didn't find it, but wasn't deterred. She would have to be extra careful from now on. Nikki was watching her and she knew others around were, too. She would put a lock on her door. And when she went to work, she would put one there too.

She slathered peach-scented lotion on and lit a candle in hopes of chasing away the bad feelings.

Chapter 91

William hung up the phone following his conversation with Psalm, happy to hear her voice. He scowled though, when he recalled how terse Nikki had been with him. He had hoped she'd be calm by now, but she seemed just as set today on not talking with him as she had been earlier. When she phoned him, she had said Psalm had been asking to speak with him. But she didn't say much beyond that.

"You look worried; you want me to rub your shoulders?" Olivia asked, walking across the living room in a soft, blue terry cloth robe.

"No, I'm fine," William said, standing. "I'm going to head to my room."

Olivia stopped in front of him. "You don't have to go to that room if you don't want to."

"And where would I go?" William looked at her, with his right brow raised quizzically.

"You could . . . you could go to my room," she said, and reached out to touch his chest.

William sidestepped her. "Better yet, I think I need to go see my wife." He grabbed his keys and made a quick exit.

He drove to Danielle's condo and knocked on the door. Nikki opened the door, and he saw the surprise in her eyes.

The surprise was quickly replaced by anger, and Nikki moved to slam the door when Psalm squealed. "Daddy!" the child squeezed past her mother and hugged her father's legs. He picked her up, kissing the top of her head. His eyes were on Nikki.

"I wasn't expecting you," she said sharply, and turned. She didn't close the door though, and William walked in behind her. "Psalm was on her way to bed. It's late."

"Mommy, can I stay up with my daddy, please?"

"Psalm, you have school tomorrow," Nikki said.

"Nikki, I've not spent any time with her lately," William said softly. "Come on. Let me see her for a little while."

"Please, Mommy!" Psalm begged and clutched her father, who sat on the couch.

Nikki rolled her eyes and nodded. "Sure, but just for a little while." To William, she whispered, "You shouldn't be here."

William ignored the comment. "Did you have a good day?" he asked Psalm.

"I miss, you, Daddy," Psalm said and leaned into him.

William's eyes sought Nikki, but she ignored him. He returned his attention to Psalm. "I know, baby. We'll do something fun really soon, okay?"

Nikki pursed her lips. "So, what brings you here?"

"I miss you," William said.

Nikki folded her arms across her chest. "That's nice."

"Baby, you can't still be mad at me. You know in your heart that I didn't . . ." he looked down at the child in his lap, eagerly hanging on to his words. "I didn't do the thing you think I did."

Nikki, also conscious of Psalm, shot back: "Well, these days, I don't know what I know."

"Baby, I promise you, nothing has happened," William said. "Let's make this work. Let's go back home."

"Yeah, let's go back home!" Psalm chimed in.

"Psalm, tell your daddy goodnight. It's time for bed."

"But, Mommy. . . ."

"Don't 'but Mommy' me, little girl," Nikki said. "Now, tell him goodnight."

A sad-eyed Psalm turned and hugged her father, then scrambled from his lap.

"We're about to go to bed," Nikki said pointedly. She walked across the room and jerked open the door. William slowly stood and walked toward it. He paused at the doorway and searched her face for a long time.

Finding no invitation, he turned. "Fine, Nikki. Goodnight."

William climbed back into his vehicle and slammed the door. A passerby glanced up sharply, but he didn't care. "She's being totally unreasonable," he fumed. "I keep trying to get next to her, and she keeps pushing me off."

She kept accusing him of cheating, and he hadn't even kissed Olivia. He thought to just drive to their empty house. But he headed, instead, back to Olivia's.

William strode into Olivia's house and she greeted him with a glass of wine at the door. He took it from her, with a surprised smile. "Thanks. How did you know I'd need this?"

"Because I know you," she said, ushering him to the big armchair. "And I knew if you were going to see Nikki, she would do something to upset you."

At the mention of his wife's name, William's jaw tensed. "Don't talk about my wife like that."

Olivia took a step back and held up her free hand. "Hey,

I didn't mean any harm. I just know things have been so strained and I thought you might need something to take the edge off. That's all I was trying to say."

William sighed. He knew Olivia had gone out of her way to be helpful to him. She had moved from running her father's campaign to stepping in to manage his. She had been his one constant supporter, even when all the bad news erupted. She had been the cheerleader in his corner, had even offered him a roof. He stretched out his hand. She placed hers in his.

"Thanks for everything."

Chapter 92

Nikki spent the remainder of the week looking for employment. She pushed her resume all over town, but each time, she received a rejection. Either she didn't have the right type of experience, or she didn't have enough. Or, they told her flat-out that she wasn't welcome there.

She spent hours on the Internet posting her resume on job sites, but no one responded. "What does it take to get a job in this city?" she exclaimed in frustration, pushing back from the computer desk in Danielle's bedroom. For some reason, a padlock was lying on the desk.

The last time Nikki had been so desperate for money and a job, Spencer had provided the answer. Thoughts of her past shamed her and she pushed them deep into her consciousness.

"May I have some of your cookies for Psalm?" Nikki asked Danielle after arriving home from a long day of searching for work.

"Yes, you may," Danielle said, getting up from the couch

where she had been sprawled before Nikki stepped into the condo.

"Thank you," Nikki said, reaching for the cabinet.

"You're welcome," Danielle said and went into her bedroom, closing the door behind her. Nikki heard the lock click and sighed. Things between them had been cool ever since their argument. They were cordial, but the tension rippled through the condo like electricity.

Nikki passed two cookies to Psalm and then she paused. She glanced at Danielle's bedroom door and made a decision. She knocked. She waited but didn't hear an answer; she knocked again, louder this time.

She raised her hand to knock again when the door suddenly flew open and Danielle stood there.

"Is something the matter?" Danielle's tone was cool.

"I'm sorry about the other day," Nikki said.

Danielle sighed. "Me too."

The admission caught Nikki by surprise. Her mouth fell open, but no words came.

"Don't look so shocked," Danielle said. "I can admit when I'm wrong. I'm not totally bad."

"I didn't say you were bad," Nikki said, returning to the kitchen and pulling out a skillet and chopping block. She grabbed bell pepper and onion from the refrigerator. "It's just—"

"I know, I can be a bit much sometimes," Danielle said, following her into the kitchen. "It's just that I get so stressed sometimes, and I just always feel like I have to be on my guard."

"But you don't have to be on guard with me."

Danielle sat on a bar stool. "I know," she said, watching her friend chop the vegetables. "You're the only true friend I've ever had."

"You don't have to feel that the world is against you," Nikki said softly.

Neither woman said anything as Nikki washed thin strips of steak and dropped them into the hot skillet and let them sizzle, then put the onion and pepper on top. She washed her hands, then leaned on the counter next to Danielle. "So tell me what's been bugging you lately. And why'd you tell Raymond my baby was dead?"

But before Danielle could answer, her cell phone rang. "Hello?"

She cast a quick glance at Nikki, then sidled off the stool. "I have to take this," she said and jetted to her bedroom, carefully closing and locking the door behind her.

Nikki stared after her friend. She did not like all these secrets. She would find out what Danielle was keeping from her.

After they ate, Nikki dropped Psalm off at Keedra's for a play date and drove to the house she had not been to in a week since moving in with Danielle. She was ready to face the fact that her marriage was over. She dragged a large, cardboard box from the Protégé. She would fill it with some items—clothes for Psalm and her, a few toys, some photos and odd items—and leave the rest. Almost seven years, and she had nothing to show. She was feeling sorry for herself.

She placed the box on the ground and unlocked the door. The house seemed to be just as she had left it, though it had the desolate feel of a deserted home. She picked the box up and placed it on the table in the kitchen and walked to the bedroom. Her steps slowed as she approached the room she had so briefly shared with her husband. She stopped at the threshold and took a deep breath and held it. Tears welled in her eyes and she let the breath out slowly, blinking away the water she would not let fall.

"Well, there is no sense in feeling all sad," she chided herself, standing in the walk-in closet. "You fell for the wrong man. And he left you."

"That's the stupidest thing I've ever heard."

Nikki whirled around and her eyes widened. She quickly regained her composure and ice laced her words. "How long have you been standing there? Those were my private thoughts."

William crossed the room in two long steps, stopping just short of her. "There was a time when there was nothing private between us."

"Well, those days are gone," she said, trying to step around him, but he blocked her way. She glared at him. "Will you get out of my way? Since you're sneaking up on me, I'm leaving."

"I wasn't sneaking up on you," William said. "I was actually coming to stay the night, and when I saw your car, I thought that might have meant you had come back."

"Not a chance," she said. "What, you're telling me you're not with Ms. High and Mighty anymore?"

She could see a muscle tick in his jaw, but his voice was controlled when he spoke. "I was never *with* anyone but you," he said. "Which you know very well. And I was coming here since this is my home."

Nikki could feel herself thawing. He looked so sincere, like he was telling the truth. She had never known him to lie to her. No, she had been the one who lied. Their eyes caught and the room temperature immediately shot up. Nikki tried to look away, but she could not. When William pulled her to him, she didn't resist. Instead, she heaved toward him, meeting the crushing assault of his kiss. He picked her up and carried her to the bed, placing her on the flowered bedspread, where he tugged off her clothes. She made no move to stop him.

"Baby, I've missed you so much," he said, burying his head in her soft flesh. He looked back up, his eyes full of words. "I'm sorry for so much drama. I know—"

"Shhh," Nikki put her forefinger to his lips. "Don't talk."

"But I just want you to know that—"

"Shhh," she insisted. She didn't want to think about anything but the feelings being exchanged between them. She reached to undress him as he had done her, but he moved her hands away. She lay there as he quickly stepped out of his shoes and trousers, his shirt already on the floor, then climbed onto the bed, taking her into his arms.

William plied her with kisses and caresses. He pulled her as close as he could, breathing deeply to take in all he had missed these last long weeks.

Nikki closed her eyes as wave after wave of pent up energy escaped her and her voice grew hoarse with letting it out. With every movement, they told each other just how much they had missed.

Chapter 93

Danielle's cell phone rang and she put down the book she was reading to answer it. She glanced at the caller ID. "Hello?"

"Hey, it's me," the voice was crisp.

"I know who this is," Danielle said and rolled her eyes. "You sure have been calling me a lot lately."

"So, what's your point?"

"My point is just that, you've been calling me a lot," Danielle repeated. "Just the other day, I was in the kitchen talking to Nikki and I know she was all suspicious when I said I had to take this call, and I went to my bedroom and closed the door."

"I told you letting her move in was a bad idea."

"She's my friend," Danielle's voice was small.

"So, what about me?" the caller asked.

"What about you?" Danielle wanted to know.

"Do you love her more than you love me?"

Danielle shook her head but realized her caller could not see her. "No, you know I don't love anybody more than you."

"You sure about that?"

"Yes."

"And who is it that has always bailed you out of trouble?"

"You."

"And who is it that got you out of that bad place so long ago?"

"You."

"And who is it that never asks anything of you, but is always there for you?"

"You."

"Okay then," the caller said. "Just make sure you remember that. I'd really hate to find that I've trusted the wrong person."

"Oh, no, you've not trusted the wrong person."

"Good. This is what I need you to do."

Chapter 94

The first rays of light peeked through the partially opened curtains and Nikki's eyes fluttered open. She groaned and buried her head in the pillow, knowing it was too early to be awake. A delicious soreness radiated throughout her body and she breathed in thoughts of remembrance. Her eyes flew open as she realized she wasn't daydreaming. She twisted and saw William lying on his stomach next to her, one arm draped across her middle. Warmth flooded her as she recalled how he declared his love to her in his actions just the night before. But that didn't change anything, she thought in the harsh light of morning.

Nikki inched to the edge of the bed until she let his arm fall softly to the mattress. When he grumbled, she paused, afraid she had awakened him. Then she realized he was still asleep. She sighed with relief and planted both feet on the floor. The cool air flirted with her skin and it tingled at memories of mere hours before.

She rummaged through the drawers as quickly as she could, casting furtive glances over her shoulder to make sure her husband was still asleep. He twisted and scratched his chest.

She paused, her back rigid as she waited to see if his eyes would pop open. When he began snoring, she grabbed clothes and zipped down the hall to the other bathroom and showered, raced the toothbrush around her mouth and pulled on her clothes. Then she dumped a few items in the cardboard box, not as many as she would have liked, but she couldn't think about that. She fled, leaving William alone in bed.

Chapter 95

Danielle woke up with a start. Something had awakened her. She slowly sat up and looked around. Was somebody there? She held her breath, struggling to hear movement. She got up and walked through the condo, opening the closet doors and looking under the beds.

Satisfied that she was alone, she went back to her spot on the couch. Nikki still wasn't there. At the thought of her best friend, so many emotions battled. Nikki was the one person she had been able to trust and open up to all those years ago, but even then there were just some things even Nikki didn't know about her.

And lately, so many weird things had been happening. Nikki was acting so suspicious, and at every turn it seemed they were fighting.

But still, Danielle felt a knot in her stomach at what she had done. She hadn't wanted to, not really. But she could never decline a request from the person who had lately seemed to have her on speed dial. Danielle shrugged off the feelings. "It's no big deal. I didn't really do anything. Nikki will never know."

Chapter 96

Nikki called Keedra. "Hey, I'm so sorry!" Nikki gushed when her friend answered. "I went by the house and William showed up and. . . ."

"It's okay," Keedra said. "Psalm was great company for my son. They entertained each other and gave me some time to get some things done."

"I am such a bad mother!"

"No, you're not," Keedra soothed. "You went to handle some business and if I was able to ease your mind by watching your child, then I'm glad to have been a part of it. So you said William was there. Does this mean you two are back together?"

"No!" Nikki's response was immediate. She let her voice relax. "I mean . . . I don't know. I mean, yes I do. No. It was just sex."

"It doesn't sound like that's all it was."

"He can't just think he can come back and everything is all right. It's not that easy. And he cheated on me."

"Do you really believe that?"

"I—" the question caught Nikki off guard. "Well, why

else would he stay at Olivia's house? And I told you what she said. She's been after him for I-don't-know-how-long."

"Yeah, but just because she wants your husband doesn't mean he wants her," Keedra said. "You know your husband better than anyone. You know the type of man he is. And you know two things: He loves God and he loves his family. And neither of those would allow him to stoop to the level you are accusing him of."

Nikki wasn't ready to accept that she was wrong and that William had been telling her the truth all this time. Especially when it was her lie that had sent them down this path in the first place. "Well, look, I don't know what to believe these days. I'm just in a place where I'm starting to realize just how much I sacrificed for him. I don't want to go back there. I'm not the meek, timid little housewife he married."

"Well, that's all right," Keedra said. "Just talk to him. Don't lose your marriage because of some stuff you guys can fix."

"It's not that easy."

"All I know is that I'm raising a child on my own because I got with a man who really was a cheater and no good for me. You—you're not with someone like that. William is a good man."

"Look, I don't want to talk about this right now," Nikki said.

"Well, just think about what you are doing," Keedra insisted. "And pray about it."

"Praying hasn't done me much good."

"Don't be like that," Keedra said. "Prayer always works."

"Yeah, well, enough of all that," Nikki said. "I'm going to come get Psalm."

"Why don't you wait a few hours?" Keedra said. "She's still sleeping."

Nikki nodded, eyeing the periwinkle sky. "Yeah, you're

right. It's just now getting to be daylight. Okay, well, I'm going to get myself together. I'll call you in a few hours."

"Okay."

Nikki continued her drive, covering the few blocks to Danielle's condo in short order and parked. When she climbed out of her car, a slight breeze stirred the air. The temperature was dropping and it was starting to be jacket weather. She quickly walked to the door and jammed the key into the lock.

She let herself in and a startled gasp escaped her lips. Danielle was asleep on the couch. At the sound of noise at the door, Danielle jumped, pointing a butcher knife Nikki's way.

"What's up with the knife?" Nikki asked, shutting the door behind her.

"Is somebody with you?" Danielle's eyes were wild.

Nikki looked around. "Somebody like who?"

Danielle's eyes narrowed suspiciously. "You know. Somebody."

Nikki dropped her purse on the kitchen counter and looked at Danielle curiously. "No. Nobody is with me, Danielle," she said. "I'm not sure what's going on, but shouldn't you be in bed? And why are you sleeping with a knife?"

Danielle slowly stood up, still clutching the knife. She kept her eyes on Nikki as she walked to the door, then opened it and peeked outside, glancing in both directions. She closed the door and placed the knife on the counter. "I waited up all night for you," she said accusingly. "I was worried. I thought something had happened to you. That somebody had gotten you."

Nikki almost laughed, but caught herself. She spoke deliberately. "I was fine," she said slowly, pouring a glass of orange juice. "I went by the house and William showed up. Why were you worried?"

"Because I know somebody's trying to get me and I thought maybe they had gotten you."

This time, Nikki did laugh. "Have you been hitting the ripple a little too hard?" She leaned in and pretended to sniff her friend's breath. "No, I don't smell any alcohol. But you sound drunk."

"You think this is a joke?" Danielle shot back.

Nikki instantly stopped laughing. "Who is trying to get you?" she asked, concern drawing her brows together.

A knowing look came into Danielle's eyes. "Never mind. I can't say anything else." Her eyes narrowed again. "So where is Psalm? Did you leave her with protection while you came over here?"

Nikki put down her glass and looked at Danielle in puzzlement. "Danielle, I'm really not following you. What are you talking about?"

Danielle repeated her question. "Where is Psalm?"

"She's at Keedra's."

At the mention of the woman's name, Danielle's voice rose. "You left my godchild with that woman? What, you didn't want me to watch her? See, I knew Keedra was trying to steal you away."

Nikki threw her hands in the air. "Danielle, I don't know what is up with you, but you are being really weird right now. I told you, I'm not in the market for a new best friend. Keedra is just a friend. She can't replace you."

"Then why did you go and give away my godchild to her? You think I don't know, don't you? You think I don't see how you've been treating me lately. You're trying to get rid of me."

Nikki cast a sidelong glance at Danielle and waved her off. "Look, I'm going to bed. When you start talking where somebody can understand you, then come see me."

Nikki turned to go to her bedroom and Danielle snatched her back around by the shoulder. The action caught Nikki by surprise and caused her head to snap back. Danielle snarled. "Don't you turn your back on me when I'm talking to you!"

"Danielle, have you lost your mind?" Nikki twisted free of Danielle's hand and glared at her friend. "Keep your hands off me!"

Danielle glowered back at her. "Are you yelling at me? You know what? You can take your junk and get out of my place!" Nikki couldn't move. Danielle railed on. "I mean it, get out! Now! I don't have to take this. I've tried to be the best friend I know how to be and all you do is throw my kindness in my face. You go rummaging through my stuff, spying on me. You call me a liar. And now you're yelling at me and calling me crazy. Just get your stuff and get out!"

Nikki's eyes widened and her mouth fell open as she struggled to reason with her friend. "Danielle, just calm down. I'm sorry if I said something wrong."

"I don't want to hear it," Danielle said. "Get out! And take your stuff."

Nikki looked around, not knowing what to say. She had never seen Danielle be so erratic. "Danielle, maybe we should calm down. Like I said, I'm sorry if I said something to offend you."

"Look, I'm getting ready to get dressed for work. And when I come out of my bedroom, I want you out of my house."

Ch

Nikki drove away fr
where to turn. She was
was there? What would
had shared? She couldr
woman had kicked her
and she sniffed hard to
blurred her vision.

She pulled into the j
shifted the gear to p
Nikki leaned back on
the tears finally seepin
had tried not to cry in a
was just too much. S
"God, I just—"

But she stopped the
since she had prayed wi
couraged at church, but
imperfection. She felt t
too blocked from God b

and you have onl
papers, all of our

"Bye, Olivia."

"You're not be
"I don't know w
continue to ignor
you and she'll n
know you moved
have feelings for
great heights, you

"You've said e
could freeze wate
fore it turns into a

"Fine," Olivia
just wait. You'll se

much, had been too bad. That's what her mother had told her; that Nikki had run her daddy off with her incessant complaints and whining. And so Nikki vowed she would never complain again—even when William told her he wanted her home and not working, she bit back protests.

She knew what could happen when someone complained. When her mother remarried and all but ignored her in favor of the new husband and stepdaughter, Nikki had retreated into herself, making herself invisible.

When Danielle slept with Nikki's boyfriend that early summer at college, Nikki hid her hurt. After all, she had a new best friend, someone who would be there for her, and why would she give up her friend over some guy? So she again lost her voice.

That's why she allowed Spencer to pull her into his scheme back in college. He had come along and soothed her hurt feelings. He looked so good, so handsome and said the right sweet things that she had easily fallen for . . . so grateful that someone like him would want her. When he asked her to join his network, she had, at first, balked; but his words seeped into her consciousness.

"If you loved me, you'd do it," he had said, looking at her with sad eyes. "I love you; that's why I want you to be my best girl."

And so she had. Nikki tried to squeeze the images from her mind, to push the secret back into the dark recesses of her consciousness. She had lost her voice in all that, speechless to voice her protest.

She had found comfort in joining William's church, because it was nice to have people who seemed to genuinely care about her, and hearing about God's love was something new to her. She soaked in the idea of a God who loved her no matter what, but somehow, she sometimes doubted that He could love her unconditionally. Not her; this flawed woman who had made so many missteps.

Even at church, Nikki felt she didn't have a voice. At church, she did what she was told, and never dared to go against something or someone. That's why she hadn't told Sister James she simply could not afford to purchase a new usher's uniform. She was afraid of the rejection.

Leaving William was the first time Nikki had found her voice. It frightened her, this newfound speech. But something inside told her she had to finally stand up for herself. Even faced with nowhere to turn, she knew she couldn't go back. She couldn't survive another betrayal. Especially one that came from her husband.

Her phone rang again. She looked down. It was Danielle.

William slammed his hand against his steering wheel as again Nikki sent his call to voicemail. He sat outside Danielle's job, more determined than ever to speak with his wife following his conversation with Danielle. Danielle had walked down to the lobby, smiling. But when he questioned her, her expression had immediately changed.

"Where is Nikki?" he had asked.

"I wouldn't know," came the short retort.

"What do you mean, you wouldn't know?" William demanded.

"Just that," Danielle said. "I kicked her out of my house."

"You did what?" William's eyes bored into hers.

"Yeah, she was being mean and bossy to me," Danielle said. "I told her she could get out. I have no idea where she went."

"Danielle, you have got to be kidding me." William stared at her. "I know you did not put my wife and child out on the street. Where did she say she was going?"

"I just told you, I don't know," Danielle said. "That should teach her to smart off at me. But look, I've got to get back to work. So if you'll excuse me . . ."

She moved to turn around, but William caught her fore-arm. Danielle gasped and the receptionist's eyes bugged. William dropped Danielle's arm, but his voice was serious. "If something happens to my wife because of some stupid fight you two had, I will see that you pay," he hissed. "You've always been so full of yourself. I can't believe you'd be so selfish."

Danielle narrowed her eyes at him. "You probably already know where she is. You probably came here snooping around for information on me. Just like she did. I know you two are in this together."

"What are you talking about?"

"You, Nikki, even the people I work with," she said, extending her hand to the lobby. "I know every one of you are trying to get me."

"Danielle, I don't know what kind of off-the-wall stuff you are talking about," William said. "Look, I've got to go. I need to find my wife."

He turned to leave, then glanced at her quizzically. "I had the weirdest conversation with somebody today. Now, I don't put much stock into what was told to me, and I know you probably won't know what I'm talking about but, what's the Welcome Wagon Contingent?"

Danielle's head snapped back as if struck. "The . . . who told you about that?"

William's heart sank. "So you know what it is?"

"I can't discuss this with you."

Back in the car, William replayed the conversation with Danielle in his mind. He let his head fall to the steering wheel, feeling as if someone had kicked him in the stomach.

Chapter 104

Nikki took a few bites of Psalm's leftovers and then dropped five of her $27 on the table and left the restaurant. She walked back to the car, unsure of what to do next. She could just go back to the house she had shared with William. But she shook her head. No, she could not do that. She could make it without him and without anything he touched.

Nikki got into the car and listened to her voicemail messages. She had three from William, each tersely asking her to call him. She deleted them. The last was from Danielle. "Look, call me. It's important."

"Fat chance," Nikki muttered and deleted that message as well.

Chapter 105

"William, where are you, man?" Winston said when William answered his cell phone.

"I'm out," William said. "I had to handle some business."

"Well, the only business you need to be taking care of now is campaign business," Winston said. "I had to stall the people for the meeting this morning. You were supposed to speak to the Kiwanis Club. And you have an afternoon meeting with the black chamber. I think they'll endorse you after this meeting."

"You know what? It's dang near time to cast ballots," William said. "Tell them I needed their endorsement weeks ago. What the heck do I need it for now?"

"Calm down, bro," Winston said. "You are losing your composure. What's going on? I heard about the altercation from this morning, but Olivia refused to tell me what it was about. Does that have something to do with the fact that you are MIA right now?"

"Look, Winston, I can't talk right now. I'll be at the

meeting with the chamber." William hung up and sighed. After trying Nikki's phone once again and getting the same result, he started the vehicle. "Let me get back to this campaign trail. I'll deal with this other stuff later."

Chapter 106

Nikki spent the day darting in and out of buildings, applying for jobs. She was terrified to leave Psalm in the car. "Psalm, do not even touch those doors," she threatened. "If you do, I will be very angry, little girl!"

"I won't," Psalm said. "Can I go with you?"

Nikki's face fell. "No, no. You can't. I'm just going in here to find a job so I can make us some money. But I need you to just be a very good girl and stay in the car. Mommy won't be long."

"But I don't want to."

"Sweetie, I know," Nikki said. "Hey, if you're really good, I'll buy you some ice cream tonight."

Psalm's eyes lit up. "Oh, okay!"

Nikki wished she could have taken Psalm to school, but today was a teacher in-service day and students were out. She kissed her daughter on the cheek and slammed the door. She glanced around, almost abandoning her plan to go into the building and leave her child in the car. She tried her best to straighten her blouse and knock the wrinkles out of the knees of her trousers when she stood next to the car. She held her mouth open to breathe out, trying to calm her stomach. She had to land a job somewhere.

Nikki emerged from the building ten minutes later, dejected. The office manager said they were not hiring receptionists, despite a sign in the window that said otherwise.

Nikki climbed back into the car and moved to the next business on her list. She hadn't done much praying lately, but she uttered a silent prayer as she walked toward the building. "Please God, let somebody hire me. I don't care. I'll sweep floors. I just need to pay for a place for my baby and me to lay our heads."

Chapter 107

Nurse Smart tapped Danielle on the shoulder, and Danielle jumped. "Sorry, I didn't mean to startle you," Nurse Smart said with a tiny smile. Her brow creased. "I'm not really sure what's going on, but you know we can't wear street clothes on duty."

Danielle flashed a brilliant smile at the woman. "But don't you think I look much prettier in this than in those old, dull scrubs?"

Nurse Smart's eyes roamed over Danielle's body, stopping at her bust before lingering on her long expanse of leg. She nodded. "I have to hand it to you, you do look good," she said, then cleared her throat. "And if it was up to me, I'd certainly let you wear what you have on. You are beautiful. But my boss is on me about not addressing this with you this morning. Danielle, you've got to go home and change."

"Come on," Danielle said, leaning a tad closer to the woman. "You just said I look good. What harm could it be in me wearing this?"

"Danielle, I really can't allow it," Nurse Smart said, reluctance lacing her tone. "I wish it could be different. You really must go put on your scrubs."

Danielle's eyes flashed. "I knew it! I knew you were in on it!"

"What are you talking about?"

"Don't 'What are you talking about' me!" Danielle yelled. "I knew you were part of the scheme. You want to force me to wear those scrubs so you can spy on me. Well, I'm not going to do it!"

Nurse Smart waved her hands in front of her, trying to calm Danielle. "Danielle, just try to get a hold of yourself. I'm not sure what you're talking about, but whatever it is, we can get to the bottom of it. I'm not part of anything."

Nurse Smart advanced on Danielle and reached for her arm. When she did, Danielle whirled on her and grabbed a pen from the desk next to her and stabbed it into the woman's fleshy upper arm.

Nurse Smart looked down at the trickle of blood mixed with ink and then back up at Danielle, shock written all over her face. "Danielle!"

"Stay away from me!" Danielle screamed, brandishing the pen in front of her.

Heads whipped around and Nurse Smart took a step back, one hand pressed against her injury. A security officer rushed toward them, but Nurse Smart held up her hand. "It's all right. It's all right," she said. "It was just a misunderstanding."

As night fell, Nikki's spirits did too. "Mommy, I'm tired of being in the car all day," Psalm whined from the backseat.

"Sweetie, I know," Nikki said.

"I want to go home."

"We can't really do that right now," Nikki said. "But shhh, Mommy needs to think."

"I want my daddy," Psalm pouted.

"Psalm, just be quiet," Nikki said sharply and her tone immediately softened. "I'm sorry, baby. Mommy just has to figure some things out. It'll be better soon."

Nikki sat in the parking lot of a motel, counting and recounting her money. Minus the pancake breakfast, a shared hamburger meal for lunch and the sandwich and ice cream she had just given Psalm for dinner, she had $7 to her name.

Not enough to get a motel room.

Nikki's mind flashed back to her freshman year at college. Money had been tight then, too. She was a scholarship student, but the money ran out long before the bills. Spencer had approached her about a quick way to make some dollars. She shook her head to banish the memory.

No, she could not go back there. She would never again be that person. Nikki's cheeks grew hot as she recalled all she had done for money. Her only solace was in knowing her secret had remained hidden.

Nobody ever had to know she was once that girl.

Chapter 108

Broussard's Wife Part Of Sex-For-Hire Ring.

The headline slapped William. He stayed at the house the night before in hopes that Nikki would show up. He walked back inside after picking up the paper from the driveway. He didn't notice the chill in the air because the heat of his temper consumed him.

The story in the newspaper unfolded as Olivia had told him. Only he was too dumb to believe it. He read the story:

"Nikki Broussard, 27, wife of underdog mayoral candidate William Broussard was a one-time member of an underground college sex ring. Mrs. Broussard apparently was among several freshmen who performed sexual favors for visiting football team members and some of the college's faculty in exchange for money.

"The sex ring was disbanded after several months, but not before Mrs. Broussard and others provided services for a reputed legion of clients. The chain was run by Mrs. Broussard's steady boyfriend at the time, Spencer Cason. Neither Mrs. Broussard nor Mr. Cason could be reached for comment."

My wife was a prostitute. William balled up the paper in his fist. After a moment, he smoothed it back out and reread the last part. Nikki and Spencer had been together like that? He clenched his teeth until his jaw hurt.

Nikki stretched, trying to get the strain out of her neck after sleeping on the backseat of the tiny car with her daughter. She climbed out of the car and stood up, letting her legs feel freedom. The house would have been more comfortable, but she refused to go back there. She would finally make it on her own.

"Mommy, I don't like this!" Psalm whined. "I'm hungry and my leg hurts and my breath smells funny."

"Psalm, baby, I know this is not fun," Nikki said. "Mommy will find us a place soon."

"Why can't we just go home? I want to go back to my own room."

Nikki bit the inside of her cheek. She couldn't have her child living on the street. A well-dressed, clean-shaven man walked by, eyeing her. She averted her eyes, but the thoughts she had been trying to make disappear resurfaced. They mocked her: *You know how to get money when you're in a pinch. It's not like you've not done it before.*

The election was the next day. "I think it's pretty suspicious that they ran this story the day before the election," William said to Winston and Olivia who stood around his desk.

"Yeah, you'd think they wouldn't run something like this so close to the time for people to cast their votes," Winston said.

"Yeah, that's true, but it's not like this was some made-up story. It's obviously true," Olivia reminded them both.

Olivia's French manicured nail stabbed at the smiling face of Nikki staring back at them. "I can't believe not only that she did something as sick as this, but that she hadn't confided all this in you, William," Olivia said. "I thought marriage was about honesty."

The words stung and William had no answer. "Well, it just goes to show, we can all be wrong, huh?" He cleared his throat. "Okay, well, let's give it one last hurrah today. Let's work hard, at least to make a good showing so we don't get beaten too badly. I know there is no way I can win after this story."

"I noticed you just standing out here." Nikki whipped around and recognized the clean-shaven man who had passed by her earlier.

"Oh yeah?" she said.

"Yeah," he said, and let a sly smile break across his face. "You looking for some company?"

Nikki shook her head. "No, I'm cool."

He took a step closer, reaching into his pocket and pulling out a designer wallet full of crisp bills. "I can make it worth your while."

"I said, 'I'm cool,' " she insisted, turning her eyes away from the money.

He took a step back and held up his hand, grabbing the newspaper he had been holding under his arm. "I just thought you might be interested in a little business," he said. "That's all. I saw the story in the paper."

"What story?" Oh, goodness, not another campaign story. What did this one say?

He smirked at her and opened his mouth, but his attention was drawn by a man who called to him. "Hey, the conference is about to start, man. Come on!"

The man shrugged and winked at her. "Maybe next time," he said, shoving his wallet back into his pocket. He cast a glance back at her and walked away, shaking his head.

Nikki climbed back into the car and leaned against the

headrest. She could still see the thick roll of money the man had held out to her, but she squeezed her eyes shut against the memory. There had to be another way. She would not go back there.

She stuck the key into the ignition and started the car; she would swallow her pride and go back to the house she had shared with William. Psalm deserved to sleep in her own bed, and not in a car. Nikki drove the short distance and let herself in, surveying the living room. A necktie lay across the back of the couch. The memories of their last night there washed over her and she caught her breath at the force of them.

She could not think about that, though. She felt she and William would never again be a couple.

Psalm flashed a sweet smile at her mother and went to her bedroom. Nikki sighed and flicked on the television.

". . . William Broussard has refused comment on the matter. Spencer Cason has been fired from the Lo Dark campaign, after it was revealed he was the ringleader of the now infamous Welcome Wagon Contingent, which sent out young women, including Nikki Broussard, to have sex with . . ."

Nikki's legs buckled beneath her and she groped for the back of the chair to steady herself. The remote slipped from her fingers and she fell to the chair, weak as the words washed over her. Her secret was no secret anymore.

"Oh no!"

Danielle hung up the phone with her sister. Their telephone conversations were usually brief. Today's was no different. Danielle had called her after the story about Nikki ran. "Did you see the newspaper?"

Her sister's voice was curt. "I did," she said. "It's a shame, isn't it?"

"Yes," Danielle said. "But I have a few comments about that."

Her sister cut her short. "Well, look, I can't talk right now."

"Well, I need to talk to you now," Danielle said. The past few days had been stressful for her. First, Nikki had left her, and then Nurse Smart made her go home after that unfortunate incident with the pen. And now this.

"Look, I said I can't talk to you now." Her sister's voice was firm.

"But I have to talk to you about this thing," Danielle said plaintively. "It's just too much. I've been under so much stress lately."

"Well, you know what happens when you get stressed," her sister said as if speaking with a child. "Try your breathing exercises. And try not to think about too much. I don't want you to have to go back to the hospital."

"I don't need to go to a hospital!" Danielle snapped. She had spent her teen years in and out of mental hospitals. She had missed so many days of school that she was a year older than all her classmates at graduation. Nobody, outside her family, knew the reason she had missed so much class.

"Okay, well, you behave yourself and you won't have to go back there," her sister said. "But if you don't let me work, something very bad may happen to you. Don't you know they're still watching you? Don't you know they're just waiting for you to slip up? If they catch you, they're going to come and get you."

Danielle dropped the phone and put her hands to her ears. "They're not going to get me!"

Nikki's discomfiture lasted for a moment before anger replaced it. She quickly hopped onto the Internet and found the newspaper's website to read the full story. It was brief, but it had all she needed. While her name was there, and Spencer's, there was no mention of Danielle.

She nodded grimly. Danielle had stabbed her in the back in the worst way. Nikki's mind went back to all those years before.

"Spencer, I really don't want to do this anymore," Nikki had said, sipping on a sweet tea with two lemons as they waited for their food at the campus grill.

"Okay," Spencer had replied. "You can quit whenever you want. But you know, you're my best girl. All the guys like you. That's really going to hurt me if I don't have you."

"And after Spencer's been so good to you, are you really going to go out like that?" Danielle had chimed in. "I mean, if it wasn't for him, you'd be sitting back home, too broke to even finish out the semester."

Nikki looked from one to the other. "I'm really grateful," she said. "But I just feel so weird about this. You guys told me it was only going to be a one-time thing when I did it the first time. Just a quick drink with that quarterback."

"Well, you did such a good job that special requests started coming in for you," Spencer said.

"It was more than just a drink, Spencer," Nikki reminded him.

Danielle waved that off. "Stop complaining. You're the newest girl and the guys do like young meat," she said. "I mean, I get plenty of special requests because I'm so beautiful, but the guys like you because you look so innocent."

Danielle had been one of Spencer's girls and often went on Welcome Wagon dates. She had such a date the first day Nikki met her as a tutor. Spencer had spotted Nikki later and insisted Danielle help him get Nikki involved.

Nikki had become involved, but with great reluctance. Now, she was ready to quit.

"Look, just finish out the semester," Spencer said. "That

way, we can take care of a few things. And if you just do that for me, I will love you forever. Besides, doesn't it feel good to be able to pay for all the things you need without having to call home?"

Nikki had looked down at her hands in her lap. "Okay."

Nikki picked up the phone and punched in Danielle's number. "Hello?"

"I saw the newspaper," Nikki said.

"Yeah, I did too," Danielle replied. "I tried to call you yesterday. William came up to my job asking me about all that. I was trying to let you know he found out."

"Oh. He just happened to *find out*, huh?" Nikki asked, her voice full of acid. "Funny how he just happened to find out. Also funny how your name was mentioned nowhere in the story."

There was a pause. "What? You don't think I had anything to do with that coming out, do you?"

"All I know is what I see, Danielle," Nikki spat back. "And it's that you're a lying, backstabbing—"

"I didn't tell anybody about that. I swear," Danielle jumped in. "I wouldn't do that to you."

"Yeah, like I believe that," Nikki said. "So, what was it? Did you just get so ticked at me the other day that you wanted to see how much you could ruin me? Well, you got your wish. I'll never be able to walk around this town again, without people thinking I'm some sort of easy woman." Nikki's voice caught in her throat. "And I guess, they'll be right."

"Nikki, I swear, I didn't say a word."

"Well, thanks a lot," Nikki slung the words at Danielle. "Thanks for showing me what a friend is. First, you went to the newspaper about the credit card. Then you kicked me out of your house. Then you wanted to top it off with telling the world about my most shameful secret. Well, if I had any chance of getting my husband back before, you've killed all that. But maybe that was your whole point. Maybe you want me to be a lonely, selfish fool just like you. You can take your jealous self straight to you-know-where."

Nikki slammed down the phone.

Danielle let the phone slip from her grasp and she sat down hard, her head in her hands. Her temples began to pound and the noise between her ears was deafening. She could hear bits and pieces of so many conversations from over the years, chasing each other around her head.

"You'd better watch it."

"You're going back to the hospital."

"You'd better do what I say."

"Tell me your secrets."

"You can't run."

"Arghhhh!" she screamed and stood.

Danielle walked around in circles, her hands to her ears, trying to block out the thoughts that threatened her sanity. "No! No! No!" she tried to fight the thoughts back.

Just as she calmed down and fell into her seat, exhausted, a flurry of activity at her door drew her attention. The building manager stood before her stern-faced, and Nurse Smart stepped quickly toward her desk. "Danielle, these people seem to think—"

"Danielle Esperanza? You're under arrest for the murder of Troy Baldwin."

Chapter 109

Nikki didn't know what to do next. She refused to leave the house, too embarrassed to even step into the front lawn. She picked up the telephone to call William, but dropped it, guilt and shame making her skin burn.

She somehow managed to fix some oatmeal and toast for Psalm, before locking herself in the bathroom. She sat on the edge of the tub and finally, after weeks of stress and years of living in fear of being found out, she cried hard. And for a long time.

Her shoulders shook for the little girl whose father chose her brother instead of her. Her throat tightened for the little girl whose mother chose a stepdaughter and new husband over her. Her chest tightened for the college freshman who felt she had no other option than to sell her body to men who fancied her. She even cried for the woman who had spent the past seven years lying to everyone, including herself. She cried for the woman who avoided God because she thought He didn't want anything to do with her.

When her eyes could produce no more tears and her

throat felt as thick as peanut butter-soaked cotton, she stood up, spent and tired. What would she do now?

William could not escape the cameras or the incessant ringing of the telephone. "William, you've got to stay the course," Winston pleaded, knowing their months of hard work were in real jeopardy.

"I can't do this anymore," William said, his head in his hands. "The cameras. The stories. I can't."

"You can and you will," Olivia said, putting a hand on his shoulder. "I'm sorry you've had to go through all of this, but maybe it's all for the better. You were able to see what kind of woman your wife truly is. And even if you don't win this election, it positions you to win the next because your name will already be out there. This is all for the better."

William looked at her incredulously. "Do you think this is a game? This is my life. I don't care anything about name recognition right now, especially when I've just realized the woman who has carried my name has been lying to me all along."

Olivia rubbed his back. "It's a shame, isn't it?"

The phone jarred Nikki from her thoughts. She slowly stood from her perch on the edge of the tub and walked with wooden steps toward the ringing. Maybe it would stop by the time she got there. She could think of no one in the world she wanted to speak to right now.

The ringing was still going on when she got to the kitchen. She sighed and picked up the receiver. "Hello." Her voice sounded dead, even to her own ears.

"You have a collect call," the automated voice informed her. She couldn't understand the name, but numbly accepted. The call connected.

"Nikki, I've been arrested, please come and get me."

you, but no, you wouldn't li[
ried to a prostitute!"

The statement ripped thr[
anger, the words hurt. "Nikk[

"Well, now, everybody air[
news makes up some stuf[
make this up. What does sh[

William wondered the sam[

"Mommy, I want to watc[
the remote from the table.

Nikki snatched the devic[

At Psalm's startled look, N[
voice, "No, baby, we're not [
one of your favorite books [
you."

"But I don't want to," Ps[
cartoons."

"Maybe later," Nikki said[
Psalm away from the televis[
seeing all those bad things ab[

Ring! Ring! The phone s[
up. "Hello?"

"Is this Nikki Broussard? [
newspaper.

"Jimmy, I can't talk to you[

"Come on, Nikki," Jimm[
going on. Give me the scoop[

"There is nothing going o[

"Nikki, all those stories w[
Jimmy tried to lean on th[
"How many stories did we [
an intern, you shooting photo[
I'll be fair to you."

"Not interested, Jimmy," N[

The voice crackled through Nikki like an electric shock. Danielle. She snapped into action, the numbness of a moment ago being replaced by fire. "I know you are not calling me to help you!"

"Please," Danielle implored. "There has been some mistake. They're saying I killed Troy. You know I didn't do that!"

"I don't care if they send you straight to the electric chair!" Nikki shouted. "I would cut off my right arm before I lifted even a finger to help you, after what you did to me."

"I didn't do anything!"

"Yeah," Nikki said. "Just like you didn't tell the press about me using that credit card. Just like you didn't sleep with my boyfriend all those years ago. Just like you didn't stab me in the back a hundred times."

"Nikki, please!"

Nikki slammed down the telephone.

"I need to run an errand," William said. If Winston or Olivia or any of the rest of his staff so much as breathed another word to him, he knew he would blow up. His face felt hot with embarrassment and his gut was tight with so many other emotions. He needed to find a quiet spot.

"I'll go with you," Olivia quickly spoke up.

"No," he said, standing. "I'll go alone."

He saw Olivia and Winston exchange glances. Winston cleared his throat. "You have appointments. And the phones keep ringing; we've got to devise a plan to recover from this latest Jimmy Vaughn story."

"I said, I need to run an errand." William's words were coarse. He grabbed his keys and jacket.

"Well, when will you be back?" Olivia pressed.

He gave her a withering look and strode away, ignoring her question.

Danielle slumped a
cell in which gruff, uni
dumped her into just
her bottom lip, knowi
ing as she welcomed t

The floor was a da
covering of dust and s
only other person in t
flat mattress. Danielle
anating from the wom:
she could. She could h
shouted obscenities ar

Danielle paced back
her hands. She didn't l

William's cell phone
in the ignition. He th
instead. Whoever it v
said.

"Who are you talki
tone drilled into him.

He was instantly ch
know it was you. I'm s

"What's up is this 1
and seeing on this tele

"I really don't know

"Well, I could have
said. "I did tell you, as
good, Christian girl. Se

"Nikki does know t

"Hmmph!" his mot
knows the Lord who
She's full of sin, I tell
out with the wrong k

"Nikki—"

"Goodbye, Jimmy."

She placed the receiver back in its cradle.

The phone rang again. She sighed and rolled her eyes before snatching up the receiver. "Jimmy!"

"Excuse me?" the female voice caught Nikki off guard.

"Oh, who is this?"

"This is Jamie Nettles from Channel 12. I was looking—"

"You have the wrong number," Nikki cut the woman off.

Nikki hung up the phone. When it rang again, she took the phone off the hook.

While Psalm rummaged in her bedroom for a book, Nikki's mind went back to a time in her distant past. She had been a freshman at college—broke. The school was threatening to cancel her classes if she didn't come up with payment. She had enrolled in school, not realizing her scholarship hadn't covered all of her tuition.

She had tried asking her family. But her mother had reminded Nikki that she should have gone to school near their home, like her mother had told her to do. Nikki was fresh out of ideas when she literally bumped into Spencer Cason.

She crashed into Spencer as she walked across campus, her mind replaying that conversation with her mother. Nikki's books spilled to the ground and she immediately bent to reclaim them, but he was quicker. He scooped them up.

She had looked up at him, mesmerized by the hazel eyes twinkling back at her. His wavy hair was cut close and his smile was inviting. She felt herself blush at the attention. "I'm so sorry!" she gushed, reaching to get her books, but he had held on to them.

"It's okay," he said. "It's not every day that I get almost knocked down by someone as innocent and cute as you."

She smiled shyly and cast her eyes down. "Oh . . ."

"So, can I walk you across the Quad and buy you a burger inside the student center?" he asked. He snapped the fingers on his free hand. "Sorry. My name is Spencer."

She knew exactly who he was. He was a star athlete and the son of a rich doctor. He was always surrounded by pretty girls—she had watched this from afar. She knew he was popular.

He looked at her expectantly, then grinned even wider. "You're not going to tell me your name?"

She had realized belatedly that she had just been staring at him. She quickly recovered and stammered out her name. "Ni—Ni—Nikki."

"What a beautiful name for a beautiful woman," he said, seeming to enjoy watching her squirm under his compliments. He looked around. "So, Nikki, let's get to know each other. I think we can be really good friends."

She later found out he was one of Danielle's friends. Danielle started pushing Nikki to go out with Spencer and later, to do much more than that for him. Danielle told her to listen to Spencer's idea about making money.

The clanking of keys in the lock jolted Nikki from her thoughts. She sprang from the chair.

William stood in the doorway.

She froze.

The sight of Nikki jarred William. He had somehow known she would be here. When he rounded the corner and saw her car in the driveway, his heart had quickened. But what emotions the sight of her standing here evoked, he couldn't discern at the moment. He wanted to shake her, to hug her, to tell her the past didn't matter.

"I assume you've read the papers," he said coolly, and he could see from the way her head jerked up that she had. He wanted his words to hurt. "Seems that I should just open the newspaper to find out who my wife really is."

She raced into the street and a car screeched, swerving to miss her. "Look where you're going, lady!"

Nikki's heart pounded in her chest as she realized how close she had come to being hit by a car. She crossed the street and put a frightened Psalm down, letting the child walk. She had to get this under control. She could not start freaking out like this.

She walked up to the polling place, pulling out her ID. When she stepped to the table, she saw two women whispering behind their hands, then averting their eyes when they saw Nikki looking straight at them.

Her face grew hot with embarrassment, but she refused to retreat. She finished the identification process then followed another poll worker to the voting machine. The black woman was probably in her 60s, though she moved like she was twenty years younger. "You keep your head up, you hear?"

Nikki's eyes flew to the woman's face and she saw a steely understanding there. The woman pulled aside the curtain to the machine. "Don't let anybody make you ashamed of who you are. Never mind what happened before. All that is done. What matters is what you do going forward."

Nikki stepped into the voting booth. She gave the woman a small smile. "Thank you."

The woman stepped away, moving to the next booth. "You will be all right. You're a strong woman."

Nikki left the polling place, the woman's words on her heart. As she walked back home, she passed a sign in front of a church that read, "Prayer works. Try it."

Nikki realized she could not continue on this road alone. She didn't know the Bible as well as some others and she didn't devote as much time to church as Sister James, but she finally knew God had a place for her. She knew He hadn't been rejecting her all this time; she had been rejecting Him. She called on His name when it didn't seem to matter much, but at this critical hour, she hadn't trusted Him.

And now, as she walked back home, she just followed the advice of that sign. She would try prayer. Real, sincere prayer. As Nikki crossed the street, she prayed silently. *Lord, please forgive me for my actions and help me to trust you. Please help me to look to you and not to lean on my own understanding and make bad decisions. My life is a mess right now, but I know you have an answer. Please heal my heart and lead me the way you would have me go.*

"Mommy," Psalm said, looking up at Nikki.

"Yes, baby?"

"I love you." Psalm smiled and Nikki's heart responded.

"I love you, too."

Maybe being exposed like that in the newspaper wasn't the worst thing that could have happened to her. Now that her secret was out, she didn't have to live in fear anymore. She breathed in deeply and let the air out slowly as she realized she had spent a third of her life petrified of being found out. And now what? Her husband had left her, even before the news. Her best friend had stabbed her in the back.

And she had survived. She knew she would be all right.

She had finally found faith.

Chapter 114

The phone rang again, and it was Danielle. Nikki accepted the charges and as she waited to be connected, she knew she would give Danielle a good piece of her mind.

"I really need your help," Danielle said when the call was connected.

"You know what? I am so sick and tired of your *poor me* routine," Nikki railed. "All you do is manipulate and take advantage of people. That's why you lied to your co-workers, telling them you were grieving the death of your best friend's child. You wanted to guilt them into doing your work. And that's why you can't ever even keep a man of your own. You're too busy trying to use and abuse; trying to take advantage. What was it about Troy? Did he tick you off when he chose another woman over you? Is that why you killed him? You couldn't stand the idea that somebody wouldn't fall all over himself to be with Danielle Esperanza? Is that it? And now that you've gotten caught, you want what, for me to feel sorry for you and bail you out?

"I bet you never thought you'd need me when you were out having secret meetings with Jimmy Vaughn, dragging my name through the mud. Why did you do it? Were you jealous? Did you want to make sure Will and I didn't get back together so I could be single and miserable like you? Is that it?"

"They're out to get me," Danielle said.

"Will you stop saying that nonsense? You've been talking about *them* coming to get you. Who are *they*? You know what? I don't care. Lose my number!"

Nikki slammed down the phone.

She didn't feel the self-satisfaction she had expected, though. Instead, contrition bubbled inside, as she wondered if she could have handled that any better. She recalled a sermon she had heard months ago, based on Ephesians 4:26.

Be ye angry and sin not.

She'd have to work on that. Because she was still pretty ticked off.

Chapter 115

William and the rest of his team gathered in a meeting room at a local hotel as they waited for the election results. An untouched celebration cake perched on a table.

Olivia received calls from poll watchers, who gave her updates. The precincts were coming in slowly. It was difficult to discern any early telltale signs, one way or the other, as the precincts seemed to be evenly split.

William tried to wrap his mind around a loss, even attempting to prepare a concession speech in his mind. He wanted to be gracious. He wanted to thank his staff. He wanted the night to be over.

But he clung to a tiny sliver of hope that he could indeed pull off this upset. A couple of political bloggers had been championing his cause lately, and all his speaking at luncheons and church functions and every other public event seemed to be having an impact as well, as people had started to recognize him around town. Of course, some mentioned those bad stories in the news, but many gave him positive comments. And it certainly had not hurt that a recent news story exposed Dark's plan to cook up a sweet deal for his cronies in a move that would cost taxpayers millions.

If William could emerge the victor, he would be the city's youngest mayor. As he looked around the room, taking in the faces of those who had been with him since he had stepped into the race, he felt a yearning for his wife.

Nikki should be here.

The thought surprised him. He hadn't allowed himself to think about her much today, at least, not for long. Whenever his mind turned to her, he had tried to distract himself.

Olivia sidled up to his side and put her arm around his waist.

"We're going to pull this off," she said. "I told you, if you'd just stick with me, I'd get us to the mayor's office. I always take care of my friends."

He smiled. "What about your enemies?"

"I take care of them, too."

A guard ushered Danielle into the visiting area and Nikki couldn't hide her surprise. She had watched plenty of jailhouse shows on TV—and she herself had been behind bars not too long ago—but nothing prepared her for seeing her friend dressed in oversized, drab correctional center garb, lines etched into her unmade and usually flawless face.

"Hi," Nikki said. She had finally yielded, deciding to visit her friend.

"Hi," Danielle said.

"How are you?"

"Not good."

Silence fell between them. Nikki hadn't known what to expect, but it wasn't this. Her heart felt full as she saw her best friend humbled and afraid. She tried to muster the anger that had propelled her but it would not come. She could find no joy in her friend's anguish.

"I didn't go to the newspaper," Danielle said, but Nikki held up her hand. She didn't want to get into an argument and she knew she didn't believe a word of the denial.

"We'll talk about it later."

"No, I need to tell you something." Danielle was insistent.

"What is it?"

Nikki saw Danielle swallow and look down at her hands in her lap before proceeding. "You know how I've never talked about my family?"

"Yeah."

"And I've never really told you about them, no one, really?"

"Yeah."

"Well, there's a reason."

"I'm listening."

Danielle slowly unwound the tale, telling Nikki about the day her father left and her uncle's abuse. Nikki stared in disbelief and tears welled in her eyes. It had never occurred to her that Danielle had come from such a broken past. She had always assumed Danielle had probably gotten into it with her family over something silly, maybe over Danielle's superficial nature and big ego. But Nikki could have never guessed such a sad past—that Danielle's mother had allowed her uncle to have sex with the girl.

"It was really hard for me to deal with and for the longest time, I tried, I really did," Danielle said softly. "But one day, I couldn't take it anymore. I was so sad and depressed and I couldn't see how my life was ever going to get any better.

"I got one of my mother's razors and," she paused and drew in a shaky breath, "I went to the bathroom after I got out of school and I got in the tub and slit my wrists."

Nikki's eyes widened.

"I know it's silly and really cowardly but I didn't know what else to do," Danielle confessed. "I didn't want to live."

"Five minutes!" the guard called, holding up a hand to confirm the time.

"Well, anyway, after I got out of the hospital," Danielle continued, "things were okay for a while, but I tried to kill myself again, and I would have except they found me. I tried to overdose on some of my mom's pills. This time, they made me go to a mental hospital, despite my mother's protests."

Nikki put her hand to her mouth to keep from crying.

"I was there for a long time—a year," Danielle revealed. "I was in and out of mental hospitals from time to time, but I've been out for quite a while now. Those records are sealed, thankfully, and nobody has ever tracked them to me. But I know they're mad and they are out to get me. They want to come back for me."

"What do you mean?"

"They're after me," she lowered her voice. "Everywhere I go, I know people are watching me, waiting for me to mess up, to do something. They send spies. Maybe you're one."

Nikki could see Danielle look quickly around, surveying the room, and she wasn't sure how to respond. But she didn't want to alarm her friend, so she spoke soothingly. "It's all right. They won't get you."

"Time's up!" The guard shouted.

Nikki had so many questions. She didn't want to leave Danielle. But she also knew she couldn't bail her friend out. She had no money and hadn't come prepared to find a bail bondsman. She stood and turned to walk away, but looked back at Danielle, summoning the words the elderly woman had given her: "You will be all right."

Nikki drove home, saddened by the story Danielle had told her, and wondering just what else she didn't know about her best friend. "How well do we really know the people we claim to be closest to?" she asked herself. That must be the same thing William wondered about her. The thought of William quickened her heart. The election results should be coming in soon!

She gunned the engine and made it to the house in record time. She raced into the house and clicked on the news.

". . . newcomer to the political scene William Broussard handed incumbent Lo Dark a startling upset, despite personal chaos and scandal."

"Yes!" Nikki screamed and jumped up and down. "Whoo-hoo!" Nikki was glad Psalm was at Keedra's. Nikki's exuberance would have awakened the child, she felt certain.

She paused to listen to the rest of the story. "LSUS political science professor, Kimberly Merritt, said young voters responded to Broussard's youthful enthusiasm and older voters were turned off by recent news reports that the incumbent was devising sweetheart deals to benefit his political friends at taxpayers' expense. This startling upset could not have been guessed even a week ago."

Nikki smiled broadly, knowing William had finally realized his dream. She danced around the living room and picked up the telephone, punching in his cell number. It went straight to voicemail. "Hi, Will, I just saw the news. Congrats on your win! You deserve it."

She hung up and turned back to face the television and stopped in mid-step. A live shot of William's celebration party flashed on the screen just as Olivia leaned into his arms and he picked her up and whirled her around.

Nikki slumped into the nearest chair.

The hotel was a dizzying array of well-wishers and hungry political power seekers, each clamoring for William's attention. Already, he had fielded four job requests, two entreaties to get somebody out of jail, and a zoning change question. Somebody even asked him for Dallas Cowboys football game tickets, though he had no connection to the football team, and someone else asked for Independence Bowl tickets, though William didn't know much about that operation, either. He committed to no one, merely smiled, slapping everyone on the back as he savored the victory.

His wife's absence tugged at him, but Olivia made sure he didn't dwell on that. She was glued to his side most of the evening, watching his conversations, discouraging anyone from taking up too much of his time.

"Congratulations!"

"Thanks, sir," William turned to face someone he didn't know. But he smiled anyway.

"I was wondering if you could help my nephew get a job at City Hall," the unfamiliar man asked, leaning in confidentially.

"Thanks for stopping by the celebratory party." Olivia deftly slid between William and the man, twisting sideways to avoid bumping against the table. She turned to the man. "If you've not had a chance, please sign the registry so we know you stopped by, and be sure to drop your business card into the jar."

She put her hand on the man's back, firmly steering him away. "Now enjoy the party," she flashed a smile, "and have some cake."

Olivia stepped back to William. "You need to make sure you speak to the governor's aide, who just walked into the room; and make sure you shake hands with the black chamber's president. And—"

"I don't care anything about the black chamber president," William whispered in a tone only she could hear.

"You'll have to," she shot back. "Go over there and make nice."

"For what? They never endorsed me. Even up to the last minute, they kept jerking me around," he said. "I don't need them now."

"Well, still," Olivia said. "Go over there. You'll want them on your side."

"We'll see," he said, though he had no intention of going out of his way to greet the chamber president.

The black chamber had been not-so-quietly looking for a replacement candidate after the first story about his wife broke, but it never took off. And at every turn, the chamber had criticized him. He wouldn't be vindictive, but he wouldn't go out of his way to be super-nice, either. *And to think, I won without them.* He smiled broadly.

He was celebrating without his wife. His smile dimmed.

Chapter 116

Nikki fell asleep on the couch, an afghan covering her. She had watched the coverage, as the news station seemed to replay the same scene over and over—that of William whirling Olivia around in the air.

She kept waking up as she alternated between seeing Danielle's solemn face and the image of William and Olivia. Both dreams left a tight feeling in her chest.

The ringing of the phone shook Nikki awake. She frowned and wiped her hand over her eyes. She held up her wrist to look at her watch. It was barely six a.m. Who was calling so early? She stretched her left arm and reached for the phone on the floor. "Hello?" her voice was thick and she wiped her tongue across her front teeth, tasting sleep.

"Nikki?" an unfamiliar voice asked. "Nikki Broussard?"

"Yeah?"

"Hi, this is Skye Scott from *USA Today*."

"Look, I'm not going to do some crazy interview with you about my past."

"What about an interview for a job?"

Nikki bounced up straight, sleep forgotten. "A what?"

"I believe you know Joe, the photo editor at *The Times*?"

"Yes, I know Joe."

"Well, he and I go way back," Skye said. "He's always spoken quite highly of you and your work, ever since your internship. I believe he said he wanted to hire you some time back but you weren't interested."

"Uhm. . . . "It was more like Joe wasn't interested in hiring her.

"Well, we have a position available and I was wondering if you'd be interested in it."

Nikki automatically shook her head. "My hus—" She caught herself. What was she saying? "Yes, I'd be very interested!"

"Excellent. When can you fly out for an interview?"

When she got off the phone, Nikki sat cross-legged on the couch. She felt her heart tattooing its nervous excitement on her ribcage. Suddenly, it hit her. She had finally broken free of all the restrictions of the past seven years. Her worst fear had stared her in the face and she hadn't died. And now she was about to chase her photography dream—at a national newspaper! The thought amazed her.

She quickly ran through the shower, towel-dried her hair, zipped the toothbrush around her mouth and pulled on jeans and a sweater. She had to share her news. She stopped short. But with whom? Her husband was gone and her best friend was locked up.

Nikki decided to visit Danielle at the parish jail. She glanced at the clock on her cell phone. Visiting hours for the morning would be over shortly. She would have to hurry.

Thirty minutes later, after what seemed like a long wait, but was only a few moments, she sat across from Danielle. "We're going to get you out of this," Nikki said, but the words sounded hollow, even to her own ears. Nikki had no money, and Danielle had nowhere else to turn.

Suddenly, her good news seemed so inappropriate. Now, who was being selfish? Danielle was staring at a life behind bars and Nikki wanted to come and brag about a job interview. Nikki felt a bit guilty.

"So, how was your night?"

"It was all right," Danielle shrugged.

They sat in awkward silence for a moment. Nikki tried to find a delicate way to ask her question.

"You remember when we talked about Reverend Chance?"

"Yeah." Danielle's reply was flat.

Nikki felt like a heel for still doubting that Danielle had told her the truth, but she had come too far in the past few months to begin living in a dream world again. Now, she would face reality, whatever it was. And that meant searching for answers.

"I was wondering if you told me the whole truth about what happened," Nikki said. *Sure, kick her when she's down*, Nikki chided herself. But she was determined to know the truth.

"I was lying." Danielle admitted.

"So you knew him before?" Nikki's heart sank. Had Danielle been a part of his murder?

Danielle's voice was barely above a whisper. "Yes. Reverend Chance was my father."

Chapter 117

Olivia had convinced William to stay at her home last night, following the election victory party. His original plan was to stay in the room he had rented at the hotel after she walked in on him in the shower, but there was too much activity and he knew he wouldn't get any rest, regardless of where he slept. His phone was ringing constantly. Things had been a little awkward between them since the shower incident. He had barged out of the bathroom, and she had rushed behind him, apologizing for what she called a "misunderstanding." She hadn't meant to offend him, she claimed.

He had accepted her apology, and with so much election activity, they had been forced to work in close quarters. He had to admit, she had been a great buffer at the party, as she kept him away from people who wanted to hog his time. Olivia seemed to always be there just when he needed her.

So, he had agreed to stay at her house last night.

William walked out of his bedroom this morning, eager to open the day's newspaper. Olivia already had it spread to the front page story of his upset victory. Next to the paper was a cup of coffee, a glass of orange juice, and a plate of grits, eggs and ham.

"Good morning," Olivia smiled at him, ushering him to his seat.

He shook loose of her grasp and sat down. "Thanks," he said, "but you didn't have to do all this."

"Well, I just wanted to help you get your day started right."

"Okay, well, thanks," William said, his eyes already devouring the headline above his smiling face.

CITY ELECTS YOUNGEST MAYOR

"Well, don't you think we make a great team?" Olivia prodded.

"We do work well together," William said, not taking his eyes off the paper. "We had a good group of people. Winston, Cal . . ."

"I don't mean them. I mean you and me," she said, standing behind him, rubbing his shoulders. William shrugged her hands off and twisted around.

"Don't do that."

"Don't do what?" she asked, placing her hands on his shoulders again.

Again, he shrugged them off. "That." Then he waved his hand across the table at the food. "And this."

"I don't know what you mean," Olivia said with feigned innocence.

"Yes, you do," William said. "I appreciate your work, I do. But you've got to stop all this extra. We can't do this."

"I wanted to show you exactly what we could do, in the shower," Olivia said. "You should stop resisting. This is what we both want."

William's mind flashed back to the day in the shower and he stood. "Look, this . . . you . . . me . . . We just need to keep it professional."

"Professional?"

"Yes."

"No, no," Olivia said, stepping around to face him. "I believe you've misunderstood this whole thing."

"What are you talking about?"

"This was never just professional between us."

"It was for me," William said.

She shook her head. "That's a lie. What about the other day when I saw you naked in the shower? What about all those weeks you stayed here? All those conversations we had? What about all the late nights? What about. . . . It's too late to go back on the plan now."

"There was no plan."

"Oh, yes, William, there has always been a plan." Her voice took on a hard tone.

"Olivia, the plan was to win the election, which we weren't even sure would happen until the very end."

"The plan was to win, and then once that was accomplished, the next step was—is—for you to divorce your wife. And make me the first lady of this city."

William guffawed in her face, but Olivia didn't crack a smile. He sobered. "You can't be serious."

"Oh, yes, William; I am very serious."

William took a step away and looked around for his keys. She stood in front of him. She grabbed his arm. "Everything I do is according to a plan. And I don't let anything get in the way of what I want. And I want you. And when you said you wanted to be mayor, I gave that to you. Now, what will you give me?"

"You're crazy. You didn't give me anything."

"Oh, yeah? Who do you think convinced Reverend Hicks to back you? Who do you think got you into that fancy house, gave you and that country bumpkin wife of yours a decent vehicle to ride around in? Gave you a bank balance of more than a couple of dollars. Better than that, who do you think even gave you the opportunity to run in the first place?"

By now, she was standing within inches of William. He moved to step around her, but again, she blocked his way.

"Olivia, you're going to need to move," William warned.

"Not before I get what I want."

"Well, his wife told me I was such a pretty girl and that my mom would miss me if I left her," Danielle said. "And she said we would go and call my mom so my mom would know I was safe; and they would see if I could stay the night and go back home the next day."

"What was your dad saying as all this was going on?"

"Nothing, really," Danielle said. "I think he was too shocked. I don't think he knew his wife knew, so it was like his secret was coming out and he was just trying to take it all in."

Nikki knew what it was like to have a carefully guarded secret spill out.

"Well, anyway, we called my mom and she was so hysterical and cursing and made them drive me back home that day," Danielle said. "It was awful. She told my dad she was going to tell everybody about me if he didn't bring me back that instant. Even though his wife may have known about me, he didn't want his church members to know. So we all piled into the car.

"My brother seemed cool with finding out about me. But my sister wouldn't even speak to me. It was years before she would even speak my name. I think she resented me. But we finally started talking. She's actually the one who got me out of the hospital the last time I was there. She's gotten me out of lots of things over the years. But I know if I don't do exactly as she wants, she'll make them come get me and I'll be back at the hospital."

Nikki held up her hand. "Your sister . . . Reverend Chance . . . ." her eyes widened. "You mean Olivia is your sister?"

"Yes."

"My sister is very possessive about what she feels is hers," Danielle said. "She felt that I came in and took her dad. And so she blamed me for the longest, maybe still does. But I tried so hard to make it up, to fit in. I wanted so much for them to like me. Her, especially, because it was like suddenly, I had a big sister. But her love came at a high price."

"What do you mean?"

"Well, throughout the years, she would always tell me that I owed things to her," Danielle said. "If she wanted me to do something, she would say, 'It's because of you that I couldn't go to Europe on my senior trip.' Or she would say, 'It's because of you my dad had to travel so much, so he could earn extra money preaching to take care of you.' Anyway, these last few months, she began doing that again. Only this time . . ."

Danielle's voice trailed off and Nikki prompted her. "Only this time, what?"

"Time's almost up!" the guard bellowed.

"Only this time, she wanted information about you."

"About me?"

"Yeah," Danielle looked down, and then back up. "She started calling me all the time, asking me so many questions. At first, I didn't tell her anything, but she kept the guilt trip on me and well, I must admit, I fell for it. I told her things about your marriage." Danielle looked at Nikki.

Nikki's jaw set, but she didn't say anything. She nodded for Danielle to continue.

"At first, I thought she was just being helpful," Danielle said. "I told her about when Psalm was sick and she was the one who insisted I offer you that credit card hookup. Remember when I offered it the first time and you shot it down? Well, I told her and she said I should make sure you took it."

Realization dawned. "So she was the one who went to the press?"

Danielle squirmed. "I think so."

"And everything just fell into place like clockwork," Nikki concluded, her mouth drawing into a tight line. "I just handed her my husband on a silver platter. I lied and deceived at every turn and she was just conveniently there to help him through his time of trouble."

"I'm so sorry," Danielle said. "But it gets worse."

"How?"

"I think she's killed before."

Chapter 119

William bumped past Olivia and headed down the hall to the bedroom he had stayed in for too long. He put yesterday's clothes into his duffel bag, shaking his head the entire time. He had to admit, at least now, that he had known Olivia had expected something from him. But he had ignored what he knew to be good judgment, allowing her to help him with his campaign.

She was a powerful woman. Rich. Accomplished. And she had lavished all her attention on him. She had bought him nice things, catered to his needs—would have done even more, if he had allowed.

And now, she was demanding payment.

He knew he had to get to his wife. He had been away for much too long.

"William, you can't just walk out on me, not after I've put so much into you." Olivia shook her head. "I've invested quite a lot into you."

He heard her words and his back stiffened. "Look,

Olivia, I'm going to leave and there is nothing you can do about it." He grabbed the bag from the bed, and finally turned to face her.

He was staring straight into Olivia's narrowed eyes. And she was pointing a .22 caliber handgun at him.

Chapter 120

Nikki sprang from her seat, wildly shaking her hands in front of her. "William, I've got to get to William!"

"What?" Danielle's eyes looked frightened.

"She's going to kill my husband!" Nikki spoke as if talking to a child. It all seemed so obvious to her now.

"What are you talking about?" Danielle still didn't get it.

"You just said she kills when she doesn't get what she wants. And I know William. He's not going to go along with what she wants. My husband loves me."

Nikki had no time for explanations. She quickly said her goodbye, promising to come back. It was all Nikki could do to restrain herself from breaking out in a full run as she exited the building. When she hopped into the car, she dived into her purse for the business card she had shoved in her wallet. She punched in the number to Luke Marks, the assistant district attorney she had met with when her part in the credit card scam hit the papers.

"I know who killed Reverend Chance," Nikki exclaimed into the phone after getting Luke on the line.

"Who is this?" Luke wanted to know.

"It's Nikki Broussard. Get someone out to Ontario Street!"

"What are you talking about?"

She rattled off her suspicions, not caring that she probably sounded incoherent. She shouted out Olivia's address, a number Nikki had memorized when she found out her husband was staying there. Luke told her not to go to the property, to wait for the police, but she knew she could not sit back and do nothing, not while her husband's very life hung in the balance.

Nikki's hands were shaking and sweaty. She ran every red light she saw, laying her palm flat against the horn.

She realized that all her suspicions of the past few months had just been a weak attempt to push William away. Her lack of faith had caused her to run away from so much. She hadn't trusted God. She hadn't trusted her husband. And she hadn't trusted herself. At every turn, she rejected the idea of trust because she didn't want to be hurt. And now, it was this newfound trust that fueled her mad dash across town. She knew her husband had not cheated on her with this woman. William loved her, and what's more, he loved God. And that meant there were just some things he would not do.

And she knew she had to bring him home.

Alive.

Chapter 121

"What are you doing?" William tried to speak calmly, but his stomach fluttered and he wondered yet again why he hadn't stayed at the hotel, or better yet, gone home to his wife last night.

"I told you, you owe me," Olivia said.

"I don't owe you anything. You're crazy." He knew he probably shouldn't talk like that and make her even madder.

"Crazy or not, I don't appreciate how you've gone back on our agreement."

"We had no agreement." Maybe he shouldn't call her a liar right now either. After all, she was holding a gun.

"Yes, we did," Olivia said. "Did you think I was helping you just out of the goodness of my heart? Everything I do is calculated. Don't you know one of the fundamental laws of physics, that for every action there is an equal and opposite reaction? Well, I've just adapted it a bit. For every action done against me, there is a certain reaction, sometimes equal, but most times much worse. No deed against me goes unpunished."

"But I didn't do any deed against you," William tried to reason.

She laughed, her voice cackling and shrill. "Oh, yes you did." Olivia stepped behind him. He looked around, but she urged him forward with the gun, out of the bedroom and up the hallway. He walked, keeping his eyes straight ahead as he prepared to make a sudden move to the right and twist her up and force her to drop the gun from her hand. But she barked at him, "Right there!" The moment was lost as they finally stood in the living room and she moved again to face him.

"You tried to use me for your own gain. You thought you could get all you wanted out of me and then not pay. Life doesn't work like that. Look at my father. All my adult life I've been building him up, his credibility, his wealth, his power. And then he goes and lets what he did years ago come back and jeopardize all of us. I told him from the start to leave those casinos alone, but he wouldn't listen.

"He finally left them behind and became a changed man. Building a church, leading the community. But I knew I was going to have to punish him when those gambling stories hit the papers. If he had just listened to me, he wouldn't have had to die."

William's brows shot up. He could scarcely believe what he was hearing. "You killed your father? But why?"

"Don't you listen? I just told you. All of my hard work of positioning him to run for office was going to go up in smoke. I kept telling him to let me handle things, to let me run his campaign. But he was too stubborn. So I didn't have a choice."

William stared at her as if she had to be crazy. "You didn't have a choice?"

"You remember how he kept going against everything I said, William," Olivia said. "I had to do something quick. Then I got the idea of handing the election to you."

"How did you know I would accept?"

"Because I wanted you to. And I get what I want." Olivia said the words matter-of-factly.

William laughed, but not with mirth. It was dry and full of cynicism. "So it's like that for you? I thought you loved your dad?"

"Oh, I did," she said. "I loved him very much. And we could have run a very successful campaign, if his past hadn't compromised it. I don't play to lose. And we would have lost with his skeletons tumbling out of the closet like cans in an overstuffed pantry. I had to take care of the situation. My way."

Her eyes were cold and her voice sent icy fingers marching down his spine. How could he never have noticed how unfeeling Olivia was?

"So, all your dad was, was a *situation*?"

"Don't make it sound so bad!" Olivia said. "Did he tell you he had two illegitimate daughters, twins? One is your wife's best friend. Danielle. All he did was get himself into situations. And that would have come out too, with the election. I had to do something.

"And I chose you. You should be honored. Most men would have been. Yet, you seek to throw my generosity in my face." Olivia talked with the gun, jabbing it in his face to punctuate her sentences.

William's mind raced. How could he get her to put down the gun so he could make a break for it? If he rushed her fast and caught her off guard, it's possible he could knock the gun out of her hand. But if he faltered . . .

"Olivia, let's talk about this," he reasoned. "Maybe we can work something out after all."

She wagged the index finger of her free hand at him. "Do you think I'm dumb? I know you're just trying to say anything to save your skin. It won't work." She sighed. "It's really a shame. My late husband learned that the hard way.

I really hated to have to poison him like that. Do you know it took a week? I had to be so careful. But he had to go because I realized too late that I had married the wrong man. And you already know, I don't like failure. I couldn't have a divorce on my hands."

William couldn't believe his bad luck. There were 400,000 people in the area, and he had somehow gotten hooked up with this crazy vigilante woman who didn't like divorce but had no problem with murder.

"I had to kill my sister's boyfriend too. Danielle made such bad choices in men."

"Troy? You killed Troy? Why?"

"Two reasons," Olivia said. She seemed to gain some satisfaction out of these confessions. It was as if she needed to brag that she had outsmarted so many people. "One, he wasn't right for her. And two, she was getting out of hand. I had been able to keep a handle on her with threats to send her back to the hospital, but I needed something more. I thought pinning a murder on her would come in handy. It did, too."

"You had her arrested?" William somehow knew the answer.

"I had to find some way to shut her up," Olivia said. "She was acting really jittery and I couldn't keep watching her while I was so busy with you. And I didn't want her unstable behind to go off on a tangent."

"How could you just be so cold?" William shook his head in disgust and shock.

Olivia shook her head. "Sweetie, you just don't listen. Calculated. I'm calculated. That means I'm smart. A genius."

"If you're so smart, why are you going to ruin your life by killing me? Don't you know you're going to get caught? I mean, we're in the middle of your living room."

"Tsk, tsk. Do you really think I've not thought this

through?" Her voice rose. "I'm a bit annoyed that I have to do this. After all, I just won an election for you and now I'll have to start all over with a new candidate. But I think what I'll do is say that, well, you were just so drunk after last night's parties . . . and well, you had been coming on to me all along, I mean, you kept harassing me. And me, being the timid woman that I am, I was intimidated, which is why I allowed it to go on for so long. But finally, it got to be too much. You tried to attack me and, just thank God, I was able to grab a gun my father bought for me years ago for protection and I shot you in the struggle."

She shook her head at the sad notion. "Sadly, our newly elected mayor was just a lowlife pervert. And it really won't be a stretch of the imagination, especially with your wife's fine reputation as a call girl and a credit card thief."

William hoped Nikki would not have to come to identify his body. Maybe they would get Mac instead. "So you really do have this all planned out, huh?"

"I told you, I do," Olivia said, leveling the gun straight at William. "And I believe, this time around, I'll run for mayor myself."

Chapter 122

Nikki ran out of gas a block from Olivia's house. She had slowed at the light, but when she pressed the gas to accelerate, the car sputtered and stopped. Nikki desperately tried to get the car to start, but it was no use. She slammed her palm against the steering wheel. "Not now!"

Nikki had been riding on empty for what seemed like days now, so running out of gas wasn't a total surprise. She hopped out and started running down the street. She had to get to her husband.

She had only been to Olivia's home once before, when the woman had hosted William and her for a dinner a few months ago, back when Reverend Chance was running for office.

Her body temperature rose as her legs pumped furiously, negating the autumn's cool bite. She stumbled up the stairs to the elegantly appointed wood frame house and fell into the door. Sirens blared from behind as blue lights flashed, but Nikki didn't wait for the police. She banged on the door and twisted the knob, pushing with her body strength at the same time. Surprised that it was unlocked, she stumbled into Olivia's living room.

Olivia whirled around, a gun in her right hand.

Nikki heard a shout from William, but all she could feel was a burning sensation as a bullet tore through her upper body and she fell into darkness.

Chapter 123

It all happened so fast. William saw Nikki burst into the living room at the same time Olivia raised the gun and pulled the trigger. The bullet hit his wife a split second before he dove to disarm Olivia. He knocked her to the floor and the gun flew across the room.

The room immediately filled with uniformed officers who scurried about like ants, filling every available space. He knelt down beside his wife. From somewhere behind him, he heard two officers asking Olivia to remain still.

"Baby, baby!" William knew he shouldn't move Nikki, but he immediately scooped her into his arms, her sticky, warm blood darkening her sweater to almost purple. "Somebody, help my wife! Help my wife!"

He stumbled out the front door with her in his arms, his mouth wide open, calling for help even as paramedics rushed toward him. Flashing bulbs blinded him, but all he could see was his unconscious wife lying on a stretcher as her blood seeped out of her body.

* * *

Danielle sat on the flat mattress in the cell she had called home for the past few days, her shoulders slumped, her eyes on a spot of grime situated exactly halfway between her feet. She felt as if she had aged ten years.

"Esperanza!"

Her head snapped up. "Yes?"

"Come on with me." The female guard offered no smile, no explanation.

Danielle rose slowly to her feet and shuffled behind the woman. She did not care what would happen to her. She felt as if her life had already ended.

The woman led her to a tiny room and another woman handed Danielle the clothes she had worn the day she was arrested. She looked up, confused.

"You're free to go. Your charges have been dropped."

"Dropped?" As the realization sank in, she let out a whoop. "Oh I can't believe it!" The strength left her legs and they buckled under her. She would have fallen if the guard had not caught her.

She cast a quick glance around, wondering if this was a setup. Maybe they were out there, watching her, waiting for her to say or do something. Maybe they wanted to take her back to the hospital. Maybe Olivia was behind this. But for the moment, Danielle didn't care. All she knew was that she was free.

"Oh, I'm so happy! I thought I would never again see the outside, my house, my car, my friends."

"Well, it looks like you have some good friends indeed," said the woman who handed back Danielle's street clothes and personal belongings that had been confiscated when she was booked into the correctional facility.

Without knowing all the details, Danielle felt her release had something to do with her best friend, not Olivia, after all. Nikki had come to her rescue, again. Nikki would be there for her. Nikki would help her through whatever lay ahead. They had endured a lot. Danielle knew Nikki was the sister she had wished Olivia would be. That thought gave her comfort.

"Yes, I do have some good friends."

Danielle tightly clutched her belongings to her chest and walked out into the free world.

Chapter 124

William was the first person Nikki saw when she opened her eyes following surgery on her left arm. The bullet had made a clean exit, but because of the amount of blood she had lost, doctors wanted to keep her under observation for a while.

"Hi," William said, leaning down to kiss her forehead.

"How are you?" she asked.

William laughed. "Seems that I should be asking you that."

"Oh, I'm fine," Nikki said, shrugging the shoulder that wasn't bandaged. She recalled the events leading to her hospitalization. Danielle's confessions had unraveled the tale of Olivia's murderous plot. Nikki felt grateful to Danielle for sharing her painful past. She silently vowed to find professional help for her friend so Danielle could deal with her mental scars. But Nikki would sort all that out later. For now, she wanted to focus on her family. She looked around the hospital room.

"Where is Psalm?"

"She's at my mom's," William said.

"At your mom's?"

"Yeah, and don't worry," William said. "My mom has been calling up here every five minutes, it seems, asking how you are doing. She wants to have a big party for you when you get out of the hospital."

Nikki's brows shot up. "Your mom wants to throw a party for me?" Saying the 9-word sentence made Nikki even more tired.

Will nodded. "Yeah, she thinks you're a superhero. And so do I. I always knew you were a superwoman."

It had taken her a long time to realize her own strength. "I'm surprising myself these days. I never knew I had it in me," Nikki whispered through cracked, dry lips.

She tried to reach for a cup on the stand next to the bed, but she was too weak. William gently helped her sit up at an angle, and then he held the cup of water while she drank some through a straw.

After she had satisfied her thirst, William tenderly took her free hand in both of his and kissed it. He was on his knees next to her bed. "Baby, I'm so sorry if I ever made you feel like I didn't respect your strength."

"I think mostly I doubted it," Nikki said. "I was so afraid of just living. I didn't want to trust God because I couldn't *see* Him, and I thought that meant I couldn't rely on Him. And then I didn't want to trust myself because I always doubted what I was made of because I had made wrong choices before."

Nikki smiled weakly. "And I didn't trust you to be the man I know you are, because I was judging you based on others in my life, like my father. He ran out, so I think I expected you to run out."

William sighed. "And that's exactly what I did." His tone was sad.

Nikki shook her head. "No, you never really went anywhere. I think I always knew that, deep in my heart. But I let my fear make me think otherwise. I tried to tiptoe around you, thinking if I was just good enough, you would see my worth. And would love me if I was the perfect wife. I didn't stand up for myself. And not only that, I lied because I didn't trust God's love in you to forgive me for my past."

"I'm sorry I couldn't see your hurt," William said. "And that I tried to impose my will on you. If you'll have me back, there are going to be some changes. We're going to move to a house we can afford—on our own. The business is going better, so we'll have the money, and of course, my new mayor's salary. You were right. I was trying to fake it 'til I made it, trying to pretend that I had all this money, but I realize now that I don't need to pretend. I am the wealthiest man I know, because I have you and I have Psalm. And we're going to get our finances in order so we can have the freedom we want. We're going to do things the way you were suggesting all along."

Nikki nodded, and William continued. "And if you want to go to work, it's not fair for me to keep that from you. I know you are really good at what you do and it would be a shame to rob the world of your beautiful photography."

Nikki smiled again. "I'm glad you say that, because I have an interview next week with *USA Today*."

"*USA Today*? That's great!"

Nikki was glad he was as excited as she was. She had made the decision to go for the job even if it meant going against her husband, because she knew she was no longer the scared, timid girl who was afraid to assert herself. Now, she knew that even if nobody else would be there for her, she would be there for herself.

She knew God was the greatest ally of all, and He was right there with her, even if she could not see Him. She knew God had created, in her, strength to face whatever lay ahead. Faith allowed her to have that confidence. She could not change her past. She wasn't perfect, and she didn't have to be. God loved her anyway. And what's more, she loved herself.

"Yeah, it's kind of cool, huh?" Nikki smirked. "Imagine me. Shooting pictures for *USA Today*!"

"Yeah, so I'm going to have to step aside and let you be the big shot, huh?" William smiled.

"Maybe we can both be big shots," Nikki said. "We'll take turns. You shine, I shine. After all, you're a big-time political leader now, Mr. Mayor. So we'll just support each other's dreams. I build you up, you build me up."

"I love you." William kissed her on the lips.

"I love you more."

"I love you more than more."

Reader's Guide Questions

1. Nikki and William had two different desires for their family. Nikki wanted to be a career woman. William wanted her to be a stay-at-home mom. They had agreed early on they would follow William's plan. Was Nikki wrong to want to revise that plan, put her child in school and go to work, or was William wrong for wanting to hold her to that plan? Explain.

2. Nikki found it easier to give advice than to take it. Have you ever been in a situation where you've given advice you didn't want to take? What happened?

3. Nikki thought faith meant doing the best she could and letting God do the rest. William thought faith meant praying about a situation and then trusting God to fix it. Who was right? Why?

4. Have you ever struggled with your faith during a time of crisis? How did you face that?

5. Our key characters were professed Christians living their lives. Did their actions show them to be "true" Christians? Why or why not? How do you determine what is a "true" Christian?

6. Did those lifelong Christians around Nikki hold any responsibility for helping her along her faith walk? Why or why not?

7. Did your opinion of Danielle change over the course of the book? If so, how?

8. William had a strong desire to be the sole supporter of his family. Was this an honorable desire or was this selfish? Explain your answer.

9. Each of the primary characters faced critical choices at different points. How do their choices relate to the choices each of us face in our daily lives?

10. Did William take advantage of the situation with Olivia, or was he an innocent victim of her ploys?

11. Did Nikki show strength by yielding to her husband's wishes of having her be a stay-at-home mom, or did she show weakness? How would you have handled the situation?

12. How important was it that Nikki did not tell William about her past? Must a person share every part of his or her past with a spouse or are some things private?

13. What problems did Danielle have? Did you see her as a selfish, narcissistic woman, a hurting soul with scars, a mentally ill person, or something else entirely?

14. What kind of relationship did Nikki and Danielle have? Did one person take unfair advantage of the relationship or did they each benefit from the friendship?

15. What messages did you see in this book?

About the Author

Monica Carter is an entrepreneur, author and speaker. She and her husband own and operate RootSky Creative, a copywriting and design firm, and are the publishers of the Knowledge Wealth Series, a resource for creative entrepreneurs at *www.knowledgewealthseries.com*. Monica enjoys discussing spiritual matters and questions of faith. She is the daughter of a minister and was the granddaughter of a pastor. She lives in Shreveport, LA with her husband. Monica also is the author of *Sacrifice the One*, a story of faith and forgiveness. Learn more about her novels at *www.monicacarter.com*.